MAN BEHIND THE MASK

Edited by David Owain Hughes,
Jonathan Edward Ondrashek & Veronica Smith

Darkerwood Publishing Group
Denver, CO U.S.A.
2016

Darkerwood Publishing Group, PO Box 2011, Arvada, CO 80001

ISBN: 978-1-938839-05-4

Cover Art by Kevin Enhart

TABLE OF CONTENTS

INTRODUCTION

Hi, I'm Linnea Quigley, and I am an '80s horror scream queen! I've been involved with about 120 films (mostly horror), and you'll probably remember me most as Trash in *Return of the Living Dead*, Suzanne in *Night of the Demons*, or Denise in *Silent Night, Deadly Night*.

I've always been drawn to horror. I just love it. As a kid and teen, I'd have sleepovers and watch creature features, *Alfred Hitchcock Presents* or *The Twilight Zone* with my girlfriend, eating bad pizza and re-enacting our favorite scenes, and we'd go to the drive-in with my dad to watch films like *Four Flies on Grey Velvet* and other Dario Argento films. Many aspects in horror related to me, and I found it to be my calling as I grew older.

A lot of horror films were made in the '80s, and let's face it: even with cheesy soundtracks and shoddy footage, they remain classics. Many women had been put down in previous horror films up to that era, though. They'd been portrayed as victims, so I tried to be a pioneer in the genre by being a strong character in every film I appeared in. It was important to me to make women feel comfortable with my roles, and with their roles in real life. The '80s were the greatest because I and many other scream queens showed we didn't have to be prim and proper—we could be strong and take down those evil villains without ending up as a slab of meat. And we weren't all divas, either.

It was fun. Really fun.

And it is important to keep women in the horror genre—whether they're producing, directing, acting, or writing, real or fictional—because our viewpoints are a lot different than a man's. Women are able to portray emotions on a deeper level, I think, which allows the audience to feel more genuine fear.

Women used to be the victims, but now we're often the heroines. It's great to be a tough-ass chick who saves the day, and to be sly and devious and treacherous enough to expose the man behind the mask.

It's empowering.
Love and screams, Linnea.

HEART'S DESIRE

by Audrey Brice

He couldn't wait to slice her open and reach inside where it was warm and wet. His breath quickened as he watched her from the window where he stood safely concealed in the dark of a moonless black sky. Between his legs, his hand stroked his swollen member faster and faster. He closed his eyes, imagining what it would be like to make her cry and beg. The look of surprise and disbelief when she felt the blade slice into her gut.

He liked fucking them while he did it. Watching his dolls bleed out and take their last breaths. Feeling their insides convulse around his throbbing cock. Then their bowels released and that's always when he came.

He opened his eyes when he heard her raise her voice.

"We're not having this discussion. I already told you I won't go through with it. It's my life, my choice!" The tall brunette frowned.

When she did that, Lucas didn't like it at all. He liked his dolls smiling, scared, or crying, but not angry.

"I'm not! I respect that it's a family tradition, but what if I don't want it to be mine?" The frown deepened. Obviously a fight with her boyfriend.

Lucas lost his erection then, and that made him angry. Four orgasms. That's how many times he liked to masturbate in anticipation while watching them. Only then could he enjoy them and take their lives, adding them to his collection. It was a rule. Tonight would have been the fourth orgasm. He had been so close to coming, but now he'd have to wait until tomorrow, Friday, to complete his masturbatory rule. That meant he'd have to kill her on Saturday. He didn't like working weekends.

On the upside, her house was off the main road, set back in the forest, and it wasn't likely anyone would know she was missing for a few days. If he wanted, he could probably do it right there in the house with little to no disturbances. He hadn't seen anyone stop by in the three weeks he'd been watching. He'd just need to take the usual precautions with tarps and gloves because there was no way he'd get caught before his collection was complete. Only two more to go!

He continued watching as she slammed down the phone, rolled her eyes and took a deep breath. This one had spirit. He liked that. Those were his favorite kind of dolls. So far he had twenty-three dolls. This one would make twenty-four. When he had twenty-five, he would celebrate. Maybe have a beer or two and listen to Black Sabbath.

She would wear the maroon dress he'd picked out for her. It had a low cut bodice to accentuate her smooth, round breasts. Her breasts were bigger than many of the others. He liked them. It was the first feature that had attracted him to her when he'd first seen her at the grocery store in town. Perhaps he would pierce her nipples before killing her. Yes, that thought excited him, and his erection returned.

He continued to watch her and began pumping his erection again. This time he was able to imagine killing her all the way to the end. When he came, it shot out and hit the window. He smiled, making a mental note to wash the glass tomorrow night. For now, it turned him on to know his semen was there, mocking her, and she was blissfully unaware of how he was going to immortalize her.

The cell phone next to her rang, and she reached out and grabbed it. "I needed to cool off," she spoke into it, the frown returning.

Lucas shook his head. Tomorrow night, the ex-boyfriend wouldn't matter. He would free her from the troubles of her earthly life. He left the house behind him. There was nothing left to do now except visit his dolls and bide his time.

He walked back up the trail through the woods and past his meager cabin. Continuing for another half mile, he came to the doll house. Usually, he didn't shit where he ate. He often travelled hundreds of miles to add to his collection. But this one wasn't one of the girls who grew up around here, and she was so close it seemed ridiculous to pass her up. Unlocking the padlock on the door, he entered the cold outbuilding, grabbed the battery-powered lantern, and turned it on. He threw up the floor hatch, braced it with a metal rod, and carefully made his way down the wooden steps into the vault. It was important to keep the collection cold so it wouldn't spoil.

He held the lantern aloft so the light could reach most of the room. His collection ranged in shape, size, hair color, and ethnicity. Each of them sat posed carefully in chairs along three of the earthen walls of the doll house. Two empty wooden chairs, one draped with a carefully chosen maroon dress, sat at the end. In the middle of the room was a table with twenty-five glass jars, and all but two of them held the hearts of all the dolls, forever preserved in a formaldehyde solution.

He sat with the dolls for a few hours, touching their hair and remembering them. Each one was special to him. His first was a beautiful Asian doll with dark, course hair and smooth skin. The second was a redhead with voluptuous curves and freckled breasts. He'd sucked on them just before he'd killed her. Number fourteen – he'd removed one of her eyes and fucked the empty socket.

He finally left, locking things up behind him. With a contented smile, he made his way back to the small cabin he called home.

The following night, Lucas took time dressing in a hooded robe and put on a Donald Trump Halloween mask. Then he went through his bag one last time. He brought two knives: the carver to kill her with, and the paring knife, just in case he felt like a little foreplay. Finally, Lucas double-checked that the rope and duct tape were there, along with the upholstery needles he'd need to pierce her nipples. His cock stirred beneath the robe, and he closed his eyes to will the erection away. Not yet.

When he was satisfied with the contents of his bag, he hoisted it over his shoulder and left his remote cabin.

***

Amber didn't want to break up with Jeff. She loved him, and she liked his family. They were good people. She just didn't appreciate the family tradition insisted upon by both her family and his. It had been an arranged marriage since she was twelve and he was fourteen.

"It's not that bad," said her sister, Kristy, over the phone. In the background, Amber could hear the kids playing. "Look at Jerry and me! We're happy, and life is great."

Kris lived in a huge house in a wealthy California suburb. Amber knew if she did what they asked of her, she could have the same things too.

"It's just, so... authoritarian. Old-school. You know?" Amber shrugged. It wasn't like she hadn't bent to the will of her family before. She had, but the situations had been different.

"So you're rebelling against authority?" Her sister groaned.

"Have you always wanted to do everything Mom and Dad and Grams and Pops wanted you to do?" She felt her jaw tighten. There were drawbacks to being born into wealth and privilege whether her sister chose to see them or not.

"You can't deny who you are and where you come from, Am." Kristy had a point. "Do you love Jeff?"

Amber let out a long sigh. "Of course I do. I just don't see why—"

"Making the commitment to him is easy. It's maintaining your figure, raising the kids and keeping the house that will be the most difficult part of your marriage."

Amber rolled her eyes. She'd never seen herself as the domestic type. "I suppose you're right."

"Now get off the phone and call him," Kris said with finality in her voice.

With another unwieldy sigh, she hung up. Even her elder sister was on their side. Maybe she was just making mountains out of molehills.

Her phone rang again, and she picked it up. This time, it was Jeff. He was certainly persistent.

"I'm coming over, and I expect you to be ready for me." It wasn't a request for an invitation.

"Tonight?"

"Amber, it's been two years. Yes, tonight." His voice softened then. "I want to marry you. I need to be near you. Tonight I will make love to you by candlelight. I can't think of anything else…"

The butterflies in her stomach turned into a knot. "I'm not sure I'm ready…"

"You're ready. We both are. We've been ready. Everything is going to be okay, baby. I love you. We'll go slow, and I'll guide you." His voice sounded reassuring now. His experience most certainly outweighed hers.

"Okay," she relented, not believing she would genuinely go through with it. If she gave in now, what else would she be expected to give in on later? Regardless, it seemed easier not to fight it. Maybe Kris was right – this was the easy part. She imagined the first time was the hardest for everyone.

Once she hung up and set the phone on the coffee table, she went into the kitchen for a glass of wine. There was nothing stronger in the house. Her parents kept it as a rental, but it had been vacant for a month before she'd decided to come. They didn't keep it stocked. Hunters, families and random creatives rented the house for a month or two at a time and rarely left anything behind. Her parents brought a cleaning service in once a month and between rentals so at least it wasn't a sty. Before she left, she'd told her parents not to rent it out. While her father had protested, her mother had calmed him and said, "Amber needs some time to work this out, Reginald. Let her go."

At least her mom understood her need to think, saying it was just cold feet, and all of them went through it. Maybe Mom was right. Cold feet – that's what it was.

Amber searched the cupboards until she found a new bottle of something red in the far back of the pantry. She uncorked it and filled a large wine glass, swirling it around and letting it breathe. She took a sip and wrinkled her nose at how sweet it was. It was cheap wine.

She was on her second glass when she heard a stirring at the front door, then in the foyer. She turned from where she sat on the couch to find a dark figure in a hooded robe standing there. Once he stepped into the light cast by the living room lamps, she could tell he wore a mask. A Donald Trump mask.

A giggle escaped her lips. "Cute, Jeff."

The man stepped into the living room and dropped the duffle bag he carried next to him.

Her eyes fell on the bag and she took a deep breath. Did she dare look in there? "Do you want some wine?"

He didn't say anything, just looked at her.

Setting her glass on the table, she got up and went to the bag, lifting it up and carrying it back to the couch with her. She unzipped it, all the while oblivious to how curious he seemed that she wasn't the least bit surprised.

She pulled out the carefully wrapped-up rope and her stomach did a flip. "I guess I should have expected this."

Then she took out the knives, setting them neatly on the coffee table. She had no idea what the paring knife was for, but the hunting knife seemed obvious. For some reason, she had assumed it would be more ornate, but then it made sense to use a hunting knife.

It was the duct tape and upholstery needles that confused her though. She held up the tape. "This is overkill, don't you think?"

The hooded figure shrugged.

"And what are you doing with these?" She lifted the upholstery needles, shook her head, and threw them back into the bag. Then she tossed the bag back to the floor. "Did you bring a tarp, too?"

The man didn't move.

Just then, the front door opened and more hooded figures entered the house, this time with far more ceremony.

"Who's this?" Jeff asked, taking down the hood of his robe and revealing his long dark hair and deep gray eyes. He shot her an accusing look.

Amber could not hide her surprise and pointed at the stranger. "I thought he was you."

The man in the Donald Trump mask exchanged a look with Jeff, then turned as if to flee, but several of Jeff's brethren surrounded him, grasping his arms, wrestling him into submission.

Jeff turned to a lone figure still standing in the hall. "It looks like today is your lucky day, Roger. The Dark Lord has provided us with another sacrifice."

"Yes, Master," Roger said, bowing his head in servitude. Sacrifices were usually willing servants unless a different option showed up.

Jeff turned to examine the contents of the coffee table. "Is this what he had with him?"

Amber nodded, still a bit shocked as she looked over the items. The man in the Donald Trump mask, who wasn't part of the coven like she'd thought, was most certainly someone who had intended to harm her, and that pissed her off.

Jeff smiled. "I can see why you might have been confused. Perhaps this will make it easier for you to fulfill your commitment?"

Their prisoner began to fight his captors again until one of them knocked him over the head with a thick book. The coven Grimoire wasn't a slender, lightweight tome; it weighed at least ten pounds. The man in the Donald Trump mask slumped over, submitting to the hands holding him.

"Take off his mask. I'm rather curious what he thought he was going to do." A sly smile slid over Jeff's lips. When he saw the stranger's middle aged, unshaven face, he shook his head. "You can't get beautiful girls like Amber to fuck you so you think you can sneak in here and take what you want? You're a pathetic loser. No one makes my girl scream except me." Then he turned to his coven mates. "Prepare the ritual."

That last order caused a bustle as all but the two biggest members of the coven, who held the stranger fast, hurried about moving tables, lighting candles, and laying out a tarp they had brought along. Ritual sacrifice was a messy business.

Jeff went to Amber and pulled her up off the couch into his embrace, kissing her full on the lips. She melted into him, loving how his hard body felt against hers. He was right. They'd waited so long for this. It was a new moon. New beginnings.

Jeff's fingers slid beneath the shoulder straps of the flimsy dress she wore, pulling it down, exposing her bare breasts.

She let the dress fall to the floor, revealing her fully nude figure. One of the rules of a Satanic witch was that she was to be available to her man at all times, and that was one rule she'd held to religiously.

Her focus was on Jeff because tonight he was the only one who existed. She would make the commitment to him and consummate their marriage no matter how nervous she was. Neither of them paid any attention to the now nude stranger, whose mouth was sealed with the duct tape he'd brought. His hands and feet were also bound, leaving his chest ready and waiting. They didn't pay attention to the wild panic in his eyes as they took him to the ground, laying him out in the middle of the room on his back.

Now candlelight enveloped them, and at Jeff's order, one of the coven members opened the Grimoire and began to read the incantation to summon Lucifer. Amber kneeled before Jeff, who pulled the hood back over his head. On all fours, she turned to the terrified stranger, straddling him with her breasts in his face.

Jeff kneeled behind her as the coven began chanting, his solid penis entering her without warning. She gasped, her eyes rolling back into her head, and then pushed back on him and let out a soft moan.

Jeff's muscular forearm lifted her up until she was standing over the prisoner with one leg propped against a table that had been shoved out of the way, exposing her clean-shaven sex to the stranger so he could watch the gorgeous woman's master and high priest fuck her. One of the coven members handed Jeff the hunting knife. Then Jeff guided her back to all fours, straddling the prisoner.

He reached out and put the knife in Amber's hand, then continued to thrust into her and whispered softly in her ear, "I'll guide you. We'll do it nice and slow. You just go into the chest right below the left shoulder and across. Then reach in and pull it out. You have to pull hard."

Amber, lost in the feeling of Jeff inside her, merely whimpered against him.

"Come on, baby. Just remember that he came here tonight to hurt you. You owe him nothing. He is a sacrifice to our prosperity." Jeff released his hold on her. Then he pointed out the man's erection. "Just watching me fuck you makes this sick fucker horny."

Taking a deep breath, Amber lifted the knife. Jeff was right. The man in front of her had planned to hurt her – probably even rape her, and then kill her with this very knife. He deserved what she was going to give him.

***

Lucas saw the red glint in the eyes of the man fucking his doll. It was the devil himself, and try as he might, Lucas couldn't escape. The rope was too tight and there were more of them than he could fight.

His doll had her legs spread, and she allowed the beast to fuck her willingly. It was too bad he wouldn't get to see her nipples pierced. When she lifted the knife, it was like a dream. She had hesitated before, but whatever the beast whispered in her ear, it made the doll more resolute. In some small way, Lucas hadn't believed she would do it.

When the knife entered his chest he first felt surprised, then a tremor, then panic. The knife was sharp; he'd made sure of it. What he hadn't expected was that he'd come, and that he would still be alive to watch as her slender hand reached into his chest and ripped out his heart, or that he would see the demon take a bite out of it.

As the world faded fast around him, he wondered two things: would his semen on the window be the only evidence of him that remained once they disposed of his body, and who would take care of his dolls now?

***

Jeff took a bite out of the stranger's heart, still warm with living blood, then offered it to Amber. Watching as the light faded from the eyes of the dead man in front of her, she partook of the heart too, surprised that she enjoyed the taste.

11

Jeff dropped the heart on the ground like a piece of discarded meat, pulled out of her and turned her around, entering her again. She spread her legs wide for her master, leaned back, and closed her eyes in ecstasy. There, in the middle of the room, Jeff fucked her on the corpse.

There would be prosperity in their marriage until their dying day; she'd made the commitment – the sacrifice – and the Daemon accepted their offering.

Jeff was everything her heart desired.

MOVIE STAR

by Dani Brown

Feet pounding on cold, hard concrete. The light at the end of the tunnel, still so distant.

Each foot forward left her with more blood. A trail of it from down the corridor. A toenail missing – another ripped away with a flap of skin. Breathing hard, her lungs screaming for air.

They were on fire – not literally, but it could be arranged with the snap of fingers (not hers, of course). Sweat ran into her eyes. Everything was a blur, except the pain – only fear could cut through that.

Running through the maze for hours – cameras followed her progress. No tricks. Simple, cold, and hard concrete with a rough surface. It wasn't a gimmick to make it go for miles; the slight incline of the concrete to escape the bowels of the Earth, and all the twists and turns, made it so. It was a trick to keep the studio staff below the surface. Pictures of oxygen-starved people on the surface; giant ant people with whips, making slaves of folks in oxygen masks. The fields only reaped rocks, and everything was shrouded in midday darkness.

No one believed the posters. The entire world below was built on illusion.

Cameras broadcast her progress to people beyond the surface, in satellites orbiting around. This was the best show: live action reality.

The girl in question wore a flimsy linen nightdress. With the flick of a switch, bright spotlights made the material transparent. She wasn't aware of anything other than the light shining in her eyes.

Each night one or two girls would try to escape.

A host of surprises waited when she turned the final corner and saw the light at the end of the tunnel for the first time. These days, it was the girl's first encounter with natural sunlight. Night below would run opposite to night above for that very effect.

The maze they ran through before had been plain and boring. They knew the way out and if they slowed down for long enough, they'd notice the slight incline. Grey concrete pounded their psyches from all sides. The maze had to be large so they'd be close enough to running on empty by the time they saw the light. Weapons would be dropped for them to use to keep it fair. The viewers liked things to be fair. The girl didn't see the doors blending into the concrete next to her. It might be fairer if she did, but then again, it might frighten her into rolling into a ball, too scared to do anything other than wet herself. That wouldn't be fair.

A man in the control room, face lit by the blue light of the screen, waited, counting the pounding steps on the concrete. His fingers spread across buttons – they would know when the time came to make a move and in what order to do it. The at-home pay-per-view audience only had this glimpse behind the scenes during special televised interviews on the premium channels.

The girls stored below were rising stars. They all auditioned for movie roles. Housing was part of the contract. The mass-market movies were churned out for the people above, who didn't know what conditions their beloved actresses lived in. Deals with the tabloids and minders helped with the illusion. They'd be drugged up and sent out to play under the watchful eye of a babysitter. Once the contract was signed, it was signed.

Girls from the inner city were so excited to be offered a way out, a way to the luxury houses in the West, that they would sign anything without first reading it. Rich spoiled brats were just as likely not to read it.

The girl running towards the light – she was different, a special prize from suburbia. She needed a special sort of weapon, one daddy wouldn't approve of.

The man bathed in blue moved his fingers. The button he wanted to press was one he'd never used before. His finger hesitated, dusting it off (his boss would kill him if he ever walked into the control room and saw the state it was in). The button was pressed. The weapon wasn't as dusty but it was still rather bad.

She needed time before the last button was pressed. She stopped and would have tripped if the light at the end of the tunnel hadn't caught on something. She bent down, the spotlight highlighting the curve of her arse.

An object from the porno sets gleamed up at her. Every night before bed, all the actresses were walked through the porno sets to ensure their compliance in their lives. The threat of their parents watching their little girl spit-roasted was always present in their minds.

The girl allowed the cramps to seize her. The man cast in blue light considered this. He would allow her time to catch her breath.

A string of snot caught in the spotlight and he zoomed in. The girl didn't notice the cameras watching her. The pay-per-view audience liked the little acts of humiliation. Snot was better than nothing, but it wasn't the best these girls could do.

The girl had a name once. A bright future open to the possibilities of a career in anything. She chose acting. She didn't remember her name. She didn't even know the name that went in her place in the end credits.

The girl stood there, her snot swaying in the breeze blowing through from the end of the tunnel. The pause was too long. There would be complaints.

"Hey girl, take off your nightie."

She looked around to locate the source of the instruction. A green dot blinked at her from the concrete wall. Now that she was looking at it, she saw holes drilled in it. The voice echoed down the corridor. The concrete should have swallowed it. She took a closer look at the walls – nothing more than a facade.

"Your nightie."

The man in the control room had access to the buttons to make his voice sound more threatening. The girl in question was prudish and uptight.

"I hope you're nice and wet."

He snickered. He doubted it. There were ways to make her that way. It was for her own good (and the pleasure of the rich schmucks in orbit around the planet).

She made no signs to remove her nightie. He swirled his chair around and went to the joystick.

Out of a hidden door came metal arms. He lifted them. She didn't notice; she was too intent on the holes in the wall.

He didn't like doing this shift alone. With two of them, they could really mess her up. He couldn't reach the buttons on the main control panel. Those buttons had all the sound effects.

He ran one of the metal arms down her spine and ripped off her nightie with the other. He turned around and pressed the button for a cold breeze.

His face was turned away from the monitor and he missed the girl pissing herself. The rewind function was useful for when he wanted to get off. With understaffing being a serious issue, it was all he had these days.

He couldn't use it now. He went back to the microphone.

"Take off your panties."

She screamed. He wheeled over to the joysticks and sent the metal arms pawing at her. Her flesh was still a bit flabby. Some of the directors liked to keep them that way. The people above demanded representation on the silver screen.

The longer he prolonged this, the more enjoyment the pay-per-view customers orbiting Earth would get. He used the joystick to direct a metal finger down her spine, all the way to her panties, promising anal violation if she didn't obey. He was slow and lingering. He couldn't hear her sobs, but he could see them wracking her body on the monitor.

She moved her hand to the hem of her plain white panties (the per-pay-view people liked those even if the actress' skin was so pale they couldn't really tell if she was wearing any). She was taking too long. He moved the metal finger in circular motions around her anus. If there had been anything left in her bladder, she would have pissed herself again.

It made her move the panties down with more speed. She tripped as she pulled them off, cutting her knees. He imagined the viewers jizzing their pants. He was used to it but some of them might be new and not familiar with such sights.

He aimed to please – mainly because he wanted a pay raise – so he shoved the unlubricated metal finger up her arsehole. He waited for her to get over the initial violation and pain as he kept her pinned there.

"Now, you see that on the floor?"

She shook her head.

"Put it on. Half goes up you, and half goes up someone else."

He was of the opinion all the actresses should start out on the porn sets and work their way up. He pulled the metal finger out of her anus.

"Quickly now, I don't have all night."

She pulled it up by the straps. He was losing patience.

"Those are for stability and support. Put it up you first, it doesn't matter what side."

These actresses were always so clueless. She hesitated and he shoved the metal finger into her vagina.

"That's where it goes."

He ripped the finger away and she put it up without further complaint.

"Now strap it to you, we don't want it falling out now."

While she was busy with the buckles, he pressed the button to operate the smoke machine. It was designed to look like fog circling her ankles. As an actress, she would know that but she'd already blown a few valves in her head, which impacted her recent memories. It worked the same on all of them, making the long run for freedom (and ant people).

She didn't notice the fog until it covered her ankles. She jumped, clutching her breasts. The double-ended plastic cock jumped with her.

"That is your weapon, little princess. Use it and do me proud."

He wheeled back to the main set of controls. The fog was disorientating but what she really needed was strobe lights. There was no script for this film. He could press whatever buttons he wanted.

What he really wanted was to see just one girl escape into the clutches of the giant mechanical ants waiting outside the tunnel. That didn't translate into going easy on any of them. Once a person became a prisoner of the film industry, they were always a prisoner.

He pressed the sound effects to mimic heavy breathing behind her. She turned around but no one was there. He pressed it again so it came from behind her on the other side. He did this a few times, shining a new spotlight on her each time she jumped (the pay-per-view audience liked bouncing tits, but he wasn't sure what they thought of the plastic penis – this was the first time he had used one of them). While she was jumping and turning around at nothing, he pressed the button for the sound of footsteps on loose hardwood floorboards. He liked it when they forgot they were standing on concrete. The audience did too.

She didn't know which way to turn and ended up running into a concrete wall. Instead of letting her crash, he opened the door.

She ran right into the arms of a waiting dummy made of rancid bits of steak and covered in flies. Strobe lights didn't allow for good vision. She could only feel the flies landing on her in the dark.

There was nothing to control the dummy. It took her some time to work out the piece of flesh she'd walked into was dead. Her scream would have been enough to break glass if there had been any nearby.

Her hair tangled in it as she tried to turn around. The footsteps were coming from that direction. She instead thought to walk past the body after untangling her hair.

Limp burlap scarecrows hung from the ceiling. An actor on his first audition hid amongst them (as there were actors hidden in all the rooms waiting for their turn under the lights).

The man in the control room had no idea what the actor was armed with. Studio execs liked it better that way. He hoped a dildo would be enough to defeat him though. It always sucked when the first actor killed the girl. Even behind the control panel, where he had seen and done it all, he could feel the disappointment of the viewers orbiting Earth.

He didn't know where the actor was hiding amongst the burlap, stuffed with straw and hung up. He exchanged strobe lights for black light with a quick flick of his wrist. It didn't allow him to see any better either but it further confused the girl. He shone little lights on each scarecrow with different colours and angles to create different shadows.

She wasn't allowed to forget the metal arms. He wheeled to his joystick and stuck one out at her. Her plastic penis bounced.

He had to be certain the actor on his first audition didn't fall asleep. They were kept caged for days on end without any contact. Not even the runners with trays of dehydrated food were allowed to say so much as "good morning" to them. Their sanity needed to be flaky but intact enough to navigate a fight or flight situation.

The control operator went back to his sound effects, setting off a fog horn – that should wake the actor up. He zoomed the cameras in on the small of the girl's back and shone a light to pick up the beads of her sweat. With another operator, they could control the joysticks and metal fingers at the same time. It would have been fun to squeeze her flesh.

One of the scarecrows moved and the girl jumped. Something silver caught in a stray beam of light. The operator pressed the button for silence in the scarecrow room. He wanted the girl to have a fighting chance with her dildo. He spoke into the microphone.

"In front of you. Use your dick."

The pay-per-view audience liked crude language. The actresses were as disposable as the actors, but the audience always replaced their faces with one of a personal enemy. Hearing them further degraded made them feel warm and fuzzy inside their guts and space pants.

The knife with a serrated blade reflected off the girl's eyes. It was a perfect shot.

The actor was dressed in a burlap sack and covered in white powder. His dank hair hung in his eyes. He was meant to blend in with the scarecrows and had done a pretty good job minus his lack of pants. This particular film studio was fond of the 'less-is-more' campaign towards clothing the stars of the silver screen.

A loud noise sounded behind the actor – his cue. He lurched at the actress. She caught him up on her removable dick. The noise of his knife dropping sounded like a pin falling to metal, only the floor was concrete.

The girl screamed and clutched her breasts (this one was fond of breast clutching). The pathetic behaviour was over-the-top. It may have been an act; the glimmer in her eyes said it was.

She grabbed the detachable penis with one hand and ran at the actor, poised to poke him up the arse. The man painted in blue light behind his buttons and screens rubbed his eyes. This might be the one. He sat back and watched. There was no need to push any buttons to urge them along.

She landed on the actor's thigh. He was too dazed to jump out of the way. He forgot about his knife lying on the floor. So did she. She manoeuvred him around and penetrated his arsehole without warning.

His howl was immediate. Her breasts bounced as she rode him – liquid from his bowels squirted up her stomach. She didn't care. She would have done well on the porno sets and risen to fame instead of always being cast as the second lady.

In the control room, he took out his dick. It was against company regulations, but then again, so was smoking. The overflowing ashtray didn't give a shit and neither did he.

The way she reamed the young man made his blood flow right to his cock. It hardly required any stroking before he blew his load on the lower buttons. It would be dust before the next shift came along to deal with any possible false-daytime escapees.

The actor was still breathing. The control operator zoomed in on his chest. The girl looked tired and out of breath. She'd never really had time to catch it.

He sounded the fog horn again and covered the room in smoke. It was time for her to move on. He opened a door in front of her. Light shone from it but it was too bright to pass as daylight.

She ran for it, leaving the actor panting on the floor. He reached for her ankle but, even through the lens, it was half-hearted.

The light shone on her dildo. It was hard to say if it was blood or shit reflected off it – the man in the control room thought it a bit of both. The door closed as soon as she was behind it.

A chain rattled on the floor. Compared to the gloom of the last room, it was too bright to see. However, the pay-per-view audience could see perfectly through their television sets. He gave her a moment to adjust. After her display with the last actor, she'd earned it.

He pumped the scent of fresh cut grass into the room. The audience couldn't see it, couldn't hear it, and most wouldn't be able to smell it (these sorts of affairs always made people switch off their Smell-O-Vision). It went up her nostrils though, triggering memories of long ago.

She still had access to these. She still remembered the outside world before acting had consumed her mother. She caught her breath before catching her vision but ran in a straight line anyway – she didn't notice the slight decline to the room.

The pay-per-view audience only noticed when the man in the control room flashed subtitles onto the screen explaining it. Those with Smell-O-Vision switched to the on position (they didn't bother tucking their cocks back into their space pants).

The door at the other end of the room wouldn't open. She clawed at the concrete wall, tearing fingernails away in the process. She didn't know there was a door there. She didn't need to know.

The chains on the floor rattled again. The control operator knew an actor on his first audition lay there, covered in body paint. He wasn't going to give up the disguise by casting the room in normal light levels. It ruined the haunted illusion for the pay-per-view audience. They hadn't seen this room in a very long time.

The girl didn't notice the noise on the floor. This particular actor had been instructed not to open his eyes – his audition rested on his ability to obey directions. She was making enough noise (the operator knew without switching on the sound) for the actor to inch over as far as the chains allowed.

The actor on the floor grabbed her ankle. Without knowing where his arsehole was, she was going to have trouble violating her way to freedom with this one. The control operator still rooted for her though. He wanted to see those giant mechanical ants whipping aging film stars into Botox treatment and arse implants.

It had been a long time since his last trip to the surface. Too long. Staffing cuts meant working twelve-hour shifts, seven days a week for the past six months. There was no end in sight.

She screamed and jumped. The dildo bounced. Even her breasts did before she clutched her bleeding hands to them. This one liked to try to preserve her modesty or put up a show of doing such.

He zoomed in on her blood-stained fingers squeezing the soft flesh, a little hint of nipple poking out. A drop of blood fell. He slowed down the camera, following it. She jumped.

The chained actor was out of shot. He zoomed out again. Little hints of a shadow were cast by his arm. The girl wouldn't have noticed though.

The chains inched further up her leg. He was really reaching for it. More chains stretched around to her other ankle. The other hand felt up her knee. She shook with the unexpectedness of it. Her detachable dick shook with her.

The auditioning actor would have been unaware if he was serious about his audition. It was always hard to tell who was serious and who was there because their parents made them do it with delusions of fame and fortune dancing in their heads.

His hands moved like he was blindfolded. For all the control operator knew, the make-up team could be surgically removing eyes now. Or perhaps the invisible actor was displaying raw talent with his eyes open.

The control operator tried to get an angle but it was impossible to tell where his face was. The make-up team had been bred below for their purpose.

The chains clinked as he clawed his way up her leg. They were already growing tight from dragging across the floor. The control operator sounded a horn to her side to make her move closer to the man.

His reaction when he grasped the dildo would determine whether he was blind or not. The operator had a camera focused on where he assumed the actor's face was. The hands painted the same colour as concrete were grey against the young actress' pale flesh, traveling up.

The operator sounded the horn again, sending her to cower in the corner. She fell to the floor. That should liven things up a bit. Grey paint covered her body. Where a head had been a moment before, teeth marks were left.

When she moved, the operator lost sight of his face. The plastic dick would have been discovered by now. The girl's hands were under her body. She was left with thrusting action to free herself. Based on the movement of grey across her body, the actor was enjoying it.

She thrust her arms free and reached for him. She couldn't reach his arsehole or his cock and had to settle for his hair. The chains would have allowed him to move off her. The hidden door finally opened at the press of a button, offering a glimpse of freedom.

He went for licking her instead. His eyes were still intact, just painted over. He couldn't have opened them even if he wanted to. She could see him though, against her pale flesh.

Something crept through the door. The operator didn't know what waited beyond this one or what their instructions were. It wasn't invisible though.

Silver glittered off the grey wall. Finger blades. Another first audition actor entered. He jumped onto the other actor with his finger blades poised to slash. This didn't shake the invisible actor off the girl.

Blood couldn't be painted grey. It oozed out of his back and then poured.

The actor with the finger blades went for stabbing next. He didn't impale the full length of the blades into the invisible actor's back – he would hit the girl that way.

He pulled him off and left him to bleed out in the opposite corner. The cameras picked up both the man dying in a pool of his blood and the newcomer, offering the pay-per-view audience in space the option to watch on split screen or select their favourite.

The actress struggled beneath him. He was heavier than the dead man.

The control operator zoomed in between their legs. She clutched her plastic cock with both hands. One of those hands would be better served ripping away his clothes. Too late. He was doing it himself with the raw hunger of someone allowed to masturbate to the point of orgasm but never beyond.

Her dildo was next to go. She screamed. The man on top of her didn't care. She was naked without it.

She pushed at him, pulling away his coat. There was another layer beneath.

He stuck his tongue out and licked her face. She shut her mouth against it. He pried it open and came away after thrusting without penetration, blood dripping out. She spat the tongue free of her mouth.

This actor broke character at the faintest hit of pain. Without a tongue, he couldn't speak. He wouldn't make it past his first audition.

The girl picked up her double-ended penis and shoved it back inside. She walked away and into the next room without so much as a glance over her shoulder. The man in the control room pressed the button to mimic footsteps behind her. She threw up her middle finger at them.

The room she walked into was empty. The actor had broken ranks for a quick piece of arse. The controller left the door open but let her walk straight through without clawing at the walls.

That door slammed shut as soon as she was inside. But she wasn't inside – she was out.

She ran across yellowed grass, away from the escape hatch. The building looked like any normal house from a movie set. The grass seemed endless. A patch of land to disguise the complex below.

She never lost her dildo. The ground rose up around her. Cameras poked out of the grass to follow her progress as she fell.

The camera zoomed on a giant pit, not taking any particular scene into focus. Only a certain depth had been dug before reaching the studio below. The mechanical ants were programmed to ensure this would never be reached by the aging starlets.

The girl sat naked (apart from the dildo poking out between her legs) with her head in her hands, sobbing. It didn't take long for a giant mechanical ant to come up to her. She didn't try to fight it off as a shackle was put around her ankle. Movie stars had surprisingly long lives. But the public didn't need to know that.

Her death would be reported as a drug overdose next morning. Her parents would bury someone else's daughter.

THE TRAVELLING CIRCUS

by Alice J. Black

The bus came to a chugging stop on the side of the road, jerking Charlie forward. "Shit," she muttered under her breath, pressing her hand against the back of the seat in front just in time to stop face-planting.

Shuffling on her backside, she glanced around to make sure everyone was okay. Shock was the only thing anyone had suffered and even that was minimal. "What the fuck, Dean?" she yelled as she scooted across the seat, the fabric rough on her bare legs.

He glanced back from the driver's seat and ran his hand through his hair. She'd always loved the way he did that but not right now. Right now his arse was toast. They were headed up to the cabin for the week along with six of their friends and there was still a fair way to go if she remembered rightly.

Dean shook his head and then threw his hands up. "No idea."

"What do you mean, no idea?" She swung her legs off the seat and marched to the front of the bus, ducking to avoid hitting the roof.

"I mean, no idea," he repeated, pointing at the gauge. "Engine light is on."

She slapped his shoulder, satisfied with the smack it made. "You didn't think to check before we left?"

"Woah." He held his hands up. "I'm not the only person on this fucking bus, Charlie."

"No, but you're the driver."

"Come on, guys," James cut in, stepping up to the front of the bus. "There's no need to argue."

"Dean got us stuck in the middle of nowhere, James. You think that's something to laugh at?" Her anger was rising and she sucked in a breath.

"Listen, we must only be five miles out. We can hike the rest of the way and sort the bus out tomorrow when it's light."

"Hike?" She rounded on James. "Have you seen what I'm wearing?" She indicated her body: a pair of denim shorts that barely covered her arse and a black tank that didn't leave much to the imagination.

James' eyes travelled the length of her figure. He shrugged. "Hey, you knew we were travelling. Maybe next time you'll dress more appropriately."

Charlie scowled but James turned to address the rest of the bus. "All right guys, looks like we've got to walk from here. It's around five miles but I don't think it'll take long. We'll all have to pitch in and carry the bags."

That got a series of groans and Charlie crossed her arms over her chest. A smug smile played on her lips. James always tried too hard but he wasn't getting many likes this time around.

"What about the beer?" Scott asked.

"Hey, man, if you want to carry it, be my guest."

Charlie glanced outside. Dusk wasn't far off and it was a long hike. She shivered in anticipation and hugged her arms around her body. She was not going to enjoy this.

By the time all eight of them had clambered off the bus and got their bags from the back, it was decided the beer could wait until the morning, much to Scott's irritation. Reaching into her pack, Charlie scrounged a long-sleeved top and pulled it on. It would have to do for now.

"Are we ready?" James asked.

"How long will it take?" Marie asked. She was the smallest of the group and had the lightest pack.

Charlie envied her best friend at times, but more so now as she hefted her heavy bag onto her shoulders, already wondering why she had packed so much.

James shrugged. "Not too long, but stay together. It's getting dark out and who knows what we might come across out here."

Charlie shuddered. That's exactly what she was worried about.

The long road to the cabin in the mountain was known to be haunted. It was a story that had circulated the school and stuck. She didn't really believe in ghosts, but she didn't like to be hiking in the middle of nowhere in the dead of the night either. Tightening the straps on her pack, she shivered in the night air, wishing she had worn something more appropriate. Not that she was ever going to say that to James.

They set off, James taking the lead as always. She came somewhere in the middle of the group and that made her feel a little better - there was no way she would be last in line.

"Hey, you okay?" Marie asked, sidling up to her.

Charlie looked down. Marie barely reached the height of her shoulders and Charlie got a clear view of the girl's chest. No wonder all the boys loved her. Sighing, she nodded. "Yeah, just annoyed with Dean."

"It's not really his fault if the van is broke." Marie shrugged.

"I know. I guess I was a bit harsh with him?"

"Yeah, a little." Marie nodded. "He'll be fine."

Charlie glanced back. Her boyfriend walked alongside Amber, and she had to resist the urge to stomp back there and put an end to whatever had brought that smile to the girl's face. Instead, she snapped her head back around and continued trudging.

"Don't mind Amber," Marie said, shuffling closer. "She's harmless."

"And Dean is a sucker for any girl who'll listen."

"He knows where he's better off."

"Sometimes I wonder." She shook her head. They had been dating for eight months. Not a long relationship by any stretch, but it was *her* longest. They were beginning to get serious, moving further into third base territory, but it seemed it was never enough. He wanted the full hog and she wasn't ready to give it up. Not yet.

Shaking her head, she changed the subject. There was no way she could keep up this conversation and check her anger too. "So tell me, who are *you* dating at the minute?"

Marie grinned. "You know Jonathan?"

"The guy who plays striker?" Charlie raised her brow. "He's hot."

"I know." Her grin widened. "And well endowed."

Charlie gasped and then giggled. "You have no shame."

"Hey, I'm only going to be young once."

"Doesn't mean you have to put it out there for everyone."

"Just the hot guys." Marie winked. "Besides, it's nothing serious."

"Hell, if I was dating him, I'd make it serious."

Marie laughed. "Dean isn't so bad."

They both turned at the same time and watched as Dean playfully punched Amber in the shoulder. She giggled. Charlie scowled and turned back.

"Not so bad as long as I'm watching him." She shook her head. "I don't know, Marie. Sometimes I wonder if it's even worth it anymore."

"Relationships are tough but they shouldn't be an uphill struggle. Think about that."

Charlie bit her lip against the sting in her eye. There was no way she was going to cry. Not here, not now. She was out with her friends, plus Dean, heading to the cabin for the half-term holidays. They had done it for as long as she could remember and it was always fun. It had started as a one-off and had grown into a ritual. The eight of them had always been together in some capacity. Marie was her best friend, Dean her boyfriend for the last eight months. James was the goody-two-shoes, Nez was the nerd and his girlfriend Melissa was the quiet but nice one. Scott was the joker and always got on well with Dean. Then, of course, there was Amber. Up until recent months, Charlie and Amber had always got on but recently her attitude had begun to stink and her way-too-obvious attempts at homing in on Charlie's boyfriend were doing the girl no favours.

Maybe Marie was right. Though her relationship with Dean had been fun, things were beginning to change and they hadn't been right for a while. She felt the distance between them. Taking one last glance back, she sighed as she saw his hand brushing Amber's arm. Charlie dropped her head and kept marching. It was time to cut him free.

The group began to quieten with each step they took. The night air was chilly and the vastness of their journey swept across them. Charlie knew that five miles was nothing, and in the middle of the day she wouldn't have kicked up a fuss, but she shuddered as she remembered where they were: Old Mount Road. The place had a bad reputation. People had gone missing — even vehicles had completely vanished without a trace — and she wasn't eager to be here any longer than she had to.

An owl hooted in the distance and she lifted her head to look at the moon. The bright, round disc illuminated their way well enough but she knew this road as well as anyone else and it wouldn't be long until they passed through a copse of trees up ahead. It'd be darker then, and she was worried about what might be in the woods on either side. Shuddering, she shoved the thought away. There was no point in dwelling on it. She would only succeed in spooking herself, and after the decision she'd just made, she wasn't in any hurry to rush into Dean's arms.

"Hey, guys," James' voice cut into the night. "The trees are up ahead."

Charlie swallowed and focused on the dark patch of road. She made out the shapes of the trees and their green foliage and, most of all, the dense darkness that seemed to fill the space between the boughs. It was the sort of darkness that could hide anything, and she briefly wondered if she would pass through to the other side of that dark tunnel.

"You know what they say is in there, don't you?" Marie whispered, moving close.

Charlie gave her a sidelong glance and focused back on the road. "It's not haunted, Marie."

Marie nodded vigorously and her short, dark hair flipped around her face. "I heard it from James who heard it from Chrissy who said her friend Gemma's brother had seen it."

Charlie rolled her eyes. "Really?"

"Really." Marie nodded in all seriousness. "Apparently they were travelling to the cabin for a break away when their car broke down not far from the trees. They had to get out and walk on a night just like this when it happened."

Charlie drew a breath and realised for the first time how silent it had gone. The whole group was listening to her story. "What happened?" she asked in a breathless whisper.

"There were four of them. The girls were snatched first and hauled away screaming into the night. Then it was her brother's friend, all to the sound of circus music. Her brother was the only one who made it out alive."

"Circus music?" Amber's voice came from behind them, tinged with terror.

"They say that a travelling circus came here once, years ago. The carts got stuck and they were trapped. Some of them died and their spirits still haunt this place."

"I heard they still try to perform their skits to make people laugh before they cut their throats," Scott added.

The tension thickened as the silence continued. Charlie wrinkled her nose. "That's stupid."

"How do you know?" Amber snapped.

"Shut up." Charlie turned on the girl. "You're buying into the myth."

"And you're not opening your eyes. We're almost at the trees."

They all looked up at the boughs then. As Marie had spun her tale, they'd reached the boundary of the trees that flanked the road. Beneath the canopy of branches and leaves, the road was dark. Charlie shivered. She didn't want to go under there any more than anyone else but she had to.

Sucking in a deep breath, she ploughed forward. Behind her, she heard a deep gasp and a couple of mutters but no other footsteps. She was in this alone. She thought about swinging around, desperate to have some company, but she knew she would look like a coward if she did. Instead, she kept marching with one foot in front of the other. Staying in the centre of the road, she stared at her boots as she moved, refusing to give in to the desire to search the trees on either side for fear of what she might see. Her stomach clenched and her heart pounded. She knew it was stupid. There was no way there was some teenager-murdering ghost here. Marie's story had got under her skin and that was it.

A few moments later, she heard the familiar sound of footsteps on tarmac and knew she wasn't alone. Chancing a glance back, she watched as the rest of her friends shuffled into the tunnel of trees and began moving along the road as a pack. With a grin, she spun and carried on, glad she wasn't alone, laughing silently to herself because they had bought into the story. Everyone knew it was a myth.

On and on they marched in the darkness. Charlie's legs ached and her chest burned. She thought the road might never end but she didn't let it stop her. She had to keep moving to reach the cabin.

Soon, she saw a greyer light up ahead and knew it indicated their exit. Turning to the rest, she shouted back, "Hey, guys, we've almost made it."

That brought smiles to faces and together their pace increased. Everyone was feeling the dread under there and even Charlie had to admit, as much as she didn't buy into the story, she wanted to be out from under the dense canopy.

They were almost out, the threshold to the night within reach, when she saw something moving out of her peripheral vision. Her head snapped to the right, but where she thought she'd seen movement, there were only endless boughs of trees keening off into the distance. Nothing more. She bit her lip but resolved to forget about it. Shaking her head, she kept moving.

Finally stepping across the boundary and onto the last stretch of road, she glimpsed the cabin up ahead. They were almost there.

The sombre mood of the group lifted as they made their way along the final stretch. Marie found her way back to Charlie's side and they walked and chattered as if the last hour of silence had been nothing more than a minute. The cabin drew closer and it wasn't long until James unlocked the door and they spilled over the threshold into the relative warmth and safety it provided.

An hour later, though the beer wasn't flowing as it should have been, everyone was in better moods. The sofas and chairs were taken up by sprawling teenagers and a fire roared in the hearth, thanks to Dean. Charlie watched him work as he threw another couple of sticks into the flames and then stood to dust his hands. He shot a sidelong glance towards Amber before moving to sit beside Charlie – a duty and no more. Charlie could barely repress the sigh that escaped her. It was time to do this whether she was ready or not.

"Dean?"

"Yeah?" He looked up at her from beneath heavy eyelids.

"Come with me for a second."

That remark was met with hoots from the guys as she led him to the front door. Charlie rolled her eyes. Men never changed and that was exactly why she needed to cut Dean loose.

"What's up?" he asked as they stepped out onto the old wooden porch.

Charlie pulled the door closed, cutting off the last of the cheers, and leaned against the railing. For a moment she stared into the night. The moon was bright, illuminating the woods and, beyond, the road they had travelled. Everything looked still and there was no sound out there other than that of the bugs that revelled in the night and the wind as it swept past her ear. It was truly a beautiful place.

"Charlie?" Dean nudged her.

She felt the tension rocking through them and knew that he knew what was coming even though she hadn't said a word.

"Dean," she started, taking a deep breath, "this isn't working."

"What's not, babe?"

She glanced at him but he wouldn't look at her. "Us, Dean. We're not working. It's time to call it a day." She watched as he chewed the inside of his cheek as if debating an argument. Then he finally looked at her and nodded.

"Okay," he said.

Her heart cracked. It was just a slither, but something inside wanted to hear him fighting for her. Even just a little. "So that's it then?"

"Guess so." He nodded. "I'm gonna head back inside." And then he was gone, the door shutting after him, and another series of cheers assaulted her ears. Dean's was one of them.

Charlie leaned heavily against the railing and sighed. She felt a bit of sadness, but it wasn't because she was losing Dean. It was because she had spent the last eight months with someone who clearly wasn't worth her time and effort.

Just then, something caught her attention. A movement further down the road. Straining her eyes, she stared at the spot where she thought she'd seen something flash but there was nothing. The night was as still as it had been. She rubbed her arms and folded them over her chest. Maybe she was more spooked than she'd thought. *Time to go inside and re-join the party.* Tomorrow would be a better day.

As she spun to step inside the cabin, a tingling noise, light and child-like, rang into the night and if she had taken Marie's story seriously, she could have sworn it was circus music.

Back inside, Charlie realised something was being passed around in a plume of smoke. Instantly her hands were on her hips and she stared at Amber, who had the spliff and had taken a long draw, blowing the smoke out of her mouth slowly and giggling. She passed it down the line to James, who took a draw.

"Who in the hell brought that?"

"Me." Dean held his hands up.

She gritted her teeth. Of course he had. It seemed to her more and more that she had just made the right decision about her now ex. It also meant she couldn't really argue with him, not to the extent that she wanted to anyway.

"Hey, we haven't got the beer so I needed something." He shrugged.

"I'm sure you did," she muttered, heading over to the empty spot next to Marie. She slumped down into the old chair and sagged into the cushion.

"You okay?" Marie asked, patting her leg.

The warmth of Marie's hand felt good on her bare skin. She sighed and forced a smile. "Guess so." She nodded. "But listen, I think I saw something out there."

"Charlie, we're in the middle of nowhere. It was probably an animal or something. Don't let the story spook you."

"Yeah. You're probably right," she agreed, but it didn't stop the bubbles in her gut as she remembered the flash of colour and soft tingling chimes.

The night wore on and the atmosphere settled. Nez and Melissa started a game of cards on the only table in the place and a few joined in. Amber's voice could be heard over everything, and Charlie winced every time she heard the high-pitched laugh. She could only hope tomorrow would be better. At least then there would be beer; she could enjoy herself and forget the whole fiasco of today.

"I'm going to get some air," Amber announced, pushing herself up.

Charlie watched her departure and the extremely bronzed, long legs that carried her through the front door. Who was she kidding? Charlie didn't stand a chance against that girl. Amber was a goddess compared to her, and she wasn't surprised Dean's eyes had wandered. Hell, even her own had.

She shook her head and stood up to go to the kitchen to get a glass of water. She had just filled the glass when a scream pierced the night. It was long and loud and cut through the chatter in the cabin.

The glass dropped from Charlie's hand, hitting the stone floor and shattering. Charlie ran through the room, lunging over the coffee table and narrowly missing Dean as he flung the cabin door open. Her chest heaved as she arrived outside and stared around the porch. It was empty, though she could swear she'd seen a flash of yellow further down the trail.

"Where's she gone?" Dean asked.

Charlie was too surprised to be angry. "I don't know." She took a step forward and stared into the darkness. Nothing. Amber had vanished.

"What's this?" Melissa whispered, taking a step forward, diverting Charlie's attention to a dark stain on the wood. It was wet.

Charlie pressed her finger to it, and it came away dark. Blood. Bile rose in her throat but she shoved it back down and wiped her hand on her shorts.

"Everyone inside," she ordered. She had no idea where Amber had gone but she knew one thing: something was going on. Holding her arms out, Charlie herded everyone indoors where she was met with tears and fear. She took a deep breath and answered the first question fired at her.

"Where's Amber?" That came from James.

"I have no idea." Charlie shook her head.

"Is that blood?" Marie's eyes widened.

"Yes." There was no point in lying to her friends.

Marie gasped. "The ghosts of the travelling circus."

A ripple of hysteria rippled around the room as people muttered, cursed and sobbed. Charlie sucked in another deep breath, trying to calm herself as much as push down her frustration. "There is no ghost. It's just a story." She had to repeat it in her mind a few times. Even she was starting to wonder.

"How do you know?" Dean yelled, face going red with exertion. "Where is she?"

"Maybe she fell."

"There's no sign of her, dumbass. We're being hunted."

"Don't you think you're overreacting? We'll find her." Charlie held out her hands in a display of peace.

"You want us to go out there?" Marie asked, her lip quivering.

"I think we need to stay calm and think logically. If Amber is hurt we need to find her and get her some help."

"That makes sense," James added with a nod. He had been relatively quiet for a guy who normally liked to take charge.

"So, me, James and Scott will go scout outside, see what we can find."

They strode towards her, happy to follow.

"I'm not staying here," Marie piped, shooting up from her seat.

"Me either." Dean shook his head.

"We're coming." Melissa dragged Nez from his spot on the floor. His face twisted and turned red and Charlie knew he didn't want to go outside.

"Nez, you can stay if you want," Charlie offered, giving him permission. He performed a sort of odd little bow, muttered a thank you and dropped back down.

"You're a fucking coward," Melissa hissed at him. He wouldn't meet her eyes.

"Come on guys. We'll go outside and figure things out from there."

Charlie led the search party outside. The night continued to be still. As she made her way down the steps, followed by the others, she wondered about Amber. Sure, she wasn't exactly on friendly terms with her at the minute, but Amber was still her friend and she wouldn't want anything bad to happen. Charlie wondered if she really believed that Amber had fallen like she told the others, but she knew the girl hadn't fallen. There was blood on the porch. Her stomach clenched. Maybe there was some truth to the story after all.

At the bottom of the steps, she turned right, then moved into the shrubbery beneath the porch. She moved slowly, calling Amber's name and searching the brush. There was nothing. No other sign of Amber at all. It was like she had disappeared into thin air. Or that's what she would have believed if there hadn't been blood on the porch.

"What now?" James asked, looking to her to make the next move.

Charlie bit her lip and was about to respond when the sound of shattering glass cut through the night, followed by a thud and a scream.

"Nez!" Melissa flew up the stairs with Charlie hot on her heels. They took the steps two at a time and burst in through the cabin door, freezing on the threshold.

Blood was smeared across the centre of the floor and had been dragged through the cabin and over to the smashed window in the far corner of the room. A scrap of faded yellow cloth hung on a shard of glass still attached to the window frame, flapping in the breeze. Outside, she heard the faint chime of the all-too familiar song. Charlie's heart hammered a frantic beat on her chest. Nez was gone and now she knew this wasn't just some freak accident.

"What the fuck?" Dean muttered as he came to a stop behind her.

"I can hear music." Marie's voice was small, betraying her fear.

"We need to get out of here," Charlie muttered to herself, but it didn't take long before everyone sprang into action. Grabbing packs, the group worked quickly to get out of the cabin, leaving the bloody mess behind.

At the bottom of the steps, Charlie realised she was in front, leading her little group of friends to safety. Or so they assumed. She swallowed as she stared at the path ahead and realised their only escape from the place was through the woods. Now she knew for certain that on their way through the first time she *had* seen something in the woods, and it wasn't anything she was eager to come across again.

Marie hurried to catch up. Silver trails of tears tracked down her cheeks. "What the fuck is going on?" she asked between gritted teeth.

"Let's just get out of here and alert the police."

"But Amber... Nez..."

"We can't do anything for them now." Charlie shook her head.

"You think it's..." Marie trailed off, staring at Charlie with wide eyes.

"I don't think it's anything. Now come on. Stop thinking and keep moving."

It wasn't long before they hit the threshold of the tunnel of trees. The whole group slowed and, as they reached the boundary, they paused.

Beside Charlie, Marie stared at the dark canopy and said, "Are we really going in there?"

"We have to. It's the only way through." Charlie nodded without moving her gaze. She bit her lip. It was the last place she wanted to go. She felt the trees weigh her down, hemming her in the darkness, like they had something to do with the disappearances, like they were a part of it all. But what scared her most was whatever was hiding behind those tree trunks. Her friends were being picked off, and though she didn't buy into the story of the travelling circus, she knew something bad was happening.

"Come on." She stepped under the ceiling of leaves. Charlie was instantly swallowed by darkness and, much like the first time she'd made the crossing, all she could hope for was that the rest of them followed. It wasn't long before she heard the pounding of feet behind her. Glancing back, she saw the small silhouette of Marie close to her, followed by tear-streaked Melissa, and then the guys bringing up the rear. Eight down to six.

They stuck to the middle of the tunnel. It had taken them an hour to get through the first time but something told her it wouldn't take as long this time. Their steps were quick and light and everyone was silent, alert. Though the cabin had been a place of imagined safety, out here on the road, with no cover or protection, they were more vulnerable than ever.

A sudden flash of garish yellow to her right had Charlie freezing on the spot, head snapping. "Did you see that?" she asked nobody in particular.

"What was it?" Marie whispered.

"I don't know. Let's move."

She stepped up the game and her footfalls were heavier this time but she didn't care. Every sense in her body was on fire. Adrenaline pumped through her body and her limbs shook. They were in danger. They had to get out of here. Fast.

Something flashed to her left, this time a hint of red. She shuddered. Forcing her gaze forward, she kept moving, jogging now. Behind her, several sets of feet pounded and she felt safer knowing she wasn't alone.

Just then, a scream tore through the night. By the time Charlie spun and pushed her way through the small crowd, she saw they were missing another member. Melissa was gone, one of her trainers left resting on the road like it had lost its way. Charlie pushed her hair back and fought the tears that threatened to come.

"What the fuck is going on?" Marie screamed, her face twisted in confusion.

"We have to keep moving."

"But they're all gone."

Charlie grabbed Marie by the wrist and dragged her close. "Get a grip. We'll be next if we don't get out of here. Got it?"

Marie nodded slowly. Charlie spurred them all into action. The guys still had the rear and although she'd like to say she felt safe with them there, she knew she wasn't. They were being picked off. Their group had almost been halved. An attack could come from anywhere. They were all in danger. Her feet moved at a run, carrying her farther and farther down the road. They'd left the destruction of the cabin behind while all around them, danger loomed.

A shout behind cut through the mounting fear. When Charlie turned to look, James was gone. This time she didn't stop moving. She couldn't, not if she wanted to live. Instead, she urged the others forward. Marie ended up in the middle of them as they trotted down the tarmac in the dark, and Charlie stared ahead, hoping they would make it to the other side of the woods.

Another flash to the right, and then something lunged. Screaming, she moved to push Dean out of the way but she wasn't quick enough. He lay face up on the road, his eyes wide and vacant; the huge slit in his throat opened up like a garish grin. He was gone. She fought to keep the rising panic at bay while Marie sobbed hysterically beside her.

It took a few moments for her to gather herself as she stared down at his lifeless corpse. After all, Dean had been her first serious boyfriend despite the fact that she'd been the one to end it earlier. Before she had time to react, another shadow moved and then Scott was taken off his feet and thrust into the woods, screaming. There was a dull thud and the screaming stopped. She knew he was gone.

Only she and Marie remained.

Charlie grabbed Marie's hand and took off running. Her chest burned. Her legs ached, but she kept moving, kept dragging Marie. They had to get out.

The end of the tunnel came into view and she saw a lighter night and knew they had almost made it. Suddenly, a shape lunged out of the trees. Ducking, she whirled away, trying to yank Marie with her, but their connection was lost and she heard Marie grunt. Charlie spun around. Her jaw dropped when she saw what the shape was: a man dressed as a clown. He straddled Marie. Her arms were pinned beneath the torn sleeves of his yellow, faded suit. Garish white make-up was plastered across his face and the blackest grin she had ever seen stretched from ear to ear, the teeth exposed, sharp and tinged with red.

Charlie jumped up. She had to save her friend. At the same time, he lifted a long, curved blade. It glinted in a patch of moonlight and Marie screamed as it came down on her neck, severing it almost in half. Blood spurted from the wound and Charlie screamed.

Then his gaze locked on to her.

She was the last. She had to move. She had to get out of there.

She threw herself in the direction of the open road. Her arms pumped and her legs worked faster than they ever had. Her chest heaved as, in her peripheral vision, she saw the darkness of the boughs streaming past. Behind her, she heard heavy footsteps of pursuit and they were gaining. She didn't dare look back.

On and on she sprinted, the opening getting wider as she got closer. She was almost there.

A hand grazed the back of her neck, and she felt the cloying touch of rubber and remembered the gloves the clown wore. She poured on her speed with a feral grunt. And then she was diving away from the canopy and into the open road.

As quickly as she landed, she rolled and turned to face the darkness, where the man's leering white mask disappeared into the darkness of the trees. There she sat on the road, panting and exhausted. Her mind whirled as she realised the story had been true. But it wasn't spirits haunting the woods.

The travelling circus had come that way and never left.

CLUB CRUELTY

by Carly Holmes

As she bent to fasten her suspenders, Jazz had a sudden moment of doubt. *I could just go home*, she thought, *pick up a pizza on the way. I'll tell Ben I got through reading the files early. He won't question it; he'll be thrilled to spend the evening with me.*

She straightened and looked at herself in the mirror, running her hands up and down her body. Black boots, shiny as ink spills, covered her from mid-thigh to toe, glittering with spurs around her ankles. Her dress clung to her ripe curves like an open wound. Scarlet wasn't a colour many people would choose to wear in a place like this; it screamed: CHASE ME. HURT ME. *But damn, do I look good!* She turned from side to side, smiling at her reflection. Though the zipper that sliced the front of the dress strained against the force of her full tits and the shiny fabric squeezed every inch of her tight arse, she knew she could run if she had to, and she could fight.

Her hair was coiled around her head and fastened with a snake clip. This was her only concession to danger. She'd been caught once before when she'd left it loose, dragged to the floor by fists grabbing her dark locks and then tied down on the rack with those same curls. She hadn't been able to move without ripping hair from her scalp and couldn't see how many of them there were, or what they were doing. She'd begged and kicked but couldn't stop them when they'd tied her wrists and then surrounded her in a leaping, jeering wall of masked faces. She'd been more fearful for her hair than her life, had visions that they'd scalp her, but luckily she'd been in one of the mainstream playrooms where the night's emphasis had been more on sex than suffering. Straddling her throat, they'd taken turns riding her screaming mouth. Cock after cunt after cock, until she was raw and sticky, weeping and euphoric.

It had been left to the staff to set her free at closing time, untying her hair and wrists and pulling her onto her feet. Blood had dribbled down her neck and her legs had shaken so much they wouldn't support her; she'd had to be carried upstairs to her changing room. By the time she'd got home and slid into bed beside Ben, freshly showered and sweet smelling but still gagging with the backwash of pubic hair and come caught in her throat, the sun had been rising. She'd clung to his warm back and nuzzled the damp skin of his armpit, waking him slowly with her tongue. She'd been so horny she couldn't wait for the alarm clock to announce the morning.

There were club rules: NO WEAPONS OTHER THAN THE ONES PROVIDED. NO MAIMING EXCEPT WHERE PERMISSION IS GIVEN. STRICTLY NO KILLING. But everyone knew rules were meant to be broken, and the best nights were the ones that broke every damn rule in the book. Though she'd enjoyed the rare thrill of being so out-of-control, she'd made sure it never happened again. She was the predator, not the prey.

Okay, time to play. Her moment of doubt over, Jazz smiled at her reflection and put her black silk fox mask on, tying the knots behind her head and stroking the fabric until it lay flat against her skin. She tucked her belongings away in the locker and bolted the door that led into the corridor and out onto the street. The other door, the one she headed for, led off from her tiny changing room and into the main part of the club. She paid a premium to have her own changing room but it was worth it not to have to mingle with the other customers before she was ready. *How can they meet down there in the bowels of Club Cruelty after they've shown their daytime selves in the communal changing rooms?* She couldn't imagine being able to take the games seriously if she had to share space with men and women hopping out of their business suits and into their gimp gear, loosening ties and chatting about the weather as they pulled masks on over their heads.

She tapped on the door, which opened immediately. They never kept her waiting here. As she stepped through, she nodded at the unsmiling security guard and descended the stairs down to the badly lit holding area at the bottom. She didn't know if he was one of the ones who had carried her, reeking of come, the night she'd been caught, but she could never look him in the eye. Not anymore.

There was a burst of static from the security guard's radio. He murmured into it and wrote something on the clipboard he carried.

Counting us in and counting us back out. I wonder what happens if the numbers don't tally at the end of an evening? There must have been plenty of occasions when people walked through the doors at the start of a night and were carried out in bags at the end. She'd seen bodies so broken after hours of play there was no way they were walking anywhere anytime soon.

"Jazz, it's good to see you again."

The door had opened behind her as she watched the security guard, and a masked face floated out of the smoky darkness of the club's main room. It faded away as the person bowed and extended an arm to invite her inside, then bobbed back up. Teeth gleamed sharp and wet in the deformed face of a gargoyle and the stench of rotting breath made her gasp and pull back, her mouth twisting with disgust. Saliva hung in thick ropes from the man's top incisors and gathered on his lips in meaty clumps.

He brushed her arm as she passed him, dragging filthy fingernails across her elbow and watching her recoil. "Great outfit," he said, smirking. He liked that he was repulsive to her, she could tell.

There was something familiar about his voice but she couldn't place him. As she walked away, she knew he was staring and she guessed he'd be trouble later. She'd have to watch her back. She was often targeted during these evenings by men who saw catching her as the ultimate prize. Setting herself apart from the others, never chatting, avoiding the more standard playrooms and going straight for the basement floor made her interesting. The fact that she'd once been caught and made powerless added to the excitement. If it had happened once it could happen again, and they all wanted their cocks to be the ones filling her mouth.

Bring it on if you think you can handle me, motherfucker.

CLUB CRUELTY was spelled out in naked bulbs above the bar area, flashing on and off randomly so that the room stuttered and spurted light in a way that made you feel drunk and dizzy. There weren't many people in here but Jazz could hear screams and howls in the distance. The games were already swinging.

The barman opened a bottle of water for her, breaking the seal with a flourish so that she knew it couldn't have been tampered with. She raised it in thanks and drank a little before putting it down and moving on. She wasn't here to socialise, unlike some of the fetish-tourists who came along and stayed exclusively in the bar area, titillating themselves with the thought of their own daring while gripping the armrests of their chairs so hard their knuckles were shiny white, terrified they'd be dragged off and forced to take a more active part.

Jazz walked down one of the corridors, glancing into rooms as she passed them. Standard S&M sex games played in the first few; there were so many whips and chains and writhing bodies it was difficult to make out what end of a person was what. Men and women stood against the walls and whooped as people queued to go in the stocks to be pelted with rotten fruit or hung by their wrists from one of the many contraptions and given endless paper cuts and nipple twists. The air was thick and hot with sweat. She shook her head and moved on when hands stretched out to invite her to join the fun.

Down another short flight of stairs at the end of the corridor, the games got more stomach-turning and bizarre. *Whatever floats your boat, you weird fucks.* Jazz kept her eyes on the floor to avoid seeing the sick corruptions of board and card games going on in the rooms as she passed them. At Club Cruelty, roulette involved the loser nibbling scabs from the bodies of the other players, who grazed and cut themselves through the month, reopening the wounds time and again in order to have scabs as crusted and angry as possible. A Mad Hatter's Tea Party spilled out into the corridor as someone realised the cloudy yellow liquid in the teapot could only be one thing and tried to leave, but was chased down and dragged back, screaming, while the rest of the party pounded the table with their tea cups and hooted, "Drink! Drink! Drink!"

Yeah, and that's not potted meat in the sandwiches either, dumb arse, Jazz thought. She strode down two more flights of steps and paused by the door leading through to the most exclusive area of the club. In here, anything went. Only the most brave and deviant opened this last door, and there was only one iron-clad guarantee: there would always be fewer walking out than walking in. The focus wasn't really on sex, and it wasn't exclusively on pain either. *Think Operation for grown-ups. Grown-ups with serious sadism issues and real scalpels. A kind of carnivalesque spectacle of cruelty.* She was getting excited just thinking about it. One evening in here kept her calm for the rest of the month; it meant she could enjoy the safe, sweet confines of her relationship with Ben and her normal life, without getting restless and being a bitch or ruining what they had together.

She placed her hand on the door and breathed deeply a few times. She was alone and in absolute silence for a moment, the games on the floors above her too far away to be heard and the games on the other side of the dark wood muffled. *Maybe this is why I keep coming back. For this moment of perfect peace before the madness.* She never felt so serene in her life as at this moment every month. Only once you've spent an hour carefully, delicately snipping the skin from a person's eyelids with scissors while they whimpered and twitched on the table can you really know yourself and your soul. The exquisite precision of shaping the lids into tiny triangles so they hung like bunting over the bloodied eyeballs.

Consent was an issue for her. Let the violent gangbangers and the rape fantasists get their rocks off on one of the other floors. It was the infliction of pain, turning agony into an art form and wielding it like a tool, that she sought. That moment when she bent close to her playmate and saw the suffering was getting too much and she knew she could turn back or go further, cause more hurt or less. That moment was the pure distillation of power.

Jazz smoothed her dress and checked that her hair was safely twisted onto the top of her head, then turned the handle, opened the door, and stepped through.

The smell of antiseptic always stung the back of her nostrils for the first few minutes, until she got used to it. She walked the white corridor, stilettos clacking on the floor, past the pegs of surgical gowns (*I'm not covering up* this *dress with one of those things!*) until she reached the ward at the far end, where dozens of patients lay strapped on gurneys. She ignored the sighs and pleading whispers, reading the sheets clipped to the foot rails expressionlessly and then moving on. Something would interest her enough to make her stop and consider; sometimes she went back and read again (PATIENT REQUIRES LEG TO BE OPENED BELOW THE KNEE AND TIBIA REMOVED FROM SOCKET, REPLACED BACK TO FRONT; PATIENT REQUIRES TEETH TO BE REMOVED FROM MOUTH AND STITCHED INSIDE VAGINA) before making her decision.

Jazz preferred performing her surgeries on men. *Don't ask me why, but Daddy could hazard a guess.* For them it was always about sex. It didn't matter what screwed-up personal history made them cherish mutilation fantasies, they were in it ultimately for the intense orgasm they got from experiencing agony. The women, though, wanted to be hurt and deformed out of feelings of self-loathing, and that made Jazz want to cry.

As she wheeled her patient of choice back along the corridor and into one of the empty side rooms, the door leading through to the rest of the club flung open and slammed against the wall, making her jump. She waited for someone to appear but there was just that rectangle of murky dark and a faint smell of rot.

Irritation flared in her briefly. Everybody knew this floor of the club was to be treated with respect. Most of the other customers didn't even venture down here.

"Damn it. Don't move." She left the man waiting by the tray of surgical implements, strapped to his gurney and unable to look away from the gleaming metal. *It'll build the atmosphere a bit. It's no fun if they aren't a little scared going into it*, she thought as she went to close the door.

The stench of putrid flesh hit her hard as she neared the open doorway. She covered her mouth and reached for the handle to swing the door shut, standing for a moment in the frame to look along the length of the corridor. No-one there. The smell was making her want to puke and there was an oily stickiness on her palm where she'd touched the handle.

Some pansy tourist probably, pussying out before they got so much as one foot inside here. Jazz walked back to the side room and tried to shrug off a lingering sense of unease. *Just think about what you're going to do to that man in there. He wants to be a butterfly (how sweet), and he easily has enough flab on his podgy back to make him a pair of wings. Maybe I should snap a couple of ribs, twist them at an angle and use them to hang the flesh from. That could work, though he'll struggle to walk afterwards, let alone fly...*

She was pondering ways and means when she entered the room. At the sink she pumped liquid soap onto her hands and cleaned them thoroughly. The man behind her was silent and still on his gurney.

"Are you ready for your transformation?" Jazz asked, turning to him and smiling. His neck was at an unnatural angle, lolling forward over his chest. *He can't have fainted already! We haven't even got started.* She grabbed a handful of his hair and pulled gently. "Hey, time to play."

The broken bones in his neck ground together as his head snapped back. His eyes were wide open but unseeing. Across his forehead was carved: JAZZ XxX. Blood glistened in the letters. The scalpel was on the tray, neatly lined up with the other instruments, shreds of skin clinging to its shiny tip.

Jazz spun on her heels and stared around the room, her breath lodged in her throat. *What the fuck?*

Screaming rang out at the end of the corridor, followed by the sound of gurneys crashing against walls. More screams. Jazz stood next to the dead man and tried to calculate the distance from her room to the door that would take her back to the club and the safety of the only moderately deviant. She was only fifteen strides away? Twenty at most? She picked up the biggest blade and held it in front of her, edging towards the doorway. She chanced a quick look out, her head flicking right then left.

Bodies littered the ward area at the far end of the corridor. Standing over one of them, stamping down on his victim's head with heavy boots that crushed the woman's skull to pulp in seconds, was the man who had let Jazz into the club at the start of the evening. She remembered now where she knew him from: he'd been working the bar when she first started coming to Club Cruelty a couple of years ago. He'd pestered her and a few of the other female customers, touching them up and trying to rub his obvious stiffy against them, so she'd complained to security and had never seen him again. Until tonight.

Jazz edged back into the room and balanced herself on the balls of her feet, preparing to run. *I can make it to the door before he reaches me. I think I can, anyway...* She held the blade out in front of her and swept the air with it a few times. *And even if I can't, this little baby will slice him to ribbons. The motherfucker doesn't have a clue who he's dealing with.* She smiled. *Fuck, who am I kidding? I knew I should have just got a pizza and gone straight home.*

"JAA-AAZ! I know you're hiding in there! Come out, honey, and see what I've got for you. It's big and throbbing and it's already started dribbling. Guess what it is!"

Shit. He was coming nearer. She had to move. Now.

"Come on, sweetheart, I'm waiting. It's no fun if you don't run!"

Move, Jazz! For fuck's sake! She'd be too late to even try for the door if she waited any longer. But the foul rotting smell was all around her and she knew it was already too late. Any second now, Gargoyle Man would appear, and the room was too small and he was too powerful for her to stand a chance. That brief moment of indecision (*of fear, let's be honest, little Miss Chicken Shit*) had shut down her options.

She turned back to the dead man on the gurney and wheeled him over to the doorway. *One, two, three!* She burst through, pushing the gurney as hard as she could, spinning the back end. It swung hard and fast into the corridor, gathering speed as it crashed into the man crouched outside her door. It knocked him off his feet, clipping his jaw with a loud crack that twisted the lower half of his face to the side.

Well, at least it's a good look with the gargoyle mask.

He screamed and tried to stand up, scrabbling for her ankles as she leapt back and ran. He roared with pain and rage as she reached the door and pulled the handle.

Nothing. It wouldn't budge. She kicked it and yelled with frustration. "Fuck!"

"You stupid bitch, you're going to regret that piece of work," Gargoyle Man said.

She turned to face him, flattening herself against the wall. He was on his feet now, his hands pressed to his jaw, grinding the loose bone back into its socket. Teeth popped like cherry pits, brown and slimy, down his chest. Every time he took his hands away, his jaw flapped loose again. She could barely make out what he was saying but guessed it wasn't an apology. Blood streamed from the side of his mouth and when he spat, a flow of red spattered across the white floor.

"Do you want me to take a look at that for you?" Jazz asked. "I'm pretty handy with a needle, so they tell me around here."

He roared again and lunged for her. She ducked and threw herself past him, staying low and kicking out with her leg. One of her spurs caught his calf, tearing fabric and digging a tunnel into flesh. It split like rotting fruit, strips of putrid skin trailing from the side of her boot like a banner.

"Urgh. Do you ever wash?" she asked before running back down the length of the corridor, into the ward area at the end. *There might still be someone alive who can help me, or an emergency exit down here, or something...*

Those who weren't dead were wishing they were. Gargoyle Man had gone straight for the Maximum Impact approach. Faces no longer recognisably human were smeared across gurneys, brains leaking from flattened skulls. A club studded with nails lay among the wreckage of twitching limbs.

Jesus! Jazz risked a quick look behind her at the now empty corridor and then checked the other side rooms, whispering for help, looking for a telephone or CCTV camera. Anything that could help her. *There's got to be some other way out of here!*

"Give up yet?"

The voice seemed to float from the ceiling. Jazz stared around the white walls, trying to isolate the sound, and then stepped back into the corridor. It was stupid to feel safer out here than in one of the side rooms, but she did.

"That's one hell of a lisp you've got there," she called. "It suits you." She could hear scuffling from above and over to her right. *Might as well try and goad him out...* "Hey, my cousin is a speech therapist. I could pass her number on to you?"

The ceiling directly overhead exploded as the freak punched his fist through and swung himself down to land beside her. Jazz covered her head and fell to the side, coughing up plaster dust. Her blade spun through the air and landed a few metres away. She wriggled after it on her stomach, jack-knifing her body, but Gargoyle Man was on top of her immediately, flipping her over and kneeling either side of her chest, slapping her hard across the face. His belt was tied around his head and chin, securing his jaw. She tried to grab the buckle to twist it, but he knelt on her upper arms, forcing his weight onto her biceps so they burned in agony.

"Fucking smart-mouthed bitch," he snarled. "Got anything to say now?" He reached an arm back and grabbed her crotch, digging with his nails. "You've had this coming a long time, you stuck-up cunt. Strutting around like you're better than the rest of us. Think I'd just forget about you getting me in trouble with the boss man?"

Jazz tried to breathe slowly and deeply despite the weight and smell of him. Her ribs creaked as he settled himself and pain spasmed through her chest. *I can't faint now. I can't.* Her stomach heaved with the need to vomit but she was terrified of choking if she puked. She couldn't imagine he'd put her in the recovery position and fetch her a blanket if he saw she was struggling.

Gargoyle Man shifted slightly and unzipped his trousers, easing his cock into view. The sight of it brought a quick, acidic wave of sick spurting into Jazz's mouth. *Holy fuck, what the..?* She turned her head to the side, cleared her throat and spat.

Stroking the crusted length fondly, he pushed his cock towards her face. "Haven't washed this little feller for a year now. He needs a good soaking. Open up, bitch, and suck, or I'll break every fucking tooth in your head and make you suck anyway. It would be a shame to spoil your pretty looks."

Clenching her teeth so hard they ground together, Jazz reared her head away, bucking beneath him. *I'd rather die than suck on that. I'm probably going to die anyway.* The thought calmed her. *No. There's no way this is how I'm bowing out. Would Ben even know what happened to me, or would the staff here just get rid of the bodies and mop up the blood, ready for next month's fun?*

He struggled to balance himself on his knees and get his cock near enough to her mouth, rocking on her arms and making jabbing movements with his hips.

Jazz snorted. "You're a regular John Travolta, aren't you?" She thrust forward violently and bit the end of his cock, tearing into it and twisting her head from side to side. Her mouth filled with the rank taste of sewers as her teeth burst through the skin to the muscle beneath. Cartilage and veins popped against her tongue.

Gargoyle Man howled and punched her cheeks, trying to pull away, but Jazz hung on like a rat-crazed terrier until she knew she'd severed the freak's cock entirely. Only then did she spit the bloody mess out, choking and gagging. It lay on her chest like roadkill.

"Noooooooooo! My little feller!" Sweeping the pulpy meat up and cradling it in his hands, Gargoyle Man hunched over her and wailed, rocking back onto his heels. His knees slipped off her arms.

He was so distraught, Jazz almost felt sorry for him. Almost, but not quite.

She lurched forward and slapped his hands upwards. The dismembered cock flew over their head and splattered a few metres away. He dived after it frantically and the pressure lifted from her chest.

Where's the blade? She saw it on the floor just past the freak but wasn't sure she could stand up. She'd have to try. Right now, he had his hands full, but he was eventually going to refocus on her and she reckoned he'd be pretty pissed. Lying there, staring at the ceiling and hearing her breath whistle as her cracked ribs struggled against her lungs, Jazz felt an urge to go to sleep. *Just for a second, I'll close my eyes...* Her eyes snapped open again. *You've got your own blades, stupid! Finish this, before he finishes you.*

She brought herself onto her side and slithered towards Gargoyle Man. Scissoring her legs wide open so her thighs were spread and her ankles raised, she edged close to his shuddering back. *If he turns around now he'll have the view of a lifetime!* Tipping herself onto her tailbone, Jazz brought her feet to either side of the sobbing freak's neck, opened her legs as wide as she could, and then slammed them closed.

The spurs, sharpened last week to evil points that could cut through diamonds, plunged into Gargoyle Man's neck from both sides. Blood spurted in a hot torrent, hitting the walls and pumping over Jazz's ankles. She thrust her heels backwards and forwards, sawing through the flesh and muscle, snagging the blades on his spinal column. She panted with effort but couldn't stop until his head was removed.

Gargoyle Man's fingers clenched and jerked, curling and straightening as the nerves in his neck sprayed out like spaghetti and cascaded onto his shoulders. He tried to turn and look at her, but Jazz's blades tore through the last knotty rope of spine and his head tumbled forward into his lap. She kicked free and dragged herself away before collapsing onto the floor and vomiting. Gristle and scraps of skin erupted from her mouth and lay in the pools of sick; thick matted pubic hair floated on the top.

Getting to her feet shakily, Jazz wiped her mouth and looked around. *There it is!* She picked up the severed cock with the tips of her fingers, dragged the man's head back so his bulging dead eyes were fixed on the ceiling, and thrust the cock into his open mouth. "Something to snack on for your journey down to hell, cocksucker," she said.

She walked down the corridor and into a side room, holding the wall for support. There were sinks here she could wash in but she didn't think she'd ever feel clean again. Her reflection in the mirror above the sink forced a shocked laugh from her. *So much for making an effort!* She dampened a towel and wiped her face and arms, plucked shreds of skin from the deep crevice between her tits, then tottered to a free gurney and clambered onto it. *Someone's bound to be along at the end of the night to tidy things up*, she thought, pulling a sheet over her legs. *For now, I'll just lie here and rest up. Jesus, what a night.* She winced as she stretched and closed her eyes.

Feeble moaning cut through her tiredness. She sighed and got up, staggering through the debris of body parts. On a gurney at the end of the ward area, something moved under a pile of blankets. She lifted the fabric and stared into the pleading eyes of a young man, gagged and strapped down.

"Wow, you had a lucky escape," Jazz told him. He moaned more loudly and jerked his head toward the end of the gurney. She nodded. "Oh, okay, let's have a look."

PATIENT REQUIRES TONGUE TO BE REMOVED FROM MOUTH AND SEWN ONTO SHAFT OF PENIS, she read. "Sorry, sweetheart, I don't think I could hold a scalpel steady right now, and I've had quite enough of cocks for one evening. But maybe next month? Be a poppet and keep the noise down, would you?"

She patted the guy's cheek and wandered back to her gurney, stepping over the body parts and blood spills. *I don't envy the poor fucker who's got to clean this lot up tomorrow*, she thought as she curled onto her side and drifted off to sleep.

BEST DAMN REVENGE

By Jaime Johnesee

"**I**'m so fucking wet. Please, baby. Please, *fuck* me," Miranda Newsome begged as she played with her clit.

She'd been waiting all night for this—twenty hours edging in the back of his funky-ass van, getting herself all worked up and backing off before orgasm. After spending six hours fucking herself—with no release—all she wanted (no, all she *deserved*) was a good fuck. After all, she had spent those hours waiting for her boyfriend to buy tickets for some stupid defunct carnival's reopening

Down on her knees in the blue shag of her boyfriend's Ford Econoline van, she grabbed his stiff cock, bent her head to it, and began eagerly licking the drops of pre-come off the tip.

She stopped and sat up. "What was that?"

"I didn't hear anything. Keep going, come on." His hand fisted her hair at the back of her head and pushed her back down.

As she sucked, his other hand smacked her tight ass a couple of times before falling to the sopping slit between her legs. He toyed with her clit the exact same way her tongue toyed with the tip of his shaft—fast circular motions. She caught on to the synchronicity and changed her oral skills so to better direct him how to pleasure her.

He shoved two fingers inside her. She moaned and brought her lips all the way to his hips, his cock buried in her throat.

Momentarily distracted, she thought she saw a flash of movement from a storage box near the mattress. It looked to her as if the lid had lifted.

Her boyfriend's pinkie entered her ass, and she dismissed the movement as unimportant and continued mouth-fucking him.

When she was able to speak coherently all she could mutter was, "Fuck me."

"Why don't *you* fuck *me*?" He took his hands off her, sat back, and gestured for her to hurry, a smile spreading over his face.

She slid down onto his cock and he continued grinning, closing his eyes and enjoying the sensation. Miranda then closed her eyes, intent on her own pleasure.

Neither saw the thin-framed person unfurl from the storage bin as lithely as a leopard.

Miranda was still riding her boyfriend when the axe nearly halved his head.

She was so thrilled to have a cock inside her that she didn't register the feel of his blood spattering her breasts and neck while she bounced away, locked in her own ecstasy. In fact, she didn't notice the gore until her hands strayed up to play with her tits and she encountered the sticky mess.

As she lowered herself onto her boyfriend's cock one last time, she opened her eyes to see that half of his face was gone.

Her scream turned into a gurgle as a similar wound ripped through her visage.

***

"C'mon, you guys! We're going to be late for the grand reopening!" David Black held out the flyer he'd taken from under his windshield wiper that afternoon.

As a kid, he'd loved the Kingsland Family Fun Center. However, in 1975, when he was ten, a fire had wiped through the boardwalk. The whole thing had gone up like a bale of straw. According to the flyer, someone had raised the money needed to restore and rebuild the KFFC. As soon as David had seen it, he'd taken off work and hatched a plan to sleep in the van and spend both days at the grand reopening. Then he'd grabbed his five favorite people and insisted on a road trip.

He led his group of friends to the main gates, grinning the whole way. He couldn't wait to ride The Wildcat again. It was one of the fastest small rollercoasters in the East, according to the flyer. It also stated that The Wildcat had been restored to its former glory.

"Okay, guys, are you ready for an awesome day? C'mon, are you ready to get hammered and ride some rides until we puke?"

His group of friends let out a half-hearted, "Yeah!"

"Fuck you guys." Not letting it faze him, David pushed forward into the entrance line.

"Hey, isn't this where that couple was killed last night?"

"Okay, I get it, Azure. My exuberance should be tempered because someone died here and we ought to show respect. My apologies, pussies."

Marie stepped in as the voice of reason. "Can we just go in and have some fun? This is not a good omen for the weekend if we're already fighting."

"Yes, yes we can." He had been waiting for so long to ride The Wildcat again and, dammit, he was going to enjoy it whether his friends made fun of him or not. His girlfriend, Marie, was enjoying herself and that was good enough for him.

He reminisced, recalling how they'd met through friends at a party. The last year of his life had been so special thanks to her, and he wanted to give her something exceptional in return. He was looking forward to sharing this experience with her. There was something else he wanted to share with her too. It was glittery and pretty and she was sure to say yes.

He'd planned to pop the question this weekend anyway. The KFFC reopening was just icing on the cake.

He grinned wider as he led them up to the ticket window. After paying and being admitted, David and his friends agreed to meet at the cafeteria at noon, swarmed into the park, and headed off in differing directions to the sounds of Van Halen, AC/DC,

Whitesnake, and Metallica blasting through various speakers in front of the rides.

Marie's hand was warm in his and she smiled up at him as he pulled her toward the rollercoaster he had so loved as a kid. He pulled her along swiftly, and she chuckled at his anticipation.

"I haven't seen you this giddy in ages."

"When I was a kid I rode this thing almost every weekend for two years. The Fun Center was my getaway from reality. Man, being able to come here saved my life. After it burned down, I really missed it. It was like a cornerstone to my childhood had gone up in smoke. I was there that night and it was horrific. It haunted me for years. I just wish I could have found Miranda Newsome to come with us. She was there that horrible night and I'd bet she'd love to see the way it's been refurbished. Seeing this place open again is so awesome."

They entered the queue and didn't have far to walk to hit the end of the line.

"I totally get it." She tilted in and gave him a kiss as he leaned against the rail.

"I'm glad you do."

"I had something I loved as a kid, too. Unfortunately, it was destroyed by some assholes."

"I'm sorry to hear that. Hey, maybe your place will be rebuilt one day too."

"Thanks, but as much as I'd love it, I know that's not feasible. Sweet of you to think of me though."

"I always think of you." He wrapped his arms around her and she snuggled him, grateful for the warmth. "Hey, while we're stuck here, I just want to thank you for coming to my special spot with me. It means a lot to me. So do you."

Though it was spring, it was only in the upper forties. They were dressed in sweatshirts and jeans but Marie shivered in the wind. She had a couple of long feathered roach-clips in her hair and they tickled her nose as they caught the breeze and flew up around her face.

David wrapped his arms tighter around her before stepping back and rubbing his hands up and down her arms to help warm her.

"We'll be on the coaster soon. Once we're done, we can go to the midway to thaw."

KFFC had an indoor midway with games lining the walls and a bunch of arcade machines in the center. It was nice on a cold spring or autumn day to spend an hour inside playing ring toss or skee-ball. An indoor seating area in the cafeteria also provided relief from the elements.

"You going to win me a stuffed bear?" Marie poked him lightly in the stomach.

"If they don't have a stuffed Freddy."

She poked him again, harder. "Dick."

"Aw, you know you love me, even in your nightmares." He went to ruffle her hair. Ever since she'd swapped the Dorothy Hamill cut for the Farrah Fawcett he'd seemed to enjoy playing with her hair more.

She ducked. "Yeah, you're on thin ice, bub."

"Hey, we're moving!" He jumped up and down like a kid before running ahead.

"Now, that's the spirit. I'll bet ten-year-old you was absolutely adorable." She grinned at him when he looked back.

"I don't know. I had some bad habits. I started dipping that year."

"Dipping?"

"Chewing tobacco."

"Gross."

"Yeah, not my smartest decision."

"No, *that* would be dating me." She winked at him and moved forward with the line.

As they sat in the very back row, David noticed the safety bar stopped a couple inches short of Marie's lap. He'd have to hold her in the seat. In fact, she'd be clinging to him the whole ride, and that thought made him smile.

***

Nobody cares. All they want to do is fuck and get drunk. Death is all around them and they don't even notice it.

Bah! They didn't care back then, either. They should have. The message was unmistakable, but they foolishly ignored it. I'll show them that having this park reopen is a bad idea.

I can't believe they have rebuilt everything exactly the way it was before the fire. That is going to be their fatal error. Until then, just smile, blend in, act like you want to be here with these sheep, and prepare for the slaughter.

***

They gathered around a trash barrel fire they'd started near their van to chase off the chill. The security guys were cool about letting them keep it so long as the fire was restricted to the metal barrel.

David and Marie sat outside the van in beach chairs they'd brought along. They passed a joint back and forth, talking horror movies. Some of their friends were extolling the virtues of *Jaws* while another argued it was nothing like the book.

David was getting nervous. He had plans to wait until midnight and take her back on The Wildcat for one more ride. He'd planned to propose earlier, when they first got on it, but he'd had no clue what to say. He had just been grateful for the roar of the rides and the crowd so he could spend the day thinking of what he wanted to tell her.

Midnight struck. He managed to grab the little dark blue velvet box out of his backpack and into his pocket undetected. He stood, took Marie's hand in his and, heart beating wildly, led her back into the park. The stamps on their hands had faded from the day's adventures but were still good for gaining access. They stopped at the gate and showed them to the guards, who refreshed the marks. Then he and Marie rushed to The Wildcat.

There weren't many people in line and within minutes David had his chance. He knelt down before the next car pulled in and held out the box to Marie.

"Marie, you've been a big part of my life for the last year and I can't imagine what it would be like without you. Will you marry me?" He hoped she would smile and hug him and say yes.

"I think we need to talk."

"Not a good sign, buddy!" An onlooker guffawed.

The serious expression on her face made his heart skip a beat. "What?" He had been terrified of this.

"Stand up, silly."

"What?" He felt a little lost, slightly panicked.

"I'm not quite ready for marriage yet."

"Oh." He blinked rapidly.

"I mean, we haven't ever talked about marriage and we're still really young. I'd like to finish school first."

"Yeah. I just thought...."

"Don't misunderstand, I don't want to break up with you. Honestly, I don't want anyone else. It's just that I'm not ready for wedding bells yet."

The roller coaster pulled in and the operator looked at the couple awkwardly, mouth agape as if afraid to speak.

David shrugged and entered the car. Marie followed. Three other people were on the coaster with them. They'd also witnessed David's rejection.

His face burned with embarrassment but the rushing wind cooled it.

***

Poor guy. That was harsh. Still, better to dump someone than lead them on.

If I hold the knife just so, I should be able to get to his throat without anyone seeing anything.

Success!

Aw, fuck, no! Damn, I didn't go deep enough!

***

"David?" Marie nudged him when the coaster pulled into the station and the other guests disembarked.

As the light washed over the car and his harness released, David's light gray sweatshirt looked to be soaked through with blood.

His throat had been slashed, but he was still alive.

Marie screamed and sobbed, putting her hands against the wound in his neck to try to stop the bleeding. First responders managed to slow it with a ton of gauze until paramedics arrived.

One of her friends had come looking for her and David when the ambulance pulled into the parking lot. She sat hugging Marie and occasionally muttering the obligatory, "It's all okay."

"How is any of this okay?" Marie stopped and calmed herself.

She rode in the ambulance along with David, using the excuse that he had just proposed.

The police shut down the park and kept everyone there for questioning. In their search of the area, they found a knife spattered with blood. It had fallen under the rollercoaster. The police assumed the people who'd sat behind them had something to do with the attack. However, sometime after David's injury and before park security arrived, two of the people who had gotten on the coaster had slipped away unnoticed. They were missing; park security and the cops were unable to locate them. The third hadn't seen anything; he'd been too busy masturbating.

Marie was grateful that he'd been honest about it and stuck around.

***

They'd better keep the park closed. I swear to you, Father, that every damned time someone reopens this place I will make sure they shut it down. Like you closed it down all those years ago. You're not around to do it again, so now it's my job and I promise to make you proud.

Those dumb fuckers didn't change anything, even knowing what happened before. I can do everything exactly the same way you did.

I hope you understand that I have to add my mark to it. I hope you won't be angry that I did more than simply burn it to the ground as you did, Dad. I need my revenge.

I want to paint it with blood first, then I'll pour the gas and light a match.

***

Marie sat not-watching TV in a hotel room. Her friends slept, crammed in on either the other queen bed or two roll-away beds.

She had no idea what was happening in the movie on the screen. Instead, she was busy thinking over the evening and wondering if there was anything she could have done differently. She couldn't find a single action she had taken that could have been changed to prevent David's injury.

The hospital had sent him in for a CT scan after they'd stopped the bleeding, to see if there was any further damage. If not, he would be able to leave soon. He'd needed over eighty stitches to close his wound.

Marie and David's friends would be leaving once they got some sleep. She wanted to go to the hospital and they had agreed to drop her off before they left.

She looked at the clock and decided she'd rather go quickly than deal with divvying up the room charges. This way, when everyone woke up, they could just leave. Moving out of habit rather than any real desire, she dressed and readied herself to leave. She took her credit card and walked to the front desk to pay.

She walked past the ice machine when the sound of coins hitting the ground made her stop and look.

***

Oh, she'd be so much fun to kill. I bet she's a screamer.

No, no! I can't be spontaneous; I have to wait for the others like I planned. They need to be together to hit him the hardest. All of them in one fell swoop. Do I get them back to Kingsland?

I shouldn't have struck David so soon. I should have waited.

I'll be damned if I make that mistake again.

***

After a bit of neck craning, Marie could see the coins had fallen out of the hand of a young woman about her age. The woman was at the vending machine getting some sodas. She hadn't even noticed Marie.

Chastising herself for being so distracted, Marie continued to the office and paid the bill. She walked back to the room she'd just paid a good amount for and waited inside. *Hopefully David's friends will wake soon.*

Once they awoke, the fun could begin.

She took the axe in her hands and sat in the chair, watching. Taking them back to Kingsland Family Fun Center wasn't an option.

I'll still burn the amusement park down as my dad did. Unfortunately, there'll be no painting it with blood first.

Dad tried time and again to show them their Family Fun Center was dangerous and should be condemned. He built models and showed them how susceptible it was to an inferno. In the end, he even sacrificed his own life to save theirs.

There wasn't supposed to be anyone there that day.

Little David Black and his hoodlum friends had snuck into the amusement park after hours with his friend's mom's passkey. Her

63

father had already lit the gas when he heard them screaming. He got every one of them out safely but died in the fire from smoke inhalation on his last pass looking for anyone he may have missed. Everyone assumed with the full fire suit and oxygen tank he was carrying that he was there in his capacity as a volunteer fireman.

Marie never revealed the truth. Not even after she'd found her father's journal.

She'd learned from the diary that the KFFC was a tinderbox awaiting disaster. She read how he'd tried every legal channel to stop them. How he came up with a plan to burn it down after hours when nobody was there.

If it hadn't been for David and his delinquent friends, her father would still be alive.

While some of David's friends slept silently (thanks to a huge dose of phenobarbital she'd slipped into the commiseration whiskey a few hours ago), Marie took the hand axe to the ones who started to wake. Then she sliced, diced, chopped, and carved her way through all of David's favorite people.

When she was finished she quickly showered, changed, and left with her bloody clothes in a wastepaper bag tucked into her suitcase.

Now, to finish what I started with David.

It was her bad luck that The Wildcat was so fucking jerky. When she'd stabbed him, the car had bucked. If only she hadn't had to grab the safety bar. The damn thing hadn't fit her lap right and the coaster had tossed her around the way her Doberman did his teddy bears.

She didn't think he suspected she had done it. Either way she was glad the kids who had been smoking pot on the ride behind them had taken off, presumably to avoid being caught with the marijuana.

After showering and dressing in clean clothes, she left the gruesome room and made her way to the hospital.

She walked into the red brick building, smiling and pretending to play the role she had cast herself in for the last year. She took off her burgundy *Member's Only* jacket and walked up to the desk.

"I'm here to see David Black."

Marie smiled politely but kept a look of worry on her face. After all, he was her fiancé, or so she'd told the ambulance driver who had told the nurses in the ER.

"I'm sorry, miss. Mr. Black was transferred to another hospital four hours ago."

"I'm his fiancé. Where did you take him? I didn't authorize any of this."

"No, I did." David's mother stepped from the shadows.

"Oh. I…uh, that is, I'm sorry I didn't call last night. I was told the police would and I was pretty shaken up." Marie reached out for Mrs. Black's hands.

The older woman pulled back.

"Do you think I don't know what you did to my boy? Do you think the police didn't tell me? I'm only here now to tell you how rotten I think you are." The woman's voice was shrill and that was a large part of why Marie was relieved not to have her for a mother-in-law.

"I don't understand?"

"He asked you to marry him and you said no!"

"I told him I wanted more time before we got married. I didn't break up with him. I just want to be more financially stable when we do get married." Marie backed up. *Sure hope they buy this bullshit so I can get to the park before the midnight security guys show.*

"I am going to Holy Cross Trauma Center. If you would like to visit David there… Well, try to come when I'm not around." Mrs. Black turned on her patent leather heels and stalked away.

"Bitch," Marie muttered. Maybe she'd add her to the list. She'd never liked the old bat anyway.

She'd have to set the fire first and then go back for David. She hoped he wouldn't remember anything about her arm on his chest before she stabbed him. She'd had to try and make herself look as unlikely as possible to be the killer, and she'd taken a risk piercing him in the left side of the neck while seated on his right. Probably also why she'd lost the knife. Her left hand was far weaker than her right.

Miffed at her plan being interrupted, Marie left the hospital and hailed a cabbie. She had him drop her at the grocery store just up the road from Kingsland. She went inside and bought a box of Ohio Bluetip matches.

Her desire to fulfil her destiny pulled her to the amusement park. She arrived not long after nightfall and hid in a large drainage pipe just off the parking lot. Within sixty minutes of her arrival, the park was dark and silent. Still, she waited. She wasn't going to make the same mistake her father had. She waited until eleven o'clock, which was a shift change (when all the guards were back at base), and extricated herself from the pipe.

Stiff-legged, she hobbled from her hideout to the gas cans she'd stowed earlier in the lawn equipment shed. After a quick sweep of the amusement park, making sure to stay out of the way of guards, she was ready to get to work. It took her ten whole minutes to pour the gas the way he'd written in the journal.

"My promise to you is fulfilled, Daddy!" She dropped the match and watched the fire spread quickly.

Quicker than she had expected.

It's out of control!

She leapt through a wall of flames but was cut off by another.

No! I can't die like this!

***

After surgery, David Black regained consciousness in his hospital bed and listened to the sirens for a moment. He oriented himself and then looked out the window. He was sad to see fire trucks heading toward the inferno that was once, and had been again for a couple days, the Kingsland Family Fun Center.

The police officer next to the bed coughed and startled David into looking at him and away from the window.

What the cop had to say to him shattered his world.

This weekend was supposed to have been his best weekend ever. Instead, his Sunday had begun with the police giving him the news that all of the friends who'd come with him were dead. Except Marie, who was missing and assumed kidnapped. Worse was when David had to admit he had no clue who had stabbed him or how. He'd been too focused on holding onto Marie.

No bodies were recovered from the newest KFFC fire but the damage was brutal. The midway and cafeteria had burnt down to ashes and all of the wooden coasters were gone. The amusement park would likely never reopen.

David told the officer who had come to tell him about his friends' deaths, girlfriend's kidnapping, and fire that he hoped it never did.

A woman with oozing second degree burns on her hands and right arm stood outside David's room. Even with the burns she was invisible by way of being dressed in scrubs and surgical mask in a hospital. She ignored the pain of her injured hands and held a patient file, pretending to study it intently.

In reality she stared at her nemesis as he lay crushed, weeping for the loss of his friends and girlfriend. She heard him wail out his love for her.

She'd stopped by to see him suffer. Satisfied in her revenge, Marie ditched the file and mask and walked out of the hospital toward a whole new life.

BLACK ROSE

by Lisa Lane

Surrounded. What more could he do? At this point, all that remained to be seen was how gracefully he would find his end. And what more graceful way than to throw himself into their midst, his own body brimming with the last of the poison that might have, had he enough, saved his life?

He left detailed notes about the experiment both in hard copy and on a case-protected flash drive—not so others might replicate his work but to see to it that no one else did. God willing, no one would happen upon this place until *they* were long gone—but who was to say how long that could take? Was it possible to starve them out? If so, what would become of the next generation of foliage to be introduced here? Migrating birds dropped seeds all the time onto islands far remoter than this one. He shuddered at the possibilities.

Constricting vines…venomous mango trees…fragrance-bated jasmine patches….

At least they'd proven nonviable. That they couldn't pollinate meant migrating birds wouldn't be able to transplant them from here to any populated areas. They'd also proven sensitive to the saltwater, so they couldn't swim to new land either. So long as no one else intervened, these mistakes of science would die with him.

All he could hope for now was that he might take as many as possible with him.

He wrote in bold marker on his desktop: *The price of playing God is death.* Then he stood, steadied himself, straightened his tie, and took a belly flop off the balcony.

***

Stacy lay on the deck of the *Persephone*, working on her tan, although even that was becoming a boring pastime. She and her brother, Sam, and his girlfriend, Janet, had been confined to the yacht for far too long now, and she thought she might just jump overboard if she had to suffer one more day with the mixed company.

Sam was a decent guy, albeit spoiled. He'd flunked out of Harvard, spending more time at frat parties than class, and he'd since passed the time wasting his part of their inheritance wooing Janet. The buxom blonde was about as sweet as they came and Barbie doll gorgeous, but she was also about as dumb as a pile of rocks. While Stacy didn't have any personal qualms with the woman, she also couldn't stand the thought of her brother settling down with Janet and having a brood of beautiful, stupid babies. He was quite taken with her; however, she was quite taken with his money, so it was likely only a matter of time before he broke down, bought a rock the size of Texas, and asked her hand in marriage.

If the Fates were at all kind, they'd render one or both sterile.

Janet bounced over to Stacy's chaise lounge, looking like she might squeal. "Look!" She pointed. "We're almost there! Sammy says that's the one!"

Stacy sat up and raised a hand to block the sun from her eyes. Sure enough, land was within sight. "Thank God."

The island was larger than she'd thought it would be, but also…duller? Granted, they were still a ways off, but it didn't seem to have much color to it. From the pictures on the website, the place had looked to be a small paradise. *"Move over, Caribbean; step aside, Jamaica—the next booming tourist attraction is right in the palms of our hands,"* her brother had said after learning the land their father had invested in had been abandoned by his business partner. The man had been reported missing over a year ago, but the process of having a missing person declared dead was lengthy. Both Sam and Stacy had known about the island for years, but it had been off limits while it remained in the shareholder's possession. Their father had never told them why he'd bought an island solely for a business partner's private use, but he was gone now and it no longer mattered.

The engine kicked into high gear as their leisurely stroll toward the island became a race to the finish line. Janet hopped around a little more, her double D's nearly falling out of her bikini top. Stacy turned away in anticipation of the wardrobe malfunction.

"We should pop open some bubbly and have a toast," Janet said. "What do you think Sammy would prefer, the Armand de Brignac Brut or the Champagne Krug Vintage?"

Stacy suppressed a cringe at the woman's crude pronunciations. They both tasted pretty much the same—subtly dry with a light finish—and they were coming from Sam's personal collection, not hers. As far as she was concerned, they could open both and sample a glass from each. She gave Janet a smile and a shrug. "Why don't you go ask *Sammy*?"

He hated being called that. Janet was the only one who could get away with using the nickname without a hostile correction. It seemed double D's opened the gate to the double-m-y. That, and she wasn't bright enough to have caught on the first fifty times he'd tried to correct her.

C'est la vie.

Janet hurried off to determine the champagne, leaving Stacy to gather her thoughts. Sam's idea to turn the island into a resort had seemed a good one at the time, but now she wasn't so sure. She hadn't committed too much of her own money to it, but she was having second thoughts about spending any money at all. How many other people had tried to turn private islands into hot tourist spots? How much money would it cost just to get this place on the map? Sam had shown her all sorts of graphs and plans—a water park here, a health spa there—but they hadn't talked a whole lot about how they were going to get people to choose their luxury resort over all the others already spread across the tropics.

Janet returned with a glass of champagne, stayed just long enough to hand it over, and then hurried off to drink at her beau's side. Stacy tasted it. Whichever brut Janet had chosen, it tasted good. Her nerves getting the better of her, she downed the glass and followed Janet to pour another.

By the time they reached land, Stacy was feeling better about the situation. The three glasses of champagne hadn't hurt. She watched as Janet ran barefoot across the beach. The sand was pristine, the water rolling into it clear and blue. That, however, was as far as the beauty stretched. Beyond the beach, dead foliage spread as far as the eye could see. Not one hint of green; not one bright, tropical flower; not a single sign of life.

Sam stopped beside Stacy, looking just as taken aback.

"Do you think it's safe?" she asked him.

He shrugged. "Maybe it just needs some proper irrigation?"

"You ever see a tropical island that needed 'proper irrigation'?"

He sighed and scratched his head.

"You might want to stop your girlfriend before she heads off into the jungle of death."

"She's not that stupid, Stacy. She —" He stopped short when he saw her reach the edge of the beach. "Hey, Janet, hold off for a few, wouldja?"

She stopped and turned. "Everything's so brown."

"Yeah, it's brown all right."

"Think it could be radiation?" Stacy asked him.

"I think it could be anything. Toxic waste for all we know."

Janet hopped across a few rocks, slipping and falling to her knees. "Dammit!"

Stacy stayed put while Sam went to retrieve his fallen girlfriend. "Well, I guess we'll find out if it is toxic waste," she muttered when Sam helped Janet hobble back to the beach. She'd skinned one of her knees, and blood trickled down her shin. He stole a long peek at her rack while he helped her along, and Stacy looked away when she saw the bulge forming in his shorts.

Although Janet didn't seem any worse for the wear, they agreed to seek out more information before returning to land. They were able to access low-bandwidth Internet through Sam's satellite phone, but no one really knew what they were searching for. They tried to find more information using their specific coordinates, but nothing came up. There were no mentions of anything related to the island. Nothing about the potential hazards. Not even a word about the previous owner or what type of research his business partner did. Nothing.

Sam and Stacy found themselves in disagreement over what to do next. Stacy wanted to turn around. Sam wanted to trek to the mansion about a quarter of a mile inland and see if anything else might turn up there. Janet was just as adamant, although Stacy suspected the stance came from either her attachment to Sam or the desire to find more privacy with him. The yacht was nice, very roomy as far as luxury boats were concerned, but not roomy enough for a young couple whose favorite pastime appeared to be sneaking off to perform whatever kinky sexcapades they were into. The walls were cardboard thin, and the two hated to fuck quietly. When finally Stacy had suggested he stuff a sock in Janet's mouth the next time they got frisky, a strange tension dropped over the trio like a sheer curtain—noticeable and weighty enough to put a damper on their fun but not substantial enough to throw everyone off too terribly.

Had the yacht belonged to her, Stacy would have had it back into the open sea by now. She'd never been much into toys—well, rich men's toys, anyway. The yacht was Sam's, of course, and so she was screwed.

Janet climbed on deck, dragging a small luggage case behind her. She still wore her bikini, but now she had on boots appropriate for hiking through dead foliage and hopping between rocks like a ten-year-old. Well, at least her chances of scuffing the other knee—or maybe an elbow…or her face—weren't as bad as they'd been on her original venture.

Sam came up to them carrying a backpack of supplies. He looked at the luggage case. "You really think you're going to need all that?"

"Well, a girl needs some bare essentials, even in a place like this. Please tell me you're bringing at least a change of clothes."

"A few. I don't foresee us being gone that long."

"Well, I for one am not willing to take a chance that a storm comes through or something else happens to delay our return. You want me looking my best for you, don't you?"

"You do know those wheels are going to stick as soon as we start across the beach. Bag's not going to roll over the sand, you know." Before she could respond, he added, "And I'm not carrying it for you."

"It'll be fine." She hurried off, Sam not too far behind her.

He turned back to his sister one last time before hitting the beach. "Sure you want to stay here?"

"Sure you really want to go?"

He waved off the question as though it were a pesky fly buzzing nearby.

"There's nothing I can say to stop you. I mean, look at—" She stopped short when she noticed a small patch of green grass bordering the beach and the desolation beyond.

He noticed it too. Must've taken it as a good sign, because he met Janet on the beach, took her hand, and started for the mansion.

"Okay, then. Be safe."

Neither he nor Janet said another word; instead, they slipped into their little world where only they existed and nothing terrible could burst that bubble. Janet lugged her bag for all of twenty feet before handing it over to Sam, who took it without as much as a groan.

"Yeah, have fun," Stacy breathed.

It would be nice to have some privacy of her own—but what to do? She'd decided not far into their journey that she hated the yacht. For as many luxuries as it provided, it was nothing more than a glorified prison cell.

Another bottle of Sam's finest might make the stay more tolerable.

***

By evening, she was ready to crash wherever her spinning world would take her. She tried to make it to the bedroom, but the chaise lounge on the deck came quicker and easier, so she went with it. Somewhere along the way, she'd lost her clothes.

The tropics were damn hot.

A hint of worry over her brother crept in, but her thoughts had become too scattered for them to linger. She let her mind drift, willing her consciousness to allow her some respite. Tomorrow would be a new day—she just hoped it would involve her brother coming to his senses and agreeing to get away from this godforsaken place.

The alcohol, while making her groggy, made sleep difficult, and yet she found herself drifting in and out of a dream. She'd been bound on her stomach in four-point restraints and her eyes were blindfolded. She could sense the presence of someone there. Watching. Waiting. Something caressed her inner thigh. The gentle graze of fingertips, maybe? As in most erotic dreams, despite the bondage she hadn't remembered consenting to, she found herself aroused, waiting for whatever her captor had planned for her next.

She shivered, feeling herself go wet at the feel of something more substantial moving in for a harder feel. Between her legs, teasing, testing her excitement. Whoever her mystery dream lover was, it seemed he was into toys. Something cool pressed between her labia, prompting the lips apart, and she held her breath while the object eased into her.

The dream took a hideous turn when a crawling sensation took hold, as though the object had released hundreds of tiny bugs inside her. She tugged at the restraints and struggled to work off the blindfold, kicking and writhing in an attempt to free herself of both her bonds and whatever continued to violate her. She cried out.

Whatever was holding her released all at once just as she gasped awake. She sat up and looked around, her heart racing, but she saw nothing. The crawling sensation continued, however, prompting her to spring from the chair and examine it.

Nothing.

When the sensation subsided, she chalked it up to hypnogogic phantoms, although she did retreat to the cabin to finish the night's rest.

***

Even left unmaintained as long as it had, the mansion was exquisite. The exterior would need a lot of work, especially to take down all the dead vines that had yet to release their hold along the masonry and balcony railings. The interior was dusty but otherwise in good shape. The electricity wasn't working, but there were plenty of candles and matchbooks to go around. The pantry and refrigerator contained some spoiled food, but the wine cellar held some fine vintages. Sam and Janet shared a bottle of L'Apparita while they explored the place.

By the time they reached the desk in the upstairs study, both were feeling tipsy.

The hard copy notes lay in the same perfect stack they'd been left in the day the good doctor—or more fittingly, albeit somewhat clichéd, *mad scientist*—took his life. He'd printed them from a file, more of a computer diary than a scientific log, but had also added some longhand notes in the margins. Sam and Janet went from stunned and saddened to out-loud laughter after deciding to read some of the entries. The first one was dated February 25, just over two years ago:

> *I've succeeded in my efforts to create fully mobile flora, capable of escaping their natural predators and moving to richer soil when needed. My colleagues had deemed me insane when I'd suggested genetic engineering to introduce not only different types of plant DNA, but also that of humans and a few different animals. "It's not possible," they said. "There's no chance of compatibility." Ha!*
>
> *One unexpected result I've perceived is their eating habits; all three species appear to be omnivorous. Even more interestingly, they behave as if in direct competition with one another for food, some fighting over insects and rodents while some are consuming other species of plants. The passion flowers are the most noteworthy, actually constricting their prey. I'm hoping they won't prove protective of their fruit, as the strength of their vines is impressive and I fear their defenses might be too good.*

"Is this guy for real?" Janet asked while Sam skimmed through some of the later entries. She took a long pull straight from the bottle, nearing its end.

"Total nut case." He pointed to the March 20 entry from that same year, and Janet read it over his shoulder.

> *They've killed my sweet, beautiful Isabel! God, I wish I'd never come here, let alone dragged my poor wife along. How was I to foresee that the roses would see her as a threat? It wasn't for trying to clip them—the mutation turned their flowers into a hideous, black, shriveled mess. And why were the vines trying to protect her? Or did it just look like protection?*

Sam took the final swig before he shuffled to the bottom of the stack. The final entries were short, some just single sentences:

How has the mutated DNA spread? The only explanation is that the pollen from the genetically engineered samples contains whatever RNA vehicles are necessary to transform both new and established growths.

The term "growing like a weed" has taken on a whole new meaning. How are they growing so quickly? Exponentially. I've never seen anything like it. One single plant spread over half the house in a matter of days.

Why didn't I radio for help while I still had the chance? Hubris, maybe? They've cut the power and destroyed all means of outside communications.

I'm afraid I'm going to die here.

Waited for the perennials to go to seed and die, hoping I might make it out of here if there were fewer threats. After a prolonged wait and still no seeds, I was able to take a sample of one of their pods, but I was rewarded with a cloud of what appeared to be spores when I dissected it. As quickly as the plants have grown and matured, I would think I'd have seen the next generation spring forth by now, but I've yet to find any evidence of it. Given I'd used my own DNA as a catalyst, it's probably safe to presume they're all male. At least, as quickly as they are growing, they appear to be incapable of procreation.

I've concocted an herbicide, and it's effective, but I just don't have enough to kill them all, nor do I have the makings for much more. Even worse, they've become much more aggressive now that they know I'm trying to kill them. I can't open any windows ... and it's so hot.

So hot.

They're taunting me. Can I possibly starve them out?

Then, there was the final entry, which had his shaky signature at the bottom:

I'm at the last of the poison. If I die here, I'm going to die on my own terms. If you read this, you must know that the island is dangerous. If any of the plants survive, they will see you as either a threat or prey. Vacate the premises immediately. Bring my lab notes with you. Don't let this scourge travel beyond this place. Please don't let all of my efforts to stop them be in vain and PLEASE do not try to replicate my work. It's too dangerous.

The price of playing God is death.

"I wonder what really happened to him—and his wife," Sam thought aloud.

Janet shrugged. "Maybe the plants really ate him."

They burst out in laughter together as if perfectly timed. Janet took the wine bottle from Sam and shook the last drops onto her tongue, nearly falling over when her head tilted back.

"What do you say we dust off one of the beds and play a little God ourselves?" Sam said, taking the bottle back and setting it down on the desk.

"Lead the way, sailor."

They entered the first bedroom they came across, and Janet's bikini was on the floor before they made it through the threshold. He tossed her to the bed and she bounced with a giggle. He dropped his pants before diving beside her, and she rolled on top, taking him aggressively. He closed his eyes with a light groan.

When he opened them again, he could've sworn the vines along the balcony were staring in, watching them through the French windows.

***

Patches of green were everywhere. Overnight, passionflower vines had taken over the house. Through the downstairs windows, they could see the roses had sprung back to life. Just as Doctor Whatever-His-Name-Was had described, the flowers were black and shriveled. They also had what appeared to be seed pods, just as hideous, in place of some of the flowers. There were several other types of plants as well, and none of them looked like their original species. They were more robust.

And they moved around like snakes and worms, some attacking one another while others pressed against windows and slithered along the balconies.

"It's impossible," Janet said.

Sam paced the room. "God, I hope Stacy's okay."

"I hope she didn't leave us."

"No, she wouldn't do that."

She crossed her arms, unconvinced.

"Whatever sparked those things back to life, they're going to keep growing. We know that much from the lab notes. The longer we wait here, the harder it's going to be to get back to the boat."

She shook her head. "I don't want to go out there."

"Yeah…" He sighed, peeking through windows as he passed them. "Maybe Stacy used the satellite phone to call for help."

"We should've brought it with us."

"How was I supposed to know we'd wake up to a shit-storm?"

She took another peek out the window, and black, shriveled versions of passionflowers stared back, their little faces following hers.

Sam walked out and made a beeline for the kitchen.

Janet followed. "What are you doing?"

"We've got to get back to the boat." He went for the butcher block and picked out the two largest knives. He handed one to Janet.

She scoffed. "You can't possibly think we can cut our way through."

"You have a better idea?"

"Maybe we can burn them."

"If this island goes up, we go up with it." He led her to the front door, where they both paused, struggling to summon the courage to open it.

He took a deep breath. "I'll go first. Try to stay right behind me."

She nodded, although fearful tears were already pooling in her baby blue eyes. That in itself offered him the bump in testosterone he needed to swing open the door and start hacking at everything that came their way.

The vines found their ankles first, twisting around them and slowing the couple's forward movement. Janet screamed, useless, frozen in terror. Sam chopped away the vines that had taken hold, cringing to see red blood oozing from the plants' severed appendages. Just as quickly as he could cut them off, more vines curled around their legs.

"I can't get them all, Janet—you need to help me out a little here!"

She steadied herself and began cutting, her movements frantic and aimless. Sam continued to pick up the slack, but the rose bushes had worked their way in, as had the ferns. A few coconut trees inched their way forward, still far off in the distance.

Janet screeched when the vines started hissing. Blood spatter came from all directions, and still arms of vines and thorny rose branches continued to advance. Those that weren't fighting off the others fought for their hold on Janet. A rose bush grasped one leg while a passionflower vine wrapped around the other. Sam tried to free her, but he couldn't move quickly enough to save them both.

She screamed again when one good yank from the vine threw her off her feet. Her legs went in two separate directions when each plant tried to drag her away. Then they had her arms, and she looked like someone had ordered her drawn and quartered. One of the rose limbs took advantage of her prone position and wrestled a pod up her shorts leg.

The last vision Sam had of his girlfriend was of thorns and flailing limbs and blood. The rose bush dragged away its prize, the vines and ferns giving up when the mass of thorny branches had claimed her bleeding orifice. She stopped fighting, dropped her knife, and stared Sam down, her jaw agape, while he cut away the last of the vines holding him and scampered away.

The passionflowers, by far the quickest moving of the species, slithered after him. They tripped him up several times, but he managed to remain on his feet. The beach came within view, and he nearly froze when the boat was nowhere to be seen.

"No—Stacy!" he cried, still holding out in the back of his mind that she hadn't left him, that he just wasn't looking in the right direction. In his distraction, he failed to catch a vine as it snatched his left leg. He dove forward, hitting the ground face first.

He righted himself and slashed as quickly as he could, but they had his arms fast enough. The ferns tried to fight their way through only to be smothered in vine. Bulbs searched his pants, probing for the right spot, and then, finding him useless for anything else, the plants wrapped around him as tightly as they could, breaking bones, crushing his ribcage into his lungs, and then tearing him limb from limb.

***

Stacy woke with a horrific hangover. Her body ached. Her stomach cramped. She felt disoriented and weak, and when she realized she'd somehow been set out to sea—the engine shot and the satellite phone lost—all she could do was stare out at the ocean that spread in every direction and pray someone would find her.

A pang of nausea hit her, and she retched over the railing. She looked with surprise at the broken tangles of vines still clinging to the side, destroyed by the saltwater.

When another yacht came into view, she scrambled for the flare gun. Three flares later, a lovely middle-aged couple steered to her aid, and they agreed to call for a tugboat and take her to the nearest port.

She rested on the deck, struggling to make sense of her luck—worried to death that her brother might not have any clean water or edible food, unsure how many days it would take for help to find him—and the middle-aged woman sat beside her and gave a reassuring pat.

"Don't worry, dear, you'll all be okay."

Stacy managed a nod.

The woman sniffed. "You've got to tell me the name of that perfume you're wearing. It's so delightfully floral."

Stacy shook her head. "I'm not wearing any perfume."

The woman shrugged. "I'm going to make some tea. Want some?"

"Yes, thank you."

The woman gave her another quick pat then walked off.

Stacy squirmed, a grimace stretching across her face, when the first of the sprouts began to wriggle their way out.

CAMP COUNSELORS WANTED

by Stevie Kopas

"Jamie! Hey, Jamie, wait up!"

Jamie stopped and turned around, squinting into the sun. A short, buxom blonde with a big smile came into view, jogging up with an armful of books.

"Oh, hey, Linda!" Jamie shouted, giving a wave. Linda was a new friend of hers. They'd only just met this semester and her other friends thought she was a little strange, but Jamie was always one to root for the underdog and had welcomed her into the circle.

"I tried to stop you after class. Didn't you hear me calling your name?" Linda asked, panting slightly.

Jamie stepped off to the side, taking refuge from the harsh sun in the shade of a large tree. "No, sorry. What's up?"

"I found this in the student center this morning." Linda thrust out an arm, balancing her books in the other.

Jamie took a yellow sheet of paper from her classmate and read the large, bold headline at the top of the page: *Summer Camp Counselors Wanted.*

"I remembered you telling me over lunch the other day that you were worried about losing your housing assistance. Thought this would be helpful."

Jamie chewed her bottom lip. "It doesn't say how much it pays."

"I already called the number. Evidently they're working with the university and any student that participates in the program gets free housing next semester. How amazing is that?" Linda's enthusiasm was contagious, and Jamie smiled.

"What's the catch, though?" she asked the blonde, knowing it was just too good to be true.

Linda giggled and snatched the paper back from Jamie, shoving it in her back pocket. "That would be spending six weeks with a bunch of unruly brats aged eight to twelve."

Jamie cringed, laughing. "Oh God, Linda, you know I can't stand kids. I don't even like my younger brother."

"Aw, c'mon, please? I could use the help next semester and I know you damn well need it too. Don't make me go with a bunch of knucklehead strangers. I was hoping you could get your drama major friends to sign up. There are only a few spots left. Pretty please?" Linda batted her eyes and gave Jamie her best pout.

Jamie narrowed her eyes, wondering how her boyfriend Bruce would feel about it. They'd planned on taking a road trip this summer, but with their funds running low, she wondered how far they would have gotten anyway.

"I don't know, Linda. I'd have to talk to Bruce first."

Linda looked disheartened for a moment, setting her books on the grass. She sat down and rifled through her bag, looking up at Jamie with a peculiar smile. "Well, I guess I'll just have to smoke all this with those other lamebrain counselors that sign up."

Jamie's eyes went wide at the sight of the hugest bag of marijuana she'd ever seen. She crouched down and shoved it back into Linda's bag. The two girls giggled.

"Oh my God, you're crazy! You're carrying that around with you? What if you get caught?"

Linda giggled and shrugged. "I just bought it before class. Tell the gang it's an added incentive."

Jamie smiled. She really had nothing better to do this summer and getting some lame part-time job in town couldn't be any worse; plus, the money she'd make would be put right back into paying for school costs anyway. The camp counselor gig might end up being fun, especially if all her friends were there too. It couldn't hurt to ask.

"Okay, I'll talk to them about it." Jamie's eyes flicked down to the massive bag of dope in Linda's bag.

It couldn't hurt to ask at all.

***

Jamie rushed through the woods, Linda close behind. Jamie pulled her along and the shorter girl sobbed and stumbled.

"We can't stop, Linda!"

She couldn't remember how many times she'd already yelled that phrase during their trek through the woods. She couldn't remember how long they'd been running either. Scenes of the massacre they'd escaped kept flashing through her mind and it took every ounce of life she had left in her just to keep running. Her bare feet screamed at her, bloody and filthy, aching with each pounding footfall. She'd come away nearly unscathed. She could only imagine how poor Linda must be feeling.

Jamie stole a quick glance at her friend who plodded along behind her, uncontrollable sobs wracking her frame. Linda was covered head to toe in blood, some of it her own, most of it from her friends. One hand clutched Jamie's and the other held a bunched-up cloth to her bleeding side. She'd managed to hide under the body of Janet's boyfriend, Vincent, and pissed herself as the killer disemboweled him on top of her. One of the killer's vicious strikes had plunged through Vincent and straight into Linda's side. Lucky for her, she'd passed out from the pain and had been able to uphold her lifeless façade as the masked madman continued to hack up a screaming Vincent with an oversized machete.

When Jamie had found her, it had all been too much at that point. She'd been too quiet for too long. Jamie had to threaten to leave her behind if she didn't stop screaming, and now, as the girls fled through the dark forest that surrounded Camp Elmwood, she was unable to stop crying.

Jamie kept replaying the night's surreal moments through her mind…

***

The children wouldn't arrive until the following morning and the tight-knit group was enjoying their first night of a summer full of party-filled nights and long days of glorified babysitting. She cuddled up with Bruce by the campfire, melting into his oversized arms. The group of eighteen and nineteen-year-olds laughed and passed around bottles of stolen liquor along with several poorly rolled joints. They shared silly stories and laughed until their faces stung and their bellies ached.

It was the perfect night, Jamie thought, glancing around at her friends' stoned faces. Shelley and Tommy were the only ones not there; they decided to lock themselves in one of the bunks with a bottle full of Tequila for some playtime. Looking up at Bruce and smiling, Jamie wondered if they should have opted out of the campfire and sprung for some alone time themselves. She reached up and caressed his chin, getting his attention. He responded by giving her nipple a playful pinch and attempting to slide a hand up her skirt. Jamie let out a squeal and the rest of the group doubled over in laughter, until the sickening sound of a blade burying itself into Bruce's skull interrupted them.

"Bruce!" Jamie let out a scream as the life left her lover's blue eyes and a stream of blood worked its way down his handsome face.

The others screamed and scattered in different directions around her. She struggled to get up, but Bruce's heavy body toppled over and pinned her to the earth. She cried as the man above her worked the machete from Bruce's skull, spraying her with his fresh, warm blood. She tried desperately to free herself; her thin tank top snagged on something and tore, adding insult to injury. She felt around for something on the ground to defend herself with, never taking her eyes off her attacker. Their eyes met—she would never forget those piercing, dark eyes. Though his sick smile lay hidden behind a patchwork mask, she could still see it expressed in his stare.

The killer laughed as he raised his weapon and prepared to sink it into Jamie's exposed chest, but she was able to grab hold of one of the loose logs from the fire. She cried out, her hand burning, but she cringed through it and struck him with the glowing log. He shouted and recoiled far enough for her to give it her all and shove Bruce's body off of her. The madman flailed, focused on the glowing embers burning holes in his thick clothing, and Jamie took her chance, fleeing for the bunkhouses.

She ran topless through the trees, stumbling once, twice, three times, knowing all the while that her hulking attacker pursued not far behind. When she finally made it to the bunks, she found Shelley butchered in her bed. Jamie stifled a scream, bringing her hands up to cover her mouth, and swallowed the bile creeping up her throat. Shelley's amputated legs lay near her head and her left forearm had been shoved into her mouth like a gag. There was no time to mourn Shelley's death, though. Tears streamed down Jamie's cheeks as she rifled through the dresser drawers, pulling out the first shirt she could find. The attacker hadn't followed her; he'd chosen instead to prey upon her fellow counselors. She slipped in a thick pool of Shelley's blood and landed hard on her ass. Jamie could hear her friends' screams as she cowered on the floor, curled up in a ball. She tried willing herself to move, but with every scream that echoed in the trees, she seemed to have less and less control of her body. When all had finally fallen silent, she'd worked up enough courage to crack the door open and peer out into the darkness. She knew her life depended on it, that she needed to make a run for it, but she couldn't bring herself to leave any survivors behind.

She worked her way through the campground in silence, holding back tears as she came across the bodies of her murdered friends: Tommy, tied to a nearby tree, his innards draped around his neck like a scarf; Janet's decapitated head perched atop a totem pole; Wes and Sidney in the cafeteria, their torsos propped up on folding chairs and their limbs laid out neatly on the table before them. Jamie was living a nightmare. She soon stumbled upon Vincent's mutilated corpse in the kitchen and had all but given up hope when she heard Linda whimpering beneath the bloody heap.

She promised Linda they'd make it out of there alive and find safety. There was no way in hell that after hours of utter torment she was going to let the masked madman win.

***

Jamie spotted a break in the trees up ahead.

"Linda!" she shouted, unable to contain the excitement in her voice. "I think I see the road!"

She turned to her friend and watched her collapse to the forest floor.

"Linda?" Jamie dropped to her knees and shook her pale-faced friend. "Linda, answer me!"

Linda groaned and grimaced. "I can't..."

"Yes, you can! You have to!"

Linda let out a few more painful sobs. "No, Jamie, please. I can't, it hurts too much." She glanced down at the blood-drenched cloth that she clutched to her side.

"Let me see." Jamie pulled the cloth away and cringed at the stab wound. Linda lay there groaning as Jamie worked on ripping the cloth into strips, securing them around her and hoping to staunch any further bleeding.

"Listen to me." Jamie gripped her friend's shoulders. "You have to keep going. We've made it this far, you can't give up now."

Linda shook her head and pushed Jamie's hands away. "No, *you* have to keep going. I trust you. You'll come back for me. I know you will." Linda's eyes fluttered and her head slumped over to one side.

"Linda!" Jamie shouted and shook her limp frame. Panicking, she checked for a pulse and relaxed when she found the faint thump in Linda's neck. She wiped tears from her eyes and pulled Linda's body over to a large tree, setting her upright. "I'll come back for you. I'll bring help, I promise."

She kissed Linda on the cheek and started to head off, but returned to her friend. She pulled Linda's tennis shoes off in a hurry and put them on her bloodied, bare feet; they were snug, but they would keep her going. Jamie took off again, her body begging her to stop. It had been miles upon miles, she knew that much, and after what seemed like an eternity, she could feel the exhaustion finally setting in. Her adrenaline was winding down and her stomach was doing unending backflips. As she fought back her nausea and tried to focus on the road ahead, she almost didn't believe what was right in front of her eyes. About fifty yards ahead she could make out the unmistakable glow of a neon sign, and that's when she caught her second wind.

She pumped her arms as she grew nearer to the large sign, finally able to make out what it read: *Crystal's Diner*. The parking lot was just about empty; only an Oldsmobile and a few pick-up trucks were in it. She made a beeline for the diner's entrance, but spied a lone payphone off to the side and changed course, collapsing to the pavement in front of it. She snatched the phone from off the hook and punched in 0 for the operator. She panted, clutching the phone to her face, waiting for someone on the other end, but there was dead silence. She cried out in desperation, punching 0 over and over before realizing her efforts were futile.

She hobbled to the diner entrance and threw open the door. The portly waitress behind the counter turned around and made a face, clearly disapproving of Jamie's noisy entrance and ghastly appearance.

"Do you have a working phone?" Jamie asked, her eyes wide.

"Heavens to Betsy, honey, you look a mess," the waitress said, placing a pudgy hand on her hip.

Jamie scanned the room; the few patrons in the rundown diner whispered to one another and cast looks of disdain her way.

"I need a phone!" Jamie shouted, her body shaking, voice quivering. "There's been an attack!"

The waitress shook her head and stepped out from behind the counter, moving toward Jamie. "Now, now, sugar, just have a seat. What's all the fuss about?"

Jamie backed away from the woman, frustrated and suddenly feeling like a scared animal. "They're dead! They're all dead!"

"Who's dead, darlin'?" the woman cooed, still making her way toward Jamie.

Jamie's chest began to heave; all eyes in the diner were on her. Her butt bumped against the table behind her and she realized she had nowhere left to move. She was trapped.

The waitress put a hand out and stopped just inches away. "It's all right, it's all right. Who's dead, honey? Why don't you have a seat and tell me what happened?"

Jamie let out a frustrated wail and collapsed into the booth behind her. She pulled her knees into her chest and began to sob. "Please," she choked out, "they're all dead, all of my friends. Please, just call the police."

The waitress stood over her for a moment and shook her head. "My, my, you must have been through somethin' wicked. You stay here, I'll be right back." She returned to the counter and pulled a rotary phone down from a shelf.

Jamie managed to sit upright and scooted to the rear of the booth, her back pressed flat against the wall. The other diners returned to their coffees and slices of cherry pie, paying Jamie no further attention. She hugged her knees and shivered. The air conditioner must have been set to sixty; she was freezing.

Jamie kept glancing out the grimy windows, convinced the madman would appear at any moment to finish her off. She turned her attention back to the waitress and noticed a round, red face appear in the drop window. The cook met Jamie's gaze and frowned.

"John, do me a favor, will ya'?" the waitress asked the cook. "Get the girl some of your famous coffee for me. I'm tryin' to get a hold of someone at the Sheriff's Department."

The cook muttered something and his face disappeared. Moments later he rushed through the kitchen door, coffee pot in hand, and grabbed a filthy-looking mug from the counter. Brown liquid sloshed over the sides of the pot as he made his way over to Jamie, leaving a trail of liquid behind him. He slammed both items down on the table, causing Jamie to jump. He grunted, pointing at the coffee, fixing his intimidating eyes on her.

Jamie nodded her thanks and reached out her trembling hands, pouring herself a cup of coffee. She held the mug in both hands and absorbed its warmth. He stood there, staring at her until she finally took a long sip. She was surprised the coffee was so sweet, and she gulped it down. The cook seemed satisfied enough and he finally turned around and headed back to the kitchen. She set the empty mug back down on the table and pushed it away from her.

"Weaver?" the waitress asked in her loud, shrill voice. "Yes, honey, it's me, Dee. I hate to bother you so late and all, but we got ourselves quite the interesting customer tonight."

Jamie's ears perked up and she leaned forward; Dee noticed and turned her back to Jamie, speaking in a hushed tone. Jamie's frustration grew and she rose from the booth, tip-toeing toward the far end of the counter.

"Mm-hmm, yeah, I'm just not real sure," Dee continued. "She's real young, and she's filthy too, like she's been runnin' around in them woods out there. Yep, I think so. Says a bunch of people got killed but I can't be too sure she knows what she's sayin'. I think she's been smokin' the reefer."

Jamie clenched her fists. After all she'd been through she'd be damned if some hillbilly waitress was going to downplay the gravity of her situation. She slammed one of her fists down on the counter and every eye in the diner was back on her.

"Is that the police? Let me talk to them!" Jamie demanded, startling Dee.

Dee cupped the receiver with her free hand and whispered something into the phone.

"Did you not fucking hear me? I want to talk to the police!" Jamie screamed, her nails digging into her palms.

"Okay, thank ya kindly. We'll see ya real soon." Dee hung up the phone and plastered fake concern all over her face. "Now, honey, pretty girls shouldn't use language like that. You nearly scared the dickens outta me just then! Go on," Dee said, waving a hand back toward the booth. "Go have a sit back down and someone will be here to help in no time. No need to cause a scene."

Jamie suddenly had an uneasy feeling in her gut and her head swam. Her skin felt warm—too warm. Dee came up behind her and placed a hand on her shoulder; the woman's hand was ice cold on Jamie's boiling skin. She guided Jamie back to the booth in the rear of the diner and helped her sit down.

"I don't... I don't feel so well." Jamie's mouth was drier than a desert and her words were slurred. She looked up at the waitress with wide eyes, a sick realization dawning on her. "What... What was in the coffee?"

"Nothin' but a little sugar!" Dee grinned down at Jamie and a laugh escaped her. She patted her on the shoulder and helped lay her head down on the table.

Jamie could barely move, let alone keep her eyes open. As her eyes glued themselves shut, she could hear Dee talking to the other customers in the diner and then laughter filled the room around her.
***

Jamie's skin was hot and sticky with humidity. Her eyes fluttered open and she strained to see anything around her. Her vision was still a bit blurry and her head pounded. As her vision adjusted, she swallowed hard and tried to ignore the lump of horror building in her chest. She was back at the camp.

"No…" she whispered.

She heard something to her left and jumped. It was an odd sound, like muffled crying. Scanning her surroundings, she rose to her feet, uneasy. There was something up ahead, and that's where the noise was coming from. As she made her way nearer she could see Tommy's decaying body still tied to the tree in front of her. Her stomach turned. At the base of the tree, something moved.

Jamie's heart pounded with each step she took closer to the writhing mound and she held her breath as she finally figured out what it was. There was someone trapped inside a large burlap sack.

"Linda?" Jamie squeaked out, keeping her voice as low as possible.

The sack on the ground shook and Linda screamed out for Jamie. Jamie rushed to the tree and dropped to her knees, desperately trying to free her friend, but the expert knots proved to be too much for her trembling fingers. She looked up at Tommy's corpse and jumped to her feet. He always had a knife on him. She ignored the gaping hole in his torso and the sickening smell of his exposed innards as she searched his pockets. She pulled a small folding knife from one of them and dropped back down to Linda's side. Knife in hand, she tore open the sack and freed her friend. Linda's panicked, wet eyes met Jamie's and she sobbed through her gag. Jamie quickly removed it and cut through the ties around her wrists and ankles.

"Jamie, why are we back here?" Linda asked between gasping breaths.

"I don't know. These people are sick. I found a diner—they drugged me. I think they're all in on it."

"What are we gonna do, Jamie? I don't want to die." Linda wailed as Jamie helped her to her feet.

"We have to keep running, but this time we run the other way. We're not going to die here, Linda."

"I can't!" Linda sobbed and stumbled, falling back to the ground.

"Linda, you have to! Get up! Please!" Jamie shouted, attempting to get her back on her feet.

A branch snapped behind the girls and they froze in place. Jamie slowly turned her head to find the masked madman standing there, machete in hand. He let out a menacing laugh.

Linda screamed and crawled along on hands and knees. Jamie hollered at her, pleading with her to get up, pulling her along as the madman began his pursuit. Jamie finally got the hysterical girl up off the ground and they tore off through the campground, terror-filled screams penetrating the darkness around them. They zigzagged through trees, nearly falling multiple times, and found themselves trapped at the end of the long row of bunk houses.

Jamie's mind raced. She was right back at square one. She should have never left the first bunk she'd found earlier that night. If she had just stayed hidden until daylight, she might have already been in the safety of the police.

Linda's whimpering snapped her from her thoughts and she was filled with a selfish remorse. Linda would be dead if she hadn't found her, but then again, they both might have been better off had Jamie just stayed put.

"We have to hide, come on." She pulled Linda along and headed for the last bunk on the left.

"I'm so scared," Linda whispered, squeezing Jamie's hand as they snuck into the dark bunk.

Jamie closed the door and led them to the back. "Can you help me move one of these beds to the door?"

Linda shook her head, clutching her side.

Jamie sighed and took hold of one of the heavy bed frames. She grunted as she shoved it forward, but stopped immediately as it screeched against the hardwood floor. She cringed at the loud sound. Linda placed her hands over her ears, crying again.

"Linda, we have to block the door. We can't let him get in here."

Like clockwork, the door shook in its frame and the girls jumped. Linda screamed and ran behind Jamie for cover. The madman's laughter grew louder with each earth-shaking blow he delivered to the door. Jamie knew it wouldn't hold for long. She held out Tommy's knife in front of her, knowing damn well it wouldn't do much to protect them, but she wouldn't go down without a fight.

The door burst inward and Linda screamed in Jamie's ear, startling her even more than the shattering door, causing her to drop the knife. The madman entered the bunk, his weapon at his side, eyes still smiling through that patchwork mask. The only thing Jamie could do was to try and make a run for it; she would have to leave Linda behind.

The madman took another step forward and raised his machete, laughing.

Linda made a sudden move for the knife on the floor and caught Jamie off-guard. She wrapped an arm around Jamie and dragged the blade across her exposed throat. Jamie's eyes went wide and the madman stopped laughing; the only sound filling the bunk was the sound of Jamie choking on her own blood.

Linda pushed her forward and Jamie dropped to her knees, bringing her hands up to her throat in a pathetic attempt to stop the bleeding.

"What the hell, Linda?" the madman asked, pulling his mask off and glaring at her.

"That's for stabbing me so deep, you asshole!" Linda shouted back, tossing the knife aside.

Jamie continued to choke on the floor between them, tears streaming down her face. She toppled over onto her side, hands still over her wounded throat. A car pulled up outside and harsh headlights flooded the cabin.

"I'm telling Mom. You're gonna be in big trouble," the madman said, throwing the mask at his sister and storming outside.

As Jamie lay dying on the floor, she could hear the madman outside complaining. A familiar voice asked him what was wrong.

"God, he's such a fuckin' baby," Linda said, hands on her hips. She stared down at Jamie and shook her head. "Sorry about all this. He would have done much worse to you anyway. Consider it a token of our short-lived friendship."

Jamie struggled to breathe. She stared in disbelief at Linda. She could feel the life slowly leaving her; after everything, this was how things would end.

The madman and a short, portly woman entered the bunk.

"What's the meaning of all this, young lady?" Dee asked, her hands on her hips. "You spoiled Weaver's entire birthday present."

"Mom, look." Linda pulled up her shirt and exposed the wound in her side. "He cut me too deep!"

"It was an accident, Linda! God!" Weaver folded his arms over his chest and pouted.

"Honey, that ain't even that bad. Now, apologize to your brother this instant!" Dee demanded, pointing a finger at Linda.

"Yes, ma'am." Linda looked down at her dirty, bare feet. "Sorry, Weaver."

"Whatever," he grumbled.

Dee looked down at Jamie, who was barely wheezing on the floor, the blood-flow from her neck slowing. "She ain't dead yet?"

"She's about to be." Weaver gave Jamie a hard kick and she flopped over onto her back, her bloody hands falling from her neck. Her head slumped to the side and she lay lifeless below them.

Dee shrugged and patted her son on the shoulder. "Now, you two hug it out and let's get goin'. Gotta get up early and clean all this up before church tomorrow."

"Yes, Mom," they said in unison, hugging over Jamie's lifeless body.

The trio exited the bunk and piled into Dee's Oldsmobile.

The Harvest

by S. L. Mewse

The door to the dingy little bedsit swung inwards on creaky, rust-laden hinges. Jennifer rested her hand upon it, then grimaced at the slick feeling of damp and mould beneath her fingers. As she stepped into the darkness within the tiny flat, she resolved to give the place a good clean on her next free day. It couldn't be good for the patients on the ward if she was working covered in spores, but when she had so little free time, she simply didn't have the opportunity to clean.

Dropping her overstuffed brown handbag to the floor by the door, she kicked off her shoes and stuffed her aching feet into a pair of fluffy slippers. She wriggled her toes and wondered if the sharp feeling against her digits was a crumb of food or if they were coming apart. On her pittance of a wage it was not likely she would be able to afford a new pair for another month, so she hoped it was the former.

Reaching behind her head, the weary student pulled the hair tie from her long, golden tresses and ruffled them with her fingers to rub out the remnants of that morning's hairspray. The freshly loosened hair cascaded down around her shoulders and in it she could faintly smell medical soap mixed with the sweet scent of her shampoo. She had not been away from the wards since the previous morning, and after having had only an hour of sleep in the staff rest room she was about ready to drop. She wanted nothing more than to fall into bed, but first she had to put her work clothes into the washing machine and grab herself a bite to eat. It was six in the morning and almost time to crawl into bed, but she was starving.

She crossed over to a dingy little archway and moved from the living area into the kitchen. Having spent so long under the harsh glow of artificial lighting, she was relieved to finally be in her own home and in the comfort of the half-light. There would be no buzzing machines, beeping pagers or moaning patients for the day. No, she could finally rest. A quiet, grateful sigh escaped her as she thought of the sleep she would soon be getting; she could think of nothing better than sinking into the black oblivion of a dreamless slumber.

In the tiny kitchen, she pulled her pale blue scrubs top over her head and bent down to open the washing machine. Throwing the top half of her uniform into the gaping maw of the empty drum, she heard a faint thump somewhere in the main room. Stopping dead, she held her breath and listened, awaiting another sound, but nothing came. She stood up straight and peered into the main room.

When she saw nothing in her brief scan, she exhaled, deciding it must have been something falling from the table loaded with old takeaway boxes. She returned to her undressing with another quiet sigh. She slid her thumbs into the elastic waistband of her unflattering trousers and pushed them down past the curved mounds of her buttocks. She stepped out of the pool of material they had created around her feet and reached down to pick them up, throwing them on top of the rest of her uniform inside the machine. Stepping back, she fumbled about on the kitchen countertop until her searching fingers found the curves of a washing detergent bottle. She hesitated, realising that to wash just two items would be a waste of money and resources.

She reached behind her back and unclasped her bra, then slipped it off over her arms. She slung it into the washer before beginning the ungainly dance of removing her socks, and then lastly slipped off her lace thong and threw everything into the washer on top of the rest of her clothes. She stood naked in the darkness, debating whether to throw in more. She decided she may as well, and turned to make her way over to the washing bin. The room seemed suddenly darker to her then, but she put it down to her increasing tiredness and stepped into the lounge.

As the first of her slipper-clad feet touched the plush, dirty carpet, a hand slammed against the side of her face. She fell, her ample breasts swinging as she tumbled, her slender arms crumpling beneath her as she went down. Her lip exploded in a burst of crimson as the fist made contact again. A sharp gasp escaped her. She landed heavily on her front, her legs kicking out against the shins of her attacker.

She opened her mouth to scream only for it to be filled with a dirty rag. She bit down, hoping to find fingers, but only found more fabric as it was pushed deeper into her throat. A sweet, strange smell filled her nostrils as she struggled to breathe past the suffocating scent and invading material. Her vision swam. Blackness shrouded her as a heavy weight pushed down on her back, and she slipped into unconsciousness.

***

Jennifer groaned. Every muscle in her body ached; her throat felt like sandpaper. Sluggishly she wormed her limbs around, feeling the deep, dull ache of bruising as she tried to reach up to rub her eyes. Her limbs moved heavily, and her arm fell and hit her cheek.

"Argh!" she gasped, flinching at the sudden pain, conscious that her hands were numb.

Forcing her heavy-lidded eyes open, she blinked against the glare of harsh, artificial light. Screwing up her face, she turned her head and pressed her cheek to the scratchy material beneath her. She tried not to panic as the memory of a stranger in her home came back to her, but a cold feeling of dread crept through her. Her heart raced, and she opened her eyes again with more determination. She could hear the insistent whir of a generator in the distance, but that was not what had stirred her. A sudden sharp sound cut through the droning of the generator. There was a brief moment of quiet and then it came again: the unmistakable sound of a scream.

Gripping at the sheets beneath her, she forced herself to sit upright with shaking arms and tried to take in her surroundings past the blurred vision. She realised quickly that she was naked. Gooseflesh scrambled over her tanned skin as she clamped her slender legs together to try and hide her most private part. It was freezing cold; her breath misted in the air with each ragged gasp for oxygen. Her chest felt as though her lungs were full of lead, and she desperately rubbed at the smooth skin between her exposed breasts as if she could coax air into them. Hot tears prickled at her eyes as another sharp scream rang through the place. Gulping air like a fish out of water, she swiped away the tears with two dirty palms before another scream jolted her back into awareness. She had no time for self-pity. She had to get out of there. Wherever *there* was.

She peered around her surroundings and her fright turned to outright terror. She was in a small, squalid room lit by one flickering strip light in the centre of the ceiling. The walls were covered with filthy white tiles and the floor was thick with grime. Metal-topped counters lined one edge of the room. She noticed a large, grubby sink beside the only door, and loose papers strewn across the surface beside it. Casting her gaze to the floor, she noticed a set of footprints through a line of disturbed dirt leading to where she sat on a metal medical table. Beneath her was a thin blanket and a grimy old pillow, but there was no mistaking the shape of the gurney she had been left on. With a quick fumble of her fingers she felt a raised lip around the edge of the bed, and the pillow she had woken on rested snugly in a sink with two small taps hanging over it.

She was on an autopsy table.

Swinging her legs over the edge of the table, she dropped to the ground and crumpled in the dirt. Her limbs were half-numb and sluggish, but she needed to flee. As more screams rang through the strange place, she dragged herself across the floor on her belly towards the door. She grimaced at the greasy feel of filth as it clung to her breasts and belly, willing her legs to work and regain feeling in them as she squirmed across the ground. By the time she reached the door the screams were at fever pitch, and she knew she would not have long to make her escape.

She scrambled upright, testing the steadiness of her legs. She leant against the back of the door and peered through the crosshatching of the wire-reinforced window set into the wood. The hallway beyond was so dark she could not see the wall opposite the door, which sent a small spike of hope through her. She would have more chance of escape in the darkness.

Carefully she lowered the handle of the door, feeling its cold steel against the soft warmth of her belly as she slipped into the blackness of the corridor. The screams were louder here, almost deafening, and more frequent. She ran to the far side of the hallway, pressing herself to the tile wall and allowing the darkness to wash over her. She moved away from the light spilling through the doorway of the room she had exited. Her bare feet crunched over debris hidden by the darkness and she winced as she half-walked, half-ran along the passageway, careful not to make a sound.

When she had finally got far enough away that she could no longer see the room, a slow smile spread across her lips. She was going to make it!

But as her hope swelled, her searching fingers found a dead end. The corridor ended in a wide double doorway that she could not open. She scrabbled at it with her hands, the sound of the doors rattling against their hinges filling the air around her. It was only then that she noticed the screaming had stopped. She froze, her heart pounding as she listened for any signs that she had been discovered. For what seemed like an eternity, she heard nothing, and then a groan of pain sounded somewhere in the distance.

Jennifer knew she would have to go back towards the sounds of torture. She had no other choice. She moved faster on her way back, no longer flinching when her feet found sharp stones or rubbish. She had wasted time by heading in the wrong direction, and time was precious. Since the screams had died down into groans and moans, she knew whatever was happening would soon reach its climax. Once that occurred, she had no doubt she was next on her kidnapper's to-do list.

As she approached the square of flickering light filtering through the glass in the door, the terrified student nurse held her breath. Her heart pounded faster in her chest, and soon she was stood trembling beside the shaft of bright, artificial light. For a second she could not bring herself to move through it, but then the unmistakable sound of a slamming door echoed down the corridor.

Shit. Her time was up. He was on his way; she could hear his heavy footfalls and the sound of keys rattling.

She inhaled deeply and shot forward across the beam of light, briefly exposed before she was lost in the darkness again. She stood against the cold wall and panicked. He was getting closer; she could hear his breathing then and knew he was relaxed and unsuspecting. She closed her eyes and tried to calm herself. If she could hear him, then he could surely hear her.

And yet he passed her, by some miracle avoiding touching her as he went.

Terrified and trembling, she turned her head and watched the patch of light on the wall, waiting with bated breath for him to appear. Suddenly he was there, tall, slender and starkly lit. His dark hair protruded from beneath a surgical cap, and a surgical mask almost completely hid his face—all but for a strip of flesh around his eyes, which were covered with thick goggles smeared with red. As she watched, he removed them and wiped them on the front of the filthy surgical gown that draped his thin physique. The light did not descend far enough for her to see his feet, but she knew by the heavy footfalls that they were clad in boots.

Jennifer backed away into the shadows as the surgeon pressed his goggles back into place on his face, threw open the door to the room and stalked inside.

Seizing her chance, she turned and ran, the sounds of her footsteps masked by the clashing of metal on tile as he searched the vacant room. Her heart hammered in her chest as her naked feet pounded on the grimy floor. She held her arms in front of her, feeling for any obstacles as she fled blindly down the dark hallway, her breasts swinging heavily and her feet stinging more with every step.

She seemed to run forever before another brightly lit doorway loomed to her left. She skidded to a halt at the shaft of piercing light and approached the window in the door. What if there was second kidnapper? Or a team of them?

She tried to peer through the window without moving into the light, but she could not. Crouching low, she crept into the shadows below the glow and slowly raised her head. She pressed her nose to the door, and the contents of the room revealed themselves. Her heart seemed to stop beating as she saw what lay within those four walls. A breath hitched in her throat, and her legs trembled as though they might give way.

The room was a morgue, but one that had not been used for its intended purpose for a long time. The walls were splattered with red and brown patches of blood and the floor was awash with it. The far wall was a mass of open metal drawers, rusted with age and piled high with things the shadows mercifully concealed. But that was far from the worst of it. In the centre of the room stood a filthy metal autopsy table flanked by small portable tables laden with medical instruments. The gurney itself was covered with a thick sheet that had once been white, the shape of a female body beneath it. Her blood-splattered feet protruded from the end of the table, strapped tightly into a set of rusted makeshift birthing stirrups.

Jennifer stumbled backwards, her hands rising to her face as a tiny gasp escaped her. Further down the corridor a door rattled on its hinges as it was thrown open. It hit the wall and tiles shattered against the floor. Footsteps stormed in her direction. She was rooted to the spot with fear. What could she do? If she ran he would hear her and make chase. If she stayed in the dark she risked being stumbled across.

She could see only one option.

She fumbled with the handle on the door in front of her and pulled it open. She slipped through the gap and closed it behind her with a soft click, the sound masked by the heavy footfalls echoing down the hall. Exposed in the flickering light, she ducked down and crept across the room to the cold chambers on the far wall. As she skulked by the autopsy table, she held her breath against the scent of decay that rolled from the compartments in what had once been a chilled storage system for the deceased. The sound of footsteps grew louder; she searched the cabinets in the wall for a space she could cram herself into. Her fingers found slick wetness in the first compartment, a sticky substance that made her gag in the second, and a pool of slimy mess in the third. They were all occupied.

She darted to the centre of the room as his shadow loomed into view. As the door handle rattled, she slithered under the autopsy table, pressing tight to the floor as she writhed through a puddle of stagnant, congealing blood. She squatted on the balls of her feet below the table as he stormed into the room and threw open the drawers in the wall. A heavy, wet slap sounded as he pulled the occupants from their resting places and onto the tiled floor. She scrambled backwards, her breathing ragged, as a misshapen eyeball skittered across the floor and struck the wheel of the gurney. She followed its grisly progress until it came to rest at the base of one of the medical tables, and suddenly she remembered the surgical equipment.

She lowered herself to the floor again. Her breasts and belly sank into the blood beneath her as she looked out through the gap below the sheet. His boots faced away from her and he was scrabbling around in the drawers. She knew she might not get a better chance, and cautiously slithered over to the base of one of the instrument tables. She ignored the blood dripping from the end of the table, reached up between the bound feet above her and fumbled on the surface for the first thing she could reach. Her fingers closed around the handle of something. She pulled it over the edge. It caught on something, and a muffled groan sounded from the table above her.

The woman was still alive!

Flinching away from the feet in the stirrups, Jennifer raised the item she had stolen to her face. It was a surgical scalpel tipped with a curved blade, short but sharp. But she did not have time to feel relief at her acquisition of a weapon. The sound from the table had drawn the man's attention. His feet snapped around to face his previous victim and he stomped over, his boots coming to rest almost beneath the sheet.

Jennifer held her breath as the filthy shroud was thrown from the woman above her. It fluttered to the ground at the head of the table, and the boots moved until he was stood between those wide spread legs.

"You look well!" He laughed.

Jennifer saw his body lower as he inspected his work. A wet, slapping sound reverberated in the room, and more blood trickled over the edge of the metal table to the floor between his feet. A quiet moan escaped the woman. Jennifer heard a rattling, and his feet spread on the tiles in front of her. He chuckled as the sound of a zipper being slowly pulled down filled the air.

"The other little bitch can wait." The smile on his face was audible in his voice. "She's got enough sedative in her to knock out a horse. She won't get far. Besides, we're not done here, are we, sweetheart?"

His blood-splattered trousers fell around his ankles. The woman on the table screamed, her voice breaking as he slammed something down onto her. Quiet sobs broke out. Jennifer crept forward over the bloodied tiles, squatting on the balls of her feet with the knife in hand as he sank lower. She saw everything before he plunged himself forward.

Screaming with rage, Jennifer flung herself forward and sank the scalpel deep into the soft white flesh at the top of his inner thigh. She stabbed at him again and again; blood jetted out of the wounds and splashed onto her. He screamed and dropped to the ground. Snarling like an animal, she scrambled from beneath the table and tore into him with her weapon, slashing at his shins, working her way up to his thighs and crawling over his twitching body to bury the blade deep into his belly.

His hands grasped at the handle, his fingers sliding on his own blood as he tried to pull the weapon free, but his movements quickly deteriorated into twitches and jerks. She had severed his femoral artery. He would bleed out in a matter of minutes.

Jennifer scrabbled away from him, slipping across the gore-slicked floor. Coated in blood, she screamed at him, "Fuck you!" She raked back her bloodied hair from her face. "Fuck you!"

She got to her feet and leaned forward to spit onto his mask-covered face. "A fucking medical student?" she screamed. "I know every system in your body. You've got less than three minutes to live, you fucking monster!"

The man squirmed and moaned, his hands sinking from the blade in his belly to his exposed groin. She kicked him away, slamming her toes into his unprotected bollocks. A jet of bright blood spurted from his leg onto her shins. She reached down and tore the blade from his belly, ripping it sideways to spill his steaming intestines onto the tiles.

"Fuck you!" she spat one last time, before turning to the woman on the table.

The sight was worse than she had expected. Far worse. She could not move, rooted to the spot with shock and disgust.

The woman had once been dark-haired if the tone of her eyebrows was anything to go by, but every other hair on her head and body had been meticulously shaved away. She was hooked up to a small IV stand by the bedside, and the needlepoint in her arm was buried deep into a pus-oozing wound. That lesion was only the tip of the iceberg. Almost every scrap of skin below her neck had been peeled away to expose the raw tissue beneath. Her eyelids were stitched shut, but the hollowness of the sockets indicated the eyes had been taken from her skull.

Instantly, Jennifer knew what she was looking at. She was being harvested.

Jennifer managed to choke out a whimper, tears streaming down her cheeks. She stepped closer and forced herself to ask, "Can you hear me?"

The woman's mouth opened and she groaned quietly. The inside was utterly devoid of teeth.

Jennifer could not contain the reflexive shower of vomit that burst from her mouth. She bent double, crying fitfully at the knowledge of what the woman had been used for and vomiting until her stomach was empty.

When she had nothing more to expel, she straightened up and looked the woman over with a clinical eye, assessing her like a patient, judging her chances of survival. They were zero. It was only a matter of time before her infection levels soared or shock claimed her life.

Jennifer knew what she had to do. With a heavy heart, she reached over to the nearest table of equipment and chose a savage-looking blade. There were syringes, but she did not trust their contents to offer kind relief.

She moved closer to the head of the table, scalpel in hand. As she leaned in to find an artery, the door slammed open behind her and a shot rang through the air. She slumped to the ground, blood pouring from a hole in her chest. She gasped for air while blood filled her lungs.

"Fuck," a deep voice swore. A man wearing clean surgical gear rushed across the room to the table. He fumbled with a pager at his belt, his brow knitted above the mask covering his mouth and nose. "We'll have to hollow these out now and get it all on ice before it rots."

He sighed out at his fallen comrade as the sound of more hurried footsteps echoed in the corridor.

BAG LADY

by Dawn Cano

On the outside, Emma seemed like an ordinary bag lady lazily walking through the streets of Dallas, Texas, pulling her cart behind her. What nobody knew was that she starred in several B-horror films during the 1980s. In her movies, Emma portrayed the stereotypical big-breasted blonde teenager who seemed to get killed at the beginning of every film (or more likely, after having sex with the star of the show). Although the films were bad in the eyes of critics and audiences, today, more than 30 years later, she was still proud that she was once an actress and had appeared on screen.

Despite making plenty of money during her short-lived film career, Emma was now completely broke and had been living on the street for the last three years. Parties with too many drugs and alcohol and extravagant purchases had ensured she'd blown through her earnings in no time. Looking back, she wished she had the chance to do things differently. Now in her early 50s, Emma was depressed, lonely, and insecure, though she did her best to keep up with her good appearance and looked better than most of the women she encountered on the street. Her large tits and long blonde hair still captured the attention of men all around, and more than once she had been mistaken for a prostitute.

On the street, Emma kept to herself, not caring what anyone thought of her – she only worried about her day-to-day survival. Her life might be shit now, but she had her memories to keep her warm on cold, lonely nights. Besides, not wanting to face the uncertainty of her future, Emma preferred to live in the past. Some of the other transients would sit and watch her talk to herself, but that wasn't what she was doing at all. She loved reciting lines from her past films, thinking that if she could remember them, she'd hold on to her sanity in this fucked up world a little while longer.

In her cart, Emma had all the things you might expect to find in a homeless person's collection: dirty clothes, cardboard, a couple of trash bags, newspaper, and an old, worn blanket. She also carried mementos from her younger days, items that were so special she kept them to herself. At the bottom of her cart sat a torn and wrinkled poster from one of her films, *I Am Death*. It showed her as a young starlet running from a masked man wielding an axe. In one of her trash bags, she carried a large, razor-sharp knife, given to her by her father, an avid hunter. Each night before she found a place to sleep, Emma always made sure to check that her most prized possessions were still there.

Over the last six weeks, Dallas had become far less safe than it ever had before. There were areas Emma knew to stay away from (Elm Street being one of the main danger spots), but usually she felt safe walking around at all hours of the day and night. Now, she feared for her safety as well as the others.

Someone was killing Dallas' homeless and prostitutes in the most horrific ways possible. The killer would lure the homeless away from their spots, and after a day or two, their bodies would turn up in another part of the city raped, mutilated and gutted. Whoever was killing these people took a lot of pleasure in their activities, often carving words into the chests of their victims, removing their eyes, or cutting off their genitals. Although the homeless walking around downtown Dallas rarely saw the news, they did read the newspapers, and when a report of a new murder surfaced, the fear among them would increase only to quickly be replaced with the task of trying to survive.

Crime scene investigators assured the public that there was only one killer, but he was extremely dangerous. Dubbed "Dallas' Jack the Ripper", his attacks were becoming more frequent and increasingly violent. Police found little in the way of forensic evidence to link anyone to the crimes so the killer had little to fear from the cops, and that made him ever more terrifying.

Emma had started keeping her knife on her person, wrapping it in a small trash bag and putting it in her waistband, which made her feel a little safer. Besides, there were dozens of homeless on the streets, so the odds of him choosing her were slim.

Luckily, Emma also had a protective friend: Charlie "Killer" Wilkes, a 60-something black man who spent most days sitting alone, talking to himself. He'd been on the streets much longer than Emma and had received the nickname "Killer" due to his hot temper and small size. His friends made fun of him daily, but their teasing didn't bother Charlie. Emma spoke with him regularly and on the rare occasion she had extra food, she would share it with him.

One warm spring day, Emma picked up a couple of candy bars with the change dropped at her feet while she'd slept, and she thought of Charlie. Dragging her cart behind her, she went to where she knew she'd find him, snuggled in between two abandoned buildings on Elm Street – a place she didn't want to be.

She called out as she rounded the corner, "Charlie, I brought you some breakfast!"

Charlie wasn't there, which was strange since he rarely left. When he did, he didn't go far. Emma looked up and down the street and saw no evidence that Charlie had ever been there.

Maybe someone came along and kicked him out.

She sat in Charlie's 'house', becoming nervous when gang members and drug dealers started staring at her. She took off, working her way back to a more populated area, all the while wondering where Charlie had run off to. On her way back to her spot, she found the front section of a newspaper lying on the ground. She picked it up and read the headline: "Local Homeless Man Found Dead in Fair Park. 'Jack the Ripper' Strikes Again." There, beneath the headline, was a picture of a younger Charlie.

As she read the story with tears running down her cheeks, she learned her friend was beaten, sodomized, and had choked to death on his own penis. Terror and revulsion mixed with her grief. She slowly made her way back to her spot. Suddenly, Emma wasn't feeling hungry and gave both candy bars to those she encountered on her walk.

Emma grieved for her friend, but as always, life quickly got in the way, and she became complacent again. She still carried her knife, but the fear had all but disappeared. She went back to scrounging for food, begging for spare change, and finding places to sleep each night.

***

It was during a particularly warm summer evening in early June when an attractive young man who obviously had plenty of money approached Emma. As she sat on the pavement, feeling sorry for herself, he walked up and called her by name.

"Emma? You're Emma Lincoln, aren't you? From *I am Death?*" The man appeared genuinely excited to meet her.

"Yes, that's me. You know me?"

"Not only do I know you, I love you! Your performance in that movie was amazing. I can't believe I'm actually standing here talking to a real movie star." He smiled, making her feel at ease with his friendly face and warm compliments.

Emma stood and smoothed out her clothes. She was wearing her favorite outfit from the two she still possessed: her khaki cargo pants and black Iron Maiden t-shirt, which were the cleanest things she owned.

The man offered a hand. "Forgive me. My name is David. I'm starstruck. I...wow."

Emma took his hand and shook it. "Thank you. I don't know what to say. I suppose you didn't expect to meet an actor living on the streets. I'm more than a little embarrassed."

David ignored her comment. "What do you say we go and get something to eat? One of my favorite burger places is not too far from here and I'd love to hear about *I Am Death.*"

"That actually sounds like fun, if you're sure you have nothing better to do. But I can't leave my cart here. Someone will steal it."

David thought for a moment, then said, "I have an SUV, and I bet if we lay it down, it'll fit in the back. What do you think? Grab a bite, talk about one of my favorite horror movies, then I'll bring you back here if you like."

Emma smiled, feeling more important than she had in years. "Lead the way, David."

They walked down the street to David's waiting SUV. He clicked the button on the key fob to unlock the doors and walked around to the back, opening it up. "See, there's plenty of space."

Together they grabbed the cart and laid it in the spacious cargo area. David closed the hatch and ran around to open the passenger door. Emma climbed in. A few seconds later, he appeared at the driver's side, opening the door and jumping in. He inserted the key into the ignition and offered her a water bottle.

"Thirsty?"

Emma took and opened it, drinking deeply. She never noticed that the seal was broken.

In less than five minutes, she was fast asleep.

***

Emma awoke on a cold slab of concrete in a place she'd never seen, not knowing how long she'd been unconscious. At first glance, as the fog in her mind cleared, it looked like a warehouse of sorts, but she couldn't be sure.

She sat up, still dizzy, and looked around. The room must have been 20 feet wide by 40 feet long, and every wall was made of metal. It was empty except for a long table in the middle, with a small door set in the far wall. As Emma stood up to investigate, David walked into the room through the door, slamming it shut behind him. At least she thought it was David. She couldn't quite remember what he'd been wearing, and now he sported a Michael Myers mask.

"Good morning, sleepy head. I thought you'd never wake up."

Emma stood rooted to her spot and didn't speak. David approached her, and she retreated until she found herself backed into a corner. He stopped mere inches from her face. She stared into his eyes through the mask, becoming more terrified with each passing second. David was a large man, something she hadn't noticed on the street. He stood more than six feet tall and weighed around 250 pounds. That alone made him intimidating; she only stood about five feet tall.

Although she wanted to appear strong just like the heroines in her movies, her voice trembled as she asked, "*You're* the one killing us - killing homeless people, aren't you?"

When he spoke, she could tell he was smiling. "That's me! I'm so glad word of my service has spread throughout the land, even to the peasants. Anyway, would you like to know why? Sure you do.

"You see, the government has no idea how to handle the homeless problem in this city so I stepped in to help. Nothing ever gets done and the vagrant population continues to grow, so I took it upon myself to remove the vermin littering the streets of our fine city. Granted, it's a slow process, but as the media continues covering the murders, I suspect many of you people will move on, taking your filth and disease with you. Soon, the city leaders will thank me."

Emma stood staring at him, not believing what she was hearing. "Why the mask? I already know what you look like."

"Why not? It's fun and I've always wondered what it's like to be the villain in a horror movie. I wear a different mask for every one of you stinking pukes I kill. And besides, you're a former scream queen, so I thought you'd find the humor in it.

"Now it's my turn to ask the questions. What the hell are you doing out on the streets? Did you squander all your money? Drugs? Booze? What was it?"

Although she couldn't explain it, Emma felt ashamed. Here was a serial killer judging *her* life choices? As tears blurred her vision, she didn't say a word and defiantly stared into David's eyes.

"Too good to answer me, huh?"

David reached up, slapping her hard on the left side of her face. Emma stumbled but remained standing. He laughed like a kid at a carnival and slapped her again, harder this time. As she doubled over from the blow, she felt blood trickle from her nose.

The knife.

She wanted to kick herself for not remembering it sooner, but that would have to wait. She needed to find a way to get the knife out of the back of her pants. If David wanted a fight, she'd gladly give him one. She didn't believe in God, but at that moment, she prayed a silent prayer.

Please, God. Please let him turn around. Just for a minute.

Emma straightened up, filled with confidence, and stared him in the eyes. "Yes, I wasted all my film earnings on drugs, drinking, and expensive things. Is that what you wanted to hear? Are you happy now?" She looked away and wiped the blood from her face.

David laughed loudly, causing Emma to jump and look back at him. "Whoa, where did the attitude come from?" He peeled the mask up, spit in her face, backed away from her slowly, and turned around, pacing the room. "So, let me get this straight. You fucked up your life and we, the taxpayers, are supposed to take care of you? You wasted all your money and now you want us to waste ours? How is that fair? That makes you no better than the rest of the homeless scum lining the streets of Dallas. You had a good job, but instead of saving your money and spending it wisely, you decided to blow it all, and now you expect the city, and the people walking by, probably on their way to actual jobs, to support you? To survive, you beg, borrow and steal, and the government spends hundreds of thousands of dollars each year to provide food and shelter for you and your cockroach friends, as well as cleaning up the mess you fucking people make?"

When Emma didn't answer, he turned to face her - just as she went after him with the knife raised. Her technique was clumsy, but her attack was powerful. She plunged it at his face. David was too slow in his response and the knife went through his right cheek, almost nicking his eye. Blood poured from the wound, staining the floor crimson. David screamed and lunged for Emma, but slipped in his own blood. He fell, his head making a sickening crack when it hit the concrete floor, and he was out cold.

Catching her breath, Emma ripped the mask off David's face. Laughing, she put it on and felt more powerful than she had in years.

Death has come to your little town, Sheriff.

Using the knife, Emma cut away David's shirt, unbuttoned his pants, and although it was more effort than she'd expected, pulled his pants and boxers down around his ankles. Removing the dirty belt from her cargo pants, she used it to tie David's arms together at the wrists, behind his back. When she was confident he couldn't move, she straddled his chest.

When he woke up, she'd be ready.

111

***

It took a long time for David to finally wake up, or at least it felt like a long time to Emma. While he was unconscious, she searched his pockets, finding more than $100 in cash, his car keys, and a cell phone. She stuck the items in her pocket and when he began to stir, knew exactly what she was going to do. She'd played it out in her head like a movie script.

Action!

David's eyes fluttered open and he stared in horror at Emma.

Stealing a line from *Jason Lives*, Emma said, "I've seen enough horror movies to know that any weirdo wearing a mask is never friendly."

David remained silent, staring up at her as she laughed.

"Cat got your tongue?" Emma slapped David hard across the face, making sure to hit the spot she'd cut earlier. David hissed, but didn't cry out. "Since you seem to love horror movies so much, I'm sure you realize you're beyond fucked."

David gritted his teeth and growled, "You fucking whore. When I get out of this, I'm gonna gut you with that fucking blade. I'll strangle you with your own intestines."

Emma laughed again. "Silly man. You're in no position to make threats. Right now, all we're doing is talking. There's nothing wrong with talking, is there?" Her question was met with silence. "Since you admitted you're the one slaughtering the homeless – my friends – I thought maybe you'd want to brag about your kills. You know, try to scare me by telling me what you did to them. After all, you are the big, scary man and I'm the weak, helpless female."

David grinned. "You mean like the old bitch whose tongue I cut out because she wouldn't shut the fuck up when I told her to? Or the guy whose cock I shoved down his throat? I'm really proud of those two."

The mention of her friend Charlie got Emma's blood boiling. "Let me tell you about the guy whose dick you cut off. His name was Charlie. He had a daughter and three grandchildren. He served his country during Vietnam. He didn't have many friends and the people he knew teased him relentlessly, yet he never raised a hand to them, never said a bad word about anyone. He was my friend. Now his daughter has to live without her father and his grandchildren without their grandpa."

David smiled. "Sounds like a pussy to me."

Emma raised the knife with her right hand and plunged it deep into David's left shoulder, leaving it there. He screamed. She was really beginning to enjoy this. Smiling inside the mask, she said, "Now who's the pussy?"

"Look, what do you want from me? An apology? Fine, I'm sorry. Okay? I'm sorry! Now let me up."

"Beg for me. Beg me to let you get up. Beg me to let you live."

David spat, "Fuck you."

Emma twisted the knife. He screamed again and she shouted over him, "Fuck me? Fuck you. This is for all the innocent people you killed. This is for all the sons and daughters who had to bury their parents. This is for the grandbabies who will never get the chance to know their grandparents."

Tears flowed from David's eyes, staining the concrete below his head. When he got himself under control he said, "You doing this won't bring them back."

"Oh, I know, but if there's a Heaven and Hell, you can bet your fat ass all your victims are smiling right now. That's reason enough to do this. Besides, since you like wearing masks and are so well versed in horror movies, I thought this would be fun for you. You're the victim in your very own horror story!"

Emma removed the knife from David's shoulder and marvelled at the amount of blood that spilled out of the hole she'd made. Unlike the films she'd starred in, where the woman always got killed, this time, she was doing the killing. She liked the feeling of administering vigilante justice to this piece of shit.

She leaned down, placed her mouth close to David's ear and whispered, "You've killed at least six people who couldn't defend themselves. I'm going to cause you pain in six different ways before I finally let you die." She sat back up and plunged the knife into David's other shoulder, laughing as he screamed and cried.

"That's one."

Scooting down, she sat on his knees, removed the mask and placed her mouth over his exposed penis. She teased the head with her tongue and was amazed that, despite the obvious pain she'd caused him, he was getting hard. *It's true. Men always think with the little head when they should be thinking with the big one.*

"That's a boy. Mmmm."

She continued teasing and sucking until he was standing at full attention. Although she really wasn't horny, the power she felt coursing through her was amazing. She wanted to maximize the adrenaline flowing through her system. In all her favorite '80s horror films, there was always a little sex before the massacre began, so why not include it here?

Emma looked up at David's face and noticed him looking down at her. His eyes were moist and red, but it was obvious he was enjoying the moment. "How does it feel to get a blowjob from a scream queen?"

He closed his eyes and laid his head down, enjoying the feeling. As his breathing increased, she stopped. David moaned deep in his throat. "Please, don't stop now," he whispered.

"You want me to keep going? Do you want me to let you come? Ask me."

Breathlessly he whispered, "Please, make me come."

Emma took him in her mouth again, sucking hard and, just as he was about to shoot his load, she bit down as hard as she could. David bucked and screamed, almost knocking Emma off his lap.

She sat up, smiling as she said, "That's two."

After David calmed down, Emma slid back up. "I have something special planned for number three."

"Please, no more. Please stop. I'm sorry."

Emma put the mask back on. "I'm sure the people you tortured and killed begged for their lives, didn't they?"

David stayed silent.

"Didn't they, David? Is that even your real name? It doesn't matter, I suppose. So, they begged you not to kill them, didn't they?"

Without looking at her, he said, "Yes."

"They begged you to stop hurting them, didn't they?"

"Yes."

"Yet you didn't stop. You never stopped until they were dead and even then you mutilated their bodies." Emma ran the knife down David's chest from his collarbone to his navel, deep enough to draw blood. David hissed through his teeth. She made another cut from one nipple to the other.

"Stop! What the fuck do you want?"

"I want you to feel the pain you caused the others. I want you to suffer. Then, I want you to fucking die." In one fluid motion, Emma grabbed David's left nipple, holding it taut. Using the knife, she sliced it off. *It's just like cutting butter.*

David's eyes rolled back in his head as blood ran down his chest onto the floor. His scream came out breathy, weak and desperate. She did the same on the right side. Emma remained sitting on David's stomach, holding the nipple in her hand, seemingly lost in her madness. It took her a moment to realize he'd passed out.

"Damn. That's three," she muttered under her breath.

While David remained unconscious, she kneeled next to him and used the knife to carve the word 'Cunt' into his chest. That was number four. She wasn't sure what to do for the last two, but they had to be good. She also knew he needed to be awake for the finale. To wake him, she poked him repeatedly in both thighs with the tip of the knife. As she did, she couldn't help but smile at the blood covering the blade. Eventually, David woke up.

"What was it you said to me? 'Good morning, sleepy head. I thought you'd never wake up.'"

David groaned. He was becoming weak from the blood loss so Emma knew she had to work fast. She smiled as she figured out what came next. "I'll tell you what I'm gonna do for you, David. I'm going to put an end to this quickly. Would you like that? Would you like to die without more pain?"

David moaned but didn't say anything.

Emma slid down and looked at David's battered penis. She noticed the blood oozing from the bite marks she'd left behind.

As she stared, David raised his head. "What are you doing?"

Emma grabbed his penis with her left hand and brought the knife up to rest against the base. David squirmed and bucked, but Emma put all her weight into holding him down. "I'm sorry, but numbers five and six will have to happen a little more quickly than I wanted. I hope you'll forgive me, but I really can't have you bleeding out before I'm finished."

With that, she sliced off his penis. She was disappointed to discover the knife wasn't as sharp as when she'd started this little adventure, so she had to saw part of the skin off. David screamed before slipping into unconsciousness once again.

"Fuck," Emma whispered. *He's going to miss number six.* She scooted through all the blood, moving up to his face. Dropping the knife, she forced his mouth open with her left hand and with her right, shoved his penis as far in as it would go.

David gasped as he awoke, but with a dick in his throat, it was a futile effort. Emma watched as his face turned a variety of interesting colors and his eyes streamed tears. It didn't take long for him to die and after several seconds, it was over. As she breathed a sigh of relief, she performed one last act of defiance. She picked her knife up off the blood-soaked floor and stabbed David's right eyeball.

"And that, motherfucker, was for what you planned to do to me. Burn in Hell, bitch."

By this point, the adrenaline had worn off and Emma trembled. She left the knife in the now bloody socket and fought to stand. Her stomach flip-flopped. Before she could try to stop it, Emma tore off the mask and vomited on David's face.

What have I done?

You've saved a lot of innocent people, that's what.

Once she found her footing, Emma did her best to avoid slipping in the blood on the floor and walked toward the door David had come through. Her clothes were covered in blood and the metallic stench was all she could smell. The door led to the outside and as she headed out, she remembered that her cart was still in the back of his SUV.

On shaky legs, she walked over to the vehicle, thankful to find it unlocked, forgetting she had the keys. With a strength she didn't know she possessed, she removed the cart from the back and immediately dug to the bottom to pull out her old movie poster.

In every film Emma had made, she died a horrific death at the beginning. She was *always* one of the first victims.

Today, Emma was the heroine.

KILLER TIMES AT RIDGEWAY MALL

by Debby Dodds

Timbo felt his sweat cutting a tortuous, flesh-colored path down his meticulously applied white clown makeup. A normal-looking person barreling through the crowded shopping center this time of year would barely cause a raised eyebrow in his or her wake. However, even grown men leaving the 24 Hour Fitness after pumping some serious iron felt themselves involuntarily flinching, instinctively clenching their butt cheeks as Timbo passed by. Small children who happened to catch a glimpse of Timbo unabashedly sobbed in fear, unable to articulate beyond, "Mama, that a scary man." What they wanted to say was, "There's something in that man's eyes, a great otherworldly passion, lighting him from within. On this mortal coil that I'm admittedly new to, I've never seen anything so unnerving!"

The sound of *Silent Night*, vocals by Tiffany, screeched over the tinny mall speakers. Garish red and green decorations seemed to infect every nook of this monolith to capitalism, but Timbo paid little attention. He was on a sacred mission. Timbo had heard what he believed to be the voice of God Himself.

"Leave your twisty balloons and your air pump at home today, Timbo. Instead, go to the garage and find the Omni Hunter 12PT your father uses to skin and quarter his fresh kills and bring that to the mall with you."

Timbo's father prided himself on not only being an avid deer hunter, but also one who did his own field dressing. Timbo had been forced to watch the process from the tender age of four—the exposing of the meat, red and shiny. He knew the knife the Almighty voice in his head was referring to.

"I will provide further instruction when you arrive at your destination." This part made Timbo even more convinced it was truly God because he'd read enough of the Bible in Sunday school to know how vague God could be with His instructions.

Since Timbo had graduated high school, he'd stopped going to church. Frankly, it was all he could do to get out of bed most days. If the air mattress in his parents' basement could even be called a bed. He was so lonely.

He bolted past the Orange Julius stand, not even trying to make his usual furtive eye contact with the cute blonde, Stacy, who he thought might be his soulmate. The last time he'd gazed in her direction, she quickly looked away as if Bloody Mary had appeared in the mirror in front of her. He'd tried to talk to her once, but she'd gotten 'distracted' by her friend Linda. He often fantasized that one day she'd see the *real* Tim, not just Timbo the Clown, and that she'd be awestruck by his magnificence. He knew she'd had an older boyfriend who'd broken up with her and he often imagined finding the creep and separating his limbs from his body with a chainsaw, one by one.

Timbo knew he'd finally have his chance to make a difference, to rewrite the script, to change this miserable world he'd been forced to live in. Make the girl of his dreams notice him. Working as a children's birthday party entertainer was not what Timbo had aspired to. But after his heavy metal band Deep Fried Cornhole had split up, he'd realized he had limited prospects. Being a clown was all he could think of to fall back on. At least his years of applying Kiss Army makeup when he was younger came in handy. He'd been working a gig in the mall the past two weeks for the holidays, earning whatever he could in tips, making balloon crowns, poodles, and swords for kids in the center court area by the fountain.

He scurried past his arch-nemesis, Damone, who lounged on a wall near the arcade with his sunglasses on. Damone had recently sold Timbo Def Leppard tickets, promising totally righteous seats, but instead Timbo had gotten shafted with partially obstructed view seats, almost completely behind the stage and the one-armed drummer. At the time, Timbo had imagined hanging Damone up on the gutting hooks in his dad's garage and slowly gouging his eyeballs out with one of his mom's delicately engraved tea spoons.

Then he spotted *her*: the chubby gray-haired lady wearing a wide smile and a comically large wreath pin over her ample left breast on her standard issued red apron. This was his *destination*. He felt it with every bit of marrow in his bones. She blithely stood ringing her bell. Timbo thought she looked less beatific and more like she was considering whether she'd prefer a stale tuna fish sandwich from Circle K to another Hungry Man Salisbury Steak TV dinner tonight. But Timbo knew if he was successful in completing his sacred mission, her future held neither of those.

"You must act quickly. You do not have much time," The Voice commanded. He knew he was close to ending this. He felt another line of sweat originating at his bushy orange wig line, burning a swath through his bright blue eyeshadow, smearing it even more, and he realized how deranged he must look. But he didn't care.

Timbo reeled back, unsheathing his Instrument of Justice.

"Get away from that collection bucket, bitch!" he screamed, paraphrasing something he'd seen in a movie once.

But he hesitated.

For a spilt second, he doubted.

And before he could lunge forward to sink the knife up to its hilt in the granny, a shot rang out.

Stacy, his crush, the ultimate dream girl, held the gun.

She looks just like Heather Locklear on T.J. Hooker, Timbo thought as he lay writhing in pain, his red life juice seeping from him.

"I knew you were up to no good, you creepy clown." Stacy's lips curled down in disgust. She still pointed her gun in his direction.

"You noticed me..." Timbo croaked. But his joy was short-lived as he saw Stacy jerk forward, dropping her gun. Her mouth opened and bubbly blood gushed out like puke. Her eyes glazed over and she fell forward. Dead.

Behind her stood the Salvation Army woman, smiling wide, holding her own knife in her right hand.

"This is for my grandson, Bobby. You're all filthy maggots in this mall. The mall is evil." She glared at him, daring Timbo to disagree. But he didn't.

"All that boy ever wanted to do, all day long, was to hang out here in the arcade. He never wanted to spend time with his grandma anymore, rubbing her calloused feet, learning bridge. Well, he's gone now. He died from an infection on his trigger finger from all that dirty video game playing. And the rotten losers in this mall must pay! They will know my—"

"Oh, for God's sake! You want revenge. No, duh. Got it." Timbo said with his last breath, "Stop monologuing and get on with it."

"For Bobby," she whispered. With that, the old lady reached into her bucket and set off a series of bombs that had been placed throughout the mall. The explosions lit the place on fire, blasting bodies into chunks and killing every last person.

When the first responders found Timbo's head blown off to the side of some of the worst damage, they noted that a single tear had blazed the last of many sloppy lines of smudge through Timbo's happy clown face.

"Jesus!" the paramedic said, looking at him. "Clowns have always freaked me out." Then he shivered and stepped over what was left of Timbo.

PAPER, ROCK, SCISSORS

by Michelle Garza and Melissa Lason

"**A**re you gettin' in or not?" Detective Simons asked.

The two women were obviously twin sisters judging by their mirror resemblance, but what made his smile broaden was that the two dark-haired young ladies were dressed in matching halter tops and leather miniskirts. His suit jacket was thrown in the seat, the top three buttons of his shirt undone. He was ready for a few hours off work, maybe a few drinks with the sirens he'd found on the roadside. He anxiously checked his appearance in the rearview mirror. His blond hair looked fine but his eyes were puffy from lack of sleep.

Valerie grinned from the side of the road. "There's only one thing that will help us decide."

The sisters turned to each other, hands extended. The driver shook his head and laughed softly as they played a game of paper, rock, scissors to determine if he was someone they would accept a ride from. It was a childish game where both players pounded their fists in the air in unison and let their hand fall in the shape of paper, rock or scissors on the third pound. He couldn't remember what each object in the game beat, and he didn't really care. Something told him they would be climbing into the truck beside him; it was his lucky night.

Vickie was victorious, throwing out the rock to beat her sister's scissors.

"DARN!" Valerie spat.

"I win!" Vickie proclaimed. "I call shotgun!"

The women threw their backpacks into the truck bed, climbed into the seat, and settled in.

"Buckle up," Detective Simons reminded them as he crumpled up his suit jacket and threw it in the well at their feet.

"Yes, Officer!" Valerie said.

Simons couldn't help but watch the obvious way she slid the belt across her ample chest, how it rested between her perky breasts. His eyes roved up to see the knowing smile on her face—she was teasing him. Her sister sat right beside him in the single cab truck. The scent of her perfume reminded him of women performing in the nudie bars down the highway.

"Where are you girls coming from?" he asked.

"We just got off work," Valerie answered as she rolled down her window. "Mind if we smoke?"

"Go right ahead," Simons said. "I just got off work too."

"I thought detectives were always on the clock," Vickie said.

"We usually get enough time to shit, shower and shave, maybe sleep a few hours."

"Must be stressful," Vickie said, puffing on a cigarette and then handing it to her sister.

"It is. Especially of late." Simons stopped himself from giving them too much information but couldn't resist warning them. "There's a real weirdo out here. You shouldn't be hitchhiking."

"Is that why you gave us a ride? That's so chivalrous." Valerie said.

"Yeah, we don't see guys like you very often," Vickie said as she patted the detective's thigh.

Her touch warmed him through his slacks and sent a tremor up to his groin. He could feel himself leap to attention when she kept her hand there, kneading the muscles in his upper leg.

"To protect and serve." He winked.

"We do some services on occasion," Vickie whispered.

Simons looked over at them, slack-jawed, cock pressing against his pants in an almost painful display of how long it had been since he had been 'serviced'.

"It's the least we could do for a man who was gentleman enough to give us a safe ride home," Vickie purred, her hand sliding upward to grip his erection.

A deep sigh escaped him as he nodded his head.

***

By the time they reached their destination, a house in a rural area surrounded by cornfields, he wasn't sure if his balls wouldn't burst beneath her teasing hand. Vickie was busy sucking a hickey on his neck, causing him to nearly miss the driveway.

"Slow down, cowboy!" Valerie giggled, pointing to their home. "Let's go inside and get comfortable."

Detective Simons waddled after the scantily clad pair of dancers and through the front door of a small, dark house.

"Take a seat, Detective." Valerie smiled and pushed him down into a well-worn recliner. They were in a cramped living room; sparse light came from a kitchen adjacent to it, illuminating a couch covered in laundry, a small television and a coffee table lined with liquor bottles.

"Would you like a drink?" Vickie asked.

"Yes, ma'am," he said with a grin.

"Pick your poison." She smiled, though he could hardly see it in the dim lighting.

"Anything will do."

"All right then," she answered.

She nudged Valerie, who instantly stuck her hand out. Their hands bounced up and down in another game of paper, rock, scissors. Detective Simons mused how much it looked like they were engaged in giving hand jobs to invisible men. He chuckled aloud.

"What's so funny?" Vickie questioned.

"Just looks like you two are jerkin' off some ghosts or something every time you do that."

She giggled. "We do this for every decision. It's fairer that way."

"Yeah, we've done it since we were little girls. Helps us decide."

"That's how you make decisions?" He laughed. "That's cute. I like it."

"Sure hope you do. It keeps our arms strong." Valerie did the motion again and winked.

He hardly caught the flirtatious gesture in the lighting but he was well aware what she had in mind.

Valerie picked up a bottle of tequila, slid it along her body and seductively ran her tongue up its side. "This is what you'll be havin', Detective."

Vickie took a seat on the edge of the crowded couch beside the recliner and poured herself a drink. "Tell us about the sicko you're tryin' to catch. He's all over the news."

"You don't want to hear about him. It will ruin the mood," he said. "Well, I suppose I can tell you a little bit. Our suspect is merciless. Would kill two little things like you with no remorse." Simons added, not really caring anymore if he gave away any vital information as long as the sisters kept on seducing him.

"Actually, if we knew how dangerous he is and what kind of guy you're protecting us from, it would only make us more...thankful," Valerie said as she knelt on the floor before him, handing him a glass of straight tequila.

"Thank you, my dear," he said, taking the cup. "I will share more, if you're willing to keep it a secret."

"Of course!" Vickie said.

"Is he a real sicko?" Valerie asked.

"One of the sickest I've ever seen." His erection began to shrink as he thought about the dismembered corpses that had begun showing up along the riverbanks for the last six months.

"How sick?" Vickie asked.

"You really don't wanna know."

"Yes, we do," she said, running her hand up his thigh.

"Does it turn you on?" he asked.

"Yeah, and knowing you're here to protect us... It's sexy," Vickie said.

Detective Simons had dated a few women like this pair—they insisted on hearing about all the rapists and murderers he had put away. His dominance turned them on.

"Take off your clothes and I will tell you just how sick he is," he whispered.

"Kinky! I like that!" Valerie answered and stood up from the floor.

"We'll do it one piece at a time, but you gotta tell us all the nasty shit," Vickie said.

"You got a deal," he said as he unbuttoned his pants.

"Who were they?" Valerie asked as she slid her black miniskirt down her pale thighs. She was wearing a thong that barely covered her shaved pussy.

"All kinds of people: black, white, old, and young."

"Don't you coppers look for patterns?" Vickie snickered.

"Take it off and I'll tell you," he answered, sliding his pants down around his ankles and then kicking them off to the carpet.

She followed his instructions and pulled her skirt off, revealing that she was wearing no panties.

His dick leapt to attention and he teased, "I thought twins dressed exactly alike?"

"I left my undies at work," she said, winking. "Now go on."

"Yes, we always look for patterns, connections, motives, but these cases have none, other than the victims end up in pieces," he answered. "It seems so random—the choices of victims and what is done to them before death."

He sipped his drink, feeling full of himself now that the sultry sisters were completely enamored with his knowledge. He would have them eating from his palm. He'd never made it with twins before. Actually, he hadn't made it with anyone in almost six months and his balls were screaming for release.

"Tell us how they died," Vickie said as she toyed with the string holding her crimson halter top up.

"I already told you," he said.

"We said *all* the details. Don't keep secrets," she said and pretended to pout.

"All right." He blushed as he stared at the shape of her full breasts beneath the flimsy layer of clothing. Her nipples were erect, and by the way her tits sat on her chest he could tell they were natural and perky, just like her sister's. "Some were strangled, some had their throats cut and one was smothered with a plastic bag,"

Vickie let the halter top fall. She stood naked in the faint light. It drove him mad with arousal; he felt himself dribbling with anticipation.

"Keep going." Valerie sighed as she too shed her halter top, and then ran her hands down to toy with her tiny g-string. "Stroke yourself as you tell us."

He would have found the request morbid had his erection not stolen the blood from his brain. He hurriedly yanked off his tighty-whities and sat back on the recliner, running his hand over himself slowly. His swollen cock pulsed with excitement.

"One woman was completely gutted. Her insides were found drifting along the bottom of the river...fish food."

Valerie stripped off her thong and moved closer to him, swaying her body. He knew she was a dancer and from her moves he would say a damn good one at that.

"Dance for me and I will tell you more."

Valerie began winding her body seductively.

He used his free hand to point at Vickie. "You, too."

She joined in and they danced together. He bit his lip, worried he might blow his load, so he slowed his stroking and told them more about the grotesque assortment of deaths he had encountered in the riverbank butcher killings.

"A lady had her eyes gouged out and we never found them. They could've been kept as a trophy."

Valerie fell to her knees and crawled up onto his lap. She kissed him as he feverishly stroked himself.

"Do me," he said, his voice pleading.

"Do you have any suspects?" she whispered.

"Huh?"

"In the riverbank butcher case. Do you have any suspects?" she asked, moving his hand away and rubbing herself against him.

"None," he answered, staring down and praying to any god that would listen that she'd slide it inside her.

"Good," she whispered.

"The killer must be pretty smart," Vickie said as she slid her hands down her sister's chest from behind. She cupped her twin's breasts and pinched her nipples. Simons nearly came just watching her knead her sister's pink areolas.

"Which one gets him first?" Valerie asked.

He could feel the warm wetness of her against him. He rocked his hips, trying to coax her into letting him in.

She laughed. "Hold on, cowboy."

Valerie held her fist up to Vickie and grinned. "Best of three."

Simons rolled his eyes, his balls throbbing. He wished the wacky bitches would hurry up and spread their legs.

The first round went to Valerie, the second to Vickie. Their faces were grim, the competition between them making him hornier—twin sisters battling over who got to bang him first. He almost lost control.

Valerie was victorious. "I WIN!!" she cheered.

"Come claim your reward," Simons said, pointing at his erection.

"Mmmmhmm," Valerie teased. "I like that. You know what else I like?"

"What would that be, honey?" he asked, stroking himself to prepare for the pleasure awaiting him.

"I like tying guys up."

"Can we use your handcuffs?" Vickie suggested.

"They're on my belt," he said, smiling. This sex game was nothing new to him; from his earliest days as a recruit he had used his handcuffs for playing naughty cop.

Vickie searched his trousers and came back with the shining set of restraints. She handed them to her sister, who danced around the detective slowly. Valerie pulled his hands behind the recliner and snapped the cuffs shut around his wrists. The way his arms were stretched around the cushioning was slightly uncomfortable but he didn't complain. It made his hips jut out, and his cock looked like a fleshy spear.

"Time to party!" Valerie said. "Excuse us while we freshen up."

The sisters disappeared into the darkness of the small house. Simons flexed his fingers and squeezed them into a fist. Vickie had cuffed him too tight and it was growing uncomfortable. He worried his dick would shrivel if he waited for them too long.

"Come on, girls! Dinner is gettin' cold!" he called.

He could hear giggling from somewhere down the hallway. Pins and needles set upon his arms. He shook his head. "This better not be some kind of prank," he said, agitation bubbling into his voice.

"Far from it," Valerie answered as they came strutting back into the tiny, half-lit room. Simons was confused as to why they were dressed in clear plastic suits; they were completely nude underneath but the costumes would definitely get in the way of penetration.

"Hey, now! You went back on our deal. I told you about the butcher but you had to get naked!" he complained.

"We thought you wanted to play?" Vickie pouted.

"I do! I do, but look, I need a little attention." He motioned his head towards his shriveling erection.

"Don't worry, baby. You'll get lots of attention before this night is over," Valerie said, then giggled, which triggered her sister into laughing.

The sound of their laughter didn't bring sexy, playful thoughts to the detective's mind; it was the cackling of people who knew a secret.

"Uncuff me. I'm not in the mood for playing anymore," he said.

"No," Vickie answered. Her face fell into a blank stare. The teasing hussy was gone, and what replaced her worried him.

"Let me go," he repeated.

The twins shook their heads in unison and then stepped forward.

Vickie kicked a pile of laundry off the couch, exposing an assortment of pinchers, saws and hammers. "You won the first round so you get to go first." She smiled. It was overly sweet; a touch of madness flared in her eyes.

"You're too kind, sissy," Valerie answered and walked over to the array of tools on the stained sofa.

Detective Simons' eyes grew wide. "What the hell are you doin'?"

"Whatever we want, pig. Now shut your mouth," Valerie answered.

"You'll hang for this, bitch! I swear! Hurting cops gets you the maximum sentence. The judge will throw the book at you!"

"That's if they catch us. You already told us you have no suspects," Vickie said.

Simons struggled in his handcuffs, his dick flopping from side to side as he tried to pull his arms over the back of the recliner.

"I like the name 'Riverbank Butcher.' It's badass!" Vickie laughed.

"If anyone really knew, it would be Riverbank Butcher*s*. Plural, as in two," Valerie added, then let her hand fall on a pair of garden shears.

"Nice choice!" her sister complimented.

"I have to outdo you and that lady you plucked the eyes from!"

"Still got them in a jar!" Vickie beamed with pride. "*Hey*! Why don't you get yourself a trophy?"

"What should I go for?" Valerie asked, turning back to eye him.

"You know exactly what I'd say!" Vickie answered, and laughed.

"I like that idea," her sister replied, then bent over her prey.

Simons fought and kicked his feet out. One foot connected with Valerie's stomach.

"You fuckin' pig!"

"I got him, sissy," Vickie said, grabbing a carpenter's hammer.

She smashed him across both knees. Her teeth were clenched in a tight smirk as she repeated the beating. His bones crunched; blood sprung out of the wounds. He vomited as agony rolled through him in waves of nauseating pain.

"Sit still, you piece of shit!" Valerie had recovered from his boot to the gut and now hovered over his flaccid penis. The cold shears pressed against his skin as she positioned them at the base of his shaft. It was only for a second, but the chill it sent through his balls and stomach was only a precursor to the sharp, hot pain as she snapped the blades closed. The scissors cut through his flesh with ease. She picked up his severed dick and swung it around like a bleeding worm as she performed a victory dance.

"Nice trophy!" Vickie complimented.

"Now it's my turn, but what should I use? The screwdriver or handsaw?" Valerie asked, prompting another round of paper, rock, scissors.

The detective ended up with a screwdriver in his ocular cavity, his toes smashed by a hammer and his nipples removed with a razor knife in a matter of a few rounds of the sisters' favorite game. At last, Valerie hovered over his right wrist with a handsaw, something that would surely send him into unconscious shock if he hadn't already died from blood loss. She whispered to him their secret, knowing dead men can tell no tales.

"You will never catch the butcher because you are looking for a connection that doesn't exist. It's all about the luck of the draw that we choose who lives, dies, and how they die… like a game of chance. Paper, rock, scissors."

24 LONE PINE LANE

by D.M. Slate

Cassie stood alone and off to the side of the crowd, waiting for her passengers to arrive. The Three Stooges – her brother Dillon and two of his best friends – waited close to the front barriers holding signs that read 'Free Rides for Babes', 'Spring Break Fling' and 'Denver Does Ya Good'. She was mortified for her cousin and her guests to step off the airplane to such a welcome, but her immature older brother happened to own a Suburban. And as her only form of transportation, Cassie had no choice but to be thankful for his company and ride.

As the throng of visitors poured into the concourse of Denver International Airport, Cassie easily spotted their guests. She'd warned her cousin Charlotte that there was a spring snowstorm expected, but sure enough, Charlotte sauntered in wearing a pair of skin-tight jeans with holes in the thighs and an overly snug tank top. Her bright pink bra straps dangled loosely over her shoulders. Cassie waved her hands in excited greeting, but Charlotte and her friends seemed to take greater pleasure in the boys' demeaning welcome signs than Cassie's jubilant expressions.

Deflated, she watched as Charlotte rushed up to Dillon and embraced him in a hug, exclaiming, "Cousin – it's been way too long! Look how handsome you are now…"

Dillon returned the gesture, beaming proudly in response. "Well, beautiful, the same could be said for you."

The awkward attraction between the two of them made Cassie fidget.

Jeff was quick to step forward, intervening. He took Charlotte's hand and dropped to one knee, proclaiming in a theatric voice, "Welcome to Colorado, m'lady."

Charlotte tossed her long, caramel-blonde hair over her shoulder and smiled at the compliment. Tiny dimples marked her flawless cheeks. She looked back over her shoulder. "These are my roommates, Alice and Daisy."

Two beautiful women emerged from behind her cousin and Cassie wanted to gag. How was it possible that they were all so gorgeous?

One of them stepped forward, raising a hand in greeting. Her dark brown hair and olive, sun-kissed skin seemed to glimmer under the terminal's florescent lights. "Hey, I'm Alice. Nice to meet you." The young woman wore little in the way of clothing: short-shorts, tall furry boots, and a So-Cal tank top.

Cassie scoffed at her stupidity. She was going to freeze to death.

Mark, however, rushed forward, removing his coat and eagerly draping it over Alice's shoulders. "Hi, I'm Mark. Here - take this. It'll help keep you warm." He gave her a sly wink, grinning mischievously.

Cassie rolled her eyes as Alice snuggled into the garment. She'd known Mark for seven years and knew he'd let her freeze before he'd offer her his coat. And just like that, he was all over Alice. Typical male.

Standing silently at the back, the third and final girl stepped to the side with her eyes downcast to the floor. She looked up briefly, waving and smiling before blushing and averting her gaze once again. A thick white headband contrasted with her short, brown curly hair. Diamond earrings sparkled in her ears and a tiny locket hung around her neck. Wearing blue jeans and a light jacket, she was the most appropriately dressed of the trio.

Dillon approached the shy girl, raising her chin so that she looked him in the face. "So that must mean you're Daisy, right?"

The girl's cheeks flushed and she gave a quick nod. Dillon's smile widened.

Cassie shook her head in shame. She'd seen her brother pull this trick time after time over the years. He knew how to take advantage of a woman's weakness. The thought made her sick to her stomach.

Grabbing Daisy by the hand, Dillon led her and their small group through the congested airport toward the parking garage. As the automatic doors to the airport opened, a gust of arctic air whipped by, taking their breaths away. The underdressed women leaned into their companions in search of body heat. The college boys dragged their guests' luggage through the parking garage, all the while trying to shield the young women from the brunt of the storm. Cassie walked at the back by herself, holding up the side panel of her coat to shield her face from the blowing snow.

Finally reaching the Suburban, Dillon rushed forward and unlocked the doors.

Charlotte was the first to comment. "Holy fuck. This piece of shit is our ride?"

Cassie tried to stifle her laugh. The late eighties Suburban sat atop massive tires. The fenders were marked with rust and decay, and a cracked windshield sealed the deal.

Dillon stood at the rear passenger door, holding it open for his guests in the raging wind and snow. "Why do you have to be so disrespectful to my baby?" he asked.

The group shared a collective chuckle as they piled into the vehicle. Cassie made her way to the front passenger seat and hopped inside, thankful for the break from the storm.

Once her brother was in and the vehicle was on, heater blasting, he turned and announced, "Welcome to spring break in Colorado."

***

Snow continued to plummet to the ground and the wind was relentless. The hour-and-a-half drive from the airport to deep within the Rocky Mountains ended up taking closer to two-and-a-half hours.

Cassie messed with her phone the entire time, attempting to get the GPS to work, to no avail.

Dillon slowed the Suburban as they approached a side road, trying to read the snow-covered street sign. Putting the vehicle into park, he hopped out of the car and rushed over to brush the snow away from the sign. "Ha! Lone Pine Lane. This is the one we're looking for."

A sigh of relief passed through the vehicle.

Rushing back into the Suburban, Dillon slammed his door and smiled. "We're almost there. According to Stacey, once we turn here it's just a few more miles."

Cassie's forehead furrowed. "And who is Stacey?"

"The chick on Craigslist that I rented the cabin from, dummy."

Even in the cold, Cassie felt her cheeks burning hot with embarrassment. Her brother could be a total asshole.

The Suburban crept down the unplowed road, leaving tire marks in the fresh white snow. The trees were thick, and in some spots they overhung the road, creating a tunnel of plant growth. On the left, a metal mailbox marked a private driveway. Dillon turned onto it, moving deeper into the trees. As they passed the mailbox, Cassie could barely make out the address through the thin blanket of snow covering it: 24 Lone Pine Lane.

A tiny cabin came into view at the end of the drive. A steady plume of smoke emerged from the chimney, and even though it was small, the structure was a welcome relief from the storm.

Putting the Suburban into park, Dillon announced, "We're here."

Cassie looked around. "How are we going to get inside?"

"We're supposed to call Stacy once we get here."

Cassie gave him a blank stare. How was it possible that he was so dense? "Well, bro – my phone doesn't work in the mountains during a blizzard. Does yours?"

Digging deep into his pocket, Dillon removed his phone, holding it up and moving it around as he attempted to get service. "Shit! Do any of your phones work?"

The passengers in the back all removed their cells, staring at their screens.

Mark was the only one to respond. "Dude, you didn't think that one through very well, did ya?"

A few nervous laughs followed.

"Shit!" Dillon screamed again. He slammed his hands against the dash before bashing his forehead on the steering wheel.

Cassie caught something out of her peripheral vision and turned her head. The cabin's front door opened and a man stepped out onto the porch, raising a hand to his forehead to shield his eyes from the wind and snow.

"Ummm, are you sure this is the right cabin?" Whipping her head to the side, Cassie looked to her brother for reassurance. She could tell by his body language that he was uneasy.

Dillon cleared his throat. "I'm going to go talk to him. If it's the wrong address, I bet he can help us find the right cabin. Maybe this is a blessing… I'm sure he has a land-line that we can use to call Stacey." Smiling, Dillon hopped out of the Suburban.

Cassie's stomach jittered. Something didn't feel right. Jumping out as well, she rushed to follow behind her older brother.

He held up a hand in greeting as he approached the man. "Hello, sir. Sorry to bother you. We're looking to meet up with Stacey at 24 Lone Pine Lane. Can you tell us how to find that cabin from here?"

The skinny, balding man smiled awkwardly. "You're already there. I'm Stacey." He extended his hand in greeting.

Cassie watched as her stunned brother shook the man's hand. She had a moment of personal satisfaction at his gross mistake. This entire time he'd thought he'd been writing to a woman. Classic.

Stacey's beady black eyes traveled from Dillon to her, and Cassie wanted to hide. Outdated, wire-frame glasses sat atop his pointy nose and a layer of auburn five o'clock shadow grew on his face. His thin-lipped smile gave Cassie the creeps. She nodded in his direction before sidestepping behind her brother's muscular frame.

Stacey informed Dillon, "I knew that the cell phones wouldn't be working, so I came over to meet up with you guys whenever you arrived. I've got a nice fire going already so the cabin is toasty warm."

Cassie found herself staring at the wide gap between Stacey's front teeth as he talked. Not wanting to be rude, she turned and made her way back to the Suburban. Within two minutes, Dillon headed back to the vehicle as well, cabin keys in hand. They all watched as Stacey zipped up his coat, pulled on his hood, and walked off into the snowy abyss.

Dillon laughed. "That guy is a freak."

Charlotte broke away from Jeff's embrace, sitting forward on her seat. "Where the hell is he walking to?"

"He said his cabin isn't far from here. I guess he's walking home."

Cassie reached down and grabbed her purse, slinging it over her shoulder. "Well, what are we waiting for? Let's go check out our spring break *casa*."

***

They'd only been inside the cabin for an hour before Mark and Alice snuck away to a room for some private time. Dillon and Daisy sat cuddled together next to the fireplace, and Jeff continued to make passes at Charlotte as he used the microwave to make a bag of popcorn. Cassie sat alone at the tiny kitchen table, staring out the window into the snowstorm, pondering her decision to come on this trip.

The overhead lights flickered once before going out completely. The microwave stopped running, although several kernels of corn popped afterward. The light emitting from the fireplace was enough to allow dim vision in the main area of the cabin. There was a large *thump* from the back room, followed by Mark's cursing. Seconds later, he emerged holding his cell phone up for light. Alice clung to his arm and followed close behind.

The seven people instinctually moved toward the fireplace.

Dillon clapped his hands together once, and his voice carried an optimistic tone as he said, "I'll bet the power is back on within ten minutes." He gave Daisy a sideways glance. "And besides, I'm sure we can find a few ways to occupy ourselves in the meantime." Daisy smiled and shook her head from side to side, looking away with embarrassment.

Jeff ripped open the half-popped bag of popcorn and chomped down on a handful. Holding the bag out, he offered to share with the group. When Cassie reached for a piece, Jeff pulled the bag away from her, teasing. She snarled at him in response.

Laughing, Jeff extended the bag back Cassie's way. As she reached out again, he pulled the bag away once more, chuckling with amusement.

Irritated, Cassie growled, "Fuck off, jerk."

All three boys shared a laugh at her expense. Cassie spun on her heels and marched across the dim room into the murky darkness. She felt her way back to the kitchen table where she took a seat in a brooding frame of mind.

Charlotte flipped on her phone light. Walking over to Alice, she grabbed her roommate's arm. "I have to pee and I'm not going alone. Come with me." The two young women walked out of the room and down the hallway.

Dillon had just resumed his seat next to Daisy when they heard a car door slam. Jumping to their feet, Dillon and Jeff both made their way to the front door. They pulled the curtain away from the window and held their phones up to the glass, shining the lights outside.

Jeff's voice trembled as he asked, "Why are all of the Suburban doors open?"

Dillon didn't allow time for a response before he pulled the cabin door open and stormed outside, yelling, "Get away from my car!"

Cassie and Daisy both ran toward the door, Mark joining them at the same time. Dillon was already halfway to the vehicle as the others exited the cabin. He ran toward his Suburban at full speed.

Shining his light into the interior of the car, Dillon searched for the intruder. The vehicle was barren.

A shrill scream broke the silence of the night. Looking back toward the cabin, the vacationers all sprinted in the direction of the distress call. Once inside they found Alice banging on the bathroom door, hollering, "Charlotte – open the door, let me in!"

The bathroom door didn't budge.

Jeff screamed, "Watch out!" Charging forward, he thrust his shoulder into the wooden door. It shimmied, but didn't open. He backed up again and proclaimed, "Step back!"

Lunging ahead with all his speed, Jeff burst through the threshold of the bathroom. The door swung wide and they all gawked inside.

Charlotte wasn't there.

The bathroom window was open and the curtain fluttered with the turbulent movement of the storm. Outside, a trail of crimson blood marked the snow, leading away from the cabin.

Alice screamed in terror.

Jeff rushed toward the window, yelling into the darkness, "Charlotte! Where are you?" A massive gust of wind was his only response.

Cassie's body trembled as tears streaked down her cheeks. Alice and Daisy were on the verge of hysteria - their terrified cries filled the tiny bathroom.

Slamming the window closed, Jeff turned and pushed his way out of the cramped restroom, sprinting for the front door. Dillon and Mark trailed close behind him. The cluster of girls moved quickly to follow them, terrified of being left alone.

Cassie heard her brother yell, "I've got a hockey stick and a Taser in the Suburban."

Jeff already had the front door to the cabin open.

Dillon looked back, telling Mark, "Stay with the girls."

Darting into the storm, both Jeff and Dillon called out to Charlotte, listening for a response as Mark closed the cabin door behind them. He and the girls watched out the window as the boys rushed toward the Suburban.

Cassie's gut worked itself into a knot. Feeling like she might vomit, she backed away from the front door. She turned with her phone in her hand, and the light beam moved to the side window.

She screamed in terror and dropped her cell, pointing. "There's someone out there!"

Cassie heard the lock on the front door latch before Mark rushed over to look out the window. "Shit. Are you sure? We have to warn the guys."

Alice and Daisy stood clasped onto one another, crying in dismay. Cassie watched in terrified shock as Mark ran back to the front door, holding his light up to the window. Snapping back into motion, Cassie rushed past the other girls and peered out into the storm as well.

The wind had picked up and it was impossible to see half the distance to the Suburban at this point. Adrenaline coursed through Cassie's veins as she considered their options.

Mark's voice broke her concentration. "Look, I see something."

Straining her eyes, Cassie noticed movement in the blizzard. Her brother's form came into view – he was supporting Jeff's weight and they were stumbling back toward the cabin. Dillon kept looking back over his shoulder so Cassie knew they were being chased.

Mark saw it too. He pushed Cassie aside and whipped open the front door of the cabin. "Come on – hurry!"

The boys scrambled the short distance and Mark ushered them inside. Slamming the door closed behind them, Mark continued to watch out the window, looking for the unidentified person outside.

Tossing the hockey stick and Taser onto the floor, Dillon then lowered Jeff onto the couch. The injured man moaned in pain. Cassie stood watch next to Mark as Alice and Daisy moved to help Jeff.

Shining her light down on Jeff, Alice bellowed in horror, "Oh my God!"

Cassie's gaze moved from the front door to the couch where Jeff was seated. His arms had moved away from his abdomen, revealing a long slash in his stomach. Dark red blood soaked his shirt and jeans. His intestines seeped out of the opening in his flesh, bulging like link-sausages. Blood poured from his nose and mouth and he gasped for air in spurts.

Vomit crept up the back of Cassie's throat and she fought to keep it down.

Dillon removed his coat and tried to apply pressure to the gaping wound. Mark moved from the door to his dying friend's side. Both men sobbed as they tried to console their mortally wounded companion.

Cassie stood alone by the door, frozen in fear.

***

The comforter from the back bedroom covered Jeff's lifeless body. They'd draped the blanket over him, unable to look at his wide, dead eyes. Both college boys sat in silent shock, staring into the darkness. Cassie stood watch at the door, peeking out every few seconds. The wind and snow had subsided, leaving a quiet, frozen abyss outside.

Looking back into the main room, Cassie spoke softly to Alice and Daisy. "My phone is almost dead and that fire is almost out, too. We need to keep the fire going so we have some light. Do you have any paper that we can burn?"

Alice stared at the floor, sniffing through her cries. She shook her head.

Daisy got to her feet, replying, "I have a couple of magazines that we could use."

Alice jumped up as well, gripping onto Daisy's arm. The girls inched their way to the back bedroom to retrieve the magazines.

While they were gone, Cassie asked her brother, "Dillon, what did you see out there? Who was it?"

Dillon's head turned slowly in her direction. His eyes were wide and glossy. He shook his head slightly, lifting his shoulders in confusion. "I don't know. Some dude in a mask."

"What kind of mask?" asked Mark.

"Some weird shit I've never seen before. It covered his entire head. Like some S & M type of mask, only it wasn't black. It was a peach latex material with rosy cheeks, pink lips, and large blue eyes."

Cassie peeked back out the window again, scanning the front of the cabin. The masked image that her mind conjured sent shivers down her spine.

A loud *thud* from the back room echoed through the cabin, followed by Alice and Daisy's hell-raising screams. Both men rose, running to the back of the wooden structure. Dillon carried the hockey stick in his hand and Mark was armed with a small knife that he'd found in a kitchen drawer.

Cassie chased after the boys, terrified to stay in the main room by herself. She squeezed the Taser tighter, ready to put it to use.

They were already inside the bedroom with their phone lights on by the time she caught up with them. Cassie's breath hitched in her throat as she saw Alice crumpled on the ground, blood spraying from a deep gash across her throat. Her tiny hands tried unsuccessfully to stop the gushing blood and her terrified eyes stared up at them, pleading for help.

A trapdoor in the floor was flipped open, revealing a dark space beneath the cabin. Daisy screamed for help from the depths of the murkiness and Dillon was quick to hop down into the hole.

Mark jumped in as well, leaving Cassie alone in the room with Alice. The entire floor was pooling with her blood. Alice's torso had slumped to the side, and with every beat of her heart, more gore gushed from her punctured neck.

Cassie shook with fear as she rushed back to the main room of the cabin. Her phone began to beep, letting her know the battery was about to die. "Why?" she screamed into the darkness as her phone went completely black.

With hands outstretched, Cassie felt her way along the wall until she saw the dim glow of the coals in the hearth. She couldn't help but to glance at Jeff's covered corpse on the couch.

A sudden banging on the front door caused her to screech in terror and jump from the ground. It took only a second to recognize that it was Dillon banging and hollering.

"Cassie, we have to go. He killed Daisy too. Come on, get in the Suburban *now!*"

Darting toward the front door, she unlocked the latch and swung it open. Dillon stood outside, still holding the hockey stick. His eyes connected with her before looking around in all directions. He grabbed her arm and pulled her along behind him as he sprinted toward the Suburban. As they neared it, Cassie could see Mark already seated inside. He motioned them onward with frantic hand gestures.

Jumping in and closing the front doors, the siblings immediately hit the lock button. Dillon tossed the hockey stick on the middle console and dug deep into his pants pocket, searching for the keys. Cassie felt a temporary sense of relief as she heard them jingling. Dillon felt each in the dark to find the right one.

Jamming it into the ignition, he cranked the key forward. The Suburban did nothing in response. Repeating the motion again and again, Dillon tried to bring the vehicle to life.

From behind, there was a pained grunt, followed by a loud choking noise. Mark's feet kicked erratically and his arms thrashed about. Turning, Cassie watched in horror as the man in the mask choked Mark with a rope. He yanked, pulling Mark's body from the middle row into the back of the Suburban.

Dillon had already grabbed the hockey stick and he lunged over the console, into the back of the vehicle.

"Get back to the cabin!" he screamed at his sister.

Without a second thought, Cassie bolted from the car and sprinted back into the cabin. Slamming the door behind her, she tried to see through the window into the darkness outside. Gripping the Taser tightly did little to ease her emotions. She sobbed uncontrollably.

A loud holler caught her attention and she forced herself to be quiet. Straining her ears, Cassie could detect the sounds of a fight. Her brother was yelling at the man, but she couldn't make out his words. There was a large *whack* followed by the sound of wood splintering. Cassie hoped that Dillon had broken the hockey stick over the man's head.

She pressed her ear to the glass and anxiously waited for more noise.

Dillon's piercing scream tore through the darkness, jolting Cassie back into hysteria. Her heart raced faster than it ever had, and the beating in her ears was so loud it made her dizzy. She backed herself into the corner behind the door, crying.

Hearing footsteps in the snow, she willed herself to peek out of the window. Dillon limped in her direction, holding the broken hockey stick that protruded from his abdomen. Cassie screamed as she saw the masked man approach Dillon from behind. He raised one of his giant boots, kicking Dillon in the lower back.

The motion sent her brother flying forward to the ground, impaling the hockey stick further into his gut.

Cassie lost control and vomited across the floor. Trying to catch her breath, she looked back outside. The man in the mask stood near her brother's bleeding body, staring calmly at the cabin door.

Cassie was frozen, unsure what to do.

The lights flickered twice and then came back to life, illuminating the interior of the small cabin. The microwave resumed its cooking time and, within seconds, it emitted a loud *ding*. Cassie jumped in response and then turned to peek out the window again. The man was still standing there, staring. Cassie ducked to the side, knowing that he could see her silhouette now that the power was back on.

Remembering that the trap door was still open, Cassie sprinted to the back room. Alice's blood saturated the carpet. Ignoring her emotions, she rushed to the door, flipping it closed. She set the Taser on the bed. A surge of adrenaline helped her shove the dresser onto its side, on top of the trap door. Cassie grabbed the Taser once again and crept back down the hall to the main room.

She hesitantly looked around the corner, scanning the interior. Everything seemed to be the same as it had been. She got to her hands and knees and crawled back to the front door. Carefully standing to the side, she stole a quick glance out the window.

The man was gone.

Her brother's body remained impaled on the stick, but he was now still. Crimson stained the white snow all around him. It took all of her willpower not to cry out and rush to his side to help him.

The shattering of a window caught Cassie's attention. She whimpered.

The moment she heard a footstep crunch the broken glass, Cassie's body kicked into motion. Whipping open the cabin door, she sprinted faster than she'd ever run before. She flew past Dillon, not even glancing down at his body. Before long, she reached the

Suburban. The rear door was open and Mark's corpse lay face down in the snow not far from it.

Cassie never slowed her pace. She held on to the Taser with all of her might.

Stealing a glance over her shoulder, she saw the man in the mask coming out of the cabin, chasing after her.

A tiny scream escaped her throat and she pushed herself to run faster. The snow was fluffy, unpacked, and her feet sunk in and slipped, making it more difficult to run.

Reaching the end of the long driveway seemed to take forever. Once she spotted the mailbox and the side road, Cassie looked back again. The man wasn't anywhere on the path behind her. She was out of breath and panting hard, so she took a second to recover.

Spinning in a slow circle, she peered into the trees, searching for the killer. Cassie held on to the Taser with both hands, preparing for an attack.

The entire forest seemed calm and undisturbed.

A low rumble became audible from down the road and Cassie watched as two bright headlights made their way toward her. She waved her hands in the air, pleading for help. The vehicle slowed and came to a stop. She sprinted to the passenger door.

Cassie looked back over her shoulder again, afraid that the man in the mask was behind her. Finding no one in pursuit, she allowed herself a sigh of relief.

She yanked on the handle and whipped the truck door open.

Her breath caught in her throat when she saw Stacey in the driver's seat. Her stomach quivered with unease. He stared back at her with a questioning look.

A tree branch snapped behind her, causing Cassie to hop into the truck and slam the door closed, locking it. "Drive!" she screamed in terror.

Stacey hit the gas and the truck's tires spun in the snow before catching traction. The truck jolted forward. Cassie's face was glued to the passenger window, searching for the masked killer hidden within the trees.

The truck turned, heading down the long driveway to the cabin.

Cassie bellowed, "No! There's a psychopath running around out here. He killed all of my friends. We've got to leave!"

As her head spun back in his direction, Cassie caught a glimpse of the mask tucked underneath Stacey's pant leg. He gave her a sideways smile.

Without hesitation, Cassie lunged forward with the Taser. Pressing the weapon against Stacey's neck, she squeezed with all her might.

Stacey's back arched and his upper torso shook as electricity coursed through his body. His eyes rolled back into his head and he let go of the steering wheel, at the same time flexing his feet and pressing on the gas pedal harder.

The truck barreled down the driveway. Drifting off to the side of the road, it smashed into a small cluster of pine trees, bringing the vehicle to an abrupt stop.

The collision sent Cassie crashing into the dash, breaking the connection of the Taser to Stacey's neck. Several of her ribs snapped upon impact. Fiery-hot pain erupted in her chest and she struggled to breathe.

Stacey let out a moan.

Cassie ignored the pain and bent to the floorboard, searching for the Taser. She recovered the weapon and wasted no time before jolting electricity through Stacey's body once again. Reaching across his torso, she unlatched the driver's door. She sat back and kicked with all her might, forcing his limp body out of the truck and into the snow-drift.

She pulled the door closed and locked it, feeling temporarily safe.

Amazingly, the truck's engine was still running. Cassie switched gears into reverse and stomped on the gas. The truck moved backward, thumping once as the front tire rolled over Stacey's body.

Switching back into drive, Cassie floored the truck, hauling ass down the long, snow-covered driveway. She never slowed for the turn onto the main road - just held tight onto the steering wheel as the grill of the truck plowed over the mailbox that marked the cabin at 24 Lone Pine Lane.

BROKEN RULES

by Fox Emm

"You're grounded, young lady! Rules are rules!"

Those words had echoed against the walls of every quaint suburban living room the family had occupied since before Lauren turned 14. That year began with what her mother referred to, with no affection, as her 'troubled' period. Four years had passed, but the shrill syllables were still being parroted by her mother.

Lauren rolled her eyes, pursing her full lips into a sneer. "Fine," she growled, though her tone said what wasn't spoken.

Her mother, accustomed to her daughter's insolence and back talk, was not hindered by the reaction. "That means no phone, no TV…"

As her mother spoke, Lauren made her hand into a puppet which mocked her mother's every word.

"…And now you're not leaving this house for anything but school for the next month!"

The last remark caused the redheaded teen to freeze in her tracks. "But Jessica's birthday party is tomorrow!" The event was one she had been looking forward to for months.

Lauren's mother curled her lips into a self-satisfied smirk. "Maybe next time you won't leave your brother home alone when I'm working late. …Or perhaps, even better, you shouldn't back talk and mock me when I'm issuing your punishment."

Lauren opened her mouth to object but allowed her lips to close soundlessly instead. She knew if she continued to press she would succeed only in earning additional time on her sentence. She lowered her hand and shifted her gray eyes to the hardwood floor. "Yes, ma'am," she replied, her voice somber.

The older woman nodded curtly before she gestured down the hall with a hand. "Now, go to your room. You won't be doing anything else tonight."

Lauren nodded before she marched back across the living room. As she did, she cast a harsh glare toward the corner where her five-year-old brother was playing with his trucks. In that moment, if looks could kill, the boy would have been toast.

Once through her bedroom door, she flopped onto her back on the bed, arms sprawling across the mattress. She heaved a sigh before she picked up one of her pillows and covered her face. The down-filled pillow caught and muffled the brunt of her frustrated screams. She felt the cotton case go moist from her saliva and the tears that she hadn't realized were falling. Once she had thoroughly drenched the pillow, she tossed it to the carpeted floor.

When she rolled toward the edge of the bed, she jumped. *What was that?* She sat up, biting her lip. She couldn't be sure, but she believed she had seen something in her window. Now that she was sitting up, she saw little more than the reflection of her lamp...

She was willing to blame the phantom on the remnants of tears which still blurred her vision, but she could have sworn there was something there.

Lauren got to her feet and found herself wishing she hadn't quit playing softball. Her bat had been donated weeks before in the interest of avoiding clutter, though she wasn't sure what good it would do other than comfort her if someone were outside. (Cleaning up seemed to be the one thing Lauren's mother loved doling out more than groundings.) She crouched low, hoping she would be able to get close to the glass to investigate further without alerting whoever was nearby. She peered through the sheer, powder pink curtains, glancing from side to side. She tried to force her vision to see farther than the limited light from her room allowed. Seeing nothing, she managed a soft sigh of relief, then made sure to close the blinds.

Now that her momentary panic had subsided, she rubbed her bloodshot eyes with the back of her hand. Her gut reaction was to call and explain the unfairness of the situation and her punishment to Jessica, as well as apologize for missing her party, but that was off the table since her mother had opted to cut her off the telephone as well. *Looks like it's time for Plan B.*

She moved to her desk and unlocked the middle drawer. She tugged a worn leather-bound diary and a pen from inside it, and then took a seat. She haphazardly scrawled the events of the day to that point into the journal.

Periodically she got an eerie sensation that she was being watched, which made her feel uneasy. Each time, she glanced over her shoulder toward the window. She figured that being startled had made her edgy and there was nothing to actually be afraid of, but her logic wasn't quite enough to make the tiny hairs on the back of her neck stay flat or keep a cold sweat from forming along her forehead at her hairline.

Lauren had just placed her journal back into her drawer when a sound caused her to jolt upright. She stood, slipping the drawer closed. She spun to face—

Nothing. Again.

She leaned to the side, trying to see around the foot of her small twin bed, hoping her younger brother or cat was the culprit. No such luck. In fact, she couldn't spot any reason for why it sounded like something had fallen outside the closet opposite her bed.

Lauren took a deep breath and wished again for something firm to use as a weapon. Without a bat at her disposal, the teen grabbed the next best thing: a trophy she had earned years before. She hefted it upside down as if she were stepping up to home plate. She took a few cautious steps toward the closet and swung the door open with her empty hand.

The hanging clothes appeared untouched on their hangers, and the folded sweaters above and shoes below the hanging rack sat undisturbed. The thud she'd heard was completely source-less, and that made it much more frightening. Her heart raced and those hairs on the back of her neck raised once more. Sweat loosened her grip around the base of the trophy.

The golden memento made a thump when it hit the floor. She took a step toward the door to the hallway. She opened the door and darted through, heading toward the living room. The television was on, and as soon as Lauren got to the edge of the carpet, she heard her mother.

"No television, young lady!" she squawked.

"I wasn't going to try and watch TV, I just—"

"Back to your room!"

"But—"

"Back. To. Your. Room."

It was obvious that she wasn't going to make any headway, so Lauren decided to attempt what passed for a compromise. "After I get a glass of water."

This deflection technique was one she had used frequently in the past. It initially had started as a sneaky way for her to gain access to the phone, television, or some other forbidden thing when grounded. If Lauren's mother was aware of the ruse, she hadn't let on and continued to allow it to happen. This instance was no different.

Once her feet hit the tile, Lauren shifted back from irritated comfort to unease. She glanced around the room, looking for anything out of the ordinary. She slowly moved around the kitchen table to the counter where the knife block stood.

One of their large slicing knives was missing.

She checked the sink and the cutlery drawer, but still no knife.

"Mom?" Lauren called, hoping against hope that her mother would have an explanation. No answer came from the living room.

The girl's voice wavered as she called out again. "M-M-Mom?" She took a step toward the living room and hesitated, casting a glance back at the knives once more. She grabbed one similar to the missing blade to make herself feel more at ease, but also so that she could show her mother which of the knives was absent.

When she turned the corner to the living room, nothing seemed out of the ordinary at first. The television was on and switched to the local news. As the announcer blathered on about some festival or another taking place downtown, they showed footage of jubilant children and carnival rides. Her little brother, Benny, had his toys strewn across the floor in front of their mother's chair as usual. The only thing irregular was that neither Benny nor their mother was in sight.

"Mom?" Lauren's voice had risen in pitch and still quivered with uncertainty. Goosebumps ran all across her pale flesh, and she felt the dewy mist of sweat on her forehead and at the back of her neck. She tried to control her racing heart with deep breaths as she stepped closer to her mother's armchair and the sofa. When she stood beside it, her heart leaped into her throat and she shrieked.

Lying by the chair, its throat cut and glistening in the lamplight, was the family cat.

"Oh, Jasper!" she cried, tears welling in her eyes. Who could have done this, and where was the rest of her family?

Lauren raised the knife defensively, her elbow locked into a pose she hoped would be domineering. "I don't know who you are, but you'll pay for that!" she yelled, hoping to instill some fear into the monster who'd murdered the beloved family pet.

She made her way down the hall, glancing in her bedroom as she passed it. Nothing seemed out of place. She looked into her mother's room and noticed the lampshade knocked askew. Without hesitating, she threw the door open, satisfied with the loud thud it made as it collided with the bumper on the wall. Once inside, the first thing she noticed was the few spots of crimson on the white carpet. She followed the trail, knife still raised, and was shocked when it led to her mother's closet. She took a deep breath in an attempt to steady her shaking hands and whipped the door open.

The blood trail continued through the closet. The shelves in the back almost seemed to cut the trail off mid-stride. On impulse, Lauren tried to pull on the shelves and was disgusted when she snatched her fingers back, wet and sticky. She tried not to think about where the blood might have come from.

She felt defeated and kicked the wall of shelves. She heard a click, and a segment of the wall popped forward. *How long has this been here?* she wondered, pulling the wood toward her to reveal a passage. The blood trail continued down a dark, narrow hall, but for a moment Lauren hesitated. *What can I do?* she asked herself, gnawing at her lower lip. *More than police who might take an hour to get here, I suppose.*

Even so, she dialed 9-1-1 from the phone on her mother's night table and placed the receiver down once she heard the operator on the other end. She decided her time would be better spent trying to find her family than explaining the situation to a dispatcher. After all, how could she explain when she wasn't sure what was happening herself?

She started down the corridor toward her fate.

The passageway led between her room and her mother's and ended at a rickety ladder. At the top, there was a trap door through the ceiling. The door was open, beckoning her upward. The rungs of the frail ladder were glossed crimson. Lauren opted to carry the knife in her teeth, determined to make the ascent. She wanted to reduce her risk of cutting her hands as she climbed, something that became more likely the more weight she pressed on the sad wooden implement.

A few rungs below the opening, she did her best to gaze through the door into the darkness. She tried to remember the reasons why she was doing this. Her mother. Her little brother. They were all she had.

When Lauren finally mustered the courage to clamber through the small trapdoor, she couldn't have dreamt the scene she discovered. Her mother knelt bound, gagged, and bleeding near the far wall. Lauren had never seen anyone look as afraid as her mother did at that moment, her eyes wide and her teeth clenched around a dirty cloth fashioned into a gag.

Lauren climbed the last few rungs of the ladder and darted across the floor to reach her kneeling mother's side. The older woman groaned against the fabric as she lifted her head to look at her daughter. Her mascara and eyeliner ran down her cheeks, mingling with the filth that decorated the material which silenced her.

"I'll get you out of here," Lauren whispered as she used her knife to cut the knots binding her mother's hands behind her. It was sharp and made quick work of the rope. Her mother untied the cloth wrapped around her face as Lauren worked on the rope at her ankles.

"What happened?" she asked her mother.

The older woman finally loosened the cloth enough to drop it around her neck. In the dim light cast by a single bulb hanging bare from the ceiling, Lauren could see bruises forming a collar around the lower part of her mother's throat. The marks from where she'd been choked at some point since they'd last seen one another were only partially hidden by the fallen gag. On closer inspection, Lauren noticed several deep gashes around her mother's arms and shoulders.

"He grabbed me and brought me up here... I don't know where Benny is," her mother rasped, her voice already hoarse from crying and trying to make noise against the thick gag.

"We'll find him," Lauren whispered, finally cutting through the remainder of the rope. "You think there are more of these rooms in the closets?"

"I don't know," her mother managed, her voice escaping in sobs.

Lauren took a deep breath and nodded. It was obvious her mother wasn't going to be much help. "First, let's focus on getting you out of here. You can go get help, and I'll try to find Benny."

Lauren had barely finished speaking when a shriek sounded from somewhere in the house beneath them. The sound caused her mother to erupt into a new round of tears. Lauren placed a hand on her shoulder to comfort her, but wasn't sure that she would be able to do more than offer the empty gesture. She was beginning to regret her decision to not stay by the phone and wait for police. They would have been able to trace the call by now (at least, if the action movies she loved were any indicator). She intended to try the phone again when they got down the ladder... *if* they got down the ladder.

Her mother got to her feet and stumbled. The rope had dug into the tender flesh just above her ankle, and putting weight on the leg was a treacherous activity.

"Lean on me," Lauren instructed, extending her free hand to her mother.

The older woman cooperated. They closed the distance between them and the ladder when they heard Benny squealing again.

Lauren locked eyes with her mother and shook her head. "We need to get you out of here," she repeated. "We need to do what's best for Benny."

Her mother nodded in agreement, but she looked paler than she had moments before.

When they got to the ladder, Lauren opted to go down first in case she needed to fend off the man if he returned. Once she was safely on the floor, her mother shuffled down the ladder, holding fast with both arms when she needed to step down with her one reliable leg. It took several minutes for her to reach the floor, and during that time Benny's wailing intensified. Lauren tried to remain positive, reminding herself that as long as Benny was crying it meant he was alive.

As soon as her mother was down, Lauren went to the night table and picked up the receiver. Nothing. She pressed the button to reset the connection a few times and didn't even get a dial tone after she did so. That meant the man must have cut the phone line. She could only hope he did so after the operator had been able to determine where the call had come from. Otherwise, they were in trouble.

"If we get you outside, can you reach the Swishers?" Lauren asked.

Her mother's eyes widened at the question. "I don't think I can. You'll have to go. I'll head in that direction, but I'm too slow. By that time Benny could—" Her voice caught in her throat. "You can run there and back in the time it would take me, Laur."

There was no disputing that fact, but Lauren still didn't like the thought of it. "Okay. I'll go. You try to get to the car. Even if it won't run you can lock yourself inside until I come back with help or Benny." Lauren doubted that someone who was bright enough to cut the phone lines would have been stupid enough to leave their Sedan in well-working condition.

She helped her mother to the side door which led out to their driveway. There, her mother was able to grab a walking stick she had used on their hikes through the Appalachians the previous summer. It was one of the few mementos that had escaped her vengeful cleaning. With the stick and her keys in hand, she hobbled toward the vehicle without Lauren's help.

Once certain her mother had her footing, Lauren darted like a bullet for the Swishers' house. Since they lived in suburbs, she didn't have as far to go as she would have at their previous home in the country. She thumped on their door with her entire forearm, and the wait for someone to answer felt as though it took years.

"Lauren, what on Earth…" Mr. Swisher was a balding man in his fifties whose adopted children were long gone. He and his wife had never been able to conceive, and they had made up for it by taking in children and teens whose parents had passed away or given them up. It was obvious from his expression that he was taken aback by both Lauren's furious knocking and her disheveled, bloody appearance.

"Call the police, Mr. Swisher! Someone's in our house. He hurt Mom badly, and he's got Benny," she said.

"What do you mean, someone's in your house? Lauren, where is your mother? Is this some sort of prank?"

"Call the police, Mr. Swisher. Mom's in the car in our driveway, hiding. It's not a prank, Mr. Swisher. Let me call, if you won't."

"I'll call, I'll call," the man said, still studying her in disbelief. "Martha, it's Lauren Peterson from next door," he called over his shoulder. "Come in a moment, Lauren. They might need additional information from you."

Lauren nodded in agreement and followed the man down the hall and into his foyer. She still gripped the kitchen knife tightly, counting every second she was away from her mother and little brother. She needed to get back and protect them.

"Good evening, dear," Mrs. Swisher offered as the young woman and her husband entered the room where she sat, knitting. She raised an eyebrow as she studied Lauren's bedraggled appearance. "What've you got that knife for?"

"There's a man in our house," Lauren explained. "He killed our cat and hurt my mom, and now he's hurting Benny. We need to get the police."

Martha Swisher's eyes went wide and she looked to her husband, who was dialing the telephone. "My word, Harold." The old woman dropped her needles and raised a hand to her mouth, returning her gaze to Lauren. "That's terrible, child. Did he hurt you?" The graying woman glanced back to her husband. "Harold, he didn't say he was going to kill the cat or the boy. That seems excessive, don't you think?"

"We don't question the professionals, Martha," he replied. "He's the one the Home Owner's Association recommended."

Lauren froze in place and raised the knife in front of her chest. "W-What?" she asked, backing toward the hallway she'd just exited.

"The man, dear," Mrs. Swisher said. "He was hired to get rid of your mother. We can't have a woman living alone with two children out of wedlock in our little community. It wouldn't be proper."

"Martha, be quiet," Mr. Swisher scolded, raising the phone to his ear.

"I will not, Harold. The girl needs to know she's safe." The older woman stood, which caused Lauren to back up a few more paces. "I'm not going to hurt you, child. Neither will he. The neighborhood has drawn straws and the plan was for Harold and me to take you in after your mother was gone. The Kearns down the way were going to adopt your brother." She raised her hands to the girl, indicating she meant her no harm.

Lauren focused on the old woman's words; she couldn't believe what she was hearing. She wanted to run, but shock kept her rooted in place. "But why?" she asked.

"Yes, this is Harold Swisher from…" Mr. Swisher took the corded phone around the corner to speak to the operator.

"Your mother's a whore, darling," Mrs. Swisher replied flatly. "It was bad enough when she didn't bring you children to church, but lately, she has been coming and going at all hours and having strange men in and out. We won't have her getting knocked up again. We were too late with the Morgan girl. We hated to get rid of someone so young, but rules are rules."

"Holly Morgan?" Lauren was still in shock. "She was in my homeroom. They said she moved away."

"She *went* away. She didn't move. Her parents didn't like it, but they knew the consequences when they let her get pregnant—"

"The police are on their way," Mr. Swisher cut in as he re-entered the room. "They should be here shortly."

Lauren couldn't listen to any more of their talk. She turned on her heels and sprinted for the door. She fled into the night, running towards her house. She had to be sure her mother was okay.

***

"Who was working tonight?" Mrs. Swisher asked, unfazed by Lauren's disappearance from the room.

"Thatcher and Morgan. I told them they'd find her in the car over there, so they'll put her down. You know, Margaret, I don't know why they couldn't have done it in the first place."

"Rules are rules, Harold," Mrs. Swisher said simply.

***

When Lauren got to their car in the driveway she found her mother sprawled out in the back seat. Though it was dark, Lauren could see the black reflective sheen of blood on the leather. She began to cry as she opened the door. The foul stench of death reached her nostrils immediately, and she saw that her mother's throat had been slit from ear to ear.

Lauren drew back from the car and fell into the grass, where she vomited. *How is this real?* she wondered, struggling to maintain any sort of coherency. She felt as though she were struggling to remain on a madly spinning world.

How can any of this be real?

***

When the police arrived they found Lauren sitting in the grass, still crying and getting sick. What they didn't find was any sign of forced entry or the man who had killed her mother. In fact, the only thing they could find that matched the wounds left on the two bodies was the kitchen knife they found outside with Lauren. She had blood on her hands and shoes when they found her, allegedly from opening the car where her mother was lying dead, and blood was smeared on the blade of her knife.

They found the boy in the teen's room, his small form slashed to ribbons. A smudged handprint led them to her journal and the latest entry, which featured an angry tirade about how unfair her mother was and how much she resented her little brother for getting her into trouble. To make matters worse, the dispatchers on duty claimed to have no record of a call from the Swishers, so Lauren's account of events fell apart quickly. There was nothing to link the Swishers or anyone else in the neighborhood to a secretive assassin in either the case of Lauren's mother or of her classmate Holly Morgan, and no evidence turned up to suggest anyone else was in the house, much less had committed the attacks.

The Swishers went on record for the court proceedings saying that they bore no ill will towards the mentally troubled Lauren Peterson and they hoped she got the help she so obviously needed.

Lauren lay awake at night from her conviction onward. Occasionally the guards would pass by her cell and hear her muttering to herself, "Rules are rules. Rules are rules. Rules are rules."

HOT SAUCE

by Crystal Jeans

He pushed his finger into the dead head and crispy bits of dried yellow stamen crumbled into the vase. A petal the color of apricot fell to the carpet. When was the last time he had watered them and vacuumed this floor? He'd been distracted lately.

"My humble apologies, Mother," he murmured. "I'll bring you some fresh ones tomorrow." He smiled. "Some really pretty ones."

He took his mother's clothes out of the laundry basket, her Sunday best, and laid them on her bed for tomorrow. He paused at the door before leaving and checked that everything was in its right place.

He hated this old room but it brought a kind of comfort.

He went to the fridge and took out a quart of milk. He poured some into a clean glass and sat at the table to drink. He picked up the mask and turned it around, looking for marks or dirt. This was mask number four. The previous three had been ripped or dirtied, which was only natural.

There was a newspaper folded up on the table next to his car keys. He started to read it, methodically checking every story and article. He felt apprehensive. Birds in his belly—that's what his mother would say. *"Ya got birds in yer belly. Crows and swallers, flapping their wings in a dread panic."* Stupid Southern nonsense.

160

He reached the end of the newspaper and folded it shut. Nothing important. They invariably fell through the cracks. *Tut tut, America.*

He noticed a spot of muck under the nail of his forefinger— from the food prep, most likely. He went to the sink and washed his hands with scorching hot water and soap, using a scrubbing brush for thirty seconds on each nail. He was good at counting seconds.

He went back to the fridge and looked at the Tupperware laid out on the middle shelf. Meat should go at the bottom of the fridge—he'd learnt that in Home Ec. He could remember that horrible cross-eyed lesbian, Miss Hughes, making them write it down in their textbooks with three underlines. He couldn't remember the reason for it. Something about food poisoning, probably. Maybe her dyke lover had died of salmonella—caught it eating out her funky-smelling pussy.

No. That was crass. He was better than that.

He closed the fridge door. He should eat for strength, he knew, but there were those crows and swallers all a-flapping.

He sat again at the kitchen table, back straight, eyes on the wall ahead, waiting for night to come. When his mouth felt dry, he poured more milk. He loved milk. When his hands got restless, he picked up his car keys and ran his fingers over the tinkling charms attached to the fob ring. Otherwise, he sat still at the table, poised and achingly present.

He was good at waiting.

***

The guy behind the bar looked at her like she was a tumbleweed that'd just rolled in trailing shitty toilet paper. Just like he always did. Nancy bought a beer most nights, but still that same shitty look.

Fuck him. She hated men like that: looking down their noses like fucking puritans but secretly sitting on a lifetime's worth of suppressed nastiness. She knew his kind. If he'd been born a few centuries earlier, he'd be the guy heading the witch hunts, standing the closest to the pyre and yelling biblical quotes with foam pouring out his mouth. And come dawn, he'd be the one sticking his cock in the warm ashes.

She went to the restroom and it was empty as usual. Not many women came to this place. She couldn't think why, with that charming motherfucker behind the bar.

She pressed her face right up to the mirror. Her eyesight was the shittiest. But men seldom made passes at girls who wore glasses. She fixed her make-up, rubbing away the globs of eye-liner balled up in the innermost corner of her eyes and adding fresh concealer to the fat zit on her jawline that had yet to grow a head. "Patience, my pretty," she whispered to it.

She adjusted her wig—white blonde bob with a harsh fringe—and checked herself out, nose-tip skimming the cool mirror, eyes squinted. *Out of ten? Eight, maybe. With twenty-twenty vision? Fuck knows. Ignorance is what? Bliss.*

She got out her washbag and wet a washcloth. Then, checking the door, she hiked up her skirt, kicked off her panties and vigorously scrubbed herself down there. That's how her mom used to say it: "down there", and always whispered. Like there was some sort of monster sleeping up her pussy and it wouldn't do to wake it.

She pulled on a clean red thong, took out her perfume, sprayed it three times into the air and walked through the falling vapor as if it was an elegant snow flurry. "Like a fucking Disney princess," she said, snorting laughter through her nose.

She left the restroom and passed the bar, winking at the bartender. He gave her a look like someone had just snuck a pinky up his ass. *Fuck him, and his piss-warm beer.*

She slipped a stick of gum into her mouth and walked outside, her peach stilettos clip-clopping the sidewalk. The street was warm and stinking and full of nauseous bright lights. She stopped and lit a cigarette, skinny pink-tipped hands cupped around the flame. She could hear "Hungry Like the Wolf" by Duran Duran blasting like bad breath out of the Smith Grove's open doors.

She fucking hated that song. "Hungry like my ass," she muttered.

She didn't notice the red '58 Cadillac slow as it passed her.

***

She walked with her hips bumping in that trashy way. She had a pretty face and nice legs, but she looked cheaper than last week's off-cuts (his mother's phrase). He'd seen this girl before but in a different wig. It had been curly and red last time but certainly no less tacky. She'd stood outside a laundromat, smoking with a tall black he-she in a gold dress. She looked . . . sparky. Plucky, his mother would say.

He drove alongside her until she noticed. She coaxed her face into a smile, teeth the color of candle wax. She stooped over as he rolled down the window.

"You wanna party, mister?" Her voice was harsh. It put him in mind of a serrated blade. "'Cuz I like to party. Do you like to party?" She glanced around the interior of the car, feigning bored curiosity, but he could see cunning and caution in her eyes. Spark and pluck.

"You a dude?" he asked. 'Dude' was not a word he would normally use but he had to speak their language.

She brought her eyes back to his. Glassy and blue. There was a dark look in them. Was she offended? Was the hooker offended?

"Nuh! Hundred percent female last time I checked. And I check an awful lot."

"Show me."

She glanced both ways, then hitched up her skirt and edged her red panties to the side. He caught a patch of stubbly flesh and a dash of wet pink.

He nodded. He had to make sure. No surprises. *Not after last time.*

"What about you?" she asked. "You really a dude?" She was smiling but her eyes were all skittish, nervy. Needed a fix, probably.

"I am one hundred percent a dude. Want proof?"

She waved a hand. "Nah, I don't need to see your junk." She rooted around in her bag and pulled out some gum. Her hands were shaking.

Yes—definitely needs a fix.

She put a stick of gum in her mouth, slowly, letting her tongue pull it in. "I don't need to see it ta know I wanna put it in my mouth *so bad.*" Dead eyes.

"Get in."

"No way, daddy. What am I, a retard? Meetcha somewhere."

"Fair enough." They were getting so tetchy lately, these whores. It was almost as if there was a man on the loose deplcting their numbers. "I have a room on Sixteenth Street, east side. Balaski Motel, room eighty-two."

It was his lucky room, eighty-two. It had thick walls and the parking lot outside had a lot of cover, and it always felt like a good sign when he was able to book it—under a fake name, of course. (A necessity—he didn't bring his work home with him. Mother didn't want that in her house. The carpets were turn-of-the-century Persian.)

"It's very clean and well-lit, I promise you, and there's a mini bar. You could meet me there in, say, fifteen minutes?" He smiled. He'd practiced smiling in the mirror a heap lately. He could get it to reach his eyes, just about.

"Eighty-two?" She looked unsure.

"Yes. I booked it for the weekend. I'm here on business. And what the wife doesn't know . . ."

". . . can't hurt her," she finished.

He held a ten-dollar bill out the window. "Get a cab on me."

There was no way she was going to spend that potential drug money on a cab with the Balaski only two short blocks away. It was an investment. He'd found that if you gave them a taste, they were more likely to show up. Whores were very fickle.

She looked at the bill like it was a dead roach and snatched it. She turned away and started walking, then turned back. "A mini bar, you say?"

He nodded. "Whiskey, vodka and gin."

"What kind of whiskey?"

"Jameson."

She nodded. "See you in a tinkle, big daddy."

He smiled and lifted a hand.

He didn't like the daddy thing. He'd have to correct her on that.

**

It was a silly looking thing. He knew that. But he liked that about it— the way a contrast was slashed between the daft and the terrifying. Like a Care Bear with a purple-veined erection, or a poodle riding a unicycle with half its face melted off. He'd bought it in a dime store along the boardwalk in Coney Island. He'd seen countless kids wearing the mask every Halloween since he could remember.

He was sitting naked on the cold rim of the bathtub, the mask balanced on his thigh. The toilet seat would undoubtedly be more comfortable, but a toilet was for shitting, not sitting. Eurgh. His mother again. She had such a vulgar mouth on her, especially after a few drinks, and the worst thing was, everyone found her *so* funny. Just because she was old money. Old Southern money. Like that made it acceptable. "Oh, she's one of a kind, your mom. She brightens any party," the neighbours would say, grinning, and he would look at their bland bourgeois faces and imagine inserting a finger into their eye sockets, slowly, until his fingertip was in their brain. "You don't know her," he would say, wiggling his finger. "She's nothing but a lonely old lush and a whore who pretends otherwise, and if anyone here is one of a kind, it's me." Then a blade across the throat and a shove and a gooey red finger.

If it wasn't for him, she would be all alone. Just sitting alone for supper, drinking herself numb and dreaming about the good old days in the South. Nothing but a washed-up society whore. He was all she had.

There was a knuckle-knock on the front door. Tentative. He stood up. "It's unlocked!" he called.

He heard it open. "Hey, where are you?" she asked.

"I'm just getting out of the bath. Come in, make yourself at home."

"Okay, daddy."

He waited for the door to click shut, and then put the mask on and sucked in that familiar plastic smell. He was erect. He picked up his hunting knife from the lip of the tub. The bungee cords were in the corner next to the thick roll of plastic sheeting. Everything ready, everything in its place.

He took a deep breath and opened the door.

She stood in the middle of the room.

With a gun. Pointing. Hands steady.

"Drop that fuckin' knife, creep." She took a step forward and aimed the barrel at his slackening penis. "Do it!"

The knife dropped with a muffled thud to the carpeted floor. "Now sit down." She jerked her chin toward a wooden chair. He sat. He had birds in his belly.

"Do you know how much I wanna shoot your goddamn cock off right now? I am *this* fucking close, so you better start talkin'. What have you done with Roxy?"

Crows and swallers fluttered around in a dread panic.

"I saw her bracelet danglin' off your fuckin' car keys. Yeah, I *saw* that, you fuckin' genius. Where is she? You done to her what you was gonna do to me? Huh? You piece of fuckin' shit, you better start talkin' or so help me Jesus—"

A chubby white woman in a tight PVC tube top burst through the door, a kitchen knife gripped in both hands. "I heard shoutin', Nance. Are you—" She caught sight of him. "Ho-lee *shit*."

Hot piss dribbled down his legs.

***

Guys like him, freak shows—they always had a second wind in them. The only reason he wasn't fighting like a cat in a sack right now was because he was shocked that he'd screwed up so bad, that he'd gotten sloppy, but that wouldn't last.

Nancy just hoped the ropes were tight enough. She wasn't too strong and Ruby had arthritis in her hands, even though she was only thirty (too many hand jobs, repetitive strain, she'd joke). He didn't look like much: a skinny pale thing with a chest that dipped right in, not much hair on his body. His cock was a joke. Right now it was tucked up like a snail with only its nose out of the shell. His face was like a little boy sitting outside the principal's office—nothing like how it had been in the car, all wolfy and confident. He had the mask pulled up onto the top of his head.

"Found 'em!" Ruby said. She held a key fob overstuffed with keys, trinkets and jewels. They made a pretty tinkling sound. "Shit, Nancy, it's like you said." She brought them over, eyes sad. "Just like you said."

"It was her grandmother's, on her Irish side," Nancy said, her words coming out all tight and strange. "I always told her, I said, 'It's got sentimental value, numb nuts. You should put it somewhere safe, else someone's gonna take it from you one day.' And she was all, 'It ain't worth shit. Who'd wanna take it?'" She felt her eyes wanting to cry. *No.*

Ruby grabbed the TV remote and cracked it over his head. "What have you done with our friend?" Another crack. "Huh? Where is she?"

He had his head drawn into his shoulders and his eyelids clenched shut.

She brought the remote down once more. Batteries and pieces of black plastic exploded all over his lap. "You dirty mute *bastard!*" She had tears in her eyes.

She came and sat next to Nancy on the bed. "I've got a bad feeling, Nance. I think—hey. That ring." She pointed at a large gold ring with a cluster of diamonds. "Didn't Monique have one like that?"

"Monique?"

"The lady-boy. You know. She hangs with Crystal, works Fifteenth. The tiny Puerto Rican one that passes real well. Real pretty—you wouldn't know she was a dude 'less you looked close. You *know!* The one who blew that politician."

"Monique? She ain't Puerto Rican, dumbass. She's black."

"Well she looks Puerto—"

"You know where Crystal is?"

"What, right now?"

"No, last Christmas, doofus."

"Well, I saw her in Dunkin Donuts about an hour ago."

"Can you go and look for her?"

"What, *now?*"

"Oh, my fuckin' Christ, Ruby! Yes, now! Tell her to come by herself. Don't tell her why, just say it's about Monique and it's important, okay?"

"All right, all right. I'll try. You be careful with him. He ain't done."

Nancy raised her eyebrows. "This gun says he is."

***

"You motherfucker! This ain't Jameson, it's fuckin' gut-rot!" Nancy shook the small bottle in his face. "You lied to me." She sat down opposite him and took a resentful sip. "You thought you was so clever. And I was just some brain-dead tramp walkin' right into your trap."

"You *are* a brain-dead tramp."

She went up and slapped the side of his head. "You rotten son-of-a-bitch! I got brains enough to catch you out, ain't I?"

"I got caught because I wanted to get caught."

"Oh, save it for someone who cares." She took another sip. "I like it better when you don't talk."

She went to his jacket hanging by the door and looked in the pockets, bringing out a wallet. *Bingo*. There were credit cards, some dry cleaning receipts, two hundred dollars in new notes and a driver's licence. "Oh, I got you now, you bastard," she whispered. She removed the driver's licence and brought it up to her nose. "Kenneth Wallace," she said, squinting. She snapped her head back and laughed. "*Kenneth!*"

"Keep laughing, whore."

She turned back and he was standing up from the chair, ropes slithering down around his legs, his tiny hardened dick pointing at her like a little finger.

"Don't they teach knot skills in the Skank Academy?" He smiled and pulled the mask back over his face.

She looked at the gun on the bedside table. So did he. There was a pause like a loaded spring.

They ran.

He got there first, putting his hand on the gun. She grabbed at it and it skidded onto the floor. He heel-kicked it under the bed and reached for her, but she twisted away and he got a fistful of wig. She ran to the door and he leapt after her, sliding along the floor and grabbing her ankle. She fell to her stomach, her implants mashing into her breastbone. She kicked behind herself viciously and her stiletto heel caught something.

He made a funny noise, like he was climaxing.

She looked over her shoulder. Her stiletto heel was in his eye, skewering the mask. She pulled her bare foot free and he rolled on to his back, still making the noise.

She climbed on top of him and wrapped her thighs around his torso. He thrashed about and the stiletto popped out of his mask.

It fell to the carpet. Dark, sticky blood squirted out of his eyehole. Clinging to the stiletto point was a blob of gore like the clots she sometimes found in her panties.

He reached for her throat and sunk his fingers into the strong muscle running along her windpipe.

She brought a knee to his dick.

And brought an end to that nonsense.

"Got you again, asshole," she whispered.

***

Crystal had walked into some weird-ass situations before—nature of her work and all—but this took the fucking trophy.

Nancy was spread out on the bed in a mess of empty mini-bottles with a gun on her thigh, her little blue-white gut sticking out the top of her skirt, wig off, real comfortable, and the man . . . shit, the *man*. Such a sorry state she seldom saw: skinny, bony little white dude, all ribs and bruises, a tiny pecker and thick blood all over his chest coming out of his—what the shit, coming out of his *eye*, Lord have mercy—and the eye looking like an overused lady part, all purple and red and shredded, the eyelid a fatty bit of bacon rind. One word for that shit: nasty.

"I think I found the dude Janet Jackson be singin' about," she said.

"Shit, Ruby, you took your time!" said Nancy, rising from the bed.

"She took some convincin'," said Ruby, clutching a grocery bag to her chest.

"Damn right I did," said Crystal. "Now where is she? Where's my girl at?"

Nancy pointed her bare toes at the man in the chair. "It's him you should be askin'." She held out the key fob. "Look at this first. One with the diamonds." She tossed them to Crystal, who snatched them out of the air in a blur of red varnish and gold jewels.

Crystal held the mess of keys in her large brown palm and looked for a long time. "Ain't diamonds," she finally said in a quiet voice. "Monique couldn't afford no diamonds. Who ju think she was, the duchess of Harlem? They crystal." She clasped a hand to her mouth and shook her head.

The man let loose an easy laugh. An almost *friendly* laugh.

Crystal was on him in a second. She grabbed his face with one hand, smooshing his cheeks together. "Motherfucker, you tell me where she is and maybe I won't torture your ass as slow as I'm plannin' to."

Spitty laughter came from between his cheeks. She clamped a hand over his mouth and, with the other, she pushed a long red acrylic nail into the mess of his eye. He bucked, pushing his face further into the fingernail.

"Dude, you fuckin' yourself like Shelob the spider here. Be still or I'm 'bout to kebab your fool brain." She looked over her shoulder with a swish of straight black hair. "Ruby, help me hold this bitch."

"Hey, what about this?" said Nancy, holding up a leather wallet.

Crystal pulled out her finger and wiped it off in the freak's hair. She took the wallet and opened it. "Kenneth? Oh dear. No wonder you messin' with whores. A name like that, I'd be angry too."

"Look at the driver's licence, see where he lives," said Nancy. "I don't got my glasses." She upended a small gin into her mouth.

"The Comptons?" Crystal whistled. "This dude has *money*." She tossed the card to Ruby, who sat cross-legged on the floor eating a family-sized bag of Cheetos. "Take his car, go look."

Ruby wiped crumbs from her mouth with the back of a hand. "Bitch, anyone ever taught you how to say please?"

"Bitch, anyone ever taught you not to talk with your mouth full?"

Ruby grinned. "Yeah, your dad. When I was suckin' his dick."

Crystal raised a fanned hand to the side of her face. "Oh, my *lord*, some immature bitches out there but you win the motherfuckin' trophy. Ruby, honey, this is a serious fuckin' situation and you testin' me right now. You know I can't drive. Put the chips down and get your fat ass to the Comptons, pretty fuckin' please, cherry on top."

The man giggled through his pain.

Crystal looked at him with disgust. *Nasty little cracker pervert with a skull full of maggots and no love in his heart.* She'd met his kind plenty, dime a dozen to be sure, but this one, he was a special kind of nasty.

She planted a fist into his bruised little cock.

***

One leg crossed over the other like a woman, lipstick and big eyelashes like a woman, smoking a cigarette with la-dee-da hands like a woman, but those big quarterback shoulders and square jaw—it was a sad show. Black too. Unfortunate, to say the least.

"So what's this all about?" he asked (not she, certainly not she), waving the bloody mask. "Got any significance?"

It felt like there were fire ants crawling in his eye . . .

"Cuz I gotta say, it ain't scary. You *intendin'* it to be scary?"

. . . nibbling at the flesh, climbing inside.

He tapped the mask against his chin thoughtfully. "Now, what interests me, Kenneth—can I call you Kenneth? Thank you. What interests me, Kenneth, about this mask is how you wore it *after* you met my girl here." He tilted his chin toward the white girl passed out on the bed. "That don't make no sense to me, Kenneth. See, you wear a mask to hide your identity, right? But you already exposed your identity. Which leads me to conclude, Kenneth, that this mask here got *plenty* of significance."

He uncrossed his legs and leaned forward with elbows on knees covered in fishnet stockings. "Now, am I right here—and stop me if this is none of my business, Kenny baby—am I right in thinkin' that you got some serious mommy issues? Is that near the ball park?"

"Fuck you."

He raised his drawn on eyebrows. "Oh, I see. We gettin' somewhere now."

"You know *nothing*, you abomination. Tar baby freak."

"Oh, racist too?" He did a mock yawn. "I must admit that's caught me by surprise. Almost as much as the tiny dick and the hatred of women. You just never see those things *together*, you know what I mean?"

Kenneth tried to spit. It came out in a weak spray, only just spattering the he-she's shins. He wasn't used to spitting; it was vulgar. But what else did he have?

"Hey, keep it friendly, baby dick. Keep it classy."

171

"I'm going to string you up and cut you open like a pig."

"Is that before or after I slowly torture you, Kenneth?"

The white girl on the bed stirred, letting loose a quiet, airy fart.

"Hot sauce," he said.

"What's that?" the he-she asked, a hand cupped to his ear.

"Hot sauce."

"What?"

"Your he-she friend. He tasted good with hot sauce. But not hollandaise sauce—that didn't work. Hollandaise goes better with Caucasian meat. It's a more refined meat, more delicate."

The he-she's mouth dropped open. His big black man-hand came slowly quivering to his face.

The front door opened and the fat whore came in. She looked dazed and sick. *As she well should.*

The he-she turned to her and they exchanged a long, searching look. Fatty shook her head slowly.

The he-she dropped his chin into his neck and emitted a long, wavering wail.

Fatty spun around and vomited before running out the door into the night.

Kenneth laughed into the ceiling. He didn't see who delivered the blow to his head. He lost consciousness to a beautiful choir of screaming sobs.

***

"I just keep imaginin', you know?" said Nancy. "What she must have gone through. I can't stop *imaginin'*. And I coulda gone through it myself."

"I feel so sick," said Ruby. "I don't think I'll ever feel unsick again. Shit. I think I might call Jason."

They were sitting up against the headboard, shoulder to shoulder. Crystal was on the chair, knees on elbows, hands clasped, head down, wig hanging like a black velvet curtain.

"Don't you do that!" said Nancy. "You got your six-month chip, Ruby."

"I've slipped for shittier reasons. I finally got a real reason."

Crystal lifted her head. Her make-up was streaked and her eyes were swollen. "You gon' relapse, you do it on your own time, bitch. We need to keep a straight head. I ain't dealin' with your fat ass OD-ing on me, top of everythin' else. Keep it together, bitch."

Ruby's face crumpled.

"Aww, shit." Crystal went and sat next to her, bringing her in close and stroking her head. "Sorry, girl. I know I'm being sharp with you, but you use now and you dead in six months. Only thing Jason sells is bad news." She kissed the top of Ruby's head. "Oh honey, you gon' cry out your lashes before long."

"She found deeds in his kitchen drawer, you know," said Nancy. Her face was the color of parmesan with pink blotches, her lipstick smudged.

"Deeds? What you talkin' 'bout, 'deeds'?"

"Deeds to the house. We could make him sign it over to us. Gotta be worth a few mill, a house in the Comptons. We could split it."

"We are doing no such thing. We ain't profitin' from this."

Ruby rubbed her eyes with the back of her hand, sniffling. "I was thinkin' though, Crys, we could, you know, sell it and give half to Roxy's kids. Monique's mom too."

"Bitch, please! You think them kids wanna profit from the house where we found they mother's head in a fuckin' freezer? You wanna go to Monique's mom and say, 'Hey, Mrs. C, we found your firstborn in some Tupperware, but hey, here's a few dollars. Go fix yourself up nice, buy a couple'a handbags.'" She shook her head. "Just sayin' the words, man . . . I just—I just cannot *fathom* . . ."

There was a sick silence.

"You think he ate his mother?" Nancy asked, finally.

Ruby shrugged. "He's got that shrine, don't he? With the mannequin and the clothes and all them pictures. It's like that bedroom's stuck in a time warp, straight outta the sixties."

"I wonder what he does with them. The clothes."

"Beats me. Probably dresses up like mommy dearest and jacks off into that creepy mask of his." Ruby took out four cigarettes and passed them round. "I tell you what though," she said, taking in a sharp hiss of smoke, "he's got this dinin' room with a snooty-lookin' table and there are two places set, one either end. But he lives alone. You know what I reckon? I reckon he dresses up Mommy for dinner—the mannequin, you know? It's a bendy one—he dresses her up all nice and he seats her at the table and pretends like she's alive. And we *know* what's for supper."

"You watch too many movies," said Nancy. "She's probably just livin' in some home for rich old bitches."

"Oh, I disagree," said Crystal. "This fruitcake here"—she pointed at the unconscious man—"killed his mommy dead. I just know it. I'd bet my impeccable reputation on it."

"Why's it always gotta be the mothers?" asked Nancy.

"It just has," said Crystal. "Same as it's always the daddies for us girlies here." She climbed off the bed and looked down at Kenneth thoughtfully. "Always the mothers."

"Six hours, he's been out," said Nancy. "He'll be awake real soon."

"What we gonna do with him?" said Ruby. "Ya know, specifically?"

Crystal's lips turned up into a bitter smile. "Somethin's comin' to me."

***

Something was different. Every blink felt like a heavy shutter rattling down with a bang. He felt woozy. His thoughts were like jittering pearls trying to form a necklace. There was something stuffed in his mouth, a rag perhaps, and it had a bitter, nutty taste. His vision was fogged in the one good eye, nonexistent in the other. He could make out a small table near his knee. It was familiar, the table. Mahogany perhaps. A spent syringe rested on it. That was it, that's what felt different: he'd been drugged.

No, that wasn't just it.

He began to make out the carpet. A kind of bold floral design in red and brown.

It was his mother's carpet.

Familiar framed portraits hung on the far wall, slowly coming into focus; the chesterfield in the corner where she used to keep old, ill-fitting dentures and 'secret' brandy; the bookcase full of classics she pretended to have read; the dead flowers on the table.

"He's awake." That voice, harsh and ugly and pure New Yawk—the blonde wig who'd started all this—came from behind him. From the queen-sized bed his mother hadn't slept in for almost ten years now.

A woman stepped out. The fat one.

"Rise and shine," she said, lacing her fingers together and tilting her head to the side like an airhostess. "I trust you're well-rested?"

He moaned, eyelid drooping.

"That thing in your mouth?" she said. "It's my panties."

"Her shitty panties," came a voice from behind him. Blonde Wig.

He thrashed his head around. Every movement sliced his swollen brain.

"I have a problem with leakage," said Fatty. "Especially when I'm upset."

"Like, if she finds her friend's head in a freezer," chimed Blonde Wig again.

"Yeah, that'll do it. I had sweet corn yesterday too, so bon appetite, fuck-face." Another sweet airhostess smile.

He raged through the rag.

A hand landed on his shoulder, a small warm hand stroking his bare skin. "Hush now, baby."

He looked up. *Mommy?*

"Hush-a-bye, baby. Mommy's gonna make it all better." She smiled serenely down at him. She had on the Givenchy housedress with the sunflowers on it, the green belt, the pearl-pink lipstick and Cartier earrings.

Grateful tears welled up in his eyes. "I'm sorry," he tried to say.

She squeezed his shoulder. "I want you to know something, baby," she whispered. She brought her head down to his ear. "Mommy doesn't love you. Mommy's never loved you." She gripped his face by the jaw and twisted his head around to her, and he could smell the whiskey and chewing gum and see her blue eyes—hard, blue eyes, not the hard brown eyes of his mother. "Abortion woulda been too good for you, ya string of cunt phlegm."

He hunched his head into his shoulders and shut tight his eyes. He wouldn't look at her, *couldn't* look at her. Why was she being so mean?

"Hey, baby cock," came a voice, a new, deeper voice. "Hey, motherfucker!"

He felt a sharp sting to his cheek. A slap.

"Open your eyes, baby cock."

Another slap. He bit into the rag and whimpered.

"Open your eyes, fetus dick."

Cruel fingers grasped his testicles, twisting them.

"I said open them!"

A green, grinning frog face floated there. The drugs—what drugs had they given him? He blinked away tears and refocused. No. The mask.

The he-she was wearing his mask.

Him and Mommy watching *Sesame Street* together the night of Daddy's funeral—his only happy memory. Sharing cookies and milk, laughing, relaxed for the first time ever. Her hand holding his across the couch, thanking him with her beautiful brown eyes. She didn't stay thankful for long.

How's that for significance, Tar Baby?

"Look what I got." He-she held up a small bottle. Hot sauce. "I couldn't find no hollandaise, but I reckon this shit'll do just fine. Us niggers put hot sauce on *everythin'*. Guess we ain't refined as you." He-she grabbed his hair, yanked back his head and dribbled some sauce onto his bad eye.

Fire! Fire in his eye! He screeched into the rag, face squinted up, and thrashed against the ropes.

The he-she grabbed his penis and pulled it out like taffy. "Such an itty-bitty little thing."

The white one dressed as Mother crouched down. She was holding a surgical blade. From his own medical bag. She pressed the blade to the shaft.

He strained against the ropes but they were tight. He roared into the rag, tears pouring out of his good eye.

"Keep still, angel," she said in a soothing voice. And she cut.

Nnnnnngggggghhhhhaaaaaaaaaaaaaaaahhhhhhhhhhhhhh!

An explosion of the deepest, ugliest pain. Blood pumped out like burning ice water.

"Shit, it's like steak gristle . . . almost got it, keep him still, almost—Ah. I got it."

A shrivelled chunk of slippery white flesh on Mommy's palm. Shredded muscle and oozing blood. Held out like a sacrificial offering.

"Ain't it beautiful?" asked Mommy in hushed awe. "Little Kenneth Junior!" She beamed at the other whores. "I'm a grandma! I'm so fuckin' proud!"

ORIGINAL SIN

by Suzanne Fox

*T*hump...*thump*...*thump*.

Adam squinted as daggers of late morning sunshine sliced through his skull. *Oh Jesus, my head,* he thought. *How much did I drink last night?* He rolled onto his side, looking for the alarm clock that sat on the bedside table. It was missing. Puzzled, he raised himself onto one elbow and looked around the room, the movement causing a new level of pain to assault his brain. Shattered remains of the clock littered the floor beside the door. *Guess I didn't want to go to work today.*

He stretched out his arm and picked up the phone, intending to call the Speaking clock. The urgent, blinking light of the answer machine checked him. He reached out an unsteady finger and pressed the play button. Danny's voice breached the silence.

"Pick up the fucking phone, Adam. Where the hell are you?" A crackle of static betrayed the fact that Danny hadn't hung up. "Call me as soon as you get this message!"

Adam deleted it and listened to the second one. Danny's angry voice returned.

"Bob's pissed off and I can't cover for you anymore. He knows you were out last night. Get to work now. He's already stopped your bonus for this month."

Adam pressed delete again and listened to the final message.

"You're fucking screwed, mate. Hope she was worth it!"

Adam's brow creased. *Hope* who *was worth it?* He couldn't remember any woman from last night. He couldn't remember *anything* of last night.

Slowly, he turned his head, searching for evidence of a woman's presence. No abandoned undies. No hastily torn open condom packets. It didn't matter how pissed or how high he got, he would never fuck anyone without a condom. It all equalled no woman.

He pushed a hand through his damp hair. God, he was hot — practically feverish. He threw the sweat-soaked duvet to the floor, letting the cool air stroke his body. The heating had switched off hours earlier and the March sunshine had done little to warm the room. Pushing aside his discomfort from the heat, he realised he was parched. His tongue clung to the roof of his mouth like a slug to pavement on which some sadistic bastard had sprinkled salt.

Easing his legs over the edge of the bed, Adam sat hunched with his eyes closed, letting his spinning brain come to rest. It wasn't only his head that tortured him. It felt like every single bone, muscle and sinew had been subjected to the most extreme workout imaginable. Perhaps he was coming down with something. Flu maybe? He definitely wasn't feeling himself. He hauled himself to his feet and made his way towards the kitchen, ignoring his robe, which hung from the bedroom door.

Sunlight flooded the kitchen as Adam shambled to the sink, his eyes still half-closed. He grabbed a coffee-stained mug from the counter, turned on the tap and gulped down a couple of beakers of water without pausing for breath. He allowed the third to slip slowly down his parched throat before filling it again. He sipped at his drink as he returned to the bedroom. His eyes were fully open and the water had relieved a lot of the throbbing that had threatened to explode his brain.

What the... He stopped dead. Water splashed from his mug and ran down his trembling legs. Suddenly he was wide-eyed and alert. A white-faced stranger stood before him, staring at him from within the huge mirror on the bedroom wall. He gaped at the image in the glass.

The telephone burst to life and yet another call went straight to answerphone as Adam stood transfixed by what he saw.

The light was poor, but it was bright enough for him to see the wretched condition of his body. A patchwork of deep scratches and maroon streaks of dried blood smeared his skin. Tiny welts and bruises speckled his torso, but what shocked Adam most were the constellations of bite marks scattered across his body and limbs. He shuffled around and peeked over his shoulder. His back was shredded. He assumed fingernails had repeatedly gouged his flesh. The usually soft bathrobe scraped his tender skin as he wrapped it around himself and covered his abused body. He drained the mug of its dregs and wandered back to the kitchen for another refill. *That must have been one hell of a night.*

He slumped into a chair, trying to recall the previous night. The day was as clear as glass. It had been a regular crazy day at work. He was a commodities trader, one of the best. He had spent a prosperous time on the trading floor making a fortune for the bank. Like his friend Danny, he liked to work and play hard, but recently things had changed. Adam was good at this job – some would say he was the best. He'd hungered for triumph, clawing his way up the corporate ladder and devouring anyone who ventured to steal the success he thought was rightfully his. Lately though, he'd found his hunger deserting him. The thrill of the trading floor no longer excited him. He was still an accomplished trader but he needed more. The risk of losing a fortune from a bad decision no longer gave him the adrenaline surge he yearned for. Something was missing from his life and not just his memories of last night. He screwed up his eyes in concentration, but try as he might he couldn't recall anything that happened after leaving the bank. It was like trying to remember a dream hours after waking. Echoes of pulsing music, darkness, heat, but nothing more.

Come on, man. Think. His fingers circled his temples as though the movement could summon his absent memories. Slowly, snatches of the evening started to emerge from the dense fog.

He'd gone to a bar with Danny. Last month's bonus had been smouldering away in their wallets. They'd blown a wad of cash in a swanky, uptown wine bar on a couple of girls in the hope of getting laid, but neither had even wrangled a blow-job for their expense. He could recall leaving the bar and heading for…where, exactly? His brain fog evaporated and he remembered.

A brand new and exclusive club had recently opened in the city: Temptation. It was cool and the girls were classier than the bitches they'd tried to pick up in the wine bar. They'd downed a couple of drinks before heading into the toilets to score some lines of coke.

They had left the toilets together and headed towards the dance floor. Danny had singled out a skinny girl with big hair and big tits, and gyrated his body against hers. She'd responded by moving her hips against his in a parody of sex. Adam had stood on the sidelines, studying the other girls and trying to choose who would win the star prize of sucking his cock later, but none matched his standards. He'd turned his back on the dance floor to return to the bar for another drink when a hand reached out and squeezed his thigh.

Startled, Adam had spun around and come face-to-face with a stunning, raven-haired woman. His throat had tightened and his heart galloped as he stared at her. Her hair cascaded in waves of silk around her face and she had an aura of sophistication which seemed to cross over from an altogether more elegant era, outclassing all the other women in the club. His eyes had drowned in the image of her hourglass figure that reminded him of a Burlesque queen.

She'd released her grip on his thigh and he'd drawn in a deep breath as icy, electrical pulses radiated from where her hand had gripped him. She'd dragged him onto the dance floor like a leashed dog and he'd offered no resistance to the beautiful siren. Curling her cool fingers around the back of his neck, she'd swayed against his body in time to the music, her ice-blue eyes never losing contact with his. *Tonight just got better,* Adam had thought. As he moved his body in rhythm with hers, his balls had tightened and tingled with anticipation of where the night could lead.

"Can I buy you a drink?" Adam had asked after a couple of dances.

She'd shaken her head, her soft hair whipping his cheek, and then raised her lips to his in a kiss that demanded more. She'd tasted of ripe summer fruit, and it was far more intoxicating than the coke he had snorted. Adam had returned her kiss, wanting much more from her. He hadn't known her name but he hadn't cared. It hadn't been important.

She'd withdrawn from his kiss, moving her lips to his ear, and her tongue had delved deep, electrifying his senses and radiating waves of heat and desire though his body. But there had been another sensation. Beneath the heat of arousal there had swam a cold current that hinted of darkness and malice, and he had felt his lost spring of adrenaline begin to flow. She'd spoken. Her voice was hushed but Adam had heard it ring clearly above the sound of the pounding music. "I. Want. You." The words had dripped like warm honey into his ear. "Let's go someplace else."

Grinning, Adam had grabbed her hand and pulled her from the club into the night, ready to embrace whatever she had planned for him.

It was at this point that clouds of amnesia rolled in again, blanketing his memory. What had happened next and where was his mystery woman now? She sure as hell wasn't in his flat. Adam didn't think he'd brought her home.

He stood up. His swollen bladder was jostling for space with his other organs. Standing in the bathroom and enjoying the relief that came from emptying his stretched bladder, he had an idea. He would return to Temptation tonight and see if he could find her. He didn't know her name, or if she had told him, but maybe she had and he'd forgotten. He could recall her addictive kisses though, and he craved more.

Adam filled the mug again, unplugged the telephone to stop Danny's annoying calls and crawled back into bed. The sheets were cold and damp against his burning skin, but he was exhausted and didn't care. He fell into the void of a dreamless sleep.

**

The sleep had worked its magic and now Adam entered Temptation looking and feeling his usual self. The club was heaving. It was Friday night and everyone was celebrating surviving another week.

Clutching a Perrier and determined to keep a clear head, he searched the club for his mystery woman. Strobes charred his retinas and jagged music clawed his ears, his chest throbbing to the beat of its bass. His senses sharpened and the world looked as though he was seeing it for the very first time. The miasma of the daytime had departed and everything was so much brighter and alive.

The night grew older and Adam realised his siren wasn't going to show. His disappointment was painful, but displeasure aside, he felt strangely energized - he wasn't ready for the night to end. *I need a real drink*, he thought. He battled his way to the bar and ordered a Vodka. Sipping the warm liquid, he turned and froze. A familiar curvy, dark-haired woman stood with her back to him.

His heart pounded as he grabbed her arm and pulled her towards him. Ecstasy flowed through his blood at his discovery. She spun around. A face, disfigured by anger, glared at him.

"Oh, I'm sorry," he mumbled. "I thought you were someone else."

Her face relaxed at his genuinely apologetic look. "That's okay." She smiled. "Been stood up, have you?"

"Not exactly." *She is attractive,* thought Adam, *and it would be a pity to waste the evening.* "Look, can I buy you a drink?"

"Thanks. Vodka and tonic, please."

Adam ordered the drinks and introduced himself. She said her name was Melanie. They danced, drank and talked, and Adam, forgetting all about his mystery woman, discovered he was having a great time. Melanie was pretty. She was also funny and obviously attracted to him. Adam found himself not just attracted to her, but drawn to her. Lusting for her.

"Shall we get out of here?" he whispered into her ear, inhaling her scent.

"Why not?"

They stumbled out of the club, the chilly March air gnawing at their skin and their breath clouding before them. Adam pulled Melanie close and kissed her mouth. It was weird. Was he really feeling her heartbeat thrumming against his lips?

She gasped at the intensity of his kiss and stepped back. "I...I don't normally do this," she said. "But I only live a few streets away. Would you like to come in?"

Adam nodded eagerly and she led him to her home.

Melanie pulled him through the door of her flat and slammed him against the wall. His head hit it with the force of her kisses. Goosebumps erupted on his tender skin as her hands explored his chest before reaching around his waist.

"Wait," he muttered pushing her away. "I'm thirsty. Can I have some water?"

She led him into the kitchen and took a bottle from the fridge.

Adam gulped down the chilled liquid in one. "That's better." He rubbed his mouth with the back of his hand. Then, taking hers, they went into the small living room.

Adam threw his jacket onto the sofa. His fingers tugged at the buttons of Melanie's coat before slipping it off her shoulders. He threw it atop his and gazed at her, standing before him in her tight satin dress. She was pretty. Not beautiful like his mystery woman, but cute and definitely fuckable.

He took her in his arms, kissed her and once again felt the beating of her heart through her lips. He inhaled deeply, savoring her scent. She smelt pure, like mountain air and exotic orchids. He lowered her to the floor and lay beside her, kissing and stroking her warm skin. Her perfume grew stronger and heavier. Musky. Nuzzling into her neck, Adam took in a deep breath, relishing the aroma. Its kick was more intense than the most potent cocaine he had ever used.

He needed more.

He grabbed her wrist, extended her arm and sniffed from wrist to shoulder. The room spun. He wanted more than just the scent of her. Adam was weakened by desire and simultaneously stronger than he had ever felt in his life. The dizziness consumed him, yet still he continued to inhale her sweetness.

"Hey, are you all right?"

There was concern in Melanie's voice but he didn't hear it. She struggled to sit up but he pushed her back and straddled her legs, forcing her to remain on the floor. He was oblivious as Melanie's body tensed through fear, not arousal. He was lost in his passion, unable to control the urgency he felt. He hungered to taste her.

Adam stuck out his tongue and ran it along her skin, from her neck to her arm, down to her wrist. She squirmed and wriggled, desperate to escape his grasp, but his weight pinned her down.

"Stop it! Let me go," Melanie squealed.

Adam couldn't hear her. He licked back into the crook of her arm and opened his lips wider. Her skin felt inviting and soft against his mouth, offering gentle resistance to the pressure of his teeth.

Crack!

Adam reeled as the shoe Melanie had managed to grab connected with his head. Her screaming finally breached the trance that had enveloped him, and his teeth sank into the soft flesh of his tongue, filling his mouth with warm blood. He swallowed without a second thought, the salty, ferrous tang tasting like ambrosia to him.

Melanie pushed him away and jumped to her feet, screaming. Stumbling backwards, she collided with the sofa and crashed back to the floor. "What the fuck do you think you're doing?!" she yelled, still brandishing the stiletto in a shaking hand.

"I'm sorry," he whispered. "I...I don't know what came over me." Conversely, he didn't feel sorry. His conscience and mouth spoke words of platitude whilst his body demanded that he grab the terrified girl and take everything he wanted from her.

The coffee table bruised his shin as he jumped to his feet and grabbed his jacket, his better judgment winning this fight. What had he done? What had he been thinking? He had to get out quickly. Sudden shame at his loss of control burned him.

He reeled backwards as Melanie flew across the room, hitting, pushing and screaming obscenities. He reached out to hold her back and stop her screams with his hand, but her fingers hooked into his shirt. Buttons whistled across the room and his torso became exposed. The scratches, bruises and bite marks remained livid against his pale skin.

Melanie recoiled. "What kind of sick freak are you?!" she yelled, backing away. "Get out! Get out now, before I call the police!"

A mumbled apology escaped his lips as Adam tugged his torn shirt around him in embarrassment and fled. Snooping neighbours desperate to know what was happening stared from their doorways as he raced down the steps. An elderly man tried to block his escape but

Adam shoved him aside, relishing the snap of bone as the man tumbled to the floor. He didn't stop running until he reached his flat.

Slamming the door behind him, he collapsed against it panting and crying. How could he lose control like that? Adam was no saint but he barely recognized himself. Perhaps the cocaine had been a bad batch, making him crazy. He rubbed his mouth with the back of his hand. It came away red – his tongue was still bleeding. He stared at the slick stain, mesmerized, before licking it clean.

Adam stumbled into the bathroom and turned on the taps. He splashed his face with handfuls of cold water, which stung his burning skin. Scooping up more water, he rinsed his mouth, watching in disgusted fascination as the blood-streaked liquid swirled down the plughole. The whole time his other hand absentmindedly rubbed his stiffening cock.

Sobbing, Adam crawled into bed, dragged the covers over his head and spent a long dark night lamenting his degradation. He eventually slipped into unconsciousness, minutes before dawn broke through the blackness.

Adam awoke late afternoon as the light was beginning to fade. He raised his head from the pillow, anticipating a surge of pain. None came. He sat up and looked around. The heating had failed to kick in and mist clouds formed before his lips with each breath. He didn't care. He didn't feel cold. He felt…alive, energised.

He leapt from his bed and stretched, aware of each muscle and sinew singing their way back to life. *I must have just needed a good sleep,* he mused. After all, it had been a stressful few weeks at work. Making money in the city wasn't easy despite what people thought. The players on Wall Street had a lot to answer for.

He strolled to the bathroom and created a fountain worthy of challenging any of the watery monuments across the globe as he peed for what felt like hours. Finished, he turned towards the wash basin and was, once more, shocked into stillness. He barely recognised the pale and striking face of the stranger who gazed back from the mirrored cabinet. Sure, the face had his dark eyes, except now they seemed blacker. The lips were his too, but richer and fuller. No scars or blemishes blighted the perfect mask reflected in the glass. Even his crooked nose appeared straight. Perfect.

Adam smiled and his teeth glistened whiter than he remembered. *Work must have been taking its toll,* he thought as he turned his head from left to right, almost lusting after the perfect creature that beamed back at him. It seemed all he had needed was a break from the stresses of work and a good long sleep to right everything. Except he wasn't just right.

He was better. Improved.

***

Later that evening, he swaggered through the doors of Temptation. His complete being thrummed with the anticipation of booze, good company and hot sex. He felt amazing, ablaze with energy and horny as hell. He heard all the whispered comments and saw every leering gaze as he strutted past groups of women all desperate to catch his eye. But what amazed him more were their scents. Every breath he drew captured the aroma of their arousal. Hot female musk mingled with the lighter scents of chemical fragrances assaulting his nostrils. His cock stirred at the promised delights. Fingers - some gentle, some urgent – stroked him as he passed. It seemed he was irresistible tonight.

He reached the bar and ordered a vodka and tonic, pulling out his wallet to pay for his drink. The barmaid pushed the glass towards him, her fingers lingering on his longer than necessary. "This one's on me," she whispered and ran her tongue across her lips.

Adam took his glass, turned around and re-entered the throng of revellers.

His arm flew up and vodka splashed onto his shirt.

"Oh, Jesus, I'm so sorry," said a familiar voice.

Adam looked at the girl who had stumbled into him. Dark hair spilled onto her shoulders. Curvy breasts stretched against the shiny fabric of her strapless top and her short skirt flicked tantalisingly to reveal pale thighs as she regained her balance. It was Melanie. He held his breath, waiting for her to scream at him, to call security and have him thrown out.

Her eyes briefly widened in alarm before a blankness descended on her face. She shook her head, then smiled and took a step closer, no sign of recognition in her eyes. "Can I replace your drink?" she said.

187

"It's okay, thanks." He grinned. Did she really not recognise him? It had been less than twenty-four hours since she had thrown him out of her flat and threatened to call the police. He drew in a deep breath and her familiar aroma rekindled the feelings of desire he had experienced last night.

Adam took hold of her hand and pulled her to the dance floor. She offered no resistance, following him like an eager puppy. Pulling her close, he pressed his granite-hard cock against her stomach, expecting her to push him away. Instead, she forced her body closer and he leaned his face into her hair. Her mouth met his as his fingers raised her chin towards his face. Her lips pulsed in time with the beat of her heart and her fragrance intensified as his tongue delved deep, searching. The music and dancers faded into the distance as their bodies battled to occupy one space.

His fingers brushed aside her hair and she quivered at the touch. "Can we go somewhere else?" he whispered, though he was sure his lips hadn't moved.

Melanie was keen, pulling his hand as she headed for the exit, oblivious to the bitter stares she was attracting from other women. Adam stumbled after her, a grin splitting his face and revealing his sharp, ice-white teeth.

Now it was his turn to lead her. He pulled her hand, dragging her far away from Temptation, not stopping until he had reached a deserted, industrial area of town. She followed unquestioningly, in thrall of the beautiful and sexy stranger who possessed her hand and her will.

He forged his way to the dark recessed doorway of a large warehouse, dragging Melanie behind him before slamming her against its door. Her breath gushed in a heady haze of vodka fumes and white fog, and the door rattled on rusted hinges with her impact. She should have been panicked but his forcefulness did nothing to stem her lust, and Adam was past the point of stopping. His cock throbbed painfully against the constraints of his trousers. He had never experienced a level of hunger and desire as all-consuming as the one that controlled him now. Every inhalation filled him with a medley of her scents: alcohol, perfume, hairspray and the dark sweet aroma of her arousal.

A splitting sound pierced the night air as the front of Melanie's dress tore apart under Adam's hands, revealing her pale round breasts rising from the lacy confines of her bra. He snatched at it. Her squeals of pain as the elastic bit into her soft flesh made his already impossibly hard cock swell more. He pushed her to the grimy floor atop a pile of wind-drifted leaves and fag ends.

Other scents permeated the air. Rancid oil and dog piss mingled with Melanie's sweet hot aroma to scorch Adam's acutely sensitive nose. He buried his hands beneath her short dress and hooked his fingers into her panties, shredding the flimsy satin until her pussy was bared to him. Melanie's warm wetness wrapped around his fingers as they plunged deep and hard inside her.

Déjà vu hit him like a punch to the chest as the familiar feeling from their first kiss vibrated within him. But now, he felt the rhythm of her heart pulsing through her soft tightness. Melanie's moans resonated throughout his mind and chest.

Using his free hand, Adam released the animal threatening to tear its way out of his pants. Within seconds he was deep inside Melanie, his hips rocking with a ferocity that verged on madness. A fiery heat wrapped itself around him, scorching his skin, his muscles and his bones. He could not have burned anymore had he been dropped into the pits of Hell. But he felt no pain, only an all-encompassing desire to consume.

As Adam buried himself harder and deeper, he grew oblivious to the whimpering and crying girl beneath him. Cries that had once more morphed from arousal to terror. A new scent curled from her panicked flesh: an acidic tang that blended with her sweat and reeked of fear. Melanie's screams echoed across the deserted industrial estate, bouncing from the shabby warehouse and factories like a demonic choir's mantra.

The squealing girl wriggling beneath him smelt divine. Her scent of fear melded with her hot muskiness and flooded his mouth with saliva. His fingers disappeared into the soft flesh of her breast as he squeezed and pulled it towards his face, inhaling deeply before letting his tongue slither and lap along her skin.

Melanie's screams fractured the air like the discordant chiming of a cracked bell, but it only served to fuel Adam's appetite.

He had savoured enough.

It was time.

Hot blood flooded his mouth as his teeth tore into the soft warm flesh around her nipple. Small rivulets of blood escaped his lips and tracked a tickling path along his chin, whilst most flowed down his parched throat, cooling and sating his thirst.

The agony of ripping flesh ignited Melanie's fight, sending Adam crashing to the ground beside her. Lights danced across his vision as the girl's fist collided with his temple. He gulped and the chunk of torn flesh from Melanie's breast slipped down his throat. His sick laughter almost equalled her shrieks of pain and fear as she stumbled away in her high heels.

He was on his feet with a feline speed, turning to pursue his prey, when Melanie's voice froze him in his tracks.

"Oh, thank God. Please help me. Please," she sobbed. "He's going to kill me."

A surge of adrenaline had him poised on the knife-edge between flight and fight. Melanie, alone, posed no challenge, but now she had an ally. A saviour.

The stranger spoke to Melanie in a dark, hypnotic tone. "It's okay, honey. You're going to be safe with me. Come to me. I'll take care of you."

Adam turned his head and watched Melanie collapse into the arms of a dark-haired, beautiful woman. She slowly raised her head to meet Adam's gaze and smiled, revealing small, sharp white teeth from behind scarlet lips.

"Hello again, my sweet baby," she purred.

Adam's cock pulsed back to life at the vision before him: the woman of his recent dreams holding his next meal. "*Eve?*" he mumbled as her evasive name formed in his head. "Are you really there?"

"I'm here, sweet boy. I'm so proud of what you've become. Come and eat your supper, baby." Eve grabbed the girl's hair and snapped her head back, baring the long line of her throat. She raked a long fingernail across Melanie's cheek. The flesh parted, creating a second mouth that oozed crimson vomit.

The hunger and thirst in Adam erupted at the image before him. He leapt forward, teeth bared, and sank them into Melanie's throat. He tore at stringy tendons and crushed gristle and cartilage as she threw back her head to scream. Blood sprayed his face in a cascade of sticky heat as the girl's screams faded to gurgling whimpers.

Eve released her grip and Melanie hit the ground. She watched with pride as her progeny ripped and tore the pale and tender flesh from the dying girl. She raised her arms and beckoned to the shadows. A cruel smile blighted her face as her other offspring emerged from the darkness to join them.

LOVE WILL TEAR YOU APART

by Rose Garnett

The lunch rush in the Torphichen Inn had consisted of a geriatric greyhound and two drunks who had long since staggered back out to sleep it off. Not so for Willie McBain, who lingered in the darkest nook of the pub, fertilising old grievances with fresh liquor. He eyed his pint and whisky chaser with indecision before reaching for the spirit, downing it in one. He didn't belong in this dingy boozer, or in this arse-end-of-nowhere village either, truth be told. Worst of all, his bitch ex, Jackie, was milking him like a frigging cow, and he was forced to go along with it if he wanted to keep seeing the wee man.

His eyes misted over as he drank his pint. It wasn't his fault he'd been forced to slug Jackie, breaking her front teeth and busting that enormous hooter of hers like an overripe tomato. Cow had called the law on him and now he couldn't even go back to his own fucking house.

Bitch.

They were all bitches though, weren't they? Flaunting their wares at a man; promising the earth with no intentions of delivering the goods. Come to think of it, he hadn't actually sampled anybody's goods since he couldn't remember when. He'd never had any complaints though. Well, not serious ones. That night he'd spent in the cells had just been a small misunderstanding and she – whatever her name was – hadn't pressed charges.

Over in the corner, the fruit machine sang a siren song trying to tempt some poor mug into parting with their hard-earned cash. Just like Jackie - why did everything always come back to her? He should've killed the fat slut, never mind just punching her one in the face. There had been a moment when she was on her knees in front of him, hands shielding her bloody nose and screaming at him to get the hell out, when a voice at the back of his head had said, "What are you waiting for, ya diddy – kill the wee slag."

But they'd have put him away for that even though the dirty skank deserved all she got and more. He'd seen the programmes on television where the ex was the first suspect the polis looked at. Christ alive, a man couldn't do anything or anyone these days.

"Willie," said Rab, the barman, "I've got a delivery to see to. Can you give me a shout if anyone comes in?"

Ten minutes later, Rab hadn't returned and Willie was gasping for a pint. He was just about to hunt the useless fucker down when an icy blast and a skitter of dried leaves announced the arrival of three gorgeous bits of stuff. He'd met them before but hadn't been in any state to do anything about it.

Well, he was now.

They sat down at the bar, white, silky dresses riding up to reveal succulent thighs atop long, slender legs. They must have been triplets or something because they were all identical: long, arctic-blond hair framing delicate features flushed from the February cold. Had they told him their names last time?

The ancient Torphichen Inn, named after the village it served, wasn't usually what you'd call a good pulling spot. No, Inspirationz down the road, in the not-so-Big-Apple of Bathgate, was the place for that kind of nonsense. The only problem was that it was full of underage minge and he'd been caught out more than once on that score.

Not being one to look three gift-slappers in the mouth, he heaved himself upright and weaved his way to the bar. Was it his imagination, or did the lighting flicker just then?

"You just couldn't keep away, eh?" he asked, checking out his reflection in the mirror and flashing his best gap-toothed 'come hither' smile.

Three pairs of dark-brown eyes swivelled round to fix on him with unblinking stares. Yes, there was no doubt about it: he still had the old one, two magic and no mistake.

One of the girls squirmed on her seat, blond hair so long she was sitting on it. She'd be sitting on something else before the afternoon was out if she played her cards right. Little tart. She'd love everything he had to give and be begging for more, if he knew women.

"It's more of a mercy mission," the bird nearest him said, adjusting her dress. "We like to take pity on the afflicted."

"What, you mean me?" He smiled as he said it but he was not amused. Where did this hoity-toity bitch get off talking to a real man like that?

"Bingo," said the blond furthest away, applying lip-gloss to a pouting pink mouth, making him forget what he'd been about to say.

The middle one yawned and stretched, giving him a good view of the dark aureoles of her nipples through the semi-transparent material of the dress, proof positive the manky wee midden wasn't wearing a bra. Never mind making one lucky lady's day, this could turn into a four-way fuck-fest if he kept his patter and his pecker up. Although maybe he shouldn't have had those last five pints after all. Ah hell, they'd just have to up their game to keep him interested.

At close quarters, the girls' features were a little sharper than they'd first appeared. The dark gazes, warm and inviting from a distance, were somehow blank, as though no one was home. He choked back the acid reflux that threatened to resurrect his last pint and dodgy lunchtime scotch egg. Even he would have a hard time recovering from spewing on the minge before they got jiggy.

"Are you having a heart attack?" the middle one piped up. She smiled, teeth small and gleaming in the pub murk.

Cheeky cow. Was she laughing at him? Stuck-up bint might need taken down a peg or ten.

"No, I'm not having a bloody heart attack," he said, giving a long, eggy belch. Three blond heads cocked to the side at the same time, a bird-like movement that gave him a twinge of unease.

"Rab," Willie bellowed, "you've got customers, you lazy bastard."

"You probably don't remember, judging by the state you were in before," she continued, "but I'm Marjorie, this is Morgan" – she gestured to the girl on the middle stool – "and Megan's at the end there."

Morgan reached out a slender white hand and ran her fingers through Megan's hair. Megan sighed, tilted her head back, and leaned into the caress, eyes closed.

"Maj, Mog and Meg," said Willie, trying and failing to recall when he'd last had a wash after getting a whiff of armpit, "you will, of course remember me. I'm the one and only—"

"William McBain," the three chorused.

Oh, he was a right smooth bastard when he wanted to be, even if he was a bit the worse for wear. Where the hell was Rab? The fucker better not mess up his prime leg-over opportunity. Everyone knew you needed to get birds pissed if you wanted them to let you do stuff.

"Maj, why don't you and the girls come back to mine? I've got enough booze and fags to choke a horse, not to mention that I'm also hung like one. Whaddya say lay-dees?" he asked in a bad American accent, waggling his eyebrows.

"I'd say you'd be in a lot of trouble," said Morgan, blowing a kiss.

"Aye, you look like you'd be a right wee handful," he said, reaching over to give her breast a hard squeeze. "C'mon lasses, get your coats. Your luck's in. You've pulled a real man for a change."

"Not so fast," said Megan, running pale hands down the length of Morgan's body and under the hem of her dress.

Willie's excitement grew despite a musky scent he'd just noticed. Was that what passed for perfume now amongst these posh hoors? Oh well, he could always hold his nose and hope for the best before he plunged into this particular pubic triangle.

And what was that low, continuous sound all about? They weren't actually purring, were they? Christ, talk about pussy galore – these three were all totally up for it. Wait until Rab saw the crackers he'd pulled tonight. Where was the sleazy wee loser anyway?

Before he knew it, the three of them clustered around him, pressing themselves so close he couldn't breathe. But instead of enjoying the attention, that weird, fusty smell was making him feel dizzy. He tried to stand up but a scaly, taloned hand rammed him back down onto the seat.

"Not yet," said one of them. He couldn't tell who was who, now they'd moved from their stools.

"We've not finished with you," said another.

"I really have to go home. My wife's expecting me," stammered Willie, heart hammering. Maybe he would have a heart attack after all.

"I don't smell any female on you," said the first, to raucous laughter. "Which means you're a naughty little liar."

"He's also a peeper," said the third. "Not many people know this but it's a dying art. I mean, it's not just a matter of hiding in the bushes with a pair of panties filched off the washing line in one hand and your cock in the other, is it William?"

"Oh look, he's gone all shy."

"Rab," Willie shouted, his voice moving up an octave. "Where the hell are you mate?"

"Rab's otherwise occupied, William. So we're depending on you to keep us entertained."

"You're not going to let us down now, are you?"

"It wouldn't do to disappoint a *lay-dee*."

"Or us for that matter."

That hateful, shrieking laughter erupted again, but Willie was not getting the joke. Was that a spot of blood on the dress of the one in front of him? A trickle of fear curled in his belly.

"C'mon now, William, you can break the habit of a lifetime if you really try."

The three faces began to elongate, features distorting over shifting, cracking bones, and the once dark eyes were now the colour of old blood. A sudden sound like a sail snapping in the wind almost deafened him, as one of the creatures unfurled leathery, vestigial wings. The contents of Willie's bladder streamed down his legs and onto the floor.

196

He opened his mouth to shout for help, but before he could, one of the monsters seized his tongue and yanked it out of its sanctuary. Something sharp sliced over the exposed flesh and then he was choking on something thick and viscous.

Willie's attacker hefted the severed organ in her hand and threw her head back, cramming it in her mouth. She grinned, fanged teeth chewing the flesh as blood spilled down her chin.

"I really shouldn't speak with my mouth full," she said, spraying Willie with pieces of his own tongue. "But nothing excites me quite like fresh meat."

"Blnnnnnghh," screamed Willie.

"What? It's not like you have a girlfriend to complain about your new 'no oral' rule," said another as the diner gripped the tip of Willie's tongue between her blood-stained teeth, wiggling it around to jeering guffaws and catcalls.

His gorge rose, but one of the others clamped his mouth closed and he was forced to chew on his pub lunch for a second time.

"We should take him somewhere else in case anyone comes in," said the clamper.

"Why? Just bolt the doors. The pub wasn't even supposed to be open today so maybe no one else will even turn up."

"We've already done one here and it was too quick to be much fun. But if we take this guy elsewhere, we can really let our hair down and still be back in plenty of time. *She's* coming, remember, and she won't be pleased if she finds out."

"That's true, Megan. Here, you take him."

Before he knew what was happening, he was thrown over a hard, bony shoulder and carried outside. He caught sight of Rab's corpse stuffed feet first into one of the pub's wheelie bins, nose-less, lip-less face leering out from underneath the lid.

Proof positive, as if any were needed, that, of the two, Willie always had been much more of a ladies' man.

***

Slate-grey clouds hung low in the sky, evacuating a steady, soaking rain that carved clean runnels down Willie's bloody jowls. A chill North Sea wind howled around the village square with a flurry of leaves and assorted garbage escaped from an overturned bin. In the fading light, the crumbling masonry and broken chimney-pots of the Torphichen Inn had a leprous cast, as though it was rotting from the outside in.

Beyond the square, stone cottages huddled together in the pelting rain, but no lights disturbed their gloomy interiors. The village appeared uninhabited – not so much as a solitary car or pedestrian disturbed the Bathgate to Linlithgow road that ran through it.

"I'll fucking kill you," roared a statuesque woman with long scarlet hair, shades and a leopard-print coat as she strode towards them over the car park.

The three froze, causing Willie to fall from Megan's embrace onto the tarmac, cracking his head. He lay where he fell, breathing fast and shallow, unable to move.

"Mistress," said Marjorie, eyes lowered, "we were waiting for you, just as you told us to."

"One more lie," said the woman, throwing a large bag to the ground and unsheathing two copper-hilted knives from her belt, "and I'll gut you where you stand. I knew this would happen – which is why I'm early. And not a moment too soon by the looks of it."

"No, Lady, we meant no harm," whimpered Megan, sinking to her knees, arms outstretched.

"Let's ask him that, shall we?" said the woman, pointing at Willie with one of the blades.

"He's a bad man, Mistress. A barfly that drinks here every lunchtime. We met him when you brought us here to talk to the owner of the Inn and he told us all about himself. I know for a fact that no one will miss him," said Megan, punching Willie as if to prove the point.

"So you thought you'd arrive before me and have him for a little light lunch, did you? I decide who your prey is. Me," snapped the woman, stabbing Megan in the eye and rotating the blade until it scraped against bone. Megan moaned, blood and thicker matter spilling down her face and onto the pot-holed ground in a hot, wet rush.

"You're supposed to obey me, not follow your own agenda. How many times do we have to do this?" the woman said, punctuating her words with jabs of the knife. She placed a booted foot on Megan's chest and pushed, freeing the blade.

"Mistress," screamed Marjorie, "you'll kill her."

"As my old mother might have said if I'd known her, the only good Boabhan Sith vampire is a dead one."

"But we would not survive without our sister, my Lady," said Morgan.

"Me, me, me, that's all you ever think about," the woman said, shoving a knife deep into Morgan's abdomen and jerking it upwards through meat and bone, stopping just short of her heart.

"That only leaves you Marjorie," she said, withdrawing the blade. "Now, what's it to be? I could cut something off, something that won't grow back, to teach you empathy with your victims. Or maybe I should just send you back to Morgana where you belong."

Marjorie threw herself at the woman's feet, twining her arms around her ankles. "Please Mistress, no! Don't send us back. Have my eyes, my hands – they're yours and gladly given."

Scowling, the woman kicked her off. "The deal is you're supposed to serve me. But instead, you do what the hell you like and then we have to do *this* every couple of months. Nothing ever changes. Nothing. Give me one good reason not to send you back. Just one."

"She'd kill us," said the vampire, the sibilant whisper bouncing around the rain sodden tarmac and the old stone walls of the pub as though it were an enclosed echo-chamber.

"Aw, my heart bleeds," said the woman. "Just count yourselves lucky I've got a job on and don't have time for this shit. Make no mistake though," she said, waving the dripping knives, "this is last chance saloon. If you fuck up – or worse, fuck me over – one last time, I swear to the god I don't believe in you're all going back to Morgana whether you like it or not."

The vampire's lip twitched, revealing razor sharp teeth and a flickering forked tongue. "As you wish, Mistress."

"Right. Get this guy and your sisters into the pub and patched up. You did your Hammer House of Horror vamp routine on him, didn't you? I should never have left those old DVDs lying around.

And hurry it up, will you? I need to think about how I'm going to sort this."

Willie began to sob, shoulders heaving with the effort, gobbets of snot and strings of drool mingling with the fresh blood from his mutilated mouth.

The woman grimaced. "Look on the bright side," she said. "At least I got here before they cut anything vital off. I'm Rose, by the way. Rose Garnett. It's okay, don't try to speak – I can see you bit off more than you could chew with the girls here. Sadly that's not something you could ever accuse them of."

As Marjorie hoisted Willie over her shoulder and into his now familiar upside-down world, he knew that, just like the Hotel California, he would never leave the Torphichen Inn again.
***

Rose Garnett was in an even fouler mood than usual. A psychic mercenary for hire with an affinity for the dead, she had taken on a well-paid gig to rid the Torphichen Inn of whatever haunted it. Trouble was, the three vampires she'd been forced to take responsibility for six months ago were proving to be liabilities. The supposed upside was that if she could control them, they would add much needed muscle to her operation, but that was proving to be more problematic than even she had anticipated.

It didn't help that the owner of the pub had told her a disjointed, senseless tale about sightings of flayed heads free-floating in mirrors and murderous whispers in the cellar whenever staff went down there. He couldn't get anyone to work for him for any length of time and the place was now notorious. Even the most hard-bitten of the regulars had been spooked by tales of an eyeless, giggling child rumoured to be a portent of death for whoever saw her. The bottom line was, this was one of those rare occasions when Rose didn't know what she was up against - and that spelt trouble. She needed the money though, or she'd be in trouble of a different but no less dangerous kind.

She had also left strict instructions that no one was to be present and the pub was to be closed to the public. The fact that the vampires had found their victim here before she'd even arrived meant those instructions had been ignored and the situation compromised.

Sticking to her original plan, she headed towards a door at the back of the pub, fishing out the key from her pocket.

"Do exactly as I say," she said, opening the door, "and just maybe we'll forget about your little torture-porn session this afternoon."

After climbing a rickety set of stairs, they walked into a large room that had clearly gone unused for some time. Dense cobwebs decorated the broken shelving that lined the room and there were holes in the threadbare, beige carpet. Sepia photographs, taken in the Victorian era when the pub had been built, showed a series of dull-eyed men in top hats, all gazing into the camera with the same hostile intensity.

An unseen critter scuttled in a corner colonised by a pile of broken chairs and amputated table legs. Torrential rain beat a staccato tattoo on the grimy, dimpled glass of the windows, the world beyond reduced to a smeary wash. An ancient pool table had been rammed into the wall under the windows and Morgan threw herself down on it, strands of blond hair glimmering in the dying winter light. Her blood-stained white dress was in tatters, her perfect, pale skin disfigured by the long jagged knife wound through which the secret meat of her body was visible.

"Get up," said Rose, "or I'll fillet you properly this time."

The vampire obeyed, eyes averted as Rose nodded to Marjorie to lay the man down on the vacated table.

"This room is the furthest away from the epicentre of whatever the hell has been happening here, so it should be relatively safe. I suggest you make the most of it while you can."

The injured man grunted as Marjorie ripped his blood-soaked shirt off, sending buttons pinging in all directions. Tearing strips from the material, she tied one around Megan's head as a makeshift eye-patch to stop the bleeding and gave the rest to Morgan to pack the gaping hole in her abdomen.

"You're totally useless. Here," Rose said, throwing a tube of superglue at Marjorie, "seal the wound with this, then bandage her up."

The man whimpered.

"I'll take you to A and E later," Rose told him, lying through her teeth. "I can't risk you telling anyone about the girls before we leave, so you'll have to stay put for a bit. It's no use looking at me like that, you'll spill your guts - you know you will."

The truth was, tongueless or not, she wasn't worried that he'd blab about carnivorous vampires because no one would believe him. The real problem was that he was a dead man and it was only a question of when. The vampires had marked him and there was nothing that could keep him from them, not even Rose herself. If she took him to a hospital, they would finish him off there after she left. The man was doomed wherever he went, but at least if he stayed here he'd live as long as Rose was close by. Not exactly a long-term solution, but it was the best he had. She hoped Megan was right about him not being missed.

"I promise I'll take you to the hospital," she continued as though talking to a small child. "Okay?"

The man nodded, eyes closed.

She turned to the vampires. "Did you find out his name?"

"The food said it was called William McBain," said Marjorie.

"He's not food, nor is he an 'it'," said Rose.

Marjorie stared at her, a tiny frown marring her translucent skin.

"Jesus, you really are a slow learner, aren't you?" Rose said, extracting a scraper from her bag and thrusting it at the vampire. "That's why I'm giving you something to do that's more in line with your abilities. Look for sigils under this wallpaper and carpet. If there are any, they'll be here. So get scraping. Megan, Morgan - you two are coming with me."

"But I am uninjured, Mistress. Should I not go with you instead?" Marjorie asked.

"No. I think your sisters' current states may attract whatever is here, which is what we want. You've also got more control because you are uninjured, which is why you are the only one I can leave with *him*," she said, pointing at the now unconscious man. "And he better be alive and in one piece when I get back."

She turned on her heel, leaving the lone Boabhan Sith to her thankless task.

***

"What do you think haunts this place, Mistress?" asked Megan twenty minutes later as they prowled the upper floor.

"I'd assumed from what I'd been told that it was a haunting, but it's not. I can't sense anything dead in here and that's...troubling. There's always lots of ghosts in pubs, especially old ones like this."

"I don't understand, Lady," said Megan.

"Pubs are magnets for the dead in the same way they are for the living, just for different reasons. The living come to have a good time or cry into their beer. They fall in and out of love while stalking their exes, all under the same roof. Over time, the sum total of that emotion builds, becoming a beacon to those amongst the dead who don't have much else to cling to or don't possess the wit to pass over. But there's a vacuum here, as though the place has been cleaned out. That's why I think the pub may be infested by something other than just rats."

As she spoke, the two Sith stilled, all semblance of life draining away like water down a plug-hole.

Screams rent the air.

"Prey," said Morgan.

"Blood," said Megan.

"Death," whispered Morgan.

Fuck, fuck, and triple fuck. She hadn't had time to lock the doors from the inside – had more people wandered in? She had also presumed that the most dangerous creatures in the pub were the Sith, but the shrieks from downstairs told a different story.

"There is something terrible in this place, Mistress," said Megan as though reading her thoughts.

"Aw, c'mon now, don't tell me the big bad Sith are afraid?"

She strode along the dark corridor towards the noise, the two vampires trailing like pale, wounded ghosts. They came out into a mezzanine that looked down onto a dance floor surrounded by tables and chairs. A huge disco ball hung from the raftered ceiling and through a door at the far end where part of a bar was visible. A blur of motion flashed, too fast to be human, and the screaming stopped.

Resisting the urge to rush in blind, she scoured the building with her death-sense as she descended the stairs, probing from the attic to the foundations, and found nothing but an eerie, psychic silence. She had lost count of the times she had wished for a cessation of the white noise in her head, the constant, intrusive presence of the dead with their demands, threats, and obscenities. Now she'd have given anything to have it all back.

"Show yourself," said Rose, raising her voice.

The vampires hung back, chittering.

"I said, show yourself."

The lights flickered. A child's giggle fluted from upstairs seconds before a mighty crash of broken glass came from the direction of the bar, and the agonised shrieks began again.

"Don't make us go further, Lady," begged Morgan, needle-sharp teeth crowding the width of her gaping mouth.

"There's only death here," said Megan. "We should leave."

"Go into that bar and find out what's going on," Rose said, drawing out her knives. "Or I'll be dealing out some death of my own."

They ran ahead on all fours, canine hind legs and snouted faces at distressing odds with the scaled skin, human arms and glowing red eyes. While she had no confidence they'd succeed, they would at least serve as cannon fodder, taking the brunt of whatever was in there. The truth was, however, that with no clue as to what had made the Torphichen Inn its new home, there was little chance of evicting it.

Through the door was a small bar-cum-dining area with upended tables and chairs strewn around as though someone had thrown them in a fit of rage. She glimpsed another room on the other side of the bar – the source of the screaming, and now a hail of missiles.

The stench of alcohol and blood hit her like a fist as she ran through. The screaming ceased. A dry rattle from above made her look up at the wall, but it was seconds before she made sense of what hung there: both vampires had been skewered with huge glass shards, arms outstretched, legs bound together as though they had been crucified. She stepped back and tripped on something. A human leg. The body parts of three obese, middle-aged men lay on what was left of the bar, one hacked into a mere torso.

There were more. One of two dead women had also been decapitated, her grizzled head feet away from her body, mouth and eyes wide as if shocked at the sight. The other had been caught as she'd tried to run, wedged in the exit with the back of her head smashed to a pulp, gobbets of brain adorning the doorway. The huge mirror by the bar was now devoid of glass, tables and chairs crushed into blood-spattered detritus.

"Help us, Mistress," whispered Morgan.

Rose ducked as a large glass shard flew past and pierced Megan through her good eye. Above the vampires' heads, something caught her attention. There was a mural on the wall: a twilight, barren landscape in which devils reigned, hunting human prey. Except it couldn't have been a mural, because the figures depicted were *moving*.

A red sun hung low in a dark sky, illuminating carnivorous trees festooned with strips of human skin, clothing and hair, all swaying as if in a breeze. A horned demon, black with blazing yellow eyes, wore human viscera around its neck even as it clawed for more in the stomach of a struggling victim. Another demon, squat with an enormous snake-like fanged mouth, devoured a naked youth and then vomited up the still living chunks of meat before starting the process over again.

The grotesque perfection in this transformation of the living into the dead playthings of such joyous predators was becoming more alluring by the moment. Unable to help herself, Rose ran her hand along the mural landscape, and with that contact came an overwhelming rush: the first, feathered touch of a homicidal lover in a midnight lay-by; a last desperate gasp before slipping down, down, into an ocean of blood; a gourmet taste of the terror of fresh captive souls on the Highway of the Dead as they realised what was next...

A mosquito-like whine and the spill of blood on her neck snapped her out of the fugue as a glass shard sliced across her skin. The mural had been seducing her with her darkest imaginings, and only the pain had saved her from succumbing. Would she have been lost in it forever otherwise?

She ducked and rolled to the side as another dozen shards pierced the space where she'd been standing. She sprang up and ran for the exit, about to jump over the corpse blocking the door when she was struck on the side of the head. She staggered back and slid in a pool of congealed blood.

Nothing made sense anymore. A pub possessed by a sentient, soul-sucking mural? This hadn't been any part of the story she'd been told by the owner. Whatever it was, one thing was certain: it didn't want her to leave.

A noise came from behind her and she whirled, a knife in each hand. Marjorie. She was restraining the injured William McBain, who was struggling in her grip as though his life depended on it. He roared, the stump of his tongue unable to shape words as tears streamed down his face, hands outstretched towards the mural.

"He tried to escape, Mistress. I didn't notice he'd gone at first because I found this."

Rose snatched the proffered piece of wallpaper from her as a hooved foot crashed to the floor with such force that it struck sparks. A howl of rage shook the Torphichen Inn to its foundations.

The yellow-eyed demon had almost torn itself free from the mural.

"Mistress. Look, it's a sigil."

Rose stared at the design etched on the torn paper: a five-pointed star containing four circles and an inverted cross.

"You stupid bitch," she shouted. "That's the Seal of Astaroth. All this" – she waved at the mural, the corpses, and the emerging demon – "happened the instant you ripped it off the fucking wall. It was the only thing keeping that monster at bay. That," she said, pointing at the advancing demon, "is Astaroth, and we are totally screwed."

Astaroth approached, hooves clanging, a trail of steaming footprints left in its wake. Under the scarred skin of the porcine, tusked face, something burrowed and screamed. The demon bared its bloody teeth as though in response and the stench of decaying flesh and faeces became overwhelming.

William McBain broke free and threw himself down in front of the creature, raising his hands in the air in supplication.

"The man has lost his mind."

"He's being compelled, idiot. We'll be next."

Astaroth put a clawed hand on the man's head as though in benediction. William McBain beamed from ear to ear, his happy gurgling changing to raw shrieks as the monster lifted him up by the head and ripped open his belly, releasing his innards and an acrid stink. With a casual twist, the demon ripped the man's arm off and began to pulverise his face with the broken shoulder joint.

"Fuck it. I was hoping it wouldn't come to this," said Rose, scrabbling in her coat pocket. Her fingers closed around a small amulet with an inverted pentagram and goat's head inscribed on it.

She threw it.

"Catch," she said.

The demon caught the amulet before realising its mistake, eyes contracting to black, vertical slits. Its roar of protest was cut short as it winked out of existence as though it had never been, taking the living mural and the amulet with it.

"What did you throw?" asked Marjorie.

"If you must know, it was the sigil of Baphomet, a much more powerful demon. It was worked by a coven of black witches into a tool of banishment for lesser devils. Priceless, of course, and now it's gone thanks to you. Never mind that now, though. We need to clean all traces of ourselves from here and leave. The thing that really pisses me off is that I didn't get to the bottom of whatever is going on with the Inn. The mural was Astaroth's creation and he killed the folk who came into the bar."

"But didn't the Sigil of Astaroth cause the haunting before I removed it?"

"No. The fact that some arsehole summoned a demon, failed to send it back to hell and imprisoned it instead doesn't mean shit. It wouldn't have caused the sightings or all the ghosts to disappear. I'm betting that whatever was wrong with this place is still on the loose. There's no point in continuing with the job though, 'cause the owner is in that pile of bodies over there and the police will be all over it. So it's all your fucking fault that I'm not going to get paid. Get your sisters down from there, for Christ's sake."

Minutes later Rose's battered Transit screeched out of the pub car-park and headed towards Edinburgh, lights cutting tunnels into the dark sheets of rain falling from the gravid sky.

***

Inside the Torphichen Inn, something stirred.

A young girl in dirty Victorian garb picked her way over the bodies and broken furniture, her empty eye-sockets covered by the leprous skin of her face.

In one hand, she held four severed heads by their long hair. Two of them had woken, eyes rolling in their flayed faces, mouths stretched in toothless grimaces.

"We have a new companion now," she told the heads. She giggled as she held up a fifth in her other hand. "Although I rather fear the cat has got his tongue."

Willie McBain opened his eyes and began to scream.

AMBUSH

by Charlotte Ros

He checked the time on his watch by the glow of his mp3 player – nine forty-five. The bitch was forty-five minutes late already. He was beginning to get eager, hunched down in the tiny space with the darkness crushing him. But still, never mind, because he had his music and perturbed thoughts to keep him company whilst he waited for his prey.

Only one earphone was being used, and that was in his left ear. He wanted the right free, as it was pressed almost tight to the thin slats in the louvre door of the walk-in wardrobe. This was so he could hear her enter the room. God, he was so excited. He'd stalked this slag for the past four months, studying her every move, creeping in her shadows, watching her from every bush and window on her daily routes to work and friends and family houses. This was the longest he had let one live, and he was going to fucking love cutting her into tiny little sections, he thought; dissecting her like a biology frog.

His bag of sharp implements lay by his side on the carpeted floor, amongst her things: boxed clothes, toys from her childhood, photos, shoes and so forth. He'd had his nose in her clothes many a time in the past few weeks, sniffing at their crotches: trousers, shorts, panties, anything he could to try and catch the whiff of her womanly juices. God, if only she knew what he'd been doing in her room whilst she and her parents were at work. Well, the parents would not be a problem tonight, not ever again...

He'd disposed of them around an hour ago. Shelby had throttled the mother with cheese-wire whilst she'd been knitting in her rocking chair in front the fire. She'd wriggled like a virgin, he thought, sitting in the oppression of the darkness. The family cat had also been sleeping in front of the roaring blaze; he'd booted the tom into the hungry flames and watched it writhe in agony. Its ginger fur had cracked and smoked in a most impressive manner. Shelby smiled a grin to end all grins. The father had been upstairs shaving, not hearing a thing. That had left him open to an agonising attack from behind, taking a swift couple of blows to the kidneys before having his face rammed into the mirror he'd been using. Then his throat had been slit open by a jagged shard of glass. Shelby had taken a mental image of the man dying, choking on his own blood, before coming to a gargling crescendo. The clean-up had been the hardest part of the job.

Shelby wrung his hands together in the shadows of the closet, and licked his arid lips as he retraced his steps over the killings, and the way he disposed of the bodies – he'd simply dumped them in the cubbyhole under the stairs, stacking them neatly in one corner and covering them with coats. He'd carved his pseudonym into them before he had done so: T.M.M, along with a flattering music note which he always etched into the victim's necks. The police had still not made out his calling card, but that was fine. They were stupid.

He turned his head and glanced through the slats. "I Know Where You Live" began to pump out of the mp3 player; the song, and the album had helped inspire his killing spree, along with other music and musicians – not just Alice and his twisted death metal. A small lamp was aglow by the side of the queen-size bed and on top of the duvet was a stuffed toy alligator. Around its neck was a tag of some sort. A cold shudder slid down Shelby's back, for the toy had not been there when he'd walked into the room almost two hours ago; he was sure the thing had not been there. Looking at it stare back at him with its beady black eyes and chalk white teeth bearing threats of "I'm-going-to-eat-you-all-up-Shelby" gave him the chills.

His scrotum began to shrink under the dutiful eye of the soft green reptile – yummy-yummy – sadistic killer for lunch. He heard it snap.

Shelby could not contain his thirst for curiosity – it killed the cat, Shelby, remember? But he couldn't help himself. He slid his back up the wall and got himself into a standing position, all the while keeping his eyes fixed on the toy. He unplugged the restricting earpiece and let it dangle like the other one. The words spilt from both unoccupied plugs and pounded the empty-sounding wardrobe, seeping out through the slats, filling the room like a thin mist of words:

> *I watch from my car.*
> *I make sure you don't go far.*
> *I know when you sleep.*
> *Don't like the company you keep.*
> *When you're at work, I'm in your room, on the bed, and you don't know.*
> *I go through your things.*
> *The touch, the smell, what joy it all brings…*

Shelby's breathing became ragged rips of inhalation and exhalation. He faced the slats square on and slid the door to one side, still keeping his eyes fixed on the gator. He snarled, revealing prefect teeth.

"Gonna get ya now, Mr Big Bad Gator," Shelby said. He smiled as he took one step out of his hidey-hole, tucking the earphones away into one of his side pockets of the combat jacket he wore. He also removed a small knife from his other pocket. The blade was four inches in length when pulled from its channel, and erect. The steel snapped into place with a *snick*. "Gonna rip your stuffing out, Mr Gator, and pad my gerbil's cage with it. Mr Tinks will be most happy. Then afterward, I'll use my steel to hollow out your owner, Mr Gator. Let's see how much fucking smiling you'll be doing then, big boy."

His boots made the boards creak as he crossed the space between him and the bed. He picked up the cuddly toy by its thick, squashy neck and looked at the plastic tag hanging from the collar.

"Ain't that the fucking cutest thing you saw?" Shelby flicked the nametag over, and spied the nickname on it – Mr AC. "I wonder what that stands for? 'Angry Croc,' maybe."

He laughed at his own stupid joke and was about to plunge the tip of his knife into the belly of the toy and draw out the stuffing which made up its guts when he heard the front door slam shut – she was home! Shelby firmly placed the reptile back on the bed and scurried to his hideout – he just made it as Silvia Croft came bursting through her bedroom door. She was straddling *him*, the punk with slicked hair and cheap shoes.

Shelby had seen them together a couple of times over the past few weeks. He worked at Alliance Carpets in town and lived near Shelby's own home. The air in the area was immediately smothered with his sissy aftershave, which had a spicy aroma to it, Shelby thought, and that pissed him right off. He felt like stalking out there and slamming his knife into the punk's back. But that would take away the joy, for tonight he would have two for the price of one to punish, kill and deflower.

Cheap Shoes was eager – too eager – as he pushed Silvia back on to her bed. The skirt she wore rode up her body, revealing her pert arse and Shelby's favourite panties. They had little cherries on them. He'd sniffed them many a time in the past as they lay sunny-side up on the floor next to the bed. Her bare legs made Shelby moan, but not too loud. Not that they would have heard, as she was panting and her lover was clawing at her legs, making grunting sounds in the progress as he tried to pull her knickers free.

"Slow down, Gary, we got all night," she said, lightly pushing at his shoulders.

This didn't seem to cut any ice with him, as he continued to grope and claw her, burying his face in between her clothed breasts.

"The dude got the fucking horn, big time," Shelby mouthed. "This should be interesting. That's if he can get his cock out of his trousers before he erupts in his pants."

Silvia started to yield to Cheap Shoes' animal-like ravishing, and embarked on undoing his jeans by firstly loosening the belt, then tugging them down his scrawny legs – boxers and all. Then off came her clothes. It was not long before they were entwined in knots of passionate kisses, and he was deep inside her, her short raven hair matted flat to her skull with sweat, his forehead glistening as he rammed her again and again. The headboard pounded in sync with Shelby's galloping heart as he watched on, listening to his music in one ear whilst keeping the other free to hear their moans of pleasure. Now's the time, he thought, to catch them by surprise. He picked up his small bag of tricks by his side, and was about to slide the wardrobe door back, but a sudden outburst from Silvia stopped him.

She was squealing like a pig having its throat cut open. Shelby looked out at the couple, and he could see her driving her head back into the pillows, embracing a thunderous orgasm.

"Cheap Shoes has done me proud," Shelby mouthed. "But his fucking days are over."

As he was about to go out into the open once again, Shelby witnessed Silvia plough her forehead into Gary's face, cracking his nose, which exploded like a popped water balloon. He tried to get off her, but she locked her legs behind his back and writhed under the fountain of blood that descended onto her, rubbing it into her naked body, lapping at it like a cat. Gary could do nothing but hold his busted nose and shake his body violently, trying to disengage. But she had him tight.

When she finally got bored, Silvia struck him in the oesophagus, once, twice, three times before it crushed under her karate-style chop. He gargled and choked on his own blood and did the jig of the dying before finally slumping down dead on Silvia. She opened her legs and pushed him off her. She reminded Shelby of a Black Widow. Then she spoke, and Shelby thought he'd been punched in the guts as he struggled for air.

"Did you enjoy that, Shelby? I know you are there." She got off the bed, walked to the end, and picked up Mr AC. "This guy here keeps an eye on the room whilst I'm not here – he's got a little camera behind his eye. Don't be scared, you can come out, I won't hurt you – much."

Shelby watched as the naked girl dropped Mr AC, and opened a drawer to the dressing table by the side of her bed. She produced a knife – a kukri – from its depths. He backed away from the slats until his back met the wall, and the words that seeped into his ear from the mp3 player almost broke him:

Just like a spider:
Trap, kill, eat…
Trap, kill, eat…

"All this time you thought you were watching me, but I was watching you, Shelby. Or 'The Music Maestro', as you like to call yourself. I also know about all the other women you have killed, plus my parents. Mr AC cannot keep a secret. Time to die, Shelby. Time I killed you, you son-of-a-bitch, and add *you* to my conquests."

She stood before the wardrobe, bathed in blood and hunched over slightly, playing the knife back and forth between her open hands. He tore the earpiece away and steadied himself, trying to calm his heartbeats. Shelby threw the door back, and stepped out into the room – his small knife in hand, the blade standing erect and ready.

"That's it," she said. "Come to mammy, you big bastard."

He lurched forward. She followed suit, and they met in the middle of the room with a clash of steel…

Introduction to DINNER

My name is Christine Elise McCarthy. Although I have been acting professionally for 28 years I am primarily recognized for my roles as the U4EA-popping bad girl, Emily Valentine, on Beverly Hills, 90210, as Harper Tracy on ER, and as Kyle, the gal who killed Chucky in Child's Play 2. Child's Play 2 was my first major role and exciting for me on every front. I remain friends with many of the players in that experience and feel very lucky to be part of such an enduring franchise. I don't self-identify as a scream queen, though – maybe because Child's Play 2 is my only true horror feature and because I don't think of Kyle as a screamer. She was remarkably matter-of-fact about what she went through and came through it all relatively unscathed. But that job remains a sentimental experience and always will.

As a writer, I wrote three episodes of Beverly Hills, 90210 as well as characters and storylines for the series, and a pilot that was optioned by Aaron Spelling. I maintain an irreverent food porn blog called www.DelightfulDeliciousDelovely.com for which I provide recipes, photographs and sometimes share details of the triumphs and, more frequently, the humiliations of my life. I have a great passion for photography http://www.redbubble.com/people/jdempsey and have shown my pin-up and decaying Americana imagery in the United States and Paris. My directorial debut, Bathing and the Single Girl, a 10-minute short film, was accepted into over 100 film festivals and won 20 awards.

Bathing and the Single Girl, inspired by the short film, is my debut novel. It is a book about the awkwardness and indignities of trying to work and date in Los Angeles. It is, by far, my proudest achievement and I promise – it is raunchy and scandalous and funny in the most cringe-worthy ways imaginable.

I hope you enjoy this story here. It is a complete departure from the tone and content of my novel.

DINNER

by Christine Elise McCarthy

"**Hi**, Daddy! You're up!" Jackie chirped with renewed perkiness as Dougie joined her and her mother, Pat, in the kitchen.

Dougie did not acknowledge Jackie's voice. His eyes, glassy, unseeing, were fixed on nothing. He staggered deeper into the room. Jackie was instantly on edge. This did not bode well.

She plowed on, pretending not to notice how out of it he seemed. "We made your favorite: steaks!" she announced, but the confidence she had mustered to begin the sentence failed her by the time she completed it.

Dougie attempted another step forward but stumbled on something unseen. Too drunk to react and save himself, he toppled forward like a felled tree, his arms limp and heavy at his sides. He landed jaw-first on the rim of the porcelain and iron sink.

Jackie's stomach lurched. The force of that fall would probably crush the bone that had made contact with the unforgiving sink. She heard her mother gasp, and was relieved that the sound masked that of what her father's chin might have made as it shattered.

Before anyone could say or do anything, Dougie's descent delayed as his jaw slid the entire length of the broad side of the sink, briefly supporting his weight. He glided along the porcelain and into the full dish rack on the far side. Plates smashed on the floor and broken glass and silverware clattered everywhere. Once his chin reached the end of the supporting surface, he landed in a flaccid heap on the floor amongst the cutlery and debris.

Jackie thought she was going to vomit. Pat must have felt similarly because she made no sound and didn't move to get up. The two of them sat there in stupefied horror. Jackie was certain her father was dead or so badly injured that death might be preferable. While she concentrated on settling her stomach, Dougie stirred on the floor.

"Dougie?" Pat asked, her voice hesitant. "Are you okay?"

Dougie didn't respond, and began the series of clumsy moves that would ultimately result in his standing.

Jackie was certain he could not respond because the lower half of his face had been pulverized and rendered useless. Her belly flip-flopped again as she anticipated the extent of the damage he had done to himself. She and Pat sat motionless, as if hypnotized, and watched as Dougie righted himself. A minute later, he stood with his back to them, weaving and unsteady on his feet. A tin lid that had fallen to the ground with the other dishes noisily completed its spinning hula-hoop motion in increasingly smaller and faster gyrations until it finally clattered flat to the floor.

"Dougie..." Pat again asked, tentative.

Silent but apparently spurred into action again by Pat's voice, Dougie continued on his intended journey and went into the bathroom, neglecting to close the door behind him. Neither Jackie nor Pat dared to move until they heard him puking.

"Is he okay"?" a now panicked Jackie asked, sotto voce, looking urgently into her mother's eyes.

"I don't know. It seems like it," Pat said, her voice hushed and betraying disbelief.

"Do you think he broke his jaw? Do you think he cut himself on the glass?"

The abrupt end to Dougie's puking silenced them. They turned their eyes to the bathroom door to get their first sight of his injuries. Emotion and revulsion crawled, intertwined, up the back of Jackie's throat and grabbed at her uvula. She might have thrown up if her throat hadn't been so constricted. She breathed open-mouthed as if winded from running. She gagged once as a breath caught in her throat.

Dougie appeared, looming in the bathroom doorway. His beard covered his chin and jaw, so Jackie could not make a complete assessment of his injuries, but he seemed to be fine. Just a few tiny bits of vomit in his beard. Not believing her own eyes, she looked to her mother for confirmation. Pat sat staring at Dougie too, mouth agape. Jackie returned her eyes to her father. He was apparently having difficulty pulling the kitchen into focus.

"You're eating dinner without me!?" he suddenly bellowed, his speech thick. He hiccupped.

They didn't answer him. They stared at him like he was the second coming of Christ. Both Jackie and Pat wondered how it could be. How was it possible his jaw wasn't broken? Why wasn't he bleeding?

"Are you okay, Dougie?" Pat at last inquired.

Dougie turned his head in the direction of her voice and moved his eyebrows around, squinting in vain attempts to see her clearly. "What?"" he yelled, suddenly irate. "*What* did you say to me?!"

"I asked if you were okay", Pat explained.

"What the *fuck* is that supposed to mean?" he slurred. "Why do you always have to be such a bitch? I wasn't fucking *doing* anything! I just fucking took a fucking"—he thought for a beat before completing his thought—"piss!"

His hand went to his face in that unpleasantly familiar mustache swiping gesture that indicated he was in the mood for a fight. As his thumb and forefinger met underneath his jaw, he grabbed his beard like it was an ice cream cone. The weight of his hand was more than his neck could support. His head lolled to his chest. He released his grip on his beard and his head popped up again, like a driver fighting the final stages of falling asleep behind the wheel. He looked at Jackie and Pat suspiciously, as if they could be responsible for his current confusion. All Jackie could think about was that he now had vomit on his hand as well.

"Why don't you go out there and go back to sleep, Dougie?" Pat suggested.

"I wasn't sleeping. I was just resting my...eyes."

"Whatever. Why don't you go back out there and 'rest your...eyes'?" Pat mocked.

Jackie could feel how much her mother hated Dougie—the contempt was almost palpable. Although Jackie had occasionally *said* she hated her father (and this was generally said directly to his face), what she *meant* was 'I love you. Why do you hate me?' Her most vile words paled in comparison to Pat's nicest words in conveying loathing for Dougie. Jackie heard that animosity in her mother's voice again now and marveled that she dared be so openly provocative.

Jackie looked nervously to her father for his reaction.

Dougie moved forward and stood, swaying, despite his thighs being braced against the edge of the table. He looked at the plate of food that sat untouched in front of his chair. He then looked at Pat, and Jackie could tell he was trying to figure out what he could do that would most irritate her mother. She had seen this dance before.

Pat stared back, throwing daggers, waiting impatiently for the next development.

Dougie looked away from her and at Jackie. Jackie tried to look as unobtrusive as possible.

"You know what, Dougie? I am sure I don't care what you do. Jackie and I are going to eat our dinner before it gets cold."

Arrrgh! Jackie thought. *Don't say my name! Don't turn his attention to me. Don't redirect his wrath.* In an effort to placate, Jackie adopted the most innocent expression she could muster. She attempted to clear all the fear and nausea from her expression before she said, " We made you a steak dinner, Daddy. Why don't you sit down and eat it? We even made the mushrooms and onions you love...so...mu..." Jackie drifted off as she saw a spark in his eye.

Dougie locked eyes with Pat again and reached toward his plate. The table slid tight to Jackie's chest, pushed forward by his weight against it. Reflexively, Jackie's hands came up to brace against the crushing table. Wide-eyed with surprise from the sharp pain of the table against her chest, she looked up at her father in panic. Oblivious to the table movement, he stayed focused on Pat. His hand fumbled, blind, knocking food off his plate and onto the table, until it found his steak. He picked it up, brought the entire steak to his mouth, and took a big, savage bite out of it.

Pat watched him unmoved. Steak blood and gristle dripped down his beard as he chewed. At least it masked the flecks of vomit still smeared there. "That's cute. *Now* will you go back into the living room and let us finish our meal?" Pat asked.

Dougie chewed louder, with his mouth open. He took a second tearing bite out of the steak. Juice ran down the back of his hand, dark droplets trickling through the hairs on his forearm like ants scurrying through blades of grass. Chewing sloppily, he leaned toward Pat's face. Jackie was afraid he might bite Pat's nose off or do some other unthinkable and violent thing.

Pat didn't flinch. She stared directly into his eyes.

Dougie hovered there a moment, threatening in his stillness like an angered cobra, and then, with his free hand, pulled his chair out.

Jackie didn't relax until he backed away from her mother and sat in the chair in front of his plate, thereby moving out of immediate striking distance. Pat had somehow escaped that one, though she hadn't ever seemed to register the danger she was in. Gently, Jackie nudged the table back toward Dougie and off her chest. She looked at the plate in front of her father. Wax beans, mushrooms and onions were strewn all around it. Her dinner intended to solidify their crumbling bond had been not just disregarded but also used as fodder for altercation. She had failed again. She promised herself to stop trying—things backfired on her too much.

But she knew it was a promise she would break even as she made it.

Jackie looked back up at her father. He was still making a display of his piggish chewing of the steak she had insisted they make especially for him. His beard shone with grease; blood trails tracked his right arm and hand, making his forearm look like an anatomy chart depicting the locations of arteries and capillaries. Jackie looked at her mother, whose face broadcast nothing but the purest form of disgust. Jackie realized her mother did not feel any of the fear or threat that she herself felt when Dougie was in these moods. Perhaps Pat had an agenda with Dougie that did not overlap her own. Where Jackie felt fear and the urge to assuage, Pat seemed made brazen by

Dougie's anger and was determined to bring it to a fearsome head, some irreversible place that Jackie had been desperately avoiding for what seemed like forever.

Jackie looked from her mother's strong expression of loathing and challenge to her father's smacking mouth and unfocused glare and, for the first time in her life, felt embarrassed for him. In the light of her mother's reaction to it, her father's menacing posturing appeared childish and impotent. As she watched him, he took another chomp out of the steak and continued his churlish mastication. He was like a kid who took a joke too far—a joke that wasn't funny to begin with—while his audience winced in awkward discomfort.

He suddenly seemed juvenile and boorishly cretin to Jackie. Kids were not supposed to feel more in control than their parents. Jackie didn't want to feel that her father was inadequate on any level. She could not afford to witness this display any longer or linger on the feelings it evoked. The horror of her being his superior was something she was unwilling to accept. It meant she was responsible for herself, with no daddy to protect her.

"Daddy…" Jackie tenderly ventured. Without knowing how she was going to do it, she intended to make him stop this ridiculous exhibition.

Dougie turned to her, all the while chewing and slurping. As if her expression alone were indication that he was falling short of his intended affront, he scooped up a handful of food from his plate and scraped it into his mouth. It was more than Jackie could take. He just looked stupid to her now. Buoyed by her own need to not see her father behave in such a meaningless fashion, and by her mother's confident presence, Jackie decided to throw her father a lifeline, and spare them both further humiliation.

"Daddy." The sound of her own voice whipped her back into reality. What the Hell was she going to say? She suddenly felt parental, and she knew that speaking that way to her father was not going to go over well.

Dougie was looking directly at her now.

"Um…" she stalled, looking for the right words.

"What the fuck is your problem now?" Dougie demanded.

"Don't swear at her, Dougie!" Pat interjected.

He pretended not to hear her. "I said, *what's your fuckin' problem*, you little asshole?" he spat at Jackie.

Jackie knew the 'asshole' remark was for Pat's benefit but it still stung. Though he called her names as a matter of course lately, tonight was different. Tonight, she had foolishly let her guard down. She had let herself believe that things were righting, that harmony was being restored. The months of insincere pandering to his moods and needs that she had grown accustomed to did not leave her feeling as vulnerable as this evening's single but heartfelt gesture of making him his favorite dinner. Tonight she felt the full impact of the 'asshole' slap. Hurt and indignation surged from deep in her belly, up her back and across her shoulders. Her cheeks felt as hot as if he had actually struck her.

We watched Jacques Cousteau! she thought. *I made steak! I made you your mushrooms and onions! I made really smooth mashed potatoes!* She wanted to scream these things in his face but didn't dare.

"Dougie! Don't call her that! I've told you..."

Dougie took yet another bite out of the steak and began his ostentatious jawing anew.

Before she could think better of it, Jackie said, "Daddy! Stop it! You look silly."

Dougie stopped chewing and glared at her. She looked back at him and gulped, trying to swallow the fear that was rising up her throat.

"I *what?*" he screamed, food flying as he spoke.

"Dougie, leave her alone," Pat said firmly.

Dougie began chewing normally but did not break his glare. "No, Jackie had something she wanted to tell me. I wanna hear it!"

"I just meant that if you use your knife and fork, you can get some of the mushrooms and onions I...we...made. *We*," she reminded him, as if to say, "Mommie's here, remember?" It was a feeble attempt to diffuse his attention. "Mushrooms and onions on steak. Your favorite."

Dougie continued his surly focus.

"Look, Dougie, I'm gonna get my purse. I'll see if I have a couple of bucks I can spare you." Pat got up from the table. "Why don't you take it and go out with Eddie or Ritchie?" she asked as she headed toward the living room.

Jackie threw a quick, nervous glance in her mother's direction.

"Look at me, you little fuck!" he roared.

Jackie obediently looked back at him.

"You think I look silly? You think I look *silly*?!"

Jackie couldn't shake her head fast enough. A tear rolled down her cheek but she remained silent.

Pat came back into the kitchen, arm outstretched and offering a few singles. "Here you go. Now, why don't you go wash your face and get out of here?" She sounded calmer than made sense to Jackie.

Dougie continued to pretend he did not hear Pat's voice. Or maybe he really didn't. "You think I look silly, huh?"

Jackie felt the tiny hairs on the back of her neck rise and her father appeared to her as some unfamiliar, snarling demon. He wasn't Daddy anymore. Daddies didn't look that malevolent.

Dougie reached back toward his plate with his left hand, still covered in food remnants from its last dip. In one fell swoop, he scooped nearly all the steaming mashed potatoes off of his plate and flung them into Jackie's unsuspecting face.

Jackie hadn't seen the potatoes coming, so she didn't duck or flinch. They hit her squarely on the bridge of her nose and spread on impact, covering the entirety of her wide-eyed expression. She sat, stunned for a second or two, trying to comprehend what had just happened.

"Dougie!" Pat screamed.

Hot potato scalded Jackie's skin until she reflexively wiped at it with her hands.

As if this pain and humiliation was not enough, Dougie stood, leaned across the table until he was only a few inches from Jackie's face and spoke in the calmest voice he had adopted since entering the kitchen and articulated perfectly:

"Who looks silly now, *asshole*?"

PROM NIGHT

by C.A. Viruet

Clare woke up to the shrieking of her alarm, but didn't open her eyes. She rolled her tongue around in her mouth. The taste of smoke and pennies woke her senses. It was an odd but welcome surprise compared to the usual sour morning breath. She stretched her legs, touching her pale toes to the cold steel bar across the end of her bed. She reached over to her alarm clock, turning it off without opening her eyes. She lay still, listening for the rest of the house; she didn't have to get up until she heard her parents' door open.

Clare heard a wet slapping sound somewhere to her right, on the opposite side of her room. "Bunny, stop licking!" The sound continued. Clare opened her eyes and rolled onto her elbow. "Bunny... Oh my God, Roger! What the hell!"

Her little brother was ejaculating into one hand and squeezing his dick with the other. The dog was lying on the floor next to him.

Clare flew off her bed in a rage, grabbing a wooden baseball bat leaning next to her nightstand.

"Mom! Mom! Clare is going to kill me!" Roger screamed as he half hopped, half stumbled out of his sister's room.

Clare pushed him out with the tip of the baseball bat and into the hallway with enough force to make him fall over. She slammed the door so hard a piece of the frame flew free. Bunny barked from her spot.

"Clare, open this door right now! Why did you hit your brother with a bat?! Clare!"

Clare ignored her mother's yelling from the hallway. She sat on the bed with her head in her hands until Bunny nudged her cold nose in between her arms. "Oh Bun-Bun, what is wrong with these people?" She scratched the dog's head until she heard her mother give up and walk back to her bedroom, possibly to get her father.

Clare slipped out of her room and into the bathroom for a shower, careful to lock the door.

***

"So, what happened this morning, kiddo?" Clare's father asked as she sat down to eat her cereal.

Roger looked into his bowl as if he'd lost something.

"Ask your pervert son who jerks off to his sleeping sister."

There was an uncomfortable silence.

Her father looked at Roger, who was blushing. He shook his head and put down his toast. "Roger, is that true?"

Roger looked up and stared at Clare. "I was sleepwalking. I didn't mean to."

Clare laughed. "Really? He's fourteen – he stopped that years ago, and it's sleep*walking*, not sleep-masturbating. He's a little psycho, and if he comes in my room again he's dead!"

Both parents looked damningly at their daughter, her sloppy bun, jeans, and faded Metallica t-shirt confirming to them that she was in fact just making trouble.

"Clare, threatening to kill someone is not funny. If it weren't your birthday and prom tonight I'd ground you!"

Clare looked at her mother, her face red with anger. "Oh, no! Not prom, the thing I don't give a shit about but you're forcing me to go to! What will I do?!"

"Young lady..."

Clare ignored the incoming scolding of her father, picked up her backpack and slammed the door on her way out of her house.

Clare marched toward the bus stop, where her friends waited in her prom date's Volvo. She slammed the door as she sulked into the back seat. No one asked what happened. All of them had issues at home and knew better than to poke the bear. No one wished her a happy birthday.

***

"Clare Bennet, please report to Mr. Hanson's office. Clare Bennet, please report to Mr. Hanson's office."

The voice boomed from every loudspeaker in the school, penetrating the corners under the stairs where students sold drugs and cigarettes, breaking up fights in the locker room and shaking Clare awake at her desk. She looked around the room. Her entire history class was staring at her.

"Welcome back to the world. Maybe Mr. Hanson wants to talk to you about that serious case of senioritis you've got there."

Clare rolled her eyes at her history teacher, gathered her things and left the room.

She walked slowly down the hall to her guidance counselor's office. She was in no rush. It was already the end of the day and if she dragged out the conversation and the walk to and from the office, she could avoid going back to class. She was still at his door too soon. Through the small pane of glass, she could see the thin, tall man with thick glasses sitting at his desk. His back was straighter than normal, his usual defeated slouch absent.

"Hey, Mr. Hanson, what can I do for you?"

He smiled a too-wide smile. "Have a seat. Let's see if our chat can get you to the end of the day."

Clare smiled back. This was new. Usually the poor guy greeted her with a look of disappointment and then spoke quickly of the usual concern for her future and took her back to class. Today, he looked happier, younger, and jovial.

"I am letting you know that you won't be getting credit for your first period class due to all the times you came in late. The good news is it doesn't matter. It won't affect your upcoming graduation."

"Thanks. I didn't think it would. I could have graduated a semester earlier if you'd let me."

The man sighed, and his shoulders slumped a bit. "I know, and I'm sorry. I should have let you do it. If I'd had any idea of how miserable school made you and you had a plan on what to do after

226

graduating, I would have let you. Speaking of plans, will you be attending prom?"

Clare laughed. "Really? You're not going to tell me that I should be thinking about my future and what I want to major in at the college down the road?"

"No. Believe it or not, I think you'll be fine once you get out of here. I'll actually miss you. You're one of few students that I happen to find particularly intelligent and engaging."

Clare was surprised, and uneasy. The man who usually looked older than he was, defeated, and worried every day was still sitting up straight and smiling. In fact, he was beaming.

"I'd love to stay longer, Mr. Hanson, but I don't want to miss one of my last history classes. I'll see you tonight at prom. I bet you'll be the best chaperone." She flashed him a fake smile and left before he could protest.

***

Dave and Clare walked arm in arm into the gym. The room had become unrecognizable, with decorations covering the basketball hoops on either end. All other traces of the regularly used room disappeared behind paper mache vines, gaudily supporting the evening's theme of "Jungle Adventure". A temple had been constructed of cardboard boxes, a small opening holding all of the night's refreshments. Fake vines hung from the catwalk above the stage behind the home side's hoop, and the DJ stood in front of a giant fake boulder.

Clare was taking it all in when she heard Dave laugh.

"Clare, where did you get your dress?" he asked.

She looked up to see her friend Alison with a girl from the junior class. Clare looked at both girls, preparing to offer compliments on what they were wearing. She looked at herself and then back at the younger girl. They were both wearing the same deep purple gown with spaghetti straps.

Dave laughed again.

"It's not funny, Dave," Alison scolded.

"Are you fucking serious?" Clare said, her anger evident.

The younger girl jumped back. "I had no idea someone would wear the same dress as me. I thought everyone was going with brighter colors and big sleeves." She shrugged, clearly embarrassed.

"Give me your keys," Clare said to Dave.

He handed them over.

"It's not that bad. You look better anyway…" With her date's keys in hand, Clare left without listening to anyone's protests.

***

Clare pulled a worn pair of Jordache jeans and a Judas Priest t-shirt out of her backpack. There was no room to change in the car so she took her dress off next to it. Everyone was inside the gym. No one saw the tall, slender Clare in her black bra and panties for the thirty seconds she was exposed. No one saw how the moon illuminated her pale skin.

After changing, she settled into the passenger seat and lit a cigarette. She decided to just smoke and read the book she had packed instead of dealing with the embarrassment of being a double. On her second cigarette, she saw her little brother, a freshman, skulking around the parking lot. He walked between the cars, randomly stopping and bending down next to them.

Clare got out and snuck up behind him. He was knelt down next to a Camaro, digging a long knife into the sidewall of the tire.

"Wow, you're such a little shit."

"Fuck off, Clare. I won't do your friends' cars."

"Get lost, fuck-face, or I'm calling the cops and then I'm calling home."

Roger looked up at his sister, his face full of contempt. He slid the knife into a sheath hanging off his belt and walked out of the lot and across the soccer field.

Clare watched until he disappeared into the woods before going back to her book.

***

Clare was halfway through *The Tommyknockers* when she looked at the small digital clock in the Volvo. It was nearly eleven-thirty and the prom would be over soon. She glanced out of the windshield and saw a couple stumbling back through the main entrance towards the

228

dance floor. *Everyone is loaded now. I may wind up being the only sober driver,* she thought.

She stretched. Someone in coveralls and a skull mask walked around the front of the building and stood by the main entrance. The masked person pulled a chain from their torso and wrapped it around the steel handles of the large doors.

"Ha. Assholes are going to dance the night away whether they want to or not."

The person walked out to the right side of the building, where a small, enclosed hallway led to the newly built gym annex. Music pumped out into the night from the gymnasium, the twinkle of the disco ball bouncing off the windows. Clare leaned forward and stared at the person in the mask. With their broad shoulders and flat chest, she decided it must be a man. He began to wind chain around the separate gym doors as well.

Clare squinted, trying to make out what the mask was, but couldn't before the man moved on and disappeared around the building. "Headed for the back door too. Man, I am so happy I left that shit show."

She lit another cigarette and got back to reading her book. She didn't look up until she heard a loud boom and a scream.

The book fell to her lap as she noticed bright flames erupting from the roof and windows of the gym. The chained doors shook furiously as people inside tried to escape. The thumping of Duran Duran's "Hungry Like the Wolf" was barely audible over the screams of her classmates.

Clare ran from her safe spot towards the chaos even knowing the doors were chained shut. Looking into the small panes of reinforced glass on each of the double doors, she could see and feel the inferno. Everybody was on fire. The building itself had hardly been touched by the flames, yet each person burned in an invisible pyre, frozen in grotesque pain.

Clare ran from the side door of the gym where her classmates were burning like torches to the main entrance of the school. She saw some of her friends through the wired glass in the top half of the door. Their faces filled with hope when they saw her.

"Open the door! Clare, open it!" They all cried the same thing, creating a terrified chorus.

Clare shook the door. It didn't budge. She looked up to see Dave, her date, and their group of friends. "I can't open it! It's chained shut!"

Their faces fell and they began the same futile and frantic banging and pulling.

Clare took off running to the back of the school. She had skipped class earlier that day, and had shoved a pencil in the way of the locking mechanism of the window to the janitor's office. She had used that window as a means of escape from high school more and more her senior year. She could only hope that the pencil was still in place.

She sighed in relief. The window was open. She climbed through quickly and looked around. The janitor had bolt cutters. She had seen them used to cut locks off lockers when the combinations had been forgotten. Clare looked around the room; it appeared the same as when she'd last seen it. She walked over to a toolbox against one wall and pulled the middle drawer open – it seemed about the right size to hold bolt cutters.

"What the fuck?" Clare whispered in disbelief as she studied the contents of the drawer. All the tools had been replaced with parts. People parts. Clare could not look away from the neatly arranged fingers, eyes and even a jaw, flesh still attached.

She finally tore her gaze away and threw open most of the remaining drawers. Each contained more pieces, neatly arranged. She opened the deepest drawer on the bottom. The torso of the janitor took up the entire space, his blue shirt covered in blood except for his nametag, still proudly declaring 'Bob'. Clare slammed the door shut and headed for the door.

"Guys! Hey, come this way!" Clare yelled as she ran down the hallway. If her friends could meet her halfway, they could all get out of the building through the window that much faster.

There was no response.

Clare had already run down two hallways and should have been at the front entrance by now. There was something else going on. She couldn't put her finger on it, but she felt as if the hallways had become longer as she tried to reach her friends.

She leaned against a wall of lockers, trying to catch her breath. "Guys! Dave!" she called again, but more to the floor than anywhere else.

"They can't hear you."

Clare looked up. The man with coveralls who had chained the doors stood in front of her. His face was painted red. An enlarged human skull covered the top half of it, from his upper jaw to just over the crest of his forehead. The orbital lobes encircled the man's blue eyes and added shadows to the red that covered his skin. His lower jaw and neck were painted black. Blood-red symbols were painted on his neck. Chains still circled his torso like a bandoleer.

Clare could now see that the red was blood; hints of coagulation made it look chunky in places.

"What did you do? Who are you?" Clare cried and shook, not out of fear, but rage.

"I only did what was necessary. I'll let you see your friends again before the ceremony. It's only right. I don't want to stop my bride from saying goodbye." The man smiled at her, his teeth a stark white that seemed to glow from the black and red covering his face.

"Who are you?" Clare yelled again.

The man faded, no longer solid and present – he was transparent, his feet entirely gone. "I am your future husband, and the father of the new gods."

Clare ran towards him, but he vanished by the time her feet stood where his had. She looked around to get her bearings. She had to think of a way to stop whatever was happening. *Think, Clare, think.*

To her left was the door to her science class. She opened it and quickly found the phone on the wall. She lifted the handset and held it to her ear. It still had a dial tone. She jammed her finger on the numbers 9-1-1. The line rang once and an operator answered.

"Nine-one-one, what is your emergency?"

Clare couldn't believe her luck. "I'm at Easton High School and there is a fire and someone is killing people." She choked on the words as she said them. She felt relieved to have reached the outside world.

"It's part of the ritual. The fire is contained, and the vessels burn for your arrival to the ceremony. The killing is necessary. Sacrifices must be made to hasten their arrival." The voice on the other end was calm and matter-of-fact.

"What did you say?" Clare's voice was a whisper of disbelief.

"Don't worry, Mother, everything is going to plan." The line went dead.

Clare slammed the phone down on its hook, once, twice, and a third time hard enough to break the cradle and the plastic beneath it.

What is happening to me?

Clare turned toward the rest of the room.

Maybe I can get out one of the windows...

She ran to the first one and tried to turn the metal crank to open it. It wouldn't budge. She threw a metal stool from one of the lab tables as hard as she could at the row of windows. It bounced off. "Fuck!" Clare screamed as she ran towards the last one in the row. She would try one more, which was the one she sat next to in class. The one she had opened countless times in an attempt to stay awake in the hot room. The metal crank turned easily and it began to open.

"Yes, yes!" Clare threw one leg over the ledge. She lowered her foot until she felt the ground. Tears flowed down her face and made it hard for her to see. Once through, she stood up and looked out into what should have been the green soccer field.

"No! No, no..." Her body shook in heavy sobs. She was back in the hallway.

A hoarse voice filled her head, superseding the sounds of her sobs. "Clare, I'm sorry I wasn't good enough."

Clare looked up to see her date suspended in mid-air. His shoes floated a foot above the ground and his hands dangled at his sides. Behind him stood the man with the red and black face, the half-skull still framing his menacing eyes. This time he held a long knife, its pristine blade shining in the fluorescent hallway lights.

"I wasn't good enough. I was going to get you drunk and high and take advantage of you. It's okay, I'm better now."

The man pushed the blade through the teenager's back and cut in a circular motion. Blood flowed from Dave's mouth. The knife punctured through his chest, and blood gushed from the holes, down his white shirt and over his shiny purple cummerbund. Finally, the body dropped to the floor. The man held a heart in his free hand.

"What do you want? Just leave them alone. Tell me what you want!" Clare screamed at him.

He paid her no attention. Instead, he wiped the knife off on his coveralls, sheathed it, and began to rifle through the chains wrapped around his chest.

"Ahh, here's one." From the length of chain, he pulled a large fishhook. He hooked the bloody heart to his chains and then looked up at Clare.

She stood with her mouth open in shock, unable to speak.

"He thought tonight he would finally get to have you. Lucky for you the universe had other plans." He bent over and dipped a finger in the blood that had dripped from the teen's mouth. With it, he began to retrace the odd symbols on his throat.

Clare averted her gaze and turned on her heels to run.

She headed for the guidance counselor's office, where there was a cabinet full of confiscated items. She was sure to find at least one knife in it, maybe even a pair of brass knuckles. The fighting had been bad this year. The jocks and metalheads seemed to enjoy a daily blood sport. The day before, she knew at least one switchblade had been taken from a junior who had started a fight with a senior football player. Yesterday, she had watched for her own amusement, and joined in with her classmates to boo the faculty that pulled the two apart. Now she hoped that the switchblade would give her a fighting chance.

Clare turned the corner to the next hallway. Her best friend stood there, in front of the door. Clare stopped in her tracks and looked her friend over. Her bright pink dress with the puffy sleeves was free of any sign of blood; her makeup was smudged and her mascara had run down her face. Otherwise, the girl with the auburn hair and green eyes that had lived across the street for Clare's entire life looked fine.

"Meghan! Are you okay?" Clare put her arms around her best friend and squeezed.

Meghan did not say anything and did not move. She felt stiff.

Clare took a step back. "Meghan, answer me – are you okay?"

Meghan suddenly looked at Clare and a wide smile spread across her face.

Clare looked past her friend's manic smile and saw the butcher standing behind her. She jumped towards the door and locked herself in the Guidance Office. Then she peered out of the small glass window in the door.

Meghan continued to smile as the man pulled his knife from its sheath and cut her chest open. Clare put her hands over her mouth to hold in a scream as he pulled Meghan's ribcage apart with his bare hands.

How can I win against someone who is stronger than a regular person?

Meghan was somehow still standing, her smile just as wide as before. The man reached into her chest with one hand.

Meghan laughed. "Oh, that tickles!"

The man smiled as he pulled her heart out. Meghan's body fell to the floor.

Clare was pressing her hand so hard over her mouth her fingernails began to cut into her cheek. She kept watching.

The door is locked. He can't get in, can he?

The man turned to look at her through the window. "I can get in, Clare, but my job is to herd you to our wedding. You have to arrive of your own free will. I can only do so much. Cornering you in a room won't get you there." He tapped the glass with the knife, then wiped the blade on his lips, covering them in fresh, wet blood. "Wisely and slow; they stumble that run fast." He kissed the glass between them, leaving a glistening red print.

Clare backed away slowly. *Did he just quote Romeo and Juliet?*

She sat down on the dirty tile floor, her back against the door. She slowed her breathing. Clare thought back to her sophomore year when she had read *Romeo and Juliet* in class and memorized several passages to perform in front of the class for extra credit. She still remembered her lines and she still remembered her teacher. He had worked at the school until this year, and he still said "Hi" to her when she saw him in the hallway.

It can't be Mr. Sheehan. It can't.

Why can't it be?

The room contained a desk, two chairs in front of it, the 'Hang in there!' poster with the cute cat, a few inspiring quotes stitched onto cloth, and a large locked wooden box. Clare walked over to the box. The lock was small and the hinges attached to the wood were already loose. She pulled and twisted the lock. The old hinge came loose and let go of the wood.

A miniscule feeling of triumph relieved some of the stress for a moment. "Yes!"

Inside the box and on the very top of the pile of contraband was the switchblade. Clare stuffed it in her pocket and pushed aside Playboy magazines, more small knives, and what she could only assume were clothing items deemed too offensive. No better alternatives.

Clare went to the desk. She pulled the drawers out until she reached one that was locked. She kicked the drawer as hard as she could. There had to be something in there, maybe a bigger knife that warranted more secure storage. The front of the drawer caved in, and Clare pulled it out of the desk. Inside was a fully loaded revolver and a box of ammunition.

Is that why Mr. Hanson was so happy? Was he going to go nuts and shoot someone?

Clare shoved bullets in her pockets and put the revolver between her jeans and skin, the cold metal providing comfort. *I'm going to the gym, and I'm ending this now.*

The hallway was empty. Clare could smell smoke and a combination of cooking meat and burning plastic. As she walked, the hallway stayed the same, the building no longer changing. It was as if the building itself knew she intended to go where the dark forces at play wanted her to.

At the end of the hallway, her brother Roger stood holding the door open to the new gym annex. The small knife he had been using to slash tires was lodged in his head, and a hole in his chest allowed Clare to see through him.

"Oh, Roger…" A few tears fell from her eyes. As horrible as he was in life, she had never really meant her threats of violence. She had always hoped he would become a better person.

"Don't worry. I finally did a good thing. I helped with your ceremony." Roger smiled at his sister. For the first time ever, Clare thought he looked peaceful.

"He's waiting for you at the altar. He says, 'Don't worry, love is a smoke raised with the fume of sighs.'"

Another line from Romeo and Juliet. It must be Mr. Sheehan. Clare approached her brother, still holding the door for her even though he should have been dead, his body just another heap of meat littering the floor.

"I'm sorry this happened to you, Roger. Even though you did a lot of ugly things, you're still my baby brother and I love you."

Clare walked through the door and into a church of death.

Her classmates were lined up on either side of her, creating a human tunnel. Each one was stuck in place, their black charred bodies still visible through the flames. The tunnel of human torches burned bright and hot, but the smoke swirled only on the outside.

Clare gripped the handle of the revolver. She cautiously walked forward while gazing toward the end of the human passageway, where her friend Alison stood, smiling wildly. She too had a hole in her chest, but she held her heart as if it was a bouquet.

Behind Alison stood the man, hearts hanging from hooks, also smiling at Clare.

Clare reached the end of the tunnel and walked past her friend. The monster that had tormented her and killed her friends and brother stood next to an altar made of flesh and bone. She recognized Mr. Hanson's head, which had been removed and now sat on his torso, which served as the tabletop. His legs and arms had been twisted and broken so that his hands and feet could stabilize it. His tongue stuck out of his mouth farther than she thought a human tongue could, and on it were two bone-white rings.

"Do you like it? If I hadn't intervened, Mr. Hanson here had planned on shooting up the place tonight. His mind was too weak to handle the torments of teenagers. Despicable."

Clare pulled the revolver out of the waist of her jeans and pointed it at the skull-wearing man. "I want to know what is going on. Now." Her voice was calm and her hands were steady. She did not reveal how terrified she was.

"This is why I chose you. Even now you are still so strong and compassionate, and that is exactly what our children will need as they grow to rule this dimension." He was still smiling, unfazed by the revolver leveled at his chest. His blue eyes shone.

"What the hell are you talking about? I am not marrying you, Mr. Sheehan, and I'm not having anyone's children. Why did you kill everyone? Tell me before I kill you."

"I knew you would figure it out if I quoted Shakespeare. That was such a special time for us. I've been places, Clare, and I've spoken to gods that have been ignored for too long. They chose me to find a mate and bring them back into the flesh. You and I are going to be the most powerful people on this plane. The parents of the gods who will crush humanity. We have to become one and eat the hearts of those you love, and then we will be ready to bring them to this world." He kept smiling. The red symbols on his neck seemed to glow.

A surge of hatred filled her body. She looked at the organs hanging from the hooks on his chains. They were still beating. The room was full of black ash and smoke. It swirled around them but didn't hinder her ability to breathe or speak. The altar of flesh, once her guidance counselor, was covered in similar bloody symbols as those on Mr. Sheehan's neck.

"Young men's love lies not truly in their hearts, but in their eyes. I love you for your soul and your brains, Clare. We can be happy, and you can have more power than you could even dream of." Mr. Sheehan held out his hand.

For a second, Clare thought she might take it. All of her life she had felt powerless; she controlled everything she could but was still treated as if her opinions didn't matter.

"I'm sick to death of people making decisions for me and treating me like I'm only here for their pleasure. I'm not doing anything with you."

The chains glistened with the blood of the pumping hearts. She raised the revolver higher, aiming right below his neck. She didn't want to hit the chain that circled his torso. She wanted to hit *him*.

She pulled the trigger. The first round hit just above the chain and punched a hole the size of a quarter through his gray coveralls.

Mr. Sheehan brought a hand to the wound, his smile breaking. Clare pulled the trigger a second time as he looked down at the damage. This bullet struck between his eyes, sending shards of bone from the half-skull that covered his face.

Mr. Sheehan didn't fall. Instead, he looked up at Clare as the bone mask fell from his face. The red hole in his forehead didn't bleed; instead, it smoked.

"What are you?!" Clare screamed and fired once more. She hit Mr. Sheehan again, this time in the stomach.

His face changed now. Where his insane smile had once framed his too-bright white teeth, his lips were now pursed. "I am no longer just a man. I have been chosen; you have been chosen. We will be together whether you want it or not. In time, you will love me and our children." He stepped toward her. "Clare, you have no idea the children you'll have. It will be wonderful."

Clare forgot that Alison was behind her. She turned to see her friend smile as she bit into her own heart.

She raised the pistol once more and fired a shot into Alison's forehead. She fell down, finally dead.

"Clare, just let this happen. I promise you will have all you ever wanted and more." Mr. Sheehan gripped Clare's left arm.

She turned to look at him. The hole in his head was still smoking. The smell of the blood he had painted his face with nauseated her. His blue eyes still looked human – the only human thing left in the horror that was his face.

"I told you, I'm not doing anything with you." Clare knew she couldn't kill him and she couldn't let him win. It only took a second for her to make up her mind on what to do, how to save herself from the darkness she knew nothing about but was desperate to have her.

She put the revolver in her mouth and pulled the trigger. She didn't hear her depraved Romeo scream as the back of her head exploded. The human torches lost their shape, and the room and Mr. Sheehan were engulfed in a vengeful fireball, burning away all traces of the failed ceremony.

***

Clare woke up to the shrieking of her alarm, but didn't open her eyes. She rolled her tongue around in her mouth. The taste of smoke and pennies woke her senses.

SLUMBER GAMES

by A. Giacomi

Running around her room like a chicken without its head, Amanda realizes she's forgotten to pack the most important thing. Dropping to all fours, she frantically runs her hands underneath her bed several times, seeking the overlooked item. As her hands roam back and forth, she soon realizes it isn't there. Panic strikes her as she continues to pat the ground.

"Where is this stupid thing?" she huffs as she adjusts her side ponytail.

Throwing her arm back under the bed, she searches again, but before she accepts defeat, something grabs her, tugging hard at the denim sleeve of her jacket and nearly dragging her beneath the cramped space.

Shrieking, Amanda rolls out of the jacket and allows it to be sucked under the bed. Staring at the ominous gap in horror, she can't bring herself to take a second look underneath. The room is silent, the bed still. Amanda's mind races. *Perhaps it's the damn cat? Perhaps the jacket snagged on something?*

Feeling a bit stupid, she works up the courage to kneel and check under the bed, but there's nothing there, not even her jacket.

Hmmm, strange.

As she lifts herself off the floor, a face meets hers and shouts "Boo!" so loudly that she collapses backward and hits her head on the dresser adjacent to her bed.

Laughter fills the room as she attempts to pick herself up. Feeling a bit disoriented, she decides to stay put instead and rubs the sore spot on her head. When she regains composure, Amanda makes out someone sitting on her bed, crouched like a rabid dog, holding her jacket in its teeth.

"Mike? What the hell? You scared the shit out of me!" she screams at him while trying to find things to throw.

"Loser. You fall for all my pranks." Mike laughs while sticking his tongue out.

Amanda is glad to discover some of her books lying on the floor behind her dresser. She begins chucking them at Mike, hoping one will meet its mark.

"*Ouch*! Stop that, you psycho! That hurts!" Mike yells while shielding his face.

"Well, then I guess you better give me back my stuff, dipstick! Before Cujo knocks you out!" she shouts as she holds the book up high, ready to launch it.

"What stuff?" Mike asks innocently, shrugging, leaving his face open for impact.

Amanda takes that moment to launch the book at him with such precision that it hits him right between the eyes. His nose starts to bleed instantly, and although she knows she shouldn't laugh, she does.

"Take that, you nerd! That'll teach you to play bogus games with your big sis," she declares with triumph.

"Mandy, what the hell is wrong with you? I didn't take your shit, okay? It was just a joke. Jesus, chill!" he says with a slight gurgle, cupping his hands beneath his nose and racing towards the bathroom.

Great, then where is it? Amanda wonders.

She decides to give the room one last search; she is already running late for Heather's slumber party. Though you wouldn't know it from her preppie exterior, Heather had a lot of love for all things witchy. She had specifically asked Mandy to bring her Ouija board as the night's main event. Everyone would be disappointed if she showed up without it.

Shoving the rest of her sleepover essentials into her neon pink duffle bag, she gives her Johnny Depp poster a smooch before leaving the room and heading downstairs.

Passing through the kitchen, Amanda catches her mother in the room shoving something into a large garbage bag. She recognizes her board immediately.

"Stop!" she shouts, but her mother ignores her request, turning away from her and tying the bag before Amanda can reach her.

"Mom! What the heck? I need that for tonight."

"I asked you to get rid of it, Amanda. You know this sort of stuff creeps me out. I don't want you bringing it over to people's homes and having them think you're some weirdo," she says with a sigh of disapproval.

"Oh, come on! You don't actually believe any of that garbage, do you? It's just for fun, Mom. Relax!" She chuckles, even though the board freaks her out too.

With her mother still unwilling to let go, Amanda lunges at the bag and clutches it, trying to pry it from her hesitant hands.

"Please, Mandy, leave it here. Let me throw it away," her mother pleads, losing her grip on the bag.

But Amanda shakes her head and finally rips the bag free. She races towards the door, making a swift getaway.

"Please, Mandy," her mother beckons after her once more. Her pleas are silenced when Amanda leaves, slamming the door in her face.

Feeling slightly guilty, Amanda races towards Heather's house, which is only two blocks away. She knows she hasn't been the best daughter as of late. She often blamed the short fuse that came along with her personality on her teenage hormones, but what it really came down to was that she couldn't take another lecture.

Being in the house felt like she was holding her breath the entire time and leaving felt as if she was finally able to fully inhale.

Her parents had constantly been on her case about grades, her future, and the colleges she should apply to, as well as the volunteer hours she should be doing to assure her entrance to them. Amanda had finally reached a breaking point – the pressure was too much, and all she wanted was to enjoy her final year of high school.

Amanda soon finds herself at Heather's door and feels her stomach turning. She has been to Heather's house over a dozen times but never has she felt so strange about entering her home. Perhaps it has something to do with the guilt her mother had placed on her shoulders moments earlier. But Amanda ignores the feeling in the pit of her stomach and refuses to give in to the guilt her mother consistently uses to manipulate her.

Not tonight, she thinks. *Tonight is about having fun.*

Gathering her confidence, Amanda knocks on the door and Heather soon throws it open to greet her.

"Mandy! Baby doll! Welcome to my *maison!*" Heather says while twirling a single blonde curl around her finger.

There was no question that Heather was the most popular girl in school. All the boys flocked to her and all the girls envied her. Next to her, Amanda felt a tad inadequate, but the mere fact that Heather spoke to her reassured Amanda that she was worthy of the cool kids at school, and hopefully even the attention of one Tommy Dean. Even his name reeked of hotness, and Amanda, like many others, was not immune to his charms.

Before heading down to the basement to join the others for the sleepover, Heather pulls Amanda aside and asks, "Did you bring it?"

Amanda opens the garbage bag to reveal the Ouija Board and an excited yet sinister grin spreads across Heather's face.

"*Excellent!* This is totally going to be the best night ever!" Heather squeals with delight.

She takes Amanda's hand and attempts to guide her downstairs, but Amanda is frozen with fear.

"What is it, babe?" Heather asks, her brow furrowed with confusion.

"Is...is Tommy down there?"

"Yeah, you know I invited boys. Why? You like him?" Heather asks with a sly grin.

"Dammit, Heather, you know I do. How do I look?"

"Listen, you look rad, and if he doesn't want to boink you by the end of the night, then he's a major butthead and you don't want one of those."

Amanda laughs. "Okay, fine. I'm ready," she says, taking a deep breath as they descend.

At the bottom of the stairs, Amanda is surprised to find many new faces; Heather's basement resembles something more like a bar than a slumber party. Everyone stops to look at her, but only momentarily – they are soon back to their banter and beer drinking, leaving Amanda feeling more awkward by the moment. She attempts to head upstairs, but Heather pulls her back, forcing her through the crowded basement towards the only thing Amanda has been looking forward to.

The crowd slows as her heart quickens at the sight of him. Amanda is face to face with the one and only Tommy Dean. She is able to, at the very least, introduce herself, but other than that, Amanda is very grateful that Heather is doing all the talking. Her hands tremble at the sight of his bedroom eyes and perfect pout. She studies his face and to her surprise, he stares back, unrelentingly. It is more than Amanda can take. She excuses herself as her heart feels like it is about to explode.

Hiding out in the bathroom, Amanda splashes some water on her face to help her cool down.

"What the hell are you doing? You're such a dweeb. Get it together!" she says to herself in the mirror, trying to reclaim some composure.

Her short pep talk is interrupted by someone barging in.

"Holy shit! Don't you knock?" she spits out in a rage before realizing who it is.

"Sorry, it's just me. Are you okay? You looked a bit sick back there… Too much to drink? I can hold your hair back," Tommy says with a playful smile.

"Sorry, you scared me... I'm all right, just not great at big groups. Heather told me it was a small get-together, but it looks more like the whole school is here," Amanda replies with a shrug.

Tommy gets uncomfortably close to Amanda's face, so much so that Amanda forgets to breathe and begins to feel faint.

"I don't like parties much either, but I think I see something I like," he says in a seductive whisper.

Tommy leans in for a kiss, which makes Amanda's knees buckle. As his kisses grow deeper, he slides his hands up her thighs, nearly all the way under her skirt. It takes everything Amanda has not to jump him right then and there, and luckily enough, Heather barges in next, saving her the embarrassment of trying to weasel out of an uncomfortable situation. She likes Tommy, but she isn't sure if he likes her or just girls in general.

"It's Ouija time, you sexy skanks! Get out here!" Heather yells without an ounce of shame. "Gather 'round, everyone. It's time for some real entertainment."

Most of the party flocks to where Heather has set up the board to play but a few of the party-goers have other plans. Heather clears her throat to get their attention, and when that doesn't work, she storms over to the trio of nerds playing Nintendo, oblivious to her request. Rather than simply tapping them on the shoulder and asking them to join the others, Heather finds her father's baseball bat and smashes the Nintendo console to pieces, ending their game immediately. She grins when the desired result is achieved.

Amanda likewise grins. Heather has always been a fan of the dramatic.

"Now, geek-a-zoids. Glad to finally have your attention. God, you can be so rude." And with that, she turns away from them. "Come over here, Mandy," Heather says, using the bat to point to the board at the centre of the room. "See, beautiful Mandy here has brought us a mystical Ouija Board and I thought it might be fun to chat with some ghosts tonight. That is…unless you're too chicken shit."

Someone in the crowd clucks mockingly, increasing Heather's annoyance.

"Let's take this a bit seriously, shall we? Dim the lights, get the candles," she says signalling to two girls Amanda has never seen before.

Heather calls Amanda next and asks her to sit across from her at the Ouija board.

Amanda is hesitant, but Heather insists, and with all eyes on her, Amanda finds it difficult to decline, especially since she is the one who brought the board in the first place. Sitting across from the over-excited Heather, Amanda's palms begin to sweat. The atmosphere is chilling, disturbing even, and she can't help but feel that something is wrong with this whole thing. Convincing herself that her mother is just getting into her head, Amanda begins the task of gathering questions to ask the spirits.

"Heather and I will work the board, but we will need some good questions to get started, and someone to write the letters down so we can translate the answers."

"Good idea!" Heather utters as she goes off to fetch a pen and paper, handing it to the trio of nerds who had pissed her off. "Here, dweebs, make it up to me," she says as she shoves the pen at one of them.

Heather and Amanda place their hands on the planchette and a booming voice shouts out their first question from the dark, candlelit room.

"Are you a dude or a chick?"

Heather rolls her eyes. "Seriously? That's your best question? Who said that, anyway?" But no one steps up to reveal themselves. "Fine... Dude or chick. What say you, board?"

The girls concentrate as the planchette glides towards the letter *F*.

"F... Oh – female! Cool. Okay, next question," Amanda says, asking the audience for more information to work with. Her hands shake with curious energy.

"Show us your tits!" another male voice shouts from the darkness.

Both Heather and Amanda roll their eyes.

"I don't think the spirits will appreciate your lack of respect," Heather says in a sinister voice. It isn't like her to lose the pep in her tone, but the room can tell she takes this game seriously.

Amanda feels the planchette moving under her fingertips. It moves violently from side to side before landing on the word '*No*.'

"Are you moving it?" she whispers to Heather, who shakes her head.

"You guys totally insulted her. See? She has no interest in your stupid games. No ghost tits for you." Heather laughs.

"Not the ghost's tits, *your* tits. Show us *your* tits!" the male voice shouts from the back of the room once more.

Heather stands up. "All right, enough now. Which one of you dickweeds said that? Show yourself!" she shouts, anger showing in her cheeks.

No one comes forward.

"Really? Now you shut up? Now, when I call you out on your bullshit? Fine, hide in the dark, little boy, but do me a favour and shut the hell up permanently."

As soon as Heather utters her venom, the candles in the room blow out, leaving them in darkness. Screams echo through the room, and Amanda feels something clutch her arm. With fear taking hold of her, she shoves it away violently, and crawls away feeling for the nearest wall for safety. Pressing her back against it, Amanda listens as the shrill screams turn silent. She knows that it is more than just fear of the dark – something terrible is silencing the crowd. Afraid to utter a word, Amanda waits until no further sounds are heard. After taking a deep breath, she continues crawling, hoping to discover the stairs and leave the basement. She has never wanted to return home so badly.

Something squishes underneath one of her hands and she worries the sound has given her position away. She crawls frantically until she realizes she is no longer crawling on dry carpet. The entire surface beneath her is warm and moist. Pulling one hand up, she feels something dripping from her fingers. Bringing them up to her nose, she smells something metallic. Amanda refuses to guess what it is; instead, she forces herself to push thoughts away and focus on finding a way out.

Stumbling over something, Amanda runs her hand over it. She finds a foot, a leg, and continues feeling upward. She knows it is a body as soon as she touches a face and forgets about remaining silent entirely. Rising to her feet, Amanda screams.

A flashlight turns on, revealing someone in a mime mask. The masked man moves towards her with a bloodied blade raised and ready. Amanda wants to run, but the flashlight reveals more than just a masked creep. Bodies are strewn about the floor, some with their throats slashed, others with puncture wounds to the chest, eyes still open in horror. The entire carpet is dyed red.

Frozen in fear, she continues to scream. With the mime mask mere inches from her face, the flashlight goes out. Amanda is braced for impact, but the knife doesn't strike. Instead, someone pulls her sideways, dragging her in another direction.

Racing up the stairs and slamming the door behind them, she sees that it's none other than Tommy Dean. He presses his finger to her lips, pleading for her silence. They both take quick breaths before coming up with a plan to contain the killer. Tommy grabs one end of a nearby sofa and Amanda helps him drag it over to the basement door, barricading it for the time being. As soon as the sofa is in place, a banging is heard at the door, causing them to jump. The thumping becomes more desperate, and soon pleas for help come from the other side.

"Oh god! It's Heather!" Amanda cries, already attempting to move the sofa.

But Tommy takes her hand and shakes his head. "Don't do it, Mandy – the killer is down there. You let her in, you let him in. Let's just call the cops and get out of here."

"Are you serious? You want to leave her down there? No! Absolutely not!"

Tommy attempts to stop her, but Amanda pushes the couch towards him, forcing him to fall backwards. Heather explodes through the door in terror and closes it behind her. She and Amanda return the couch to its position with haste.

"Okay, let's go," Tommy says, trying to recover some pride.

"I'm not going anywhere with him," Heather snarls. "He was going to leave me down there to die! You're a waste of skin, Tommy. I bet it's one of your grody friends who did this. Who was that guy shouting out all the questions, huh? Most of the invites were yours!"

"Hey, take a chill pill! I had nothing to do with this!"

"Then why didn't you want to save me?" Heather asks as she pulls a knife from her pocket.

Amanda looks from Heather to Tommy, unsure of what to do next. Tommy had saved her life, but it was true that he had been hesitant to save Heather's. *Why would he save one only to let another die? Something doesn't add up,* she thinks.

Tommy pulls on Amanda's hand. "Come with me. Trust me, Mandy. Something is wrong with this girl," he says as he stares Heather up and down with disgust.

Amanda, although secretly loving the contact, pulls her hand out of his.

"Amanda, listen to me. She was in the basement. You know who else was in the basement? That psycho killer with the mime mask. Don't you find it a bit too much of a coincidence that she happens to pop up the stairs right after we did? Who else could the killer be?" he asks, pleading with his eyes and taking Amanda's hands in his, fondling them in an almost romantic manner.

Shaking her head as if to snap out of it, Amanda refuses to let her hormones rule her common sense. She steps away and looks to Heather. "Yes, how are you still alive?"

"Are you serious right now?" Heather lashes out. "I nearly died down there. That crazy creep was chasing me with a knife and we're still standing here debating this? Mandy, it's obviously Tommy! Come on!"

"But...but he saved my life," Amanda mutters.

"Did he? Did he really? Speaking of convenient, didn't the lights go off conveniently just before he ran you upstairs? How do you know he didn't just take off his mask and decide to play the good guy? He needs someone alive for an alibi. You'll confess to seeing some guy in a mask, and that mister super-stud hero over here saved you...and then he gets away scot-free. What the hell, Amanda? I thought you were smarter than that...or do you only think with your cooch?"

Amanda is breathless, knowing that Heather could very well be right. Her head isn't clear around Tommy, and perhaps he is counting on that. She backs away from him and finds a spot beside Heather.

"I'm sorry, Tommy, she's right. Where did the mime go after that? How did you manage to even see me or get so close so quickly?"

Tommy stares at her in disbelief. "I save your life and this is what I get? Fine, you want the truth? I was hiding amongst the bodies. Playing dead like a coward…and then I see this light across the room and see your frightened face and all I can think about is, 'Holy shit, I better get over there and help her before this psycho in a mask ends her like all the others.' So I bolt towards you and I think it caught the killer off guard. That's all. I'm not the killer; I'm not that guy, Mandy," he pleads.

"He's lying," Heather shouts. "He killed everyone and he has to pay!"

Before Amanda can register what is going on, Heather flies at him with her knife, knocking him down to the ground and stabbing him multiple times. Amanda screams for her to stop as new holes are carved into him, causing blood to spurt and splatter across Heather's face and her parents' living room.

Tommy chokes on his own blood until he becomes still. The life leaves his eyes. Amanda is still screaming until Heather, bloodied and triumphant, slaps her in the face.

"Stop it! He was dangerous and now he's dead. We're safe."

Amanda wants to believe her, but the way Heather had killed him with such ease makes her think twice. She races towards Heather's bedroom and locks the door behind her. Trying to catch her breath and block out images of Tommy's death, she looks around the room for anything weapon-like. She soon finds the baseball bat that Heather had used to smash the Nintendo console.

How did it get up here if no one had ever left the basement? she thinks.

Grabbing it, she readies herself for battle.

"Mandy, please, I did the right thing. That guy – he was no good for you, he was lame. Do you know he cheated on me? Spread rumours that I had an STD? What a total dick! So you see, I met someone else, someone better - someone with brains."

Amanda begins to piece the puzzle together: tonight had been about revenge. That's why so many people had attended, and so many of Tommy's friends had been invited. Heather had wanted to squash the rumours before they could get any further.

Heather taps on the door and whispers eerily, "Hey, my new boyfriend thinks you're kinda hot. He was considering a three-way if you're interested. Somehow he knew you'd say yes. I mean, you are in my bedroom, after all. That must mean you're a bit curious…wouldn't you say?"

Amanda's heart leaps as her gaze bolts across the room and lands on the closet door that has been left slightly ajar.

He's in there, isn't he? Amanda panics.

Holding the bat high into the air, she prepares herself. The door slowly opens, and a mime mask peeks out first, teasingly, before altogether exiting the closet and running at her with a knife. Amanda takes the butt end of the bat and plunges it into his gut, winding him immediately.

"Not so tough now, are you?" she screams at him before bringing the bat down on his head over and over again. Not even the blood spattering towards her face stops her from turning his head into a bloody paste.

A switch inside Amanda's head has flipped and her rage grows within her like a fire. Throwing the door open, she hits Heather right between the eyes, breaking her nose before she can even think about attacking her with her knife.

"You bitch! You're a psycho bitch, you know that? And now it's game over!"

Heather slides the knife towards Amanda, kneeling and holding her hands up above her head, pleading for Amanda to spare her.

"I'm sorry, Mandy. I just…I just lost my head. I was so angry and you know me – I'm a bit extreme when I get mad, especially with boys. I can't help myself. Blame Tommy."

Her words only infuriate Amanda further, and as she looks from her bat to the knife, she realizes that a quick death would be too good for her. Picking up the knife at her feet, she charges Heather, who attempts to crawl away. Amanda plunges the knife into her spine over and over again, allowing her to feel every wound Tommy had felt.

Heather soon twitches beneath Amanda, gurgling sounds replacing her breaths. Throwing the blade to the ground, Amanda has one last thing to do. She heads back into the basement, through the piles of corpses, and retrieves her Ouija Board, which is covered in blood. She wipes it clean with the sleeve of her jacket and takes it with her as she ascends the stairs and leaves the house.

Still dripping with fresh blood, Amanda walks home with her Ouija Board tucked safely under her arm. She isn't one for the spirit world tonight. Instead, she is awarded the honour of The Final Girl, and she is grateful to continue breathing.

SCREAM CAMPERS, I KNOW WHAT YOU DREAMED LAST BLOODY HALLOWEEN

by Kasey Hill

"The best eighties slasher, hands down, is *Halloween*," Eric says, tilting his beer to his mouth and taking a swig.

"You're crazy. Krueger was the best. Honestly, a man that kills you in your sleep? You never want to go to sleep! You either die sleeping or from lack thereof," Sean retorts, knocking the red solo cup from Eric's hand.

"You just think that because that's your choice of costume. Michael Myers will always be the best. You may know the face behind the mask, but you will never know the man behind the mask. He was genius. A silent Ted Bundy!" Eric swoons.

"You think you're top shit because your girlfriend is named after Jamie Lee Curtis' character. Fuck you, bro. You're no better than anyone here," Sean says, glaring at Eric.

The boys square off until the girls step in between them.

"Okay, you two. Knock it off!" Laurie says. "My parents will kill me if we get beer stains on their fur rug!"

"All of us can't be blessed with parents like yours," Sydney chides as she walks past Laurie and flops down on the couch.

"What's that supposed to mean?" Eric asks

"Every Halloween, Laurie's parents give her the keys to their cabin on the lake for her to throw a small party with her friends.

Have you ever been invited?" Sydney asks, raising her eyebrow and challenging Eric.

"Fuck you, bitch," Eric howls, stepping closer to her.

"Hey!" Chris barks. "Back off!"

"Whatever," Eric huffs as he tugs his Michael Myers mask over his face. "This is supposed to be a Halloween party. Mask it up, *bitches!*" He picks up another beer and chugs it through the mouth hole in his mask.

The guys amp up the whooping and hollering as they all slide their masks on. They had coordinated their costumes this year ingeniously. They had each chosen an '80s slasher film where one of the victims or main characters shared the same name as their girlfriend. Eric and Laurie are, of course, sporting *Halloween* gear. Eric's dad is an electrician and the blue jumpsuit was easy to obtain. Laurie mimicked Jamie Lee Curtis' outfit down to the hairstyle. Sean and Nancy are decked out in *A Nightmare on Elm Street* costumes. Sean had been burned in a small fire when he was a child, so the scars on his arms replicate the Freddy costume nicely. Nancy decided to go with a sweat pants outfit, dressing casually. Alice and Jason are coincidentally named after their same slasher flick get-up characters from *Friday the 13th.* Jason's mask hides the strawberry birthmark on his face. Alice decided to wear camping gear as her costume. Jesse and Sarah are dressed as Tom Hannigan, the psycho miner, mirroring masks from *My Bloody Valentine.* Jesse had found some old mining clothes at Goodwill for both him and Sarah. However, he had rolled the sleeves up so he could still show off his brand new tattoo.

"Sarah, it's only the guys wearing masks," Alice jokes.

"I know. But this mask is cool as fuck!"

Everyone laughs as Chris steps into the room wearing the infamous *Scream* outfit.

"Dude, that's not an eighties slasher. That's from the nineties!" Jessica ribs.

"It was all the damned store had left. Bite me," Chris seethes.

Jason turns the volume up on the radio system, and the party officially starts. To the average person, this is a night that all teenagers, both in high school and college, get drunk, party, and pass out until 5 pm the next day. That's what these ten college students thought as well.

Boom! Thump! Boom! Thump! The bass on the stereo hits hard and rattles the windows. *Boom! Thump!*

SCREAM!

They stop the music.

"What the hell was that?" Laurie asks. "All right, headcount." She looks around at the faces in the room, counting everyone. "Two short…wait…where are Jason and Alice?"

"Alice mentioned they were going for a dip, if you know what I mean," Nancy replies, winking.

Laurie tugs Eric behind her and makes her way to the back of the cabin. The sliding glass door leads onto the patio where the in-ground pool is. She stands at the window peering out into the dark. She reaches for the porch light switch, but hesitates.

"Come on, Laurie," Eric whispers. "I'm sure they're fine!"

She looks behind her and sees everyone waiting on her. She takes a deep breath and hits the switch. A deafening scream fills the cabin as the four girls screech in unison at the sight on the deck. Blood is smeared all over the outer glass and handprints glide their way down. Through the smudges, they can see entrails and blood leading from the door to the pool. The water is not the usual blue tint it has when lit up at night, but a deep shade of red. Their gazes come to rest on the two bodies bobbing on the surface like a sick game of ducking apples.

Jesse tears the door open and runs outside with Sean on his heels. They pull the bodies from the water; both are naked…cold…mutilated.

"They're gutted like fish!" Sean screams, dropping Jason's body to the deck floor.

"Get the fuck back in here before you get killed, dumbasses!" Nancy shouts.

The guys back away from the bodies, eyeing their surroundings, watching for any movement. They make it to the door and run in, the others slamming it shut and locking it.

"We need to call the police!" Sydney cries.

"And tell them what? Our friends were gutted like fish but we don't have a clue who did it? Come on, are you stupid? We would all go down for murder," Sarah says.

"If we don't call them and they are reported missing, we go down for it too, you moron! Their parents know they were here. Alice fucking called her mom while sitting on the couch—I talked to her too!" Sydney screams at Sarah.

"Who would do this?" Laurie asks, rocking in her seat.

"Well, I'm sure whoever did it has gone by now. Why would they stick around? We know about them," Sarah says.

"You're such a dumb twat!" Sydney yells. "You're at an eighties-themed Halloween slasher party and don't know the rules of the movies."

"Coming from the one whose boyfriend dressed as a nineties slasher!"

"You fucking bitch," Sydney screams, running at Sarah.

Chris catches her mid-stride and stops her. "You two need to stop! We need to stick together. Who knows what that crazy person is thinking or even listening to right now. Hell, for all we know, they've found a way in."

"Don't fucking say that!" Laurie screams, crying violently.

"We need to do a perimeter check," Sean says.

"*No!* You are not leaving me to get brutally murdered while you dillydally with the boys outside!" Nancy yells. "We'll split into groups and do checks. Start in the basement and go from there. You can all decide where you want to start," she says, grabbing Sean's arm.

"You two are the most retarded people I have ever met in my life! You don't ever split up. Jeez, don't you watch the shit you argued about earlier?" Sydney asks, shaking her head in disbelief.

"We were hoping the killer would kill you pair first," Nancy replies dryly.

"Fuck you, skank!" Sydney says, swinging her fist.

Once more, Chris grabs and picks her up, and then sets her on the couch. "We'll wait here until you dumb fucks return," he replies, plopping down beside her.

"I agree," Sarah says, sitting on the adjacent couch. "We're staying as well."

"Pussies," Eric replies. "Come on, Laurie - we'll check the attic and upstairs."

"No, no, no, no. I don't want to go!"

"Move your ass!" Eric says, jerking her up.

The two couples walk through the house and go their respective ways while the remaining two stay seated.

"Sorry for being a bitch earlier," Sarah says.

"No worries," Sydney replies, sitting back in her seat.

"Who...who do you think killed them?" Sarah asks through tears.

"I have no fucking clue."

"Well, there is the one..." Chris says, trailing off.

"One what? *What?!*" Jesse asks.

"Over the summer, we got a note. Like in the movie *I Know What You Did Last Summer*. It said, 'I Know What You Did Last Halloween.' There was a smear of blood before 'Halloween.' We showed it to Laurie, who blew it off."

"Well, what happened last Halloween?" Sarah asks.

"We've partied with Laurie here at the cabin for years. That's what Sydney's snide comment to Eric meant earlier. We've known Laurie since grade school and he tries to make her push us aside," Chris replies. "Last Halloween we had a bumping party. There were tons of students from school. Everyone was drinking, getting smashed, high—you name it, they were doing it.

"There was this girl—Amelia. She was a recent transfer student and was really quiet. We were in a couple of classes together and she started to tutor me. She developed this insane notion that we were dating. She came to the party looking for me and I was there with Sydney. We've dated for ages. A couple of the football players knew her weird obsession with me and rallied around her. They poured beer over her head and humiliated her in front of the entire school. They then threw her in the pool. She screamed out for help because she couldn't swim, but we all stood by and watched her drown.

"When the ambulance arrived, she wasn't in the pool. No one had touched her. We told them we found her body floating and had thought she had gotten drunk and fallen in without anyone knowing. There was an investigation into her disappearance—her foster parents were adamant about finding her. She was never found, alive or dead."

"So, you think this chick is back for revenge?" Jesse asks. "I don't buy it."

Sarah screams as she scrolls through her phone.

"What the fuck are you screaming about?" Sydney asks.

Sarah holds her phone up for them to see. "Do you see that?" she squeals.

When they had first arrived, they had taken pictures together. Behind them in the group pictures stands a person in a fisherman's slicks and boots, their face hidden beneath a rain hat. The person holds a hook in their right hand.

"Oh, shit. Oh, shit. Oh, shit," Jesse repeats.

"How long has everybody been gone?" Sydney asks, looking at her watch.

"It's been at least an hour or two," Jesse replies.

"Well, let's all go together and look for them. Start in the basement?" Chris asks.

Jesse nods.

They each take the hand of their girlfriend and lead them through the house to the door that goes down to the basement. Chris grabs the doorknob and slowly turns it, letting it creep open on its own. The cellar is pitch black. He reaches for the string above the steps to turn on the light when Sydney stops him.

"Why would they walk into a dark basement?" she asks.

Chris pulls the chain but nothing happens. He pulls it a few more times to no avail. "Anyone got a flashlight?"

"I think there's one in the kitchen," Sarah replies.

They make their way there and rummage through the drawers and cabinets. Jesse makes a cheerful announcement, claiming his find of the flashlight. They go back to the basement door and find it closed.

"I don't like this!" Sydney whispers.

"We need to see if they're down there or have gone outside," Chris replies.

They ease down the steps one at a time, with a slow and cautious pace. They reach the bottom and peer around the steps. They shine the light from left to right, trying to see if they can make anything out other than the old, covered furniture.

"I can't see if they're down here or not. We need to check the entire basement," Chris whispers.

He moves from the bottom step and the others follow suit. They don't even make it halfway around the corner when Sarah screams hysterically. The bodies of Nancy and Sean are sprawled out on an old waterbed, shooting blood-tinged water from the puncture holes left in it. They walk closer to the bodies and find them to be shredded.

"It looks like Freddy Krueger's been at them," Jesse says.

"Jason and Alice were killed at the pool. Nancy and Sean on the waterbed with marks like Krueger. The killer is choosing how to kill everyone based on the costumes chosen for the party," Chris remarks.

"We need to get out of here and call the cops! We have proof on my phone that there was someone else here!" Sarah exclaims.

"We need to find Laurie and Eric first. No way we're leaving without them," Chris replies. "Come on. Let's go," he says, running upstairs and slamming the door behind them.

They make their way to the stairs that lead to the second floor.

"They said they were checking the attic out first, right?" Sydney asks.

"Yeah," Chris replies.

They run to the drop-down ladder and find it's still pulled out. Chris cautiously climbs up and looks around the loft with his flashlight. The beam lands on Laurie and Eric lying naked in a pool of blood. Laurie has stab wounds everywhere and it looks as if Eric's skull has been crushed. Chris rushes down the steps and leans against the wall, heaving and vomiting.

"They're dead, aren't they?" Sarah asks.

"The killer left the basement when we went to search for the flashlight. We gave him the opportunity to kill Laurie," Sydney murmurs.

"Hey, stay with me!" Chris says, grabbing her face after wiping his off.

"How were they killed?" Jesse asks.

"Stabbed."

"We need to get to the cars and get out of here," Sarah whispers.

The four run down the stairs to the front door and pull it open to find the killer dumping a can of gasoline onto the vehicles.

"Hey, asshole!" Jesse yells.

The person in the fisherman slicks turns towards Jesse, strikes a match, and sets one of the cars ablaze. The fire leaps from car to car. They are trapped, unless they walk.

Chris and Sydney turn and run back into the cabin, screaming for Jesse and Sarah to follow. They watch as the two turn to run, but both hit the ground with axes sticking out of their backs. The killer takes a dramatic bow and walks toward the house. Chris and Sydney slam and lock the door, then back away from it, waiting for the pounding to begin.

Silence.

"The sliding glass door!" Sydney yells.

They run to the kitchen and check to make sure the door is locked. It is.

"How the fuck did he get in last time?" Sydney asks.

Chris is silent for a moment. "The basement. It has a door to the side of the house where the car park is."

They run to barricade the basement door, but it's already ajar.

"Didn't we shut it when we came through?" Sydney whispers, in tears.

"I can't remember."

They tiptoe to the basement door and peer down the empty steps. They slam the door shut and Sydney holds it while Chris pushes a table in front of it. They both sit on it to gather their thoughts.

"What are we going to do? There's no cell reception. We can't drive for help and Laurie's mom took the phone out the year the guys called all of those porno lines," Sydney says.

"We could try to make a run for it. The bluff isn't even a mile away and they have an emergency phone there."

"Do you think we can make it? I mean, he threw two axes at once and nailed Jesse and Sarah."

"It would have to be a stabbing for us if he follows his own game. Ghostface's weapon was a knife. But the difference between our movie and his is that Sydney lived in the end. Somewhere along those franchises, the girl was killed. Aside from Sarah…I just don't get that one…"

"All right, let's make a run for it!"

They jump up and make their way to the front door. They peer through the peephole and see nothing but the blazing cars.

Chris opens the door and finds the coast is clear. He grabs Sydney's hand. "Whatever you do, don't let go."

She nods and they run. He has always been faster than her, so in reality, he is nearly dragging her behind him. They run through the trees, straying from the trail, following the riverbank uphill. By the time they reach the bluff's clearing, they are panting and scraped up from branches and weeds that had lashed out at them as they ran.

They catch their breath for a moment and then continue up to the light pole with the emergency phone on it. They catch a shadow of someone already standing there. Relief washes over them.

"Hey! We need help!" Chris screams.

They pick up their pace and reach the pole faster. As soon as they get within ten feet of it, the person, dressed in the fisherman's slicks, steps into the light. And this time, they can see the face hidden beneath the hat.

"Amelia! You're alive! You're the killer?!" Chris gasps.

Amelia giggles. "Oh, Chris. If you had only told everyone the truth, none of this would have ever happened. There's a lot of innocent blood on your hands. All you had to do was admit to having a relationship with me. But, *aww*, you didn't want Sydney finding out. So you told everyone I was obsessed with you. I nearly died that night. But I had a friend there with me who saved me. Too bad I had to kill her. I didn't want Sarah giving me away once she saw Jesse dead. See, Sarah knew my plot behind tonight. I just didn't expect the bitch to turn into a big baby whiner. She thought I was just going to scare you all. So, a lesson had to be learned on her part."

Amelia looks from Chris to Sydney and says, "In truth, Sydney, you really are innocent. It was all his fault and we both got played. He told me he was breaking up with you for me; he told everyone I was psycho. I had a case of this once before, and the guy ended up dead. That's why I had to transfer." Amelia gazes at Chris. "Tell her the truth. Tell her how you kissed me, how we went out for dinner on multiple occasions, and how we went on dates to the movies. *Tell* her!" she screams, pointing a knife at him.

Chris looks over at Sydney, who is shaking her head in disbelief. "No, no, no, it's not true," he defends.

"I can't believe you! I think Amelia is telling the truth. I called one night and your mom said you took her out to dinner for helping you with tutoring. When I asked the next day, you said it wasn't exactly that and changed the subject. I am an idiot!"

"Now you have to pay, Chris," Amelia says, stepping closer to him.

"Yes, you do!" Sydney says, joining Amelia.

Chris looks at them, confused. "What are you doing, Sydney?"

"Getting rid of a problem that should have been dealt with years ago," she replies, smiling.

They back Chris up against the railing of the cliff. "Sydney, please—I love you, and *only* you!"

Amelia steps closer and Sydney gets in behind her, slipping something from the back of her pants. As Amelia raises her knife, Sydney jabs a blade into her side.

"Cheater or not, no one deserves to die like this. All those people weren't at that party!" Sydney says, stabbing her again, driving the blade deeper.

Chris moves as Amelia leans up against the railing, blood trickling from her mouth.

"Your one mistake, Amelia," Sydney huffs as she drives the blade into her again, "is that this isn't the eighties anymore. Movies play by different rules now."

Sydney and Chris pick her up and toss her over the railing. They walk over to the emergency phone and place the call, then sit and wait for the police to show up. When they arrive, they give their statement and direct them to the cabin where all the bodies are. It takes a couple of hours for the cops to sift through all the mess. Chris and Sydney remain outside at the cruisers until a cop finally tells them they can return to their dorm. They give them their information to be contacted and walk away from the cabin. They realize that Laurie's car hadn't caught on fire and decide to drive it back to the dorms.

Chris and Sydney drive back to town quietly, taking the turns heading to the university.

"Everything will be okay. She's gone," Chris says, kissing Sydney's hand.

"We are going to have a talk later on this week, Chris. Not tonight—I'm too tired—but we are really having a talk."

As Sydney looks out the window, a loud groan escapes her and turns into a gasp. Chris glances over and sees blood trailing from her mouth and pooling on her stomach.

Amelia pops up in the backseat and grabs Chris by the throat, holding a switchblade to his jugular. "Sydney was so naïve. Just like you, Chris. You actually thought I was dead and you were going to get away with everything. Your mistake!" she says, slicing into his skin. "I chose a nineties killer to match you, my darling. Remember, they always come back for one last scare."

She digs the blade deeper into his neck as he struggles to breathe through the blood filling his lungs. She reaches forward, braces herself by wrapping a seatbelt around her arm, and flips the gearshift into park. Both Chris and Sydney fly through the windshield.

Although her arm is broken, she'll live. She climbs into the front seat and glances into the rearview mirror, smiling as she puts the car back into drive.

BLOODBATH

by Briana Robertson

The Poplars had been tormenting Bobby Stroud since fourth grade. Of course, they hadn't called themselves the Poplars at the time; the group title hadn't emerged until sophomore year, when the members inevitably began to pair off into couples. It was a play on the word 'popular'—which they were, the assholes—and an ode to the poplar grove down off of—go figure—Poplar Lane, where they all went to neck and screw.

Rock was the leader. He was hooked up with Jess, a buxom blonde with the IQ of a salamander. Matt and Ashleigh were currently an item, though that might not be true tomorrow. The two broke up and got back together faster than a rattler's strike. Carson wasn't with anybody. He made the rounds as he pleased, and if any of the 'bitches' complained, he dropped 'em faster than a hot fryin' pan.

Arrogant sonofabitch.

They were all richies: the sons and daughters of sons and daughters who had gotten their money from the preceding son or daughter. The world was their oyster, as the saying went, and not one of them deserved it. But they had it, lousy fuckers.

Nobody could touch them, and they knew it.

So they'd never batted an eye at making Bobby's life hell. Instead, they relished it. He didn't doubt Rock's first wet dream had been about giving him a wedgie. Of course, Jess hadn't had tits then, but still. The lot of them squeezed every ounce of pleasure they could get from his misery.

It had all started out innocently enough, he supposed. There wasn't really any lasting damage from a wedgie, or a swirly, or having a rotten egg smashed in his shoulder-length hair, just sore balls, a wet head, and a whole lot of embarrassment. He'd learned to shrug off the laughter and ignore the pointed fingers, and he'd discovered the best routes to class—and home—to avoid confrontation. Indirect? Sure. Longer? By a long shot. But he didn't mind the exercise, and it was worth the hour of being left the hell alone.

When it had all started, he'd cried about it to his old man. He learned the futility of that damn quick. Garrett Stroud was just as likely to beat his son as he was to commiserate with him. "Shut up and go gut the fish," he'd say, with a slap to Bobby's head. "Ain't got time for your whiny bullshit. Grow a pair or get the hell out." Of course, he was usually drunk when that happened. But then again, he was frequently drunk.

Bobby looked like his mother. "The spittin' image," Garrett would say. And ever since she'd died when Bobby was five, his old man could barely stand to look at him unless it was through the filter of a bottle of Scotch. On the rare occasions when he was sober, Garrett would stare at his son, mutter something like "God, I miss her," and begin to blubber. Hating himself for the show of weakness, he'd stumble into the kitchen. He couldn't get to the booze fast enough.

So Bobby learned to be a loner. There was nothing much wrong with the solitude; after finishing his schoolwork, he'd trek through the patch of woods out behind the house to the little pond nestled in the trees about a mile away. He'd fish into the wee hours of the morning, as long as the croppies were bitin'. He shot squirrels in the fall, turkey in the spring. In the winter months he'd pull out his prized possession, his bow, and take out as many deer as the state of Tennessee allowed for the year.

Once they were down, he'd remove his Bowie, gut and clean 'em. The gore didn't bother him. Death was an old acquaintance that came closer to being a friend every passing year.

Now, he and Death were about to become lovers.

Sitting in the shack behind the house, Bobby sharpened his knife. The blade was long, about twelve inches, thick'nin' in the middle, then tapering off to a sharp, curved point. The handle was made from bleached bone, with etchings carved into the side. The weight was comfortable, familiar in his hand. As he finished, he looked over his supplies: fishin' poles, bait, rifle, ammo, backpack full of camping gear, gloves, a black ski mask, and lastly, his ticket for the 9:00pm showing of *Bloodbath* at the local theatre.

Sliding the blade into its sheath at his back, he zipped his reversible down coat, shouldered the bag, lifted the poles and gun, and headed into the small, dilapidated house. Garrett Stroud was slumped in his twenty-year-old La-Z-Boy in front of the TV, some game show buzzin' in the background. The proverbial bottle of Scotch was settled snugly against his crotch.

"Hey, Pop?"

Garrett grunted in response.

"I'm headed out."

His old man grunted again, but this time, there was a slightly higher tone at the end. It was Garrett's form of a question.

"I told you I was going huntin' for the weekend, 'member? I'll be out towards the bluff. Gonna get some squirrels, maybe a coyote or two. You gonna be okay?"

Garrett's only answer was a third and final grunt, followed by a swig from the already half-empty bottle.

Shaking his head, Bobby shut the door quietly behind him. Drunk-ass bastard. Well, his father wouldn't be the most reliable alibi, but he would be enough.

Slipping into the woods, he stashed the fishin' and huntin' gear, along with the backpack, in a hollowed-out tree trunk not too far from the house and let the brush fall back into place. Stuffing the mask and gloves inside his coat, he headed in the opposite direction of the bluff, cutting through the forested area towards town.

The air was cold, the scent of imminent snow sharp in his nostrils. It was late. Christmas had come and gone two weeks prior. His breath puffed out in frosty bubbles around his head, then dissolved into nothing. He emerged from the trees behind the high school, looking out at the deserted football field.

The scene changed before his eyes. The dead leaves cracklin' beneath his feet turned bright red and orange, and reattached 'emselves to the tree branches. The field was full of people wearing their school pride get-ups, wavin' pom-poms and banners and shit. It was Homecomin' Week, three months ago.

Matt and Ashleigh had been going through one of their typical breakups. This one had lasted longer than usual. Rumors were whippin' round the school that Ashleigh was pregnant, and the baby might not be Matt's. Needless to say, he'd booted her to the corner.

That Wednesday, Bobby had headed for his path through the woods when he'd come across Ashleigh crying under the bleachers. Common sense told him to keep walking. She was a Poplar, and had never had a nice word to say about him. Or to him. She laughed just as much as the others when Rock pantsed him, or Carson asked if his dad had fucked him lately. Nothing good could come of him stoppin' to see if she was okay.

Except she'd looked so small and alone, huddled into a tight ball, tears streaming down her face. Throwing common sense out the window, he ducked down to talk to her.

She seemed genuinely surprised when she realized who he was.

"Why would you care about me, Bobby?" she asked him. "I've always been awful to you."

He shrugged that off, told her he couldn't stand to see a pretty girl cry, and asked what that asshat Matt had done to her now?

She smiled sadly, played with the crumpled tissue in her hands. Sniffled. Said it didn't really matter. They'd talked for a while, and she'd finally asked him if he would mind escortin' her to the football rally and bonfire that Friday, since she didn't have a boyfriend to take her anymore.

Suspicion danced along his consciousness, warning him, but he waved it away.

Worst mistake of his life.

Everything was going splendidly. The rally was rowdy, full of loud and rambunctious students bursting with school spirit. The six-foot high pile of oak logs crackled, the smell of smoke burning the nose, the fire bright and blazing. Ashleigh was cuddled up tightly against him, her arm linked with his. He felt ten feet tall.

He shoulda known it wouldn't last.

A strong arm wrapped round his midsection. A hand clamped down on his mouth. In the hectic festivity, no one noticed the other Poplars dragging him through the dark shadows into the cover of the trees.

"Did you really think you could get away with hanging around my girlfriend?" He recognized Matt's menacing growl.

"Did you seriously think she was into you, dude? Seriously?" Rock laughed at him, pulling Bobby's pants down around his ankles.

It wasn't until the two of them dragged him to the ground, holding his arms down, and he felt Carson come up tight behind him that he realized what was happening.

"Were you hoping you'd get lucky, Bobby? Were you?" The rasp of Carson's zipper was impossibly loud in Bobby's ears. "Well, we'd hate to disappoint you, wouldn't we, boys?"

They'd taken turns, over and over again, one after another. He struggled at first, tried to get away, but it was pointless. He was no match for the three of them. The pain was unbearable, an acute ripping and tearing that went on and on, with no end in sight.

'Cept that wasn't the worst part.

As the three Poplars raped him, Ashleigh sat there and watched, a smug and sadistic smile on her lips. She bared her breasts to him in a sick and twisted mockery of seduction, then let her hand slide beneath the waistband of her jeans. Based on the noises she made, he figured she got off at least three times.

Finally, after what seemed like hours, they had left him there, his blood and tears soaking the ground, staining it with his humiliation.

Bobby shook his head hard, erasing the horrifyin' memory from his mind. It was over and tonight, they would pay. He caressed the handle of his Bowie, imagining how it would happen. No one had recognized his screams, the danger he was in that night.

Tonight, no one would recognize theirs.

Jogging 'cross the football field, he made his way over the four blocks down to the movie theatre. Pulling his hood up, Bobby headed into the building, handed his ticket to the teller, and drifted into the crowd. Positioning himself in a dark corner beside the entrance to the theatre's small arcade, he watched the doors.

It wasn't long before the Poplars came in. There was Rock and Jess, stumblin' and laughing. Probably already drunk, or at least well on their way to being there. Well, hopefully the alcohol wouldn't dull them out too much. Behind them was Matt and Ashleigh, arm in arm, making googly-eyes that screamed sex. Bobby wondered if Matt was gonna try and fuck her during the movie. He wouldn't doubt it. And finally Carson, with a brunette Bobby didn't recognize. He studied her for a moment. Who was she? He couldn't place her, which was weird, considering the school wasn't *that* big, and they'd all been going to school together for over ten years. Whatever. If she was with Carson, the fucking douche, she deserved what was coming.

It had been sheer luck that he'd discovered they would all be at the movie tonight. The three guys had busted into the bathroom on the south side of the school, oblivious to Bobby's presence. That was only because he'd been in a stall, taking a dump instead of his usual leak at the urinal. He was grateful then for the shit, because ever since what had happened at the bonfire, they'd been brutal. He'd had to take more care than usual to avoid them. Plus, he'd taken to wettin' himself whenever he saw them. Fucking bastards, turning him into a goddamn pussy. They'd taken to calling him "fag" now, too. It was too fucking much.

He'd sat there, holding his breath, waiting for them to leave before wiping his ass. And he'd listened.

"Dude, have you seen *Bloodbath* yet?"

"Yeah, man, went with my older brother last week. That shit is sick."

"I know, right? Fucking scary as hell. And the gore's fan-fucking-tastic."

"Hey, you think the girls would go?"

"Are you kidding? We couldn't pay them to go see it."

"I don't know. Chicks love that shit. Gives 'em a chance to be all vulnerable and scared and shit. Makes 'em horny as hell, too."

"Whatever. You're full of shit."

"Nah, man, I'm serious. I took Ashleigh to see *The Surgeon* a few months back--you know, the one where the doctor goes ape-shit and starts carving people up without anesthesia? She hid her face in my shoulder for half the movie, then begged me to fuck her all night long. Needed something to make her feel safe, keep the nightmares away, or some shit like that. I'm sure you know I was more than happy to oblige."

"Yeah, I bet you were. Well, whatever, I'm down. If the girls are up for it, you wanna go this Friday?"

"Yeah, man. Carson, you in?"

"Fuck yeah. Finding a date shouldn't be hard."

They'd done their business and filed back out. Bobby had sat there, a slow grin spreading across his lips as a plan formed. That night, he'd snuck into the theatre for his own glimpse of *Bloodbath*. For research.

He watched as they stood in line at the concessions and got their collection of Cokes, popcorn, and Jujubes. As they headed for Screen 7, he slid into the throng of bodies and followed them. The theatre was already dim, but he was careful to stay in the shadow of the stairs as he watched them find places to sit. They split up, each couple heading for a different section of seats.

That was weird. Didn't friends sit together at the movies? Then again, he wouldn't really know, would he? He was a loner movie-goer. He was a loner, period. Whatever. Their seating arrangements didn't change a damn thing.

He waited for more of the seats to fill up, then skulked up to the top row. On the far end of the aisle there were two seats together, separated from the others by the stairs. He sank into one. Waited.

Eventually someone sat next to him: a middle-aged man with a beer gut. Dude smelled like his old man. And what the hell, anyway? The theatre was only half-full. He had the whole fucking place to choose from, and he was gonna sit right next to Bobby?

What a twat.

The guy nodded in greeting, but said nothing. Bobby didn't bother initiating conversation. He glanced round the theatre, again noting the positions of the three Poplar couples. Rock and Jess talked animatedly with the couple in the row behind 'em. Rock made stabbing gestures toward Jess' neck, most likely demonstrating for the others something or other about the movie. Matt and Ashleigh were necking. Carson dicked around on his phone, blatantly ignoring the brunette who sat beside him.

Fucking tool.

Eventually, the lights dimmed, then blackened completely, leaving the room in a heavy darkness made thicker by the dense atmosphere of barely concealed and anticipated terror.

"Welcome to Vickington Theatres, with surround sound by DTFX. We ask at this time that all cell phones be silenced and put away. In case of emergency, we ask that you make your way to the nearest emergency exit. Thank you for your consideration, and please enjoy the show."

The light from the screen was momentarily blinding, the sound from the speakers grating to the ear. There was the light rustling of people fidgeting in their seats, the hushed whispers of anticipation. People were already on edge, knowing, yet not knowing, what to expect.

The previews came and went. Bobby didn't care much for them, but he took note of a thriller involving a couple of hunters that got stranded in a snowstorm. That might be worth seeing.

The screen went black. In the darkness, Bobby pulled out the ski mask and gloves and slipped them on. A dull throbbing of rhythm began: *Boom. Boom boom. Boom. Ba-boom. Boom. Boom boom. Boom. Ba-boom.* Crimson streaks dripped from the top of the screen, staining the black background. Pools of blood puddled at the bottom, then bubbled up into letters, spelling out the names of the featured actors, directors, producers.

Once the opening credits had finished, the screen once again went black. A second passed. Then another. A third. An unexpected and ear-splitting scream burst from the speakers. Caught off-guard, the audience screamed in surprised response.

Bobby didn't hesitate. Ripping his knife from its sheath, he buried it deep into the gut of the man beside him. The man's eyes bulged in the light from the screen; his gaze found Bobby's, and it was wide with pain. Bobby twisted the knife, then ripped upward and out. Blood poured from the wound and splattered onto the floor.

Sorry, dude. Nothing personal. But you were in my way.

The guy slumped forward, his hands coming up to try and staunch the flow. It was futile. Bobby had nicked at least one vital organ, as well as an artery. The guy was gonna bleed out. And soon.

On the screen, a girl raced down a street, panting. She slipped into an alley, ducking behind a dumpster. Even though he couldn't see it, Bobby could feel the audience perched on the edge of their seats. Silently, he moved down three steps and slid halfway down a row behind two guys he didn't know.

Moments passed. There was a close-up of the girl's panicked face. A crossbow bolt suddenly burst from her mouth. Gore splashed the camera lens, blotching the screen. As people hollered again, Bobby thrust the Bowie down into the neck of the guy sitting directly in front of him, letting the knife pierce down to its hilt, then ripping it free.

"What the fuck?" The second guy, brought out of the movie by the spray from his buddy's jugular, looked over, obviously alarmed. Moving quickly, Bobby slapped a hand over the man's mouth, then sliced his neck wide. Both men were dead within seconds.

Bobby sank back into his seat and crossed his arms, hiding the gleam of the blade. Calmly, he glanced around. No one had noticed anything was amiss. They were all riveted by the sight of a pair of black boots as the killer placed a foot along the base of his fresh kill's skull and ripped his bolt free.

The next scene gave the audience a breather. Bobby relaxed in his seat, letting his mind wander as the film went along. He hated killin' innocents, he really did, but if only the Poplars were found dead when the lights came back up, it would be way too easy to pinpoint him as the number one suspect, even if he did have an 'airtight' alibi. The Poplars' hatred of him was no secret; it was common knowledge they fucked with him on a near-daily basis, and so he'd have plenty of motive to want 'em dead.

No one knew about the rape, though. The richies might be a pack of malicious fuckers, but they weren't stupid. A wedgie here or a swirly there might mean a slap on the wrist, maybe a day or two's suspension. And that was big maybe. But rape? Multiple counts? That meant serious jail time. No way they were admitting to that shit.

But Bobby wasn't takin' any chances. He was making sure every last one of them took that secret to their graves.

Twenty minutes passed. Then thirty. The plot progressed, not that there was much of one. What motive did a psychopath need to slice and dice, after all? It was a bit ironic, actually, considering his own course of action. But then again, he had plenty of motive, didn't he?

It wasn't long before the bloodbath began. And it was a bloodbath; the title was more than appropriate. Letting what was on the screen play out, Bobby turned his attention back to his own agenda.

Stepping back out to the stairs, he went to the top row, now empty, and made his way to the other side of the theatre.

He slipped in silently behind Carson and his date, both riveted to the screen. Pulling the knife free, he prepared to take out the brunette. But something made him hesitate.

What the fuck, dude? Just do it already!

But she's not a Poplar.

So fucking what? She's with one!

Yeah, but...

Those other two guys weren't Poplars either. Or the fat dude sitting next to you. You killed them easily enough.

Yeah, but...

But what?

They were...well, guys.

What's the fucking difference?

I don't know, it just seems...wrong...to kill a girl.

You're gonna kill Jess and Ashleigh, you dumb fuck! What are they? Cartoon characters?

More like fucking dogs. They're different.

Whatever, man. Just do it!

He couldn't. But, he couldn't have her around to be a witness either. Adjusting the angle of his grip, he brought the bone handle of the blade down on the base of her skull, hard. She slumped, unconscious.

"What the hell...?" Carson turned towards Bobby. Bobby whipped an arm around, clamping his hand down over Carson's mouth.

"Were you hoping you'd get lucky? Were you?"

Carson's eyes widened in horror, and he struggled, his hands coming up to grip Bobby's arm.

Bobby moved quickly, leaning up and over the seat. He thrust the point of the blade into Carson's crotch and twisted. Carson screamed into Bobby's hand, the sound muffled enough to blend in with the surrounding noise of the audience's terror. Raising the blade, he stabbed again, then sawed. Carson writhed in Bobby's arms, but Bobby was in control now.

"How's it feel, asshole?" He continued to move the blade, up and down, in an even rhythm. Then, setting the knife aside, he reached down and gave a sharp tug. First came the cock, followed by the balls. They weren't quite intact; a dismemberment could only be so clean when done from behind and in the dark. Still, he'd managed.

Tear streaks covered Carson's face. Bobby could see them in the light from the screen. He was panting hard around Bobby's hand.

"You'd like me to move this, huh? Well, I'm happy to oblige." He pulled his hand off Carson's mouth, then took the dude's detached penis and shoved it between his lips. Carson choked, but couldn't dispel the chunk of bloody tissue.

"Not quite as big as the rumors make it out to be, huh, buddy? By the way, who's the fucking fag now?"

Slapping him on the shoulder, Bobby rose. "Nice knowing you, *dick.*" Then he crouched down and moved through the aisle, back to the stairs.

Another loner became another innocent victim. Bobby made it quick, leaving the guy smiling from ear to ear.

Blood dripped from the Bowie's tip as Bobby made his way throughout the theatre. The silvery sheen of the blade was gone now, taken over by a wash of thick crimson turned black by shadows.

Rock and Jess were next.

The couple behind them was going to be a problem. Bobby fell smoothly into the seat at the end of the row, sheathed his knife, and contemplated how to take them out.

Just then, the guy leaned forward and vomited violently into his lap. The girl with him recoiled, then put a hesitant hand on his shoulder, patting awkwardly. They stood up. He leaned on her supporting arm, and they sidestepped, heading Bobby's way. Bobby stood and moved into the aisle to let them pass. The girl gave him a distracted "thank you," too concerned with her boyfriend to notice he was covered in blood.

You got real lucky tonight, sweetheart. You don't even know. Though he had the impulse to go after the guy and kill him anyway, just for being such a pussy. *Really, dude? A bit of fake gore has you losin' your lunch? Fucking pansyass.*

Whatever. The path to Rock and Jess was clear now.

He crept down the row. Rock was nodding off, Jess' face peeking out from his shoulder as she squealed at the gore on the screen.

"Oh, shut up, will you?" Lightning fast, Bobby slammed a fist into the front of her neck, trying to break her larynx. The first hit left her choking. The second left her silent. Her chest heaved as she struggled to breathe. Her eyes rolled crazily as she tried to figure out what was happening.

Aiming for her ample and overly exposed chest, Bobby stabbed her right breast. She lurched forward, her head rolling. He pulled the knife free and stabbed again and again. A thinner liquid than blood flowed over his hand, startling him. What the...?

Implants. Bitch's tits weren't even real. He wondered if Rock knew. He wondered if Rock would even care. *Would I mind if a girl I was dating had fake tits?* he considered while carving up Jess' other breast.

Guess I wouldn't mind all that much. Hell, it'd be nice just to have *a girl.*

Jess was unconscious by now, the bosom she was so proud of and eager to show off completely mutilated. Bobby hesitated for a moment, then grabbed a fistful of her long, blonde hair and hacked it off, leaving it in bloody clumps along the theatre floor.

Around him, the theatre's patrons still screamed every few seconds, gruntin' and groanin' and shoutin' warnings. No one realized they were real-time actors in their own version of the film.

Rock was now sound asleep, oblivious to his girlfriend's demise. Shame. Bobby'd been looking forward to hearing him yell, but honestly, this would make what he had planned for Rock that much easier to execute.

Fisting a hand in Rock's hair, Bobby yanked back his head while simultaneously jamming the Bowie hilt-deep into Rock's belly. Rock jerked. His eyes fluttered open. By that time, Bobby was sawing furiously, gutting him from side to side. Intestines bulged out, then dropped in a squelchy heap to the floor, a macabre, malfunctioned slinky. Bobby stuffed a hand into the gory gap, fisted, and pulled. He wasn't sure what came out. The stomach, maybe? Part of the liver? A kidney? Didn't matter. Whatever it was, it joined the glutinous mass on the floor. He went back in, a second time, a third, each time pulling out more of Rock's innards, until his gloves were saturated with blood.

When the guy was fully disemboweled, Bobby moved on. Slipping back out to the stairs, he headed to the top of the theatre again, avoiding the rest of the audience. He crept through the top aisle, ducking under the light of the projector. Hitting the other stairs, he slunk down them and popped into the seat behind Matt and Ashleigh, who, unlike the rest of the terrified audience, were too busy swallowing each other's tongues to be bothered by the villain's rampage.

Flipping the Bowie in his hand so the blade rested along his forearm, he raised his fist up to his opposite ear, then swung hard, driving the blade in below the base of Matt's skull. A split second later, the tip shot out Ashleigh's cheek, just below her ear. Bobby released his hold on the Bowie for a moment, studying the silhouette the two made, joined now not only by their mouths but by his well-placed strike as well. It was fascinating—the dark shadow of the hilt jutting from the back of Matt's head, the tip piercing through Ashleigh's face, their mingled blood dripping onto her shoulder.

In the flickering light from the screen, where a group of college kids were zigzagging through the woods, Bobby could see Ashleigh's eyes rolling around in their sockets. She was trying to scream, but with her mouth temporarily glued to her now dead boyfriend's, the sound was muffled. She reached up, grasped at the blade, and jerked her hand back when the sharp edge sliced her fingertips. She cried; the knife's exposed blade caught her tears, letting them mingle with the dripping blood.

"Oh, you don't like this?" Bobby caressed her head gently, mocking her with his attempt to soothe her. "Would you like me to take it out? Yeah? Okay, it's all right. Easy now."

Grabbing the hilt, he yanked hard, ripping the knife free. Matt fell forward, his head lolling against his chest. Ashleigh stared at him in horror, then slowly turned towards Bobby.

He pounced, covering her mouth with his hand before she could scream, not that anyone would discern it from the chaos taking place on the screen. Then, adjusting his grip once more, he dug the knife's tip into the bottom of her eye socket. She did scream then, biting into his hand, but her teeth couldn't penetrate the thick glove. He twisted the knife, diggin' it in and around, manipulating the blade up behind her eyeball. Then, exerting pressure, he popped it free.

She twisted and writhed in his arm, clawing at him frantically, but there was no stopping him. Not with the memory of her watching him, laughing, and fingering herself swimmin' in his head.

"Not so funny now, is it, bitch?"

He went to work on the other eye; moments later, there was nothing left but two empty sockets. Blood trickled from the blank holes, reminiscent of a newly decaying corpse.

She wasn't close to dead, though. Not yet.

It was a shame he couldn't prolong her suffering; he'd have enjoyed toying with the heartless slut. But the movie was winding down. He needed to finish up, ready to make his escape when the lights came back on.

With a sharp jerk, he slit her throat.

It seemed a bit anti-climactic after all she'd done; a bit too tame. But it was done.

Hurriedly, he wiped the blade clean on Matt's shirt. Then he slid it back into its sheath at his back and pulled his shirt down to hide it.

On the screen, the last guy to survive was wrestling with the killer, trying to gain control of the crossbow. He was strugglin' in vain; *Bloodbath* didn't have no happy ending. The killer kicked him off and into a tree, rolled away, and picked up the weapon. The college guy barely had a second to stand before the bolt caught him in the belly, securing him to the tree. Blood welled up inside his mouth, his lip quivered, and he went limp.

As the killer turned to walk off the screen, Bobby removed his coat, flipped it inside out and slid his arms back inside. Stripping the gloves off, he stuffed them into an inside pocket. The ski mask followed. He zipped the coat up, stood, and made his way down the outer stairs, heading for the emergency exit. At the last minute, he remembered to pull up his hood.

Just as the credits started to roll, he pushed the jamb, setting off the alarm. Sliding through, he let the door gently close behind him. Knowing it was risky, he stopped for a moment and waited. There was nothing but the incessant beeping of the alarm. And then, faintly beneath it, he heard the screams. He could just imagine the scene as the audience members lucky enough to still be alive looked around in confusion, finally realizing what they were seeing: a dozen people, brutally murdered, left to idle in pools of their own blood.

A small smile of satisfaction crossed his lips; then, lifting his hood, he hightailed it for the woods.

***

The weekend passed and Monday came. All anyone could talk about was the bloodbath at *Bloodbath*. Students were terrified, intrigued, curious. The theatre's outdoor cameras were just for show; they didn't actually record, and the police had no real leads. Though many students and faculty members had mentioned Bobby Stroud might have motive to want the Poplars dead, he was a nice kid, if a bit quiet, and they couldn't imagine he'd do something that vicious. Of course, the police questioned Bobby, and his father. Nothing came of it. The boy had been out hunting, with three coyote and half a dozen squirrel carcasses to prove it.

With no murder weapon, no physical evidence at the crime scene, and only circumstantial theories, the police explored other possibilities.

The police had also questioned a certain brunette who was found unconscious beside the body of one Carson Johnson. No, she didn't remember what had happened, and no, she had no idea who might have done it. She'd only just moved there a few weeks ago, and didn't really know too many people, or who might've had it out for Carson.

As for Bobby, he went about his day, going from class to class, not saying much to anyone. When asked, he gave a frank answer. No, he didn't think it was a shame the Poplars were dead; frankly, he thought they had it coming. But no, he hadn't killed them. He didn't have the balls to pull something like that off, and he wasn't ashamed to say so.

The final bell rang at quarter to three. Heading to his locker, Bobby came up short when he noticed the folded piece of paper taped to it. Reaching out, he pulled it free and unfolded it. The script was small and neat.

I know what you did. At Bloodbath. *Don't worry. It'll be our little secret. By the way, thanks. That Carson guy was a real jerk.*

Bobby's head whipped up, and he glanced around frantically. *Who...?*

Just down the hall, leaning against a locker, was the brunette. Meeting his eyes, she gave him a knowing smile, then turned and disappeared into the crowd.

THIS ISN'T THE BREAKFAST CLUB

by Delphine Quinn

The doors to St. Paul's High School stood closed. There was an ominous feeling about the building today, its brick exterior darkened by the gray clouds in the sky. To many students, it was home, but to Ryan, it was Hell. The weekdays brought nothing but sorrow and insecurity, the school a breeding ground for bullying and self-loathing. To Ryan, it resembled a prison, and on this Saturday, its appearance gave that feeling credence.

The cloud cover slowly shifted across the sky as the wind picked up, and the metal gray doors creaked, indicating they weren't actually locked. Ryan knew this already, having served many Saturday school detentions here. Clutching the ceramic hunting knife in one hand and the master keys in the other, Ryan pulled the bandana up, shielding the face which many teenagers had mocked for the last four years.

With a sigh, the teen walked up the sidewalk to the school's entrance. The doors groaned against the wind, sounding almost eager for what was to come.

***

"Fucking detention," Arielle murmured to no one in particular.

The library was musty, the scent of old books and sweaty students mingling in her nose. She knew the routine. She'd been here before, and would be again. But Arielle remained indignant that she was being punished at all. Staging a sit-in for the rights of others was a noble thing, not something to be looked down on or met with discipline. Someday, the school's staff would realize she was right. Someday, the world would realize she was right. But for now, she took her punishment, sitting at a large, wooden table that could've seated eight students but only held her.

Arielle took stock of each of her fellow students, realizing how terrible today was going to be for her. Each was here for his or her own reason, but all of them had the same forlorn, bored expressions. Kevin, the captain of the football team, sat behind her, his blonde crewcut immaculate, his letterman jacket—a permanent fixture of his wardrobe—draped over the back of his chair. Beside him was Megan, head cheerleader whose platinum blonde hair almost made her look like Kevin's sister rather than his on-again, off-again girlfriend. Her large breasts were barely contained by her low-cut tank top, which was probably the reason for her having detention in the first place. Lastly, at the table to Arielle's right, were James and Matt. James was somewhat overweight, and his skin glistened with sweat every time Arielle saw him, red and white dots speckling across his face like boils waiting to be lanced. Matt was a good-looking kid from her theater class, but the rumor mill said he wasn't into girls. Arielle thought it a waste. Matt had defined muscles, a swimmer's physique, and a totally sexy style. Today he wore a pair of skinny jeans paired with a V-neck t-shirt. A scarf playfully danced across his shoulders and his hair was styled into a bleached faux hawk that the girls loved.

Could be worse, Arielle thought. *At least Matt's here and Mrs. Peterson isn't running detention this weekend.*

Just as the thought snaked through her mind, the library doors opened and Mr. Roberts walked in. *Ugh, he'll spend the entire time looking at Megan's chest and mine.* On cue, Mr. Roberts leered at the two girls, making Arielle cringe and zip up her panda hoodie. Megan preened, loving the attention.

"Hello, students. You all know why you're here. The next four hours will be spent working on assignments and contemplating how you can behave more appropriately on campus. The assignment for this weekend is to write an essay about what is expected of you here at St. Paul's and how you plan to rise to those expectations. I'll be in and out, as I have papers to grade, but I'll be able to hear everything from the back office of the library, so no funny business. You may begin."

Disgusting Mr. Roberts waddled his way to the back office. The walls would shield his vision but not his hearing. Arielle wouldn't be able to get away with blowing the assignment off and hanging out with Matt.

Lifting her cell phone from her shoulder bag, she checked the service, more out of habit than anything. All the students knew the school electronically blocked cell service here. *A product of too much budget and too much time on their hands,* Arielle thought as she saw the infamous No Signal bar across her phone.

Returning it to her bag, she leaned back in the increasingly uncomfortable oak chair and sighed. *Only four more hours to go.*

***

"Maybe we could all write one essay and turn it in, as a sort of protest," James said, his pronounced lisp making it difficult to understand him.

"This isn't the fucking *Breakfast Club*, Lames. And we're not all gonna buddy up and become best friends either. Go play some World of Warcraft, nerd," Kevin sneered, spitting fury at the typically quiet boy.

"Hey, man. You don't have to be a dick," Matt chimed in, trying to stick up for his tablemate. He was sick of Kevin's bullshit. *All he ever does is mess with people. It's not right,* Matt thought, giving James an encouraging smile.

"I thought dicks were *your* thing, Matty." A malicious grin broke across Kevin's face.

"Whatever. You know, at the end of the day, Kevin, no one really likes you." Matt felt himself getting angry, but squelched the feeling. He didn't want Kevin to get the reaction he obviously craved.

"*I* like him," Megan chimed in, giggling. Her arm slid through Kevin's, and her enormous breasts thrust forward with her motion. Even Matt found it hard not to look, but not because of a sexual attraction. More like when you pass a train wreck and can't help but stare.

Deciding it wasn't worth the effort, Matt pulled out a notebook and a pen, and started to think about the essay. As he began to write the first sentence, he heard a strange gurgling sound behind him, like someone had left the hose on and it was running into the mud. He glanced over his shoulder.

Mr. Roberts stumbled toward them, crimson gushing from his neck and cascading over his hands, which clasped weakly to his throat, desperately trying to stop the flowing blood, to no avail. It sounded like he was drowning, liquid coalescing in his throat and lungs, making every breath ragged and moist. Matt screamed as Mr. Roberts clung to the end of the horror aisle, his hand leaving dark red imprints across the sign. Mr. Roberts then collapsed into a pile of khakis and Hawaiian shirt, stained and discolored.

"Oh my God!" Megan screeched, her hands clutching her cheeks as if the pain might wake her up from this nightmare.

"Holy shit!" Kevin yelled, rushing over to Mr. Roberts, trying to cover the gaping wound in the man's neck. Sinew and blood draped across his hands, which had inadvertently become ensnared in the huge wound. "I can't stop the bleeding! I think he's dead! Oh my God. What the fuck?"

"We have to hit the alarm! Someone's in here!" Arielle cried, hysterical. She rushed to the cream-colored wall and pulled down the red lever which closely resembled a fire alarm, except this one sent the school into lockdown in case of a shooting or terrorist attack.

The voice of their principal, Mrs. Rodish, instantly boomed over the loudspeakers:

"Please make your way to the nearest classroom. The school is now entering lockdown procedures. Remember your drills. Please make your way to the nearest classroom."

Red lights flickered throughout the school and library—an eerie sense of dread came with them. Matt heard the metallic clinks of doors locking, each bolt sliding into place, precautions taken after so many shootings had become the disturbing norm in America. As the doors were secured automatically, Matt became aware of Arielle and Megan crying, their sobs and gasps becoming so panicked that he felt his own anxiety hit its peak.

Ever since he could remember, Matt had dealt with panic attacks. Anything could set him off, from a doctor's appointment to having to order at a drive thru. Being in a situation that actually warranted panic didn't make things any better. He could feel the pressure against his lungs and heart, as if Mr. Roberts' corpse was seated on top of his chest, daring him to try to breathe, knowing he couldn't. Black spots danced across his vision, and he knew he was going to faint. Clutching the table beside him, he could no longer hear the girls crying. Blood pounded in his ears like waves of drumming agony, and with it came a taste in the back of his mouth that was part metal, part fear. *Don't pass out. If you pass out, you might never get out of here.*

Matt tried to think of something, anything to calm down. He remembered his therapist talking about steady breathing, calming thoughts. *The ocean, my dog Bruno, Mom's pot roast, Erik...* Slowly, Matt felt himself becoming more composed. He could breathe, little by little. The weight was gradually lessening, subsiding. Closing his eyes felt good, and helped him maintain his balance. But at the same time, Matt knew shutting them was dangerous. He could faint regardless.

Or worse, some crazed murderer could rush into the room and slaughter them.

The thought made him sick again. *What the hell are we going to do?*

***

Ryan listened as the students came to grips with what was happening. All the planning and waiting had come to fruition. They were going to pay, all of them, from asshole Mr. Roberts down to the airhead cheerleader and her boyfriend. They had destroyed so many lives with their evil taunts and hateful social media posts. Shooting them was too humane; a quick death was far too good for the students of St. Paul's. It was a shame that Mr. Roberts had to be done away with so quickly. Ryan would have liked to have made him suffer the same way he had made so many other students suffer, from the girls he groped to the boys he picked on.

Ryan moved from the desk in the library's office, peering cautiously out the door that Mr. Roberts had left ajar, surveying the damage and relishing the sight of the students' shock. Ryan chuckled, knowing this was merely a taste of what was to come. While the students clung to the safety provided by the lockdown of the school, Ryan had the keys and codes, and could do anything. The others were lambs waiting for slaughter.

And a slaughter it was going to be.

***

Megan couldn't breathe. It felt like there was a vice on her organs and the harder she struggled for air, the more terrified she became. Short, quick gasps brought relief to her lungs for brief moments, surrounded by extended periods of burning and crying out for air that she couldn't give them.

"I...I want, I want to go...home," Megan sputtered. The phrase had been splitting her mind with urgency for what felt like eternity. *I'd trade everything I own to be at home with my parents,* she thought.

"I think we all do, Megan," James said from behind her, his voice a strange monotone, as if he were possessed by a robot.

"What the hell are we going to do?" Arielle cried, her heavily applied mascara dripping down her face, giving her the appearance of a member of a rock band. "We have to get out of here!"

Megan looked over at the only other female in the room. Arielle had always been weird, with her raccoon eyes and bizarre choices of fashion. Drops of her mascara had scattered across her panda hoodie, which hung loosely around her thin frame, her pink-colored hair falling over the hood that zipped entirely up to become a panda face. Megan had never really thought of the girl as a person, only someone to avoid at all costs to maintain her social standing.

"Mr. Roberts is dead. It looks like someone gouged his throat out. You can see the bone," Kevin said.

"How could anyone get in the library office without us seeing them? The entrance is right here. We would've spotted them." Arielle was borderline hysterical at this point. Her head rocked as she reasoned aloud.

"There's an entrance from the back. You need a key," James replied.

"How would you know?" Kevin spat.

"I used it to get in when I messed with the school computers. That's why I'm here," James replied, gaze averted.

"Well, what if the person is still in there?" Arielle asked.

"If they're still in there it means we're trapped in here with them. We have to check it out. That asshole could be waiting for something, some way to catch us off guard. I don't want to be trapped in a building with some fucking nutjob." Kevin seemed to be reverting to his typical self, all macho and bravado, behaving as if he could somehow kick this guy's ass.

"We have to stick together. Haven't you seen horror movies? Once they split up, they're dead," Megan said, hoping they'd listen.

"That's a good idea," Kevin replied, still using his manly voice and gestures. "We'll stick together then."

The red lights shut off. The room went from a dizzying array of illumination to the normal library again, except for the dead man in front of Megan. Opening her mouth to ask why the alarm had turned off, Megan was cut off by the loudspeakers being activated again. She and the other students looked up instinctively. Over the PA came the cheerful tones of music. In a stark juxtaposition to how she was feeling, Megan's ears rang with the sounds of the '80s hit, "Girls Just Wanna Have Fun."

"What the fuck?" Megan yelled, trying to raise her voice over the disturbingly joyous track.

***

Ryan laughed, looking down at the PA system playing an iPod mix of '80s music just for this occasion. Ryan had always loved the '80s. For some reason, it felt like the perfect era. Now this was something you could move to. Something that made you want to dance, to sing, to enjoy life. It was the perfect soundtrack to Ryan's final act.

Ensuring the iPod was secured and playing, Ryan moved away from the secretary's brown desk and secured the bandana again. *Time to get to work.* The teen exited the office, singing, "My mother says, 'When you gonna live your life right...'"

***

Arielle could feel herself breaking from the inside out. Never skilled at coping with bad situations, she was barely holding it together. The sound of Cyndi Lauper was blaring so loud that she thought her ears might burst, and she would welcome the relief if they did. She just didn't want to hear this fucking song anymore. *That's all they really want!*

She put her hands over her ears and felt her thin grasp on reality fall away. She didn't care anymore. She had to get out of there by any means necessary. James tried to grab her arm and see if she was okay, but she barely noticed him. *I have to get out of here!* The thought circled through her mind like water in a drain.

Arielle ran. The other students screamed after her to stop, but it barely registered—Arielle didn't care. She was getting out. Everyone else could stay and die if they wanted, listening to godawful '80s music. She ran to the far side of the library and grabbed the metal doorknob. Eagerly, she whipped it open, not pausing to think that it should've been locked or to wonder what awaited her in the hallway beyond.

She ran, the halls adorned in lockers surrounding her, red and white paint blurring in her peripheral vision. She sprinted past classrooms and offices. The doors waited just beyond her. Freedom, air, life—she could taste it. The thought of getting out of this place and being a survivor was palpable. Reaching the gray doors, she tore at them, ready to dash outside into safety.

The doors didn't move. Her arm had pulled so hard at them, expecting them to give way, that Arielle felt a sickening agony rise up her shoulder. It felt like someone was pouring ice water and acid through her veins, from her neck to her fingertips. In the same moment, she was gripped with a horrifying feeling that she was going to vomit. Her stomach flipped, and bile rose, an acidic, bitter taste she was all too familiar with because of her eating disorder. *Oh God, if you let me get out of this, I swear I'll do better.*

As the pain grew in her shoulder, she felt the hot prick of pure suffering when something grabbed her. Arielle didn't have time to scream. She couldn't fight back. Her arm was so damaged, she knew she must've dislocated it. Staring into the eyes of a murderer, a person she realized had no soul, Arielle knew she was doomed.

"You make me sick," a voice disdainfully whispered. "All your social justice bullshit, staging sit-ins and posting on Tumblr, but you can't defend the people being tortured right here in these walls."

Arielle tried to respond, but as quickly as the voice rose, so too had a large knife. Staring at the blade and unable to jar her arm loose from the killer's grasp, Arielle couldn't move.

In one swift motion, the killer jammed the knife into the side of Arielle's neck.

***

Blood sprayed everywhere, and Ryan could taste the coppery, thick substance oozing down the bandana. Arielle's eyes were wide, but she made no sound as her legs buckled beneath her, blood still squirting over Ryan's clothes.

As she hit the linoleum floor, an idea struck Ryan. Removing the bandana, Ryan reached down to Arielle's bloodied body and removed her hoodie, which was stained crimson. Ryan lifted the hoodie and put it on. It fit; a bit snug, but still... Pulling the hoodie up overhead, and zipping the front up, the disturbed teen laughed. *Forget the bandana—now I'm a panda!* Looking out from the eye slits at the reflection in the glass panels of the door, Ryan was completely satisfied.

Softly, Ryan hummed along as Cyndi repeated that well-known mantra: "Girls Just Wanna Have Fun."

***

"Where the fuck did she go?" Kevin exclaimed, his voice barely audible over the music. "We have to get out of here."

"We should help her," James said, still staring at the ground. "She could be in trouble."

"Fuck that. She was stupid enough to go off on her own. She can deal with it herself!" shouted Kevin.

"You're a real piece of shit, Kevin," Matt spat, not caring anymore whether anyone in the room liked him or not.

"Yeah, I may be a piece of shit, but I'm an alive piece of shit. And I intend to stay that way," Kevin retorted. "We need to find our way to an exit. One that the killer wouldn't expect us to use."

"And how do you suggest we do that?" James yelled, finally surveying the situation and becoming visibly sickened by it.

"Well, we should probably split into two groups. One runs to an exit, one to another. He can't cover all the exits at once," Kevin reasoned.

"I thought we said we shouldn't split up?" Matt said sarcastically. As he finished the sentence, the music stopped. Silence filled the library, making it seem larger than it was, a chasm once furiously loud but now audibly empty. "What the fuck?"

The quiet lasted mere seconds but it seemed to stretch on for a lifetime. Another song came on. Matt couldn't believe his ears. Somehow, this track was even more disturbing than the last. "Won't you come see about me?" it sang.

"This isn't the fucking *Breakfast Club*!" Kevin screamed, his voice cracking with effort and fear. "We have to get out of here. James, come with me. We'll take the main exit. We're the strongest. We stand the best chance of fighting this guy off. Megan, go with Matt. And Matt, if you let anything happen to her, I swear to God, I'll kill you myself."

"We shouldn't split up," Matt replied, staring straight into Kevin's face, a face that had once intimidated him but now seemed infinitely less frightening than whoever waited for them in the hallway.

"No, he's right," James said, standing straighter. "He and I stand the best chance. You two should try to get out through the back exit of the theatre."

"Please, don't leave me!" Megan snapped from her daze and clutched Kevin's arm. "I don't want to die!"

"You're not going to die. We're all going to get out of this. I promise," Kevin said, softly moving Megan's arms from his. He kissed her forehead as she shuddered. "Okay, Matt, you know what to do. If anything fucked up happens, pull the lockdown alarm again. It could buy us some time."

Matt felt a sick, rolling feeling in his guts. He didn't like this. He didn't like it at all. Splitting up wasn't the way to go. But then again, the odds were good one group was going to get out. One group would survive and find safety outside this hellhole that was once a school. Maybe it would be his.

Matt nodded, grabbed Megan's hand, and walked toward the exit door of the library. He wasn't completely convinced, but in his heart he felt a slight flutter of hope. Hope that he would see Erik again. Hope that this would all be over soon.

***

Ryan waited casually by the front exit, knowing it was only a matter of time before someone else made a run for it. The hoodie was warm. The fleece caressed skin, and the blood had seeped through the fabric, soaking against Ryan's shirt.

Ryan hummed along with the beat of "Don't You Forget About Me." A better song for the occasion couldn't have been found, and it brought a smile to Ryan's lips. Turning the knife over and over, waiting for someone to make a move, Ryan felt an increasing sense of peace. This was the moment. No turning back now.

As the thought passed, Ryan heard the thudding of footsteps. One pair was agile, athletic, swift—it had to be Kevin. The other was labored, dragging slightly, accompanied by wheezes of effort. James. *This could be tricky*, Ryan realized. Overcoming two large men wasn't going to be easy.

Luckily, Ryan had a plan.

***

James ran as fast as his legs would carry him, which wasn't very fast at all. He couldn't remember the last time he'd run full force. Always opting out of gym class because of his asthma, he hadn't ever been athletic in the least. His weight showed that, as did his poor choice of footwear. The backs of the sneakers rubbed harshly against his heels, and he could feel blisters forming already. Running on pure adrenaline was fine for now, but he wasn't going to be able to keep it up. He could feel himself lagging, staring at Kevin, who was faring far better than he and only a dozen yards from the door.

James picked up the pace, using his last reserves of energy to push through the pain and his lack of breath. As he caught up to Kevin, they nearly reached the metal doors they'd entered through that morning, innocent, with no idea of what was waiting for them. *Even if we make it out*, James thought, *nothing will ever be the same*.

Just as they reached the doorway, something moved to their right. James leapt to the side, anticipating an attack, his skills obtained through years of video games. It was Arielle. She stood there, frozen, her head covered with the panda hood. The soft sound of sobbing came from beneath the fabric, and her shoulders shook. *What the hell happened to her?*

Kevin moved forward, aggressive. "What the fuck are you doing, Arielle? Why do you have that stupid hood on? Are you hurt? Where's all that blood coming from?" He reached out, trying to pull the hood from her face.

James instantly realized what was happening. He tried to scream. He wanted to reach out and grab Kevin, pull him to safety. But he was frozen to the spot. He felt something warm dripping down his leg and realized he'd wet himself. He'd never felt anything like this. Fear wasn't the word. *Terror.*

The hooded figure lashed out with a huge, gray knife, slashing Kevin's face and neck. The first swipe of the blade shocked him, his eye and nose damaged beyond recognition. Blood shot in all directions. The panda didn't stop. It slashed repeatedly, and in such a frenzy that James lost track of how many stab wounds were inflicted. Kevin fell to the ground, his face a mutilated heap of skin and visible bone and cartilage.

James knew he had to move, but couldn't. As the figure approached him, all he could do was wonder, *Who would do such a thing? Why?* The figure moved closer, and finally James snapped out of it. He turned to run, but his poor choice of footwear betrayed him. His soles slid against the growing pool of blood draining from Kevin's body. He could feel his balance waver, and James knew he was going to die. His right leg glided out from under him, and he slid like a baseball player trying to steal third.

Agony danced up his muscles. He had torn something for sure. His leg was splayed out at an awkward angle, and his back wouldn't move no matter how much he willed it. The panda figure stood over him, staring down through the small eye slits blankly.

"James, you're probably the person who deserves this least. But you still deserve it. You should've stood up for me. We were friends. But you didn't." The voice that escaped the hoodie was incredibly small, almost broken.

James recognized it and instantly knew who was behind that mask. A sea of regret washed over him, and as he opened his mouth to plead, to apologize, to beg, the knife came down in a flash, stabbing straight into his chest. Everything went black.

***

Megan ran close behind Matt. Her lungs ached and her heart pounded so loudly she wondered if she was going to have a heart attack. She didn't care. Better to die of a heart attack than be stabbed to death by some psychopath. Her hand clung to Matt's, both sweaty and slippery, like two wet fish caught together in a net. If anyone had ever told her she'd be running through the halls of St. Paul's, grasping Matt Williamson's hand, she would've laughed herself stupid. But now, as she held onto it tightly, she felt the circulation in her fingers failing.

As they reached the third hallway they'd scampered through, Megan realized that they only had a little way to go. The theatre was at the end of this hall, and from there, all they had to do was navigate the aisles between the cushioned chairs to the stage, and out the back. *We might make it.*

"Don't, don't, don't, don't!" blared over the loudspeakers, so earsplitting that Megan wondered if she might have permanent damage. As they reached the door to the theatre, relief washed over her. Only a small theatre stood between her and the rest of her life.

Matt flung open the door and rushed inside, dragging her behind him. Megan stood in complete blackness. The lights were off and the theatre was still. She had never felt terror like this in her life. Wrenching her hand from Matt's, she reached along the wall, every movement making her more certain that the killer lay waiting just beyond. But in moments, she found what she was looking for: the lockdown handle they'd used in the library. It would provide light and secure them in the theatre, so the killer couldn't get in.

Megan pulled. Red lights ravaged the scene, and along with them came a freezing cold, wet sensation. Beyond the music, whirring sounded from above.

I've pulled the fire alarm instead!

Quickly, Megan became drenched. Her thin white shirt became transparent, her nipples hard and on display for all to see. Without any thought for her modesty, she kept moving. Matt didn't even seem to notice the water showering them. He continued rushing toward the front of the house and stage. Megan kept up, her body shivering from the cold. The red cascading over the seats of the theatre and the stage gave it a deadly feeling. As they reached the stage and climbed the stairs, Megan felt confident she had finally reached the end of this journey. She was going home.

The pair turned the corner, behind the curtains of the stage, and ran full force into a hooded figure. Megan wondered if this was a dream. Why was there a bear standing between them and the doorway leading to safety?

The music ended, and this time it didn't begin again. Matt stood between Megan and the bear, the one thing she was grateful for right now. It took everything in her not to scream.

"Whoever you are, you have to stop!" Matt screamed.

"Do I?" a soft voice came from the bear.

"Let us go," Matt replied, his voice strained but confident.

"I don't think I want to do that, Matt."

The figure rushed forward and slashed at Matt. He ducked to the right, narrowly avoiding the blade's grasp.

"Why are you doing this?!" Megan begged, her body frigid from the pouring water and fear.

"Because, Megan, you always treated me like scum. You bullied me, ruined my life. You posted pictures of me all over fucking Facebook just for a laugh. Did you think you could treat people like that and nothing would happen?" the voice spat. The bear moved quickly again toward Matt, slashing forward with the blade.

Matt almost dodged the blow, but his foot slid on a puddle of water forming on the slick stage floor. Red sluiced down his arm. He grabbed at the knife before the bear could retreat and they struggled. Every time it looked like Matt was gaining control over the weapon, the rotund bear fought harder.

Megan knew what she had to do. She had to get out of here. Matt could handle himself. She slipped around the two and moved toward the exit door, its black face almost hidden but its gold knob shining. Inching forward and keeping her gaze behind her to make sure the two were distracted, Megan reached it. As she went for the knob, and freedom, someone cried out.

It was Matt. He'd been wounded somewhere near his chest. There was so much blood flowing, Megan wasn't sure where it started and ended. Realizing she didn't have much time, she clutched the knob and turned. It didn't budge. Behind her, she could hear footsteps approaching. Matt was down, so it had to be Ryan.

Ryan, the girl she'd picked on since third grade. Ryan, who had once been friends with all of them, who each of them had turned on over the last 10 years. Ryan, the pudgy girl with small boobs that they'd taken turns photoshopping into memes. Ryan, the girl who was going to kill her.

Megan turned to try to fight off the attack, but she stood no chance. Cheerleading wasn't the type of sport that would make you strong enough to fend off an attacker twice your size. Within moments, she felt a blade stab through the arm she'd raised to shield her face. Screaming, she lowered the arm instinctively and began to sob.

***

"Nice tits, Megan. You already knew that though," Ryan said as she lifted the knife and jammed it downward, directly into the chest that Megan had once been so proud of.

Megan shrank back, leaning against the doorway that would've freed her but was now her deathbed. She slid down the wood to the floor, her glazed eyes locked on Ryan's.

Ryan unzipped the hoodie and smiled. It was done. She wiped her chin with the back of her hand. She took the keys from her pocket and unlocked the door, kicking Megan's body to the side.

Hurried footsteps approached, and she paused, hand on the doorknob.

***

Matt rushed her from behind. He bashed his fists into the back of her head as hard as he could. He may not have been a football player like Kevin, but he did work out. The club scene was cutthroat and he liked to look good for Erik.

Ryan fell forward, the keys flying from her hand and the knife sliding to her left. Matt quickly moved to grab the knife, and secured it. He didn't pause. He didn't think. He just lifted the knife and turned to Ryan, who was on the ground facedown. He stabbed her, the knife finding purchase in the skin of her back. She groaned, and stopped moving.

Matt hurried to the door and turned the knob. It opened. Sunlight thrust out the disturbing redness he'd become accustomed to. Fresh air rushed into his lungs. He was free.

He jogged past the parking lot, away from the horrors, away from all the death. He didn't stop until he was away from the school, where he pulled out his cellphone and called 911, then his parents, and then Erik.

***

Sitting in the back of the ambulance, Matt knew he was lucky to be alive. The knife had grazed his abdomen, producing a lot of blood but not actually threatening his life. His arm and stomach would need stitches, and he'd be laid up for a while, but he was alive, something he couldn't say for the others and Ryan.

Erik sat beside Matt, holding his hand, tears in his eyes. "I'm so glad you're okay," he said, rubbing his thumb over Matt's good hand. "I can't believe I almost lost you."

"Hey, don't worry," Matt said comfortingly. "You know I wouldn't die that easily."

"I love you," Erik said. Tears still twinkled, but a smile played on his lips.

"I love you too," Matt replied, leaning forward despite the pain and kissing Erik on the cheek. "It'll probably be a while before we can hit the clubs or go out dancing though."

"That's okay," Erik said, grinning. "When you feel up to it. And I'm sure everyone will be glad to meet the ultimate Scream Queen."

Matt laughed along with Erik, glad to have a sense of normalcy back. Ryan was gone, and he was safe, loved. Leaning back against the gurney, he smiled and waited for the ambulance to take him to the hospital.

***

The police couldn't explain it. They'd been through the school countless times, and only found five bodies when there should have been six.

Reaching for his handheld radio, Sgt. Hepburn called in an APB on a girl in a panda hoodie.

COURTESY CALL

by Kindra Sowder

I often wondered where I went wrong in life to end up working in a call center as a telemarketer. My graphic design degree had proven useless because of an oversaturated market. No one had warned me that everyone had been told the workplace for graphics was great, causing people to flood it in tidal waves that washed me out.

I sat in my computer chair with an Excel spreadsheet open on my desktop, headset on, dreading the next call where I would be insulted, yelled at, and maybe hear new offenses that would confound me with their verbal creativity. Swiveling in my chair, I tried not to stare at the spreadsheet again. My eyes met the bright white letters on the nameplate Velcroed to the fabric walls of my cubicle. When I graduated high school, I had never thought I'd be able to introduce myself to anyone as Zoe Chandler, a college graduate at the top of my class, a graphic designer washout, and one of the most hated individuals on the face of the planet.

Chris, a high school dropout with a great body and a wonderful sense of humor, sat at the cubicle behind me. His baritone voice radiated through the tranquil atmosphere as he pitched the latest upgrade in internet service that no one wanted. Our coworker, Joanne, was a few seats down and barely spoke to anyone aside from customers. The redheaded recluse also seemed to suffer from extreme anxiety.

I sighed and ran my fingers through my shoulder-length brown hair, leaning forward to place my elbows on my desk. It took all of my energy to resist laying my head down and giving up altogether.

It didn't help that there had been a rash of violent killings over the last month in the city, each victim having worked as a telemarketer. The company had stepped up security and wouldn't let anyone walk to their cars alone, which annoyed me to my very core, especially since the police were no closer to catching the killer. While I was ecstatic there were three others in the office with me, not including the security guard making his rounds, I wasn't pleased about coming in at all with a killer on the loose. I could be a target, but corporate greed overpowered the importance each of us placed on our lives.

"Zoe, you all right?" a familiar voice asked.

I sat up, adjusted the headset, and turned to find my supervisor, Jerry, standing behind me. He leaned against the edge of my cubicle wall, hands in the pockets of his perfectly ironed khaki pants.

"Yeah, yeah, I'm okay. Just tired is all," I replied nervously.

He nodded, his deep brown eyes studying me. "I know. The murders have us all on edge. Why don't you go ahead and get out of here? I'll walk you to your car. We've got Bryan here, and I'm sure Joanne and Chris will want to go home too. Just say the word."

"Well, I could use the hou—" I began.

"I'm saying the word, bossman," Chris interjected, spinning his chair around and bringing his headset down around his neck. "I'm sure Joanne would say it too, if she could hear us down there."

Jerry rolled his eyes at Chris and moved away from them to walk the few spaces down to Joanne. I couldn't hear if she was on a call or not. I stood and peered over the wall of my workstation and watched as he approached her desk with his hands still stuffed in his pockets.

"Hey, Joanne. I'm sending you all home. With that killer out there, we're all practically sitting ducks here. This person has been able to get into every other building in the city with even more security than us. You okay with that?" he asked her.

All I could hear were the whistles of her softly spoken words as she answered.

"Yeah, of course, I'll make sure you guys still get paid for the time. That's not an issue. Plus, it'll be better if we all leave in a group."

After a few moments, Jerry smiled weakly in an attempt to be reassuring, patted the top of the cubicle wall, and looked at Chris and me with a nod. "Shut down your computers and let's get out of here."

He didn't have to tell us twice. I removed my headset and hung it up on the plastic hook that protruded from my wall, and powered down my computer in one swift motion. Reaching into the top drawer, I removed my satchel from within the deep cavern and slung it over my shoulder. Chris swiveled in his chair, stood, and walked beside Joanne as she moved quietly down the hallway towards the elevator. Bryan, the security guard, stood next to the elevator doors with his hand resting on the butt of his standard issued Glock given to all security workers after the killings had begun.

All of us made our way in a tight-knit group to the lifts, Bryan watching diligently as we closed in on his position. He pressed the down button, calling the elevator that would take us from the third floor to the underground parking lot. As we waited for the door, something seemed to pop into Jerry's mind, his eyes widening.

"Shit, I need to grab my laptop. There's some work that needs to be done before tomorrow. Go ahead and I'll meet you guys down there," he explained as he took a few steps backward.

"No, we should wait," Bryan said.

"Nope, go ahead. I'll be a minute." Jerry saluted as if affirming some kind of promise, then turned around and disappeared.

There was a ding and the light on the elevator panel lit up. The silver doors opened to let us in. The metal walls inside were so clean they looked like mirrors and the white granite floor reflected the fluorescent lights, making them far too bright.

Each of us piled in, with Bryan moving in last. The ride down was silent except for the horrible Muzak that would turn a sane person to murder. I gripped my satchel's strap and took deep even breaths in an attempt to calm my nerves. The murders had wracked the telemarketing industry in the area, hitting it hard enough that many offices were closing and paying their employees for hours missed even though only a few offices had been struck. Ours hadn't until now, but I had a feeling that after tonight they would be, especially if another took place. The madman, or woman, had already hit three offices in the late hours, making it past the best security systems the small city offices could offer. No one had made it out alive.

Then I remembered my cell phone, something a person is practically attached to these days. It was in my other desk drawer, connected to a charger that ran to the power strip under my desk. I hung my head and my hand shot to my face, covering my eyes. "Oh, my God, I can't believe I did this," I blurted.

The doors slid open and everyone but me stepped out into the hallway.

"What did you do?" Chris asked.

I groaned and pressed the up button. "Cell phone. I'll be right back. Wait for me?" I didn't hear the reply before the doors closed, and I shot back up to the third floor.

As soon as the doors opened, I dashed to my workstation. The walk was effortless, the maze of cubicles not nearly as confusing as it used to be. My hand barely brushed the handle on my desk drawer before my desk phone rang, pulling my attention to it. It was hardly ever used except for when management or higher-ups wanted to contact me, which was never because outgoing calls were typically our only calls. My hand shot to the receiver but hovered over it with hesitation at the 'unknown caller' that popped up on the ID.

It was common for me not to answer them, but this was the desk phone—my career could be at stake. It was the only reason I picked up the receiver. "This is Zoe with Urban Solutions, offering the best in hospitality services and software. How can I help you?" I even smiled as I said the empty words.

Silence greeted me on the other end of the phone.

"Hello? This is Zoe with Urban Solutions. How can I help you?" I repeated, thinking there may have been a problem with the connection.

Nothing. No reply.

Just as I was about to put the receiver down, I heard heavy breathing. Only breathing, though, not a single word uttered. I stood there in confusion. Jerry still hadn't appeared from his office. His door was shut, so I carried on with the call despite the crawling sensation that coursed over me.

"Can I help you?" I asked tentatively.

"Yes, you can," a deep male voice answered.

"We are closing for the evening, but is there a question I can answer for you quickly?" I was beyond ready to go. The husky resonance of the man's voice unnerved me, sending waves of panic through me. The hair on the back of my neck stood on end.

"There is *something* you can do for me," he replied, breathy, as if he were excited or pleased with himself.

"What can I help you with, sir?" A pit of fear formed in my stomach. My heart raced, and my palms became clammy. I wanted to drop the phone before he could reply and run back to the elevator.

His words were garbled. I could barely make them out. He was on a cell phone, that much I could tell.

"I'm sorry, what was that, sir? You're breaking up."

He took a deep breath and then laughed maniacally. I was beginning to think he'd lost his mind, but then he said something that chilled me, something that would instill fear in anyone:

"I want you to bleed for me."

I threw the receiver onto the base, fear rolling through my body at the chance that I had just spoken to the person responsible for the deaths of all those people. What had they said on the news? That there had been a call from an 'unknown' before the murders began? Was that right?

I shivered, grabbed my cell phone, threw it into my satchel, and headed back to the elevator. I walked as quickly as I could, adrenaline pushing me to move as fast as possible.

As I approached it, the light next to the lift turned green and a ding signaled that the elevator had arrived. I stopped in my tracks, waiting as I held my breath to see what or who would come through the doors. When they opened, nothing happened, and I slowly approached them.

After a few suspenseful seconds, an arm covered in blood shot through the opening, falling to the floor with a wet slap. I recognized the white cuffs of a security uniform. I closed the distance to the elevator and screamed when I saw what lay inside.

Bryan was a mess of blood, torn flesh and exposed bone—one hand held his intestines inside him as he lay there bleeding to death. I knew there was no hope for him. Chris lay in a heap on the floor, his throat slit, the floor awash with their life force. Crimson splatters covered the walls. His lifeless eyes stared up at me and nausea rose in my throat, but I swallowed it down. The only person missing from the gory scene was Joanne.

"Bryan!" I gasped as I kneeled next to him. Blood soaked into my pants, but I didn't care. I placed my hands over his and applied as much pressure as I could, knowing full well there was nothing anyone could do. "What happened? Where's Joanne?"

"Alive," Bryan choked. He tried to speak past the blood that erupted from between his lips, but I could barely understand him.

"What?" I asked. I leaned closer, putting my ear next to his mouth

"Run. Killer," he stammered.

A tear rolled down my cheek as I stared at him and shook my head. "No, I can't leave you."

He placed his hand on my shoulder and pushed with every bit of strength he had, causing him to bleed more profusely. I slid in the blood pouring from his abdomen and fell backward, hitting the portion of the door with the tracks for the gliding slabs of metal.

"Run!" he shouted.

I stood, backed out of the elevator, and fished through my satchel for my cell phone. I could use this elevator, which was the only one on our floor, or risk the stairwell—the door to the stairs was directly behind me. My hand closed around the device as the elevator door shut. I removed it and pressed the touch screen, covering it in blood as I keyed the numbers 9-1-1.

Before I could hit the green dial symbol, hands shot around me, one covering my mouth, the other holding me against a hard, unyielding body. I screamed but it was muffled. I kicked out, dropping the phone in the struggle to free myself.

With a quick jerk, my head made contact with his face. He grunted, but something felt different. Off. His grip loosened enough for me to jerk my head back again to inflict more pain. When he let me go, I nearly fell but steadied myself, even though I was seeing stars. I took off and looked back. A plain white mask kept me from seeing anything except his lips and muddy brown eyes. He gripped a large knife in his oversized hand and was dressed in all black.

My legs took me to the place my brain instantly thought of: the rows of empty cubicles. I slid to a stop on the carpet and then kneeled to hide underneath a desk. I curled my knees in to my chest and used my arms to pull them close, placing a hand over my mouth to stifle any sounds.

Footsteps came from the opposite direction of where I knew the killer to be, meaning it was either Jerry or Joanne. But I couldn't move. I was frozen there underneath someone's desk like a frightened child. Even though my mind told me to help, to stop the slaughter, to do what it took, my body refused to listen to its pleas.

"I thought you guys were waiting downstairs?" I heard Jerry exclaim as he walked through the cubicles, his feet coming into view. "Guys?"

I wanted to reach out, call to him, but couldn't make a sound as terror gripped me like a vice, rendering me completely useless. More sounds of footfalls came from the other direction, and I stopped breathing altogether. Black hiking boots entered into view in front of Jerry's polished, pristine dress shoes.

Blood caked the bottom of the boots.

"Who the fuck are you?" Jerry asked, surprise causing his voice to rise in pitch. "How did you get past security?"

Laughter, low and deep, floated into my ears—a laugh I recognized as the one that came before the caller had said he wanted me to bleed for him. My mind raced as I watched their feet, Jerry's shifting uncomfortably at the sound of the man's joy.

"This is a courtesy call, Mr. Danvers," the man slurred.

Without warning, I heard the sound of metal slice flesh in one slick, wet motion. Strands of bright red glistened in the fluorescent lights as they fell to the mucky green carpet; the blade slid free of the unseen wound. Jerry's body fell to the floor after staggering one step towards his killer. My glance shot to his lifeless face. Blood poured out from the underside of his jaw where the knife had entered, penetrating his brain and killing him outright

The man still standing above him whistled and then walked in the direction where Jerry had come from. A few seconds later, a shrill, feminine cry shattered the stillness.

Joanne. The madman had found her and would kill her if someone didn't step in.

My mind finally switched from flight to fight mode as Joanne's sobs became desperate. As gingerly as I could, I reached out and up toward the desk drawers, opening one of them quietly to find a weapon of some sort. My fingertips grazed something cold, sleek, and metallic. I moved my hand about and found its handle, wrapping my fingers around them as I pulled a pair of scissors free. Unfolding myself from under the desk, I slinked along the rows of cubicles and headed toward the screams.

When I got to the row where I could hear Joanne, I raised the scissors to strike, confident she was being held by the man who had killed our co-workers and friends. Without hesitation, I rounded the corner.

Joanne's back was turned to me, her shoulders shaking with what I had assumed were sobs but were actually bouts of laughter.

My blood turned cold, causing the fine hairs on my arms to stand on end. Confusion wrapped around my mind. "Joanne?"

She turned and looked at me, her face and lightly colored business clothes covered in blood. "Oh, Zoe." She smirked, the madness in her eyes unmistakable, a long knife gleaming in her hand.

She launched herself at me like a bullet fired from a gun, knocking us both to the ground. I struggled beneath her; the scissors were knocked from my hand and skidded along the carpet. A punch landed on my right temple, causing me to see stars.

She bent down. "I was going to leave you for him, Zoe, but I kind of want you to myself," she whispered. Her lips grazed my earlobe as she spoke, sending a chill through me.

I felt dazed but was coming out of it quickly, the one self-defense lesson I had ever taken springing to mind. "Why are you doing this?" I asked in an attempt to stall her.

She sat up and looked me in the eyes as she raised the blade over her head. It was the same one that the man had held and killed my friends and so many others with.

"Does insanity need a reason, Zoe?" she asked, tilting her head like a confused puppy.

She brought the blade down and I lashed out, sending the heel of my palm into the underside of her nose, breaking it. My arm stung as the knife slashed my skin; warm blood flowed freely. Joanne fell backward onto the ground, and I jumped to my knees, searching for the scissors. My eyes caught the glint of steel and I shot after them, taking it between my fingers, now slick with the blood pouring from my forearm. Hands clawed at my legs, and when I turned, Joanne attempted to drag me to her, the knife still in her clutches. Her nose was severely broken, blood pouring down over her mouth and chin. I kicked out and hit her there again. She cried out in pain and jerked backward to avoid another hit. With one final blow, my booted foot collided with her shattered nose, and she fell back onto the floor.

I straddled her and raised the scissors above my head in preparation to kill her. "Die, you crazy bitch!"

Striking down, I felt the scissors meet bone and then organs, barely watching where they penetrated. She stopped moving and ceased laughing, which was all I needed to know. My fingers slid from the metal and dropped down to my sides as I took a profound and shaking breath.

A thin plastic-covered wire came around my throat, and I recognized it instantly as the long chord of one of the headsets. My hands came up so my fingers could wiggle their way between my flesh and the wire, stopping him from strangling me. I kicked out and screamed past the suffocating sensation, but knew no one was coming to rescue me. It would be up to me to save myself.

My feet touched the ground and I pushed backward with all my might, sending us both into the wall behind us. His grip loosened and I slipped from his hold. I fell to the ground and choked in air, but never stopped moving. With shaking knees, I crawled toward another desk where I saw not only another pair of scissors but a letter opener and stapler as well.

The man's large hand gripped my ankle and pulled at me, but I kicked at him. He let go to avoid the heel of my boot, but reached out again, his long arms stretching toward my waist. He gripped the waistband of my slacks and yanked, but not before I was able to reach the surface of the desk. I closed my hand around the first thing to brush my fingertips without any idea if it would actually be of use. He used my hair as a handle to bring my back against his chest, resting the blade of the knife he had picked up from the floor against my throat. It was then that I realized I gripped the letter opener. I closed my eyes and prayed it would be enough.

With a feral cry, I slashed backward with the blade and felt it sink into something soft and warm. A sticky liquid gushed out and ran down my hand. He cried out in pain and let me go, but I wasn't about to stick around. After stumbling to my knees, I pushed myself to my feet and sprinted to the only place I thought he couldn't reach me: the elevator.

Grunts of pain came from behind me, but I refused to look back. It would only slow me down. In seconds, I was in front of the elevator, jabbing the button. The doors sprang open instantly—it had never left the third floor. I had almost forgotten about the massacre that was inside and, after a split second of hesitation, I lunged into the elevator and pressed the button for the ground floor.

The doors were almost closed when the killer appeared, one eye a mess of blood, tissue, and viscous fluid. It flowed down the white mask in a disgusting display, marring its perfection. I screamed and took a step back, my foot slipping in the gore beneath me. My butt hit the blood-covered floor and my back met the wall. My head missed the metal rail along it by a lucky inch. His fist slammed on the outside of the closing doors, locking me in a cocoon of metal and death.

I looked down at myself and realized I was covered in both Chris's and Bryan's blood. In my quest for safety, I hadn't realized I'd jumped over Bryan's body to make it inside in time. Silent tears rolled down my cheeks as the dinging sound alerted me that I had made it to the ground floor. I stood with determination and bolted between the doors as they opened, careening toward the glass door that would take me outside.

I pushed through it and cool fall air met my skin, causing it to break out in goosebumps. I didn't stop running, not even when I heard the police sirens and saw the lights surrounding the building.

As a cop closed the distance between us with a gun aimed and ready to fire, I collided into his chest. He cradled me in one arm, comforting me the best he could while training his gun on the door I had exited through.

"It's okay, you're going to be all right," were the only words I heard leave his mouth before my vision blurred and fatigue hit me like a tidal wave. "You're safe."

***

The paramedic insisted I go to the hospital even though he gave me a clean bill of health after stitching up my arm, but I refused. I just wanted to be home, safe and sound—if there could be such a thing ever again.

I walked into my home with a police officer stationed outside to watch over me, his partner, Officer Hardy, inside just to be safe. My hands still shook as I set my satchel down on the coffee table. Terror still ran rampant through my veins as I thought about the man who had killed my coworkers, still out there. The silence inside my home was deafening as I felt Officer Hardy's eyes on my back.

"I want to take a shower. Get all this blood off me. You can make yourself at home. I'll get you some bedding for the couch when I return," I explained, not even turning to look at him.

"That's fine, ma'am. I don't need all that. Take your time," he replied.

I wandered into the bathroom, turning on every light along the way. The shower was quick but cumbersome as I did what I could to avoid getting my stitches wet. When I emerged from the bathroom, wrapped in a clean towel, I felt a lot better, but something was off. The lights were all out.

A solid pit of uncertainty and dread formed in my stomach. I turned and looked down the hallway toward the living room, the only light filtering in coming from the streetlamps outside.

"Officer Hardy?"

I moved down the hallway slowly, crossing into the living room. I saw nothing out of the ordinary. At first.

I approached the back of the couch and placed my hands on it, seeing something out of my periphery. I covered my mouth and screamed as I took in the sight of Officer Hardy on the ground between the couch and coffee table, throat slashed from ear to ear, his eyes wide with horror. I took a step back and felt my knees nearly buckle.

"You will bleed for me, Zoe," a familiar voice sounded from behind me, causing my heart to skip a beat.

I turned to see the white mask that stood out stark against the darkness, gore dried on it. I screamed as he lashed out. His fist collided with my temple. The blow sent me backward and over the couch, landing in the pool of warm blood. He came around the sofa, the knife gleaming menacingly in the light from outside as he raised it and slashed at me. In my attempt to avoid another gash, I jerked backward and slipped in the blood, landing painfully on the hardwood floor. And then I remembered Officer Hardy's gun. Where was it?

The unknown killer raised the knife over his head for a final attack as my hands fumbled shakily at the cop's hips, finding the gun quickly and sliding it from its home. It was in that moment I was incredibly thankful for having a father who was a firearm enthusiast.

The stranger lunged at me, but I kicked out quickly enough to catch his thigh with my heel, turn off the safety, and pull the hammer back all at once. As he raised his weapon once again, I looked him straight in his remaining eye and aimed the gun at the orb, going for a fatal shot.

"Say hello to Joanne for me!" I spat right before I pulled the trigger.

The recoil sent a jolt of pain through my wrists, weak from years of working at a computer, but the bullet hit its mark. His head jerked back. He stumbled backward and fell to the ground with a loud thud, his skull cracking against the floor.

Even though I was certain he was dead, I couldn't move. I sat there on the floor covered in Officer Hardy's blood, with the gun still aimed where he had been standing. I stood and walked toward him, kicking the knife away from his hand before glancing through the window toward the cop car that was supposed to be guarding my home from the outside. It was evident that this murderer had killed him before making it inside.

"Well, go figure," I stated.

I aimed the weapon right between the stranger's eyes, not even caring to remove the mask, and fired another shot.

You could never be too sure.

LAUGH OUT LOUD

by K.M. Cox

Emily hated clowns...*hated* them. From their oversized shoes to their red ball-like nose, they scared the hell out of her. There was nothing funny about creepy men who walked around and asked kids to squeeze their nose or pull on their flowers. She couldn't understand how these grown adults, who in her opinion acted like pedophiles, were allowed to come to parties and join hands with innocent little people who knew nothing about the real world.

So how did she end up ordering two tickets to the Big Apple Circus? Her niece...her darling niece Angie, who knew how to wrap Auntie Emily around her finger and get what she wanted. Emily couldn't help it; the poor girl was stuck between parents in the midst of a horrible, semi-violent divorce. There wasn't a day that went by that her niece didn't hear her mother (Emily's estranged sister) and father arguing and throwing things at each other, literally. Emily had seen so much hate that she wanted to give Angie a little bit of joy to look forward to. And what do five year olds love? Clowns. Damn clowns.

"Hey there, Emily."

Emily cringed at the voice behind her and the breath that was hot on her neck. Turning around, Emily faced Anthony, her over-friendly co-worker, leering over her shoulder.

MAN BEHIND THE MASK

"Oh, the Big Apple Circus, huh? That's fun...elephants, clowns, fire...it sounds...exciting." Anthony's eyes brightened at the word exciting. He was practically panting.

How many times had Anthony stared at her, panting? Too many to count. He was the guy in the office that the sexual harassment trainings were about; he asked women out time and time again and never took no for an answer. And if he *did* hear a no, he made the woman's life hell for the next year. Emily had been able to avoid the harassment until recently.

"I hate clowns," Emily said, her voice deadpan, eyes void of emotion. He wouldn't get the hint, she knew that. Just like she knew that he wouldn't leave until he was good and ready. She wrinkled her nose at the stench of his breath. It was smoke mixed with Listerine to cover up the smell of whiskey.

"Aww really?" he asked. "You hate clowns? But they're fun!" He sighed, putting his hands on the back of her chair. "Don't worry, I'll protect you from the scary clowns."

"Whatever," she said, trying to turn back to the task at hand. She had only minutes to finish buying the tickets before the stupid website timed out and she had to start over. Emily had started over three times and didn't want to add a fourth.

"If you don't like clowns, what's your favorite act? I like the elephants because of their big trunks." He wiggled his eyebrows. "Because, you know, I relate to them and all."

"Is that because you're getting gray and wrinkly?" Emily shot back. She hated the way Anthony stood there, salivating like a dog over steak.

His eyes flickered but he didn't lose the smile.

"No," he replied, his voice husky. "It's because I have a big trunk too, if you know what I mean." Pausing, he gave her a onceover. "I'll be happy to show you it sometime if you want."

"Sure," she said sarcastically. "As long as you don't mind my boyfriend coming too." With that, Emily stood, rammed the chair into Anthony's crotch, and grabbed her bag.

Anthony hissed, sending daggers Emily's way. "You stupid bitch," he growled. "You'll regret that...and your mouth. You'll see."

"Stay the hell away from me Anthony," Emily said, her heels clicking on the floor as she walked towards the elevator. "I'm one girl you *don't* want to mess with."

"Oh, you're *exactly* the girl I want to mess with."

Emily didn't hear him come up behind her, but suddenly his hands were on her waist, spinning her around to face him. He locked her in place, putting both hands on the wall on either side of her. They were inches from each other and she gagged on the rancid smell of whiskey that seemed to be excreting from his pores. It was as though he bathed in that shit.

"And don't deny it, I know you want me too. I see the way you look at me across the room. You little minx, you don't even bother to hide it," he said, his voice low. "Don't you know I'm a married man?" Leaning over, Anthony sniffed her neck, grinning a Cheshire cat grin that made Emily's hair stand on end. "But for you, I'd make an exception."

"So nice to know," she said. Her heart raced, her pulse stuttering against the sensitive skin of her wrist.

"Come on, you know you want it," he said. One hand dropped from the wall to cup her ass.

Taking her chance, Emily swiftly brought her knee up, catching Anthony right in his sack. She felt it snap up before falling and Anthony's anguished cry echoed across the room. Pushing him away, she rushed from his body, which was now curled into the fetal position, and frantically pressed the button on the elevator. She had stilettos on, making the trek down the stairs dangerous. She waited, counting the seconds the elevator took at every floor, her eyes glued to Anthony's form. He stood, cupping himself, and staggered her way. The look in his eyes was nothing short of murderous and Emily's heart skyrocketed again.

"You little bitch," he said. "Do you know who you're dealing with? Do you know who I am? I can *end* you!" The faster he advanced, the more Emily pressed the button to the elevator. It wasn't coming fast enough, so, with only a moment's hesitation, she kicked off her shoes. She nearly hit Anthony a second time before sprinting down the steps.

Her bare feet made a flapping sound every time they hit a step and she could hear Anthony descending the stairs behind her, his shoes tapping on each one. Emily ran full speed to the emergency exit, charging through it. She ignored the blaring alarm and darted to her car.

Rain fell in a fast, constant pace, making it harder to see. Within seconds, Emily was soaked. Lightning flashed, followed by thunder, and she shuddered. The only thing she hated more than clowns were thunderstorms. She made sure to stay indoors until they passed. But now she had nowhere to stay. She would have to suck it up.

To add to her luck, Emily stubbed her toe on a rock and she stumbled, her bag falling, its contents flying everywhere. With a groan, she paused, bending over to retrieve her things. She heard the door bang open again and looked up. Anthony advanced towards her. His eyes narrowed; each step he took was filled with purpose. It was only when he walked into the light that Emily saw what was in his hand: a large steak knife, probably from the kitchen in their office. It gleamed against the light.

"There's no point in running, Emily," Anthony said, his steps echoing. "I'm just going to catch you and then do whatever I want to you. Do you hear me? *Whatever*. I. Want. And there's *so* much I want to do."

"Dear Jesus," Emily said. She abandoned her purse, grabbing only her wallet, phone, and keys, and ran towards her car. With her shaking hands, it took three tries before the door unlocked and she stumbled inside.

Locking the car doors, she revved the engine, peeling out of her spot just as Anthony reached it. She heard the distinct sound of the knife scraping against her door. It took all of her strength not to hit him. Instead, Emily squealed out of the parking lot, driving with one hand while she dialed 9-1-1 with the other.

Anthony's maniacal face haunted her mind as she drove. Trying to control her voice, Emily explained to the operator what had transpired. She explained that no, she wasn't there anymore and no, she didn't know if he was. She assumed not, but Anthony wasn't exactly the smartest man out there. She gave the operator Anthony's full name and work number; it was all the information she actually knew about the psycho.

With an empty promise to look into it, the operator disconnected the call, leaving Emily to fend for herself.

***

"What took you so long?" Benjamin asked as he pulled his sister inside.

Two dogs ran around them, each begging for attention. Ignoring the furbabies, Emily fell into Benjamin's arms, tears already overflowing. She felt like she had switched between crying and panicking during the thirty-minute ride home. Her eyes were puffy and hurt, but the tears still came.

"Oh my God, Emily what's wrong? Are you okay? What happened?"

Between choked sobs, she relayed the incident, describing the way Anthony had acted. Once she had gotten home, she'd checked the side of her car and, sure as shit, there was a nice scratch across it. She would never forget where the scratch came from, even after it was fixed. It would haunt her, like Anthony himself.

"Oh sis, I'm so sorry. I'm so, so sorry. Are you hurt? Did he do anything to you?"

"I'm fine," Emily said. "Just shaken up. I won't forget this and there's no way I can go back there tomorrow, especially if they don't catch him. I can't do it, Benjamin."

"And no one expects you to," he cooed, brushing her hair from her face. "I'll call your boss tomorrow and explain everything. Then I'll hunt him down myself if I have to. No one gets away with scaring my little sister."

She knew she could count on him to take care of her. With Cal, her boyfriend, out of town, there was no way she was staying home alone. She hated being by herself; hated the quietness. And now she was beyond happy she had decided to stay with her brother until Cal returned.

Rain continued to fall, lightning lit up the sky and thunder shook the ground. Emily shivered, cold from the wet clothes soaked to her skin. Goosebumps riddled her arms and legs. She jumped at the sound of thunder and Benjamin looked at her, concerned. He wrapped an arm around her shoulders, leading her to the bathroom. She stood there as he turned on the shower, testing the water with his arm.

"What are you doing?" she asked, although the intention was obvious.

"You need a shower and a nice glass of wine," he said. "The water is warming up. You stay in as long as you want and when you get out I'll get you a glass of wine. I wish I could give you something stronger but I don't have anything else."

"Wine is fine," Emily said. The adrenaline was already draining from her body, which felt like it was in alien skin. "I'll be quick, Benjamin. I'm so exhausted that I don't know if I'm going to make it to the wine, though."

"It's fine," he said. "Just relax, that's all I ask."

Emily nodded and waited for her brother to leave, closing the door behind him. She locked it before getting out of her soaked clothes. Discarding them in a pile, she stepped into the shower, moaning at the feel of the hot water against her cold skin. She stood there for a few minutes, reveling in the heat before washing her hair. Massaging her scalp, she closed her eyes and let the water rinse the suds out of her tresses. Though she loved the shower, the longer she was in the heat, the more tired she became so she rushed through washing her body and turned off the water. Wrapping a towel around her, Emily stepped out of the shower and unlocked the bathroom door.

"Ben?" she called.

There was no answer.

"Benjamin, are you there? I could totally use that glass of wine."

Still no answer.

"Ben?" She figured her brother had fallen asleep, as he was known to do. When he got comfortable, he could sleep just about anywhere.

Walking down the hall, Emily peered into the den. Benjamin sat there, on the couch, his eyes closed, the two dogs at his side. *Of course*, she thought with a wary grin. The television was blaring. She walked over to her brother's sleeping body to grab the remote off the table next to him.

She tensed when her foot touched something warm and gooey. *I better not have stepped in vomit,* she thought, silently cursing the dogs. Looking down, Emily's heart dropped to her stomach; it wasn't vomit, but blood. Snapping her head up, Emily noticed what she hadn't seen before; blood covered her brother from his neck down, and the dogs. It coated the furniture, dripping to the floor. Her brother wasn't sleeping…he was dead. And so were the hounds.

The house went dark.

She listened, her head cocked to one side, for any sign of movement. She didn't hear any doors or windows close, indicating the murderer was gone. Then again, she hadn't heard them come in either. Her heart pounded, blood rushing through her ears. Another bolt of lightning flashed, illuminating the gruesome scene in the den. She saw again her brother, neck sliced open, blood pooling over his lifeless body. Her stomach churned, forcing her to swallow back the bile that threatened to escape. She listened more, still hearing nothing, before dropping her head.

With the towel still wrapped around her, Emily felt along the walls until she came to her brother's bedroom. She knew the layout of his apartment better than her own and could walk through it with her eyes closed. Sliding over to his dresser, she opened a drawer and pulled out the first thing that felt like a shirt. Slipping it over her otherwise naked body, she sat on the bed, pondering what to do. Thunder boomed, shaking the house.

I have to call the cops, she thought. She crawled to the other side of the bed and grabbed the phone off its dock.

Fumbling, she finally managed to turn the phone on…only to hear nothing. No ring tone, no busy signal. Nothing. *No! Oh God, please no!* She tried frantically to remember where she had put her phone. Was it in the kitchen? The den? Or…oh God…she had left it in her car. *Stupid, stupid, stupid!* she thought. *How could you be so stupid?* With the rain pouring down and a murderer God knew where, Emily was not venturing out of the house any time soon. Which meant she was stuck…a sitting duck.

While she sat there, she heard a creaking sound. It was soft and slow and she probably would've missed it if her senses hadn't already been on high alert. Her pulse spiked again as her heart shot up to her throat.

The room lit up again and Emily's eyes darted to the closet. Immediately she wished they hadn't.

Standing in her brother's closet, holding a knife caked with blood, stood a clown. A clown with a creepy smile and a maniacal laugh.

The room pitched into black and then lit up again. The clown was gone. Emily blinked, unsure of whether or not what she'd seen had been real.

She heard footsteps, slow and steady, walking through the house; the murderer was there. Patrolling. Emily could only think of one reason why he hadn't killed her immediately: he was toying with her, playing with her like she was his own personal doll. *I have to get out of here,* she thought, scrambling from the bed. *I have to get into my car and drive far away. I'll call the cops as I go.* The rain was still pounding down but Emily had no other choice. She either had to make a run for it or sit and wait to die.

Grasping onto as much courage as she could, Emily dashed towards the front door. In her haste, she bumped into some things, stumbled over others. Being stealthy and quiet was out the window. She passed the room where her brother and his dogs lay and skidded to a stop. Could she really leave him there? Sure, he was dead, but he was still her brother. She felt like she was dishonoring him somehow. He never would have left her behind.

Praying she had the time, Emily walked over to her brother's dead body and tried to pull him off the couch. Blood soaked her hair and shirt as she tried to lift Benjamin up to carry him. He was heavy, heavier than expected, and Emily stumbled in the hallway, dropping him. He fell to the ground and she bit her lip in frustration. And then her brother rasped, coughing up blood.

He wasn't dead.

Oh. My. God.

"Go ahead and run, little girl. I'll take care of your brother for you."

Looking up, Emily screeched as she saw the clown standing there, mere feet from her. He was wiping his blade with a rag, and even under the smiling mask, she could see he was grinning himself. His yellowed teeth glowed in the dark, looking ominous. "I promise."

"Who are you?" Emily screamed. "What do you want from us?"

"I don't want anything *from* you," he said. "I just want *you*."

He lurched towards her, the knife tight in his hand. Emily tried to run but he was too fast and pinned her up against the wall, the blade inches from her face. He laughed a deep, dark laugh as he jammed his body against hers.

Emily fought, using all her strength to push him off, but he was relentless. Finally, she rammed her knee up, catching him between his legs. Though he didn't flinch or go down like she had expected, his grip loosened and she was able to push him away. She ran to the other side of the house, desperate to reach the back door. She pumped her arms, her feet slapping against the wooden floor. *I'm going to make it,* she thought, relief filling her. *I'm going to get out of here.*

And then a hand was around her ankle and she fell, slamming her head against the floor. Her temples pounded. She saw stars. Panic crept in as the clown crawled closer to Emily. She shrieked as he put his gloved hands on her waist, flipping her around to face him. Emily could only see during the moments that the lightning lit the room. The rest was dark.

"You didn't think you could get away from me that quickly, did you?" he hissed. "Oh no, little Miss Emily, you're not getting away from me again." The knife shone against the belt of his costume.

As he got closer, Emily caught the scent of face paint and something else: whiskey. There was only one person she knew that smelled like that. *Anthony.*

"You son of a bitch," she said. Her fear turned into bitter anger. "You killed my brother!"

Though the charade was up, Anthony advanced towards her on the floor, grinning the whole time. The knife was too far away for her to reach so she looked around, desperate to find something else. And then she spotted a lamp.

In one swift motion, Emily grabbed it, bringing it down on Anthony's head. He dropped in a heap and she slithered out from under him. Scrambling to her feet, she ran for the back door. Yanking it open, she dashed into the wet, cold night, letting the streetlamp guide her. Getting to her car, Emily grabbed the handle and pulled. Nothing happened. She yanked again but still the door didn't give. It was locked.

She looked back to the house to see Anthony stepping out the door.

She slammed her fist into the window. It didn't move. She did it again and again, each time more panicked. Finally, the window broke, slicing up her arm.

Ignoring her own blood, Emily opened the door, desperately trying to find her phone. It wasn't in there. "Goddammit!" she screamed, kicking the wheel. Something in her foot snapped and then pain engulfed her. Falling to the floor, she clutched her foot and tried not to scream. *Oh God, what am I going to do now?* she thought, watching Anthony creep towards her. She was officially up shit creek without a paddle.

"Lookie here," he said. "I guess you're not so tough after all." He pulled the knife from his belt. "I'm going to like watching the life drain from your eyes. It wasn't fun with your brother—he was here one minute and gone the next, like a light being shut off. And you...well I'd wager you're going to go down fighting. I like feisty girls." He crouched next to her, grabbed a fist full of hair, yanked her back to her feet, and poised the knife at her throat. "You should've just said yes to the sex."

"Over my dead body," she said and, despite the pain in her foot, lunged backwards, taking Anthony with her.

He was right when he'd said that she would go down fighting.

Using all her remaining strength Emily ran backwards until an agonizing scream erupted from Anthony. He dropped the knife, and her hair.

Emily quickly limped away. Lights in the neighboring houses turned on and residents emerged, shocked and horrified. Emily was covered in blood, mostly her brother's, and Anthony's body, dressed in a clown costume, was skewered onto a rusty metal pole Benjamin had kept forgetting to throw away. Blood dripped down the body and the pole, creating a gruesome scene.

"Call the police!" she cried, thinking of Benjamin inside. She had no idea if he was still alive, but if the police didn't come, he didn't stand a chance. "Hurry! There's a man inside who might die!"

One older woman ran into the house while others gathered around her. They looked at her with concern and horror.

"I'm fine," she promised them. "Just a broken foot. Please-my brother—he's inside. Please, I need the police." The adrenaline was rapidly depleting from Emily's body and she slumped to the ground. Her breath came out ragged and unsteady, and her eyes could barely stay open. "Please. My brother," she said one last time, and then darkness overtook her.

***

When Emily finally opened her eyes, she was in the hospital. Her parents, and Cal, stood around her, eyes wide with fear. Through the window in the room, Emily could see police officers milling about, probably waiting to speak to her. Anthony was dead, she was sure of it.

"Benjamin," she croaked.

Her family turned to look at her.

"Benjamin…alive?" She could barely speak but she needed to know if her brother had been saved.

Cal kissed her forehead.

"Right next to you," he said and he, along with her mother and father, stepped aside.

Benjamin was, in fact, next to her. His eyes were closed and he was hooked up to a million machines, but he was there.

"They did surgery and put him in a coma to heal. He's alive, Emily."

"And it's all because of you," her mother said, eyes tearing up. "My poor baby…I can't believe you had to face that nightmare. God, the things he could've done to you…"

Reaching over to the table beside her, Emily handed her mother the hospital tissues.

"I'm proud of you, sport," her father said. "You didn't panic. You saved both yourself and your brother. That's one big feat." He put his hand on her shoulder, squeezing it slightly, and gave her a smile. He wasn't a man of many words, but she knew he meant well.

"When do I get to go home?" Emily asked. "I can't stay here."

They all laughed.

"Calm down there, speed demon," Cal said. "Let's get you healed first. You're always in a rush!"

"Life is a rush," Emily said. She paused, looking at her mother. "Mom, you're going to have to go to the circus with Angie," she said. "Because there's no way in hell I'm ever going near another clown again. Ever."

"Of course," her mother said. "I'll take her and we'll have a blast, I promise."

Emily sighed.

"Damn clowns."

IT TAKES A LOT OF GUTS

by Rachel Nussbaum

At the end of an otherwise dark block, a car's headlights cut through the night, illumining patches of snow across the driveway. The vehicle was parked and vacant, but the engine was on and the door slightly ajar. Despite this, the home it sat in front of was shut and silent, not a sign of life from within. The only sounds that could be heard were a beeping coming from the open car door and the trembling metal of the purring engine.

Then the side door to the garage slammed open, and a shallow wave of putrid blood and bits of bone washed out into the snow. Two figures ran frantically from within, stomping through the rotten pulp as they dove into the car and swerved out of the driveway.

The two people—a young man and woman—gasped for air as they sped off, dishevelled and blood-splattered. The man clutched the wheel so hard his knuckles went white.

"Holy fuck," he sputtered when the house finally faded into darkness behind them.

The woman took a shaking breath before she glanced down at herself. Her pants were soaked purple-red up past her ankles. She looked away to keep from gagging. "Jacob?" she whispered. "You saw it, right? The jacket and the…meat? Hanging on the hook?"

Jacob nodded.

"It was Tyler's, wasn't it?" she asked.

Jacob didn't say anything, but the tears welling in his eyes said enough.

The woman balled her hand into a fist and drove it into the glove compartment. "Motherfucker!"

"Anya..."

"Why is *he* doing this?! Did he go insane? Is it revenge for leaving him? We were his friends, goddamnit!" Anya screamed.

She balled her fist again, but Jacob reached out and grabbed her hand in his. "It doesn't matter. He didn't get us, and we're still alive. We're gonna take this fucker down," he said.

Anya breathed heavily, and Jacob squeezed her hand tightly. After a few moments, she squeezed back. "We need to go to the police," she said.

"That's what we did last time, remember? Ran like fucking cowards. And by the time we convinced the cops to believe us and got back, everyone was dead. We can't make the same mistakes—we can stop him ourselves. I saw him post online—he's spending the weekend with a bunch of people. People we went to school with. We need to get there before it's too late."

Anya was still for a moment before she squeezed Jacob's hand tighter. "You're right. I'm with you all the way. Do you know where it is?"

"I can figure it out." Letting go of Anya's hand, Jacob reached into his cup holder and removed his phone. He tapped a few buttons and then nodded to himself. He drove out of town and onto the saddle road leading to a few remote country houses.

"Do you think... he just went nuts after what happened to him last year?" Jacob asked. "Or do you think that was all...do you think it was him back then too? That this was all just some long, sick game and he was the killer the whole time?"

Anya thought for a moment. "You think he cut himself apart like that just to look like another victim?"

"I don't know. After what we just saw in his basement, I wouldn't put anything past him."

Anya nodded. "Drive faster."

***

Camila was finally willing to admit she'd made a mistake spending her winter break with her friend instead of back home. Mackenzie was the sweetest friend Camila had made at college—a rosy-cheeked, honey-blonde all-American girl.

How the hell are her high school friends such trash?

Christmas at Camila's mother's and father's respective homes would have been depressing. But it would have been better than staring at a pair of pierced tits jouncing up and down.

Riley laughed as Blake bounced her on his lap, too high to tell this was *not* normal human behavior.

"Did those hurt?" Mackenzie giggled, her face bright red.

"Oh yeah. But it's so worth it, you don't even know," Riley said blissfully, taking a drag of her joint.

"Good thing you got a wonderful boyfriend to kiss them better," Blake said, bouncing her harder.

Camila cringed. Blake was far from a 'wonderful boyfriend'. Considering he'd just yanked up Riley's shirt to tit-moon a close friend and a near stranger, 'human dumpster fire' seemed more accurate.

"How 'bout you, Cam?" Riley asked. "Got any scandalous piercings?"

Don't ask if a lobotomy counts... "Does a lobotomy count?" Camila said, unable to stop herself. Lucky for her, Riley couldn't tell she was serious and burst out laughing.

Blake noticed though, and grinned smugly as he pulled at Riley's rings, twisting them in his fingers. Riley let out a moan and arched back against him. Mackenzie giggled harder, and Camila chugged her beer, praying the buzz would make this more tolerable.

For the last week, Camila had broken a record and managed to drink more booze and smoke more weed then she had since freshmen orientation. Maybe Riley's stonerism was contagious. At least she was willing to share her stash.

The stairs creaked and Hayden—the resident of the home and the only member of the group that seemed tolerable—walked down. In a swift motion as he passed, he reached out and pulled Riley's rolled-up shirt back in place. He sat on the far end of the sofa as Blake glared at him.

Camila smiled. At least one person here was willing to shut their nonsense down.

"Did you get the Wi-Fi working, Hayden?" Mackenzie asked.

"Negative. It's on, but way too slow to stream anything."

"So not only does the reception suck out here, but now I can't even check my dank memes? Why do I even hang out with you?" Blake asked.

"Yeah, Blake. Another night of drinking, burning, and soaking in a hot tub miles away from any neighbors sounds terrible." Riley laughed.

"Surprise, surprise," Camila sighed, masking her frustration with sarcasm.

"Speaking of surprises," Hayden said, "you guys will never believe who I ran into in town earlier."

"If she's not an eight or higher, I don't care," Blake said, sipping his beer.

"Casey Dunne," Hayden said stiffly.

Blake choked and Riley rolled off his lap, eyes wide. Mackenzie brought her hands to her mouth.

"Holy shit," Riley said.

Camila glanced back and forth, watching the color drain from everyone's faces. For the first time that evening, there was silence.

"How... did he look?" Mackenzie asked.

"He was wearing a surgical face mask," Hayden said with a shrug "But I talked to him for a while. He's like an entirely different person."

"I'd bet. God. Poor guy," Riley whispered.

"Who's Casey?" Camila asked.

"He...went to our school," Mackenzie said. "He was one of the popular kids."

"He was an asshole," Blake clarified.

"Blake!" Riley gasped.

"Babe. You know how many times he shoved me into a locker? What happened to him sucks, but he was an asshole. It's a fact," Blake said, nodding.

"You are such a piece of shit," Riley mumbled.

"What happened to him?" Camila asked.

"After graduation, he and his friends went on vacation." Mackenzie continued. "They were staying at a lake house, but I guess...some nut job followed them there."

Camila widened her eyes. "I remember this. It was on the news."

Hayden nodded. "It was really gruesome. Three of his friends escaped and went for help, but everyone else got left behind. By the time the cops arrived, everyone had been tortured and killed."

"And Casey?" Camila asked.

Hayden shook his head. "They found him last. He'd been burned all over with acid, mostly on his face. The killer eviscerated him and left him for dead. Somehow he lived."

"Fucking hell," Camila whispered.

"I don't think I'd want to live through that," Mackenzie said, clutching her stomach.

"Karma," Blake whispered.

Riley wound her hand up to smack him, but Hayden's shoe hit him in the face first.

"The fuck, dude?!"

"Don't be a dick," Hayden warned.

"He literally kicked my ass. Like, foot parted crack. You don't think it's ironic he got his own medicine back tenfold?" Blake asked.

Hayden snapped his fingers. "Don't. Be. A dick."

"Why not?!" Blake asked, throwing his hands up.

"Because I invited him over tonight."

Camila watched Blake blink slowly before he erupted into a flurry of swearing and insults.

Hayden didn't flinch. "He seemed really lonely," he said, aimed more at anyone other than Blake. "I kinda got the impression his friends who lived through it stopped talking to him."

"Wow," Blake huffed. "The superficial douche squad ditched him after he lost his pretty? I'd never believe it."

"Dude, come on," Mackenzie said. "Let's try to show some compassion, and be nice tonight, okay?"

"I don't wanna," Blake mumbled. But when everyone glared at him, he finally slumped back and chugged his beer.

Camila was thankful something finally shut the piece of shit up.

***

Hayden had gone outside to usher Casey into the house, and when he came back in, he was carrying a case of expensive beer.

Casey entered after him, slowly. Like Hayden had said, most of his face was obscured behind a medical mask, but Camila could make out high cheekbones and pretty green eyes. Everything about his appearance had been meticulously planned— his auburn hair had been neatly combed, and he wore clothing just a little too nice for a casual night of hanging out. This evening might actually be a big deal to Casey.

Poor bastard.

"Hey guys," he said, his eyes creasing up in a smile.

"Hi, Casey, how are you?" Riley asked, standing to give him a gentle hug.

"Better, thanks," Casey replied, his voice pleasantly surprised. "I'm...so sorry, I'm really bad at faces..."

"Riley," Riley said with a wink.

"Hey, Casey!" Mackenzie said, standing to shake his hand. "I'm Mackenzie. I didn't know you still lived around here."

"Yeah, I didn't really leave the house for a while, but I'm trying to put myself out there more. Baby steps."

"That's great!" Mackenzie smiled before turning to Camila. "This is my friend from college, Camila."

Camila looked up at Casey, who extended his hand downward. She took it and tried to think of something to say. "Thanks for the beer. That's my favorite," was the best she could come up with.

Casey laughed. "Yeah, it was mine too."

"Had a lot of those cans under the bleachers up at the baseball field. Thought that was you and your crew."

Camila snapped her head up, and Blake grinned drunkenly at Casey.

"I'm Blake. We've met," Blake slurred. "I lost my butthole virginity to your toes."

Riley gasped and Hayden shot Blake a warning glare.

"Heh, um, I'm sorry…" Casey blinked.

"Don't remember? I got ya. If I pantsed ten kids a week, they'd all start to blur together too."

Casey's brow furrowed. Slowly, realization dawned on him. "I…was a giant ass to you guys, wasn't I?"

The room went awkwardly quiet, and Blake grinned like he'd won a prize.

"I'm really sorry…" Casey mumbled, looking down.

"It's really no big deal, man," Hayden said. "It was a long time ago."

"A year is a long time?" Blake quipped.

"Casey, don't listen to him," Riley said. "He's had too much to drink."

"Hey man, it's cool. Showing up at the house of all your victims trying to act buddy-buddy?" Blake grinned evilly. "Takes a lot of *guts*."

Casey's visible facial reactions were limited, but he looked like he'd been sucker-punched. "Sorry, I um…need some air." He walked over to the sliding door that led to the balcony and stepped outside.

"Blake, you fucking piece of *horse shit*," Riley spat.

"I can't believe you!" Mackenzie said, looking close to tears.

Hayden snapped his fingers. "Go the fuck upstairs and take a time out."

Blake's eyes widened. "You're choosing that fucking asshole over me?"

"I'd kick you the fuck out of my house right now if you weren't too drunk to drive."

Camila pulled herself off the sofa, snatched up her beer, and walked out onto the balcony. Casey was leaning over the railing, shivering in the cold.

"Hey," she said, sliding up next to him. "That wasn't cool. You okay?"

Casey looked down at her. This close, it was easier to see the scarring that peeked out over the corners of his mask. Camila forced herself to keep eye contact.

"I deserved that. I was an asshole," he said quietly.

Camila wracked her brain for something to say. "You know how on sitcoms they always depict the losers as protagonists, and the popular kids are the shitballs for bullying them?"

Casey nodded hesitantly.

"I hung out with the loser crowd my first semester of college," Camila continued. "Until I realized they had no social grace and the most bloated egos I'd ever seen. Kinda made me realize maybe there was a legitimate reason they got picked on in school."

Casey brought a hand to his mask to stifle a laugh. "That's terrible."

"Made you laugh," Camila said with a smile

"Thanks. Hayden's been really nice to me though. And aside from Blake, everyone seems fine. I just wish this were easier. I wish I'd been a better person."

Camila raised her beer. "You drink?"

"I, um...can't anymore."

"Can you still burn?" Camila tried.

"Jesus Christ—yes, please," Casey said, letting all the air in his lungs out at once.

Camila pulled her lighter and pipe out of her pocket, passing them over.

"Mind looking away?" Casey asked.

"No prob," Camila said, turning around.

After a moment, a stream of smoke blew out into the cold air as Casey exhaled. "So," he started, "if this isn't your usual crowd, how come you're here?"

Camila took a swig of her beer. "Parents decided to get a trial separation."

"Ouch."

"Yeah," Camila said. "So whoever I spent Christmas with, the other would feel awful. I picked curtain number three." She looked over the balcony and at the patchy snow and skeletal trees that bordered Hayden's property. "I regret my choice."

"That really sucks," Casey mumbled, taking another drag.

"I can deal."

Casey took a final drag from the pipe before passing it to Camila. "Thanks. That...really helps," he said, adjusting his mask.

"No prob. You shouldn't feel like you gotta hide though," Camila said, gesturing to his mask.

"Heh. You sound like my therapist." Casey chuckled. "Maybe someday I won't. Baby steps."

"Did they catch the fucker?"

There was a long pause, and Camila realized she may have crossed a line.

"I killed him," Casey finally said. "We got into a struggle, and it's all kind of a blur, but… yeah. Cops never figured out who he was. No records."

"Shit," Camila whispered.

"Sorry, was that too much?"

"That's just… Sorry for bringing it up," she said. Camila couldn't imagine what it would be like. Seeing your friends die. Getting tortured. Having to fight for your life. It sounded like hell.

"I'm just glad it's over."

Camila glanced inside. "Looks like Blake's been banished. Wanna give take two a shot?"

Casey's eyes crinkled up in a smile. "Just a minute."

***

"I called you ugly?" Casey said, what was visible of his face gone bright red. "I am so sorry."

Mackenzie laughed, kicking her feet up in the hot tub. She and Riley floated drunkenly in the jets while Hayden, Casey, and Camila sat along the edge, soaking in the warmth rising from the water.

"Well," Mackenzie said, "your exact words were, '*If you got a nose job you wouldn't be such a butterface.*'"

Casey buried his face in his hands and moaned in embarrassment. "There's nothing even wrong with your nose."

"Well, not anymore. I got my deviated septum fixed last year," Mackenzie said.

Riley burst out laughing and even Hayden cackled into his beer. Casey looked between them, and started laughing himself.

Camila smiled. She'd spent the last two hours watching the tension slowly ease out of Casey, until finally, things seemed normal. Camila didn't know who Casey was before, but now he seemed like a humble person whose addition to the group made things a little more bearable.

Or maybe it was just because Blake was gloriously absent.

A light poured over the privacy fence, and gravel on the driveway crunched as someone pulled up to the house.

"That's not your parents, is it?" Mackenzie asked.

"Nah, they're not back till Tuesday. I'll see who it is," Hayden said.

As Hayden disappeared inside, Riley sat back up in the hot tub. "Casey, do you wanna come in? Water's fine," she offered.

"Ha, thanks. But trust me, you don't want to see me without my shirt on."

"Can I get a peek, sweetie?" Riley winked. "I think scars are sexy."

"Not mine."

"Show you mine if you show me yours?" she said with a mischievous grin, Casey's face going redder.

Suddenly, a scream echoed into the night air.

Mackenzie gasped. "What was that?!"

"Stay here," Camila commanded, standing quickly.

"Don't go by yourself," Casey said, following after her.

The two of them walked through the house, Camila pausing to grab a piece of firewood. They approached the front door, the yelling getting louder and more frantic.

Hayden was keeping two people at bay. Camila took a deep breath and walked out behind him.

"What's going on?" she demanded, raising her piece of wood.

To her surprise, the pair lifted their arms, one brandishing a baseball bat, the other a tire iron.

"We're trying to help you, you morons!" the man with the bat yelled.

"Let us in!" the woman shouted.

"Anya?"

Camila and Hayden turned. Casey was frozen in front of them, his eyes wide with confusion.

And then the man rushed forward and swung his bat into Casey's stomach.

Casey collapsed to the ground, coughing hard behind his mask. Hayden charged forward and slammed into the man's chest. The two of them wrestled over the bat handle, and Anya screamed in protest.

"Jacob!" she yelled.

Camila ran towards the distracted Anya. She swung the lumber at her wrists, knocking the tire iron from Anya's hands before shoving her into the ground.

"Get off of me!" Anya screamed as Camila pinned her.

"He's gonna kill all of you!" Jacob yelled, trying to yank his bat free.

"The fuck are you talking about?" Camila spat.

"You slaughtered Tyler, you piece of shit!" Anya yelled from under her, tilting her head towards Casey.

Casey slowly stood up. He hugged his abdomen, clearly in pain.

"Are you okay?" Camila called over. "Who the fuck are these people?!"

"What …what happened to Tyler?" Casey asked.

Camila looked up at Casey's pained face, and Anya squirmed out from under her.

"What happened to him?!" she spat, yanking herself up. "He's cut into chunks in your garage, you sick fucker!"

Casey swayed on his feet in shock. Camila turned and looked to Anya and Jacob—really *looked* at them—for the first time. In the dim light, both of their legs were soaked in a pulpy reddish-brown. They smelled like rotten meat.

What the fuck is going on?

"I haven't been home in two weeks," Casey whispered.

Anya froze, and Jacob stopped struggling.

"What?" Anya asked.

"We're staying with my grandma," Casey mumbled, his eyes glazing over. "She lives closer to town…my parents thought it would help me get out of the house more…"

A loud crack snapped through the air, and Jacob lurched forward with a gasp. Both Anya and Hayden were splattered in blood, and Jacob reached down to his abdomen in terror. A jagged, metal arrow tip protruded from the side of his stomach.

A harpoon.

Before anyone could react, Jacob was yanked backward like a ragdoll. He screamed as he disappeared into the darkness of the trees.

"*Jacob!*" Anya shrieked.

Hayden looked down at his blood-splattered chest, his mouth flapping like a fish.

"Inside," Casey said.

"We have to go after him!" Anya said. "We can't just leave him—"

"Get inside now," Casey said, already trudging to the door, head down, "or stay outside and die."

"Riley! Mackenzie!" Hayden said, snapping out of his trance and running.

Camila followed, pausing at the doorway. She looked out at Anya, who peered towards the trees and back at the house.

"Goddamnit," Anya spat, rushing in.

Camila slammed the door behind her.

Hayden pulled Mackenzie and Riley in through the back door and slid it closed. Anya breathed heavily and sank to her knees.

"What was all that?!" a terrified Mackenzie asked.

"What the hell is going on!?" Camila demanded, turning to Anya. She looked up, teary eyed and heaving chest. Camila struggled to give a shit.

"It's him." Casey was sitting on the sofa, knees pulled up to his chin.

"Who?" Riley whispered.

"*Him,*" he murmured.

Camila's heart flopped in her chest.

"Why...why are you all covered in blood?" Mackenzie uttered.

"I'm calling the police," Hayden said, racing to the side table to snatch up the landline. The moment it was in his hands, it rang, and he almost dropped it in surprise.

"Who is it?" Camila asked.

"It's unlisted," Hayden said.

"Don't answer it!" Mackenzie whimpered.

"Give it to me."

All eyes in the room went to Casey, who stretched his hand out. Reluctantly, Hayden passed the phone over and Casey turned it on speaker.

The phone crackled, and a deep, cheerful voice spoke. *"Hey, sweetheart. Miss me?"*

Casey closed his eyes tight. "You're dead. They found your body," he whispered.

The voice on the other end of the line cackled. *"They sure did! It's cool, I grew a new one. Speaking of bodies, yours sure has seen better days! Digging the mask. I got a new mask too, since you ruined my old one."*

Casey took a shaking breath. "Why are you doing this?"

"Funny story! I came back to town to kill all your backstabbing friends—you know, the ones who abandoned you—I just hate leaving a job undone. Found your place was empty and I thought, 'Boy, wouldn't it be funny if I framed you for their murder?'"

The voice broke off in another antagonizing cackle. Casey trembled.

"But then the little cutie-pies actually started playing detective. It was so adorable—who was I to spoil their fun? They suspected you almost immediately, too. How's it feel knowing that? Knowing your friends think so little of you? It took nothing at all to convince them you're a monster."

"Bastard." Anya looked up from the floor, staring daggers through her tears at the phone.

"Oh!" The voice on the phone gasped. *"Was that Anya? Backstabber One, my love! It's been too long. I missed that pretty face. I think I may just keep it."*

Anya twisted her hands into fists, practically growling as the static of the phone wavered. Camila realized that Anya and Jacob had been Casey's friends, the ones who escaped the murderer.

But Casey had said he'd killed him. Who the hell was on the phone?

"Hey, Backstabber One! Backstabber Two wants to say hi." The phone crackled, and heavy breathing bellowed out of the static.

Anya stood, her eyes wide in horror. "Jacob?" she yelled, snatching the phone from Casey. "Jacob, where are you?! What's he—"

"*Anya...*" Jacob rasped out in agony.

"*Hey, Backstabber One!*" the first voice interrupted. "*Here's a riddle. What's a pile of shit sound like when you run a power drill through it?*"

A loud buzz cut the static apart and Jacob started to scream.

"*No!*" Anya yelled.

The phone erupted into a flurry of gurgles, squelching, and guttural sobs. Hayden yanked the phone out of Anya's hand and turned it off. Anya's face contorted in agony.

"You guys?" Mackenzie whispered in horror, looking out the window. The buzz of a drill echoed not too far off.

"Fucking hell—he's in the toolshed," Hayden said.

"Oh my god," Riley said, whimpering.

"*Ugh.* I can't make any outgoing calls," Hayden mumbled, focusing on the phone. "I think he *did* something..."

"I'm gonna kill him," Anya said.

"Don't go out there," Casey whispered.

"You should."

Camila snapped her head over to Mackenzie, who was staring right at Anya and shaking.

"He's only after you and Casey, right?" Mackenzie asked.

Camila's stomach sank. No. This was Mackenzie. She was sweet and innocent. How the fuck could she be saying this?

"Maybe...if you go outside...he'll leave us alone..."

"Jesus Christ, Mackenzie," Hayden said. "We're not throwing anyone off the ship. The fuck?"

"I don't know, I'm just—I'm scared! I don't know what else to—"

Something smashed through the window and Mackenzie broke off in a scream.

"What the fuck!" Riley yelled.

"It's...a brick," Hayden said.

Camila followed his line of sight to the brick lying on the floor, surrounded in broken glass. A note was taped to it, one word written on the front: *Casey.*

Anya reached down and yanked the message off, and with a small pause, handed it to Casey. He took a deep sigh and unfolded it as everyone else crowded around to see.

People Who Get To Die   People Who Get to Suffer

"What does that mean?" Camila asked.

"He's saying who he'll kill and who he'll...take his time with," Casey said.

"This can't be happening," Hayden mumbled.

"I don't want to die," Mackenzie sobbed.

"You guys?" Riley asked, her voice shaking. "Why are two names crossed out?"

It wasn't hard to guess who everyone was. Camila knew she had to be Grumpy Girl. Heart of Gold was obviously Hayden, Apple Pie was Mackenzie....Chuckles had to be...

"*Blake!*" Riley screamed.

Hayden took off upstairs, Riley right behind him. Camila slowly tilted her head up. There was a big, red stain on the ceiling.

An ear-splitting scream echoed from the top of the stairs. Casey—who seemed to be operating on autopilot—stood up and slowly trudged upward.

And son of a bitch, Camila couldn't help but follow.

Riley was slumped in a pile in the hallway, sobbing into her hands. Hayden stood frozen in front of the doorway to his bedroom, and Camila got a small glimpse of the blood-soaked sheets before she stumbled back.

Blake lay splayed out in the bed, naked and bloody. Strips of his skin had been peeled off, head to toe. Camila could see the webs of his muscles, the shine of fat, and watched in horror as blood oozed out each time his chest rose and fell.

"He's….he's still alive," Hayden whispered. "How the fuck can he still be alive?"

"*He's* good at keeping his victims alive," Casey said. "I think he uses drugs." He held up the brick. "I can do it, if you want," he said robotically. "I had to do it before."

Hayden opened his mouth, but was cut short. The shatter of glass echoed from downstairs, followed by a bloodcurdling scream.

Camila was the closest to the stairs, so she swallowed her fear and took a few steps downward to look into the living room.

Mackenzie had been pulled up tight against the door. The all-too-familiar harpoon tip was lodged through her neck and she was being yanked up and down, slamming against the glass. The line was let loose, and Mackenzie's twitching body hung still for a moment before she was jerked back with extreme force, shattering the glass.

"Honey!" a voice sang. "I'm home!"

Anya ran to the back door as a pair of feet stepped over Mackenzie.

Camila turned and padded up the stairs to the others. "Get out now," she spat through her teeth.

Hayden yanked Riley off the floor and took off down the hall, and Casey sped into a bedroom. Camila found herself frozen, unsure of who to follow.

She heard footsteps on the stairs, and turned in the hall.

A window.

Camila slid it open and looked down. It was a far drop, but enough snow had fallen that it looked like it could break her fall.

The footsteps were getting closer. Even if the fall killed her, it would be better than what would happen if she stayed.

Camila took a breath, and jumped.

***

When Camila woke up, she was freezing and her head ached. How much time had passed? She stood, glancing around. About ten feet away, there was a small, wooden shack. The tool shed.

If ever there was a chance to get a weapon, it was now.

To her relief, Jacob's body wasn't inside, but there was a lot of blood. Many instruments had been piled on the workbench: knives, hacksaws, pliers, hammers. Down the line, Camila could see various syringes, already filled, and she swallowed. She picked up a knife, but something under a pile of blades caught her eye.

A book.

Camila reached down. It was old and leather bound, small enough to fit in a pocket.

The killer's journal?

"Boo."

Camila jumped, the journal tumbling to the ground. She turned and swung her knife out in front of her.

There he was, dressed all in black, heavy boots, and a hunter's jacket. His face was obscured behind a dark, featureless mask. Uneven eyeholes had been cut into its surface and antlers sprouted from the top.

"Heh, at ease, kiddo," he said, walking past Camila. "I called time out."

Camila stumbled back, knife still outstretched.

The killer turned, looked at her and laughed. "Relax," he said, reaching the table. "I got bigger fish to fry right now. You get a free pass. This time."

Camila looked at the door, wondering if she could run for it. She looked back at the killer and then down at her knife.

"By the way, your friend Heart of Gold got himself bumped up to the suffer list," he called over his shoulder.

"Hayden?" Camila asked.

"That one. Look what that punk did to me." He held up his arm, revealing a thick, bloody gash.

How the fuck is he still conscious with a wound like that?

"He jacked up my harpoon, too. I was trying to make that a thing!" He sighed, grabbing a hypodermic needle and stabbing it into himself. Camila watched with morbid fascination as he picked up a staple gun, held his arm still, and stapled his flesh back into place.

What the fuck is this person?

"Hey, Grumpy Girl." The killer turned and tossed a little bloody ring at Camila's feet.

Fucking hell. It's one of Riley's nipple rings.

"Time in," he said.

And he walked out the door laughing.

Camila stood shivering for a moment, fighting down fear and rage. She slipped her knife into her belt, picked up the killer's journal, and ran.

***

All the cars in front of Hayden's house had their tires slashed. Thwarted, Camila glanced around. Mackenzie's body had been removed from the shattered door, and Camila had to stop herself from thinking what that sick bastard could possibly want with it. With a sigh, she reached into her pocket and pulled out the journal.

It wasn't in English. Strange symbols and drawings were scattered amongst the writing and Camila couldn't make heads or tails of any of it.

"Camila?"

Camila jumped up to see someone running out from behind a grove of trees. *Casey.* "You're alive," she said, gasping.

"Barely," he mumbled behind his facemask. "I caught up with Anya, but I think he got Riley."

"*What* is he?"

Casey's eyes widened. "You saw something, didn't you?"

A shout echoed behind them and the pair leapt.

Camila glanced around as something dawned on her. "Where's Anya?"

Casey snapped back, looking behind him. "She was just here..."

Camila took a few steps to the open door. There were bloodstains down the stairs, leading across the carpet and out to the back deck. Anya was outside, standing over the hot tub and gaping in horror. As Camila and Casey approached, it was easy to see why.

The tub had been filled with bodies, propped up like they were still alive. A now clearly dead Blake and Mackenzie sat along one end; on the other, a butchered Jacob and Riley, their faces contorted in agony. So much gore had soaked through the hot tub that the water had turned viscous. Gooey bubbles popped along the surface. Camila winced at the stench.

"*Motherfucker.*" Anya shook with rage.

Camila eyed the pair of scissors in her grasp, and realized she wasn't the only one who had taken time to find a weapon.

"Anya, we need to go…" Casey said.

"I'm not leaving Jacob in here!" Anya yelled. She ducked down to put her arms around Jacob and tried to pull him back.

The surface of the water erupted, and a pair of red-stained antlers emerged from the center of the tub.

"Gotcha!" the killer roared, slashing a knife towards Anya.

Anya screamed and reflexively pushed Jacob's corpse forward, and the killer's knife lodged into his shoulder. Anya looked down at his hand and her eyes turned fiery as she slammed her scissors into his arm.

"You *bitch*," he spat, grasping at his arm.

"Run!" Casey yelled.

Anya, Casey, and Camila took off, zeroing in on the tree line. The forest was sparse, but at this point, it was their only chance.

Camila zigzagged through the trees, jumping over piles of dead brush. All around her, she could hear the crunching of feet on snow. This was a terrible place to run or hide. Where were Anya and Casey? She'd lost sight of them. She was alone in a forest of echoes, and one of them was a murdering psycho.

"*Fucking cheater!*"

Camila slid to a stop as the scream bellowed out. It was close by. She crept through the forest, trying not to make any noise. Not that it mattered. The killer erupted into frantic yelling that drowned out any other sound. When Camila finally walked up behind him, he had worked himself into a frenzy. And Camila's heart sank when she saw why.

Hayden dangled from a noose off a tree branch, lifeless. He'd killed himself. The killer stood below him, screaming at the top of his lungs as he hacked his corpse apart with a knife.

"You think it's funny?!" the killer demanded as chunks of flesh fell into the snow. "Think you're so much better than me because you're dead?! You're nothing!" His knife stuck into Hayden's skull, and he let out a screech as he tried to yank it back.   "Stop mocking me!" he shrieked.

A hand clamped down on Camila's shoulder. She jumped and looked up at Casey and Anya. Casey brought his finger to his mask and slowly led her away from the grisly scene.

When the screams finally faded into the distance, Camila slumped against a tree. "He can't be human," she said.

"What?!" Anya grimaced.

"How long do you think he was waiting in the water for someone to walk by?" Camila asked. "I saw him with a cut that should have killed him; he acted like he didn't even feel it."

"He can't die," Casey whispered.

"*What?!*" Anya demanded.

Casey took a deep breath. "He made a deal with a demon to live forever," he said. "After a thousand years, he asked the demon to undo it. And it told him...it wanted sacrifices—delivered by a blade and his hands—for every day he'd been alive first."

Demon. Camila reached into her pocket and felt the journal. All that writing. *Spells for summoning demons.*

"How do you know this?" she asked.

"He told me before," Casey said. "I spent a long time in therapy convincing myself it wasn't true. But now..."

"Casey, can you hear yourself?!" Anya cried out.

"I killed him, Anya," Casey said. "They found his body. What I left of it."

Camila thought back to what he'd said on the phone. "When he said he regrew his body, did he... mean that *literally?*"

"I think if his body gets destroyed beyond use, he just...reforms in a cave back in Europe," Casey said.

"Fuck, this is too much," Anya said, burying her head in her hands.

"You don't get to say that, Anya," Casey said. "You left me. You and Jacob and Tyler."

"Casey, I'm sorry. We thought we could make it back with help—"

"I don't mean back then," Casey cried out. "When it was all over. None of you would talk to me after I got out of the hospital. You abandoned me."

Anya looked down. "Do you know how hard it was for us to face you, knowing how bad we failed you?"

"I was so alone, Anya," Casey whispered. "How hard do you think it was for *me*?"

Anya looked up at Casey, tears forming in her eyes.

A pair of arms reached around her from behind a tree.

"Look out!" Camila shouted.

Two knives hooked in the corner of Anya's mouth, and she screamed as they were yanked backward. Skin split and muscle snapped as the blades were pulled out. Anya lurched forward, her jaw unhinged and her tongue dangling by a thread of tissue. She fell into the snow gurgling, blood pouring out of her mouth like a fountain.

The killer stepped over her, pointing a knife at Casey. "Hey, Ugly."

Casey took a step back.

"Gods, you've no idea how happy that makes me." The killer laughed. "Thinking of what a freak you gotta be beneath that rag. If it makes you feel better, under my mask? I'm hot. When I'm not murdering, I'm getting laid, eating at fancy restaurants, kicking it at the mall. Heh, that's how I found *you*."

Casey froze, and the killer laughed even harder.

"I never mentioned that, did I? I was at the mall and you and all your friends were hanging out, talking shit. The vitriol that rolled off your forked tongue…damn, I wanted to kill you right then and there. You were such a bastard!"

Casey's eyes glazed over. "I'm…different now," he whispered. "I'm not that person anymore."

The killer scoffed. "Um, yeah, because of me. You're welcome."

Camila had to do something. But all she had was a knife…

And the journal.

"You know," the killer said, sighing and wiping his blade clean, "I gave up hope of dying centuries ago. But once you kill thousands of people, it's hard to call it quits. Especially when I find people who *really* deserve it."

He raised his knife and started to charge.

"*Hey!*" Camila yelled.

The killer's mask angled toward her, and she held the journal in the air. He brought his hands up, feeling at his pockets.

"Don't move, or I'll tear it to shreds!" she shouted.

"Little girl," the killer growled, "I will fuck your eyes out."

Camila chucked the book a few yards away into the snow. The killer ran for it, ducking down on his hands and knees to fish it out of the frost.

That was when Camila charged him. She drove her knife into the back of his neck. The killer gasped and swayed on his knees.

"Oh, fuck you," he gurgled.

Camila drove the blade down, again and again. She chipped away at his neck, blood spraying out into the snow. When she finally stopped, she slumped against his twitching body, breathing hard.

"Well, congratulations, Grumpy Girl," he said, coughing. "You've paralyzed me. I think you get to move up to triple tier suffer list now."

Camila sat back. "I wish you would die."

"Dude, me too." He chuckled from under her.

Casey walked towards Camila, reaching out to help her up. "He'll heal, eventually," he said. "We have to destroy his body."

"How?"

Casey reached into his pocket and removed the lighter Camila had lent him. "Get some branches."

"You dumb fucking cunts." The killer laughed up at them. "You *know* I'll come back for you. I got all the time in the world."

Camila stared down at him. "We'll take our chances."

The killer paused before shaking what little he could of his head. "That, my dear," he said with a chuckle, "takes a *lot* of guts."

***

343

Camila sat next to Casey, the last embers of the fire dying down. They'd watched the bastard burn—watched his flesh peel back, his muscles char. He'd alternated between laughing and swearing until his mouth caved in.

"Thank you," Casey said. "For saving me."

Camila looked up at him, his still-masked face, his weary green eyes. She leaned gently against his shoulder. "No prob." The fire crackled again, and Camila flinched. "Does it ever feel okay again? After something like this happens?"

"No. But you get used to it."

"How long does it take for him to reform?"

"I don't know," Casey admitted. "But he'll be coming for us."

Camila looked down at the leather-bound journal in her hands, and gripped it tight. "We'll be ready for him," she said.

PUT ON YOUR BIRTHDAY FACE

by Tamara Fey Turner

Thunk … Thunk … Thunk …

The sound echoed as if it were techie-magnified plops of bloody water dropping into an empty bathtub in some horror movie.

The heavy wooden base hit granite, then raised and touched down again in rhythm. A thin, slow-moving stream of red eased its way down to the countertop but splattered before settling as the knife continued its methodical rhythm.

The man was dirty, like a graveyard relic. His stench went far beyond any usual funk to that of decomp. His rigid body moved robot-like.

Something caused the tall, smelly, unkempt man to slowly turn his head to the left. He did not look up or down. He did not focus. His body remained still.

The teenager folded under the baker's rack and let out a shrill scream that would have raised the man from the dead if he wasn't already in front of her. He never looked at her as he held the butcher knife in midair, a few inches from the granite. Blood pooled gently onto the countertop.

Whimpering, Lillie Beth's breath quickened, and her heart beat frantically. She kept her eyes on the man as she fought to crawl out of her hiding place.

In a swift movement, he stealthily threw the weapon in her direction. She never screamed again. In her final moments, she lay twisted on the linoleum, reaching for the object deeply impaling her substantial breast. Her tits held her half-shirt away from her flat stomach. She was beautiful even in death.

The monstrosity stepped closer, mechanically walking in her direction. When he reached her, he looked down. His left hand firmly clutched her breast as he twisted the sharp knife and removed it. His eyes smiled as the blade shaved off most of her nipple.

As the gurgles of flooding blood replaced her breaths, she tried to focus on the man's face. It seemed wrong somehow, but her vision was blurring. As the high school lovely reached for him, the man's dark blue uniform shirt overtook her range of vision. The name tag was fuzzy to her dying eyes.

***

"Why do you like it in the ass?"

He did not respond.

The young brunette's braless knockers bounced in rhythm with the guy pounding her from behind. She looked over a shoulder at him. Her short skirt was hiked over her ass, top tossed to the sidewalk, panties nowhere in sight.

"I think you're gay."

The slap to Gloria's bare ass came hard and unexpected. Although, she should have expected it. Terry was a pig. He thought like a pig, ate like a pig, and fucked like a pig.

"Be quiet so I can finish."

"You're a pig!"

"Oink, oink, baby! Hmmm ... Do you like how my fat cock feels inside you? *Ahhh ...*"

Bent over the bicycle rack behind the library after dark ... There has to be a better place to get laid, and there has to be a better partner than piggy, she thought.

"What the fuck, Terry?" she demanded as she turned in time to see her boyfriend of the evening crumble to the concrete.

Trembling at the brick wall of a man in front of her, Gloria screamed and turned to run, tripping on her discarded halter top and hip-checking the bike rail hard. The stumble did not take her aground, and she sprinted up the steps to the back door of the library where a single light still glowed.

"Help! Help me!" She smacked her palms against the wood and glass of the old door. It didn't budge. No one came. Tears became sobs, and Gloria turned to flee. She was too late.

The man stood in front of her, over her, quickly angling the huge weapon into her belly and up with all his might. He ripped into her like he was gutting an animal, spilling her intestines as she reached down to feel what reminded her of homemade strawberry preserves. She saw the man's nametag as she collapsed: 'Joe.'

***

"It's not even ten o'clock. Why are you so worried, Mandy?" Bobby asked.

"She said she was breaking up with the asshole. She should've called by now."

"Maybe they made up."

"What? She wouldn't dare!"

"I'm sure she'll call you soon."

"She better. I hope Terry didn't hurt her."

"I'm sure she's fine. Have they been going on long enough to be considered a steady thing?"

"She seems to think so. Should we continue with tomorrow night's party plans? I mean, what if she isn't fine?"

"She will be. And she'll be there. For you."

"She always is, but I don't like not hearing from her."

"Let's go to bed, please."

"Are you sure your folks won't be home tonight?"

"I'm positive. Now stop worrying."

"All right, Bobby, you win."

"'Bout damn time," he said, grabbing her soft hand and pushing it firmly between his legs. "Now, can you concentrate on this for a little while instead of worrying about everything else?"

***

"*Gloria*! Where the bloody hell are you? You better meet me at the cabin to help get ready for the party. It's the official senior skip day, remember? No classes. Meet me there by eleven! That's A-M. And ...

did you get back together with Terry last night? I don't want that jackass at the party. I'm serious!" Click.

***

"Why the hell are you driving so fast, Mandy? The cabin isn't going anywhere."

"Duh. It's not going to decorate itself either, is it, Bobby?"

"What did Gloria have to say?"

"I left her a message. Do you think I should've gone by to check on her? Shit. Now I'm worried again."

"No, she's fine. I mean, she's a big girl. Probably hung over. She'll find any reason to start drinking again today and won't be any help getting ready for tonight anyhow. I know you love her, but …"

"You're probably right."

***

"All right, all the signs are up from the main road, around the lake, to the cabin. Even a blind man should be able to find us."

"Thanks, Bobby. You're the best."

"Things are looking pretty good in here too."

"Thanks. Good thing Jerrod and Tom showed up to help with the signs."

"I hope they come back with ice soon."

"I wish the damn phone was working up here, in case Gloria is trying to call."

"Yeah. I would've expected her to be here by now, but you know what a flake she can be."

Mandy hurled the stapler she'd been using to hang glitter balls from the ceiling at Bobby. She missed. He laughed.

***

"8 P-M and all's well!" a booming male voice reverberated through the small cabin.

Eleven drunken teenagers danced to Madonna and Prince. Two jocks stood in a corner debating over Cyndi Lauper's and Bonnie Tyler's tits.

"All the food is a hit," Jen shouted into Mandy's ear.

"I think your party is going off rather well, Mandy. The decorations look great! I'm glad you decided to get everyone together in one place. Most of us have known each other since we were kids.

348

This is a nice way to say goodbye." Jerrod glanced at Bobby, who furrowed his brow at him. Feeling he'd already said too much, Jerrod slinked away.

"It doesn't have to be a farewell party, Bobby. You know most of us will stay here in Cordova after graduation. I know you are leaving, but I'm still hoping you'll figure out a way to take me with you," Mandy spoke softly. She snuggled into his neck and kissed him.

Bobby didn't respond.

Couples deserted the makeshift dancefloor. Scantily clad bodies made out in dark corners and found their way outside to vehicles and around the lake, hands and tongues finding one another. Almost everyone seemed to be paired off, creating private parties from the one larger gathering.

***

Outside, a dense blade sliced quietly and unobserved through the exposed vulnerability of a couple, spilling warm blood. As he looked down into the bulging eyes of his victims, the man's own bulge erected again. He licked the knife and listened to the final gurgles of his victims, smiling a smile not quite right, even for a serial killer. Reaching for his forehead to adjust the mask that had begun to slide from his face, the killer inhaled heavily. The mask had an unusual odor. He was growing accustomed to it.

A small sedan with three passengers pulled away. The man stood in the shadows only a moment longer before tilting his head and walking toward the back of the cabin.

One more stop along the way: another couple. She was passed out, her date on top of her. The bloody knife slid across the young man's throat like butter.

As he took the place of the boy, on his knees between the girl's legs, the man released a throbbing purple erection from his pants. The girl did not move as he stroked himself, secretly hoping she would awaken and see how excited he had already become. He imagined her waking, and this thought stimulated him more.

Removing his mask, he put it on the young woman's face. Now he could admire himself, as his victims surely admired him. His cock exploded in a milky wave before he entered her. With a grunt, he buttoned his trousers and continued to admire the mask on the girl's face. He could hear her breathing in it. The sound kept him excited. He needed more release.

Placing a large hand over her face, completely covering her nose and mouth, the butcher thrust the knife into her chest. Her eyes opened wide, but she could not scream. He rhythmically thrust the knife downward, into her stomach, her thighs. The effort was sensual. Slow. Steady. The girl was no longer breathing when the blade found her vagina, entering her repeatedly. The man's cock grew hard again as he climbed between her legs once more.

***

"Mandy, I don't think you should be driving!" Bobby reached for the keys in her hand. Even drunk and screaming at him, she was delightful. His mind considered for the millionth time how to get her out of the tiny town. He would like to take her to California with him even though she was not part of his parents' master plan.

"I need to find out what's going on with Gloria! Where the hell is she, Bobby?"

"Who the hell knows with her. She's bound to turn up any minute, and if you're off killing yourself, then you'll miss her for sure."

Sliding to the ground, the Egyptian-American beauty began to cry. She pushed Bobby away when he knelt by her side. A knife entered his kidney as he tumbled backward.

"Bobby?" Her bottom lip quivered as she reached for him, trying to clear the tequila from her head enough to process what was happening. Her eyes searched the darkness, but she saw nothing, no one. "Bobby!"

She didn't have the car keys. Did Bobby have them? Did she drop them? Her mind raced.

"I'm here, Mandy. I've always been here." It was the high-pitched voice of a child, but not exactly. "I'll always be here, Mandy. And I want you to always be with me."

The voice sounded familiar, but she couldn't place it. Her head wagged from side to side as she crawfished on the heels of her feet and hands.

A massive figure emerged out of the night. From the ground, she could see his dirty pants and a knife dripping with Bobby's blood at his side. The scream she needed to release caught in her throat.

Mandy heard a woman scream behind her. One of the twins, Carrie or Cassie.

Scrambling to her feet, she was caught in a reverse bear hug. The man who held her was a good deal smaller than the tree trunk who stood in front of her. When the man behind her spoke, her eyes widened.

"Hi there, Mandy-cane. Miss me?"

Shakily she tried to find her voice. She could only manage a whimper. "Terry? I d-don't understand."

"I know. Not yet. But you will. Soon. I'm sorry about the twins, Man. I always liked them. I hated hurting those girls. Their boyfriends, not so much. Killing them was no real loss."

Mandy tried to squirm away from his foul breath as he kept a strong hold on her and continued to speak directly in her ear.

"Tonight is all about you, right, Man? This party was a great excuse. You thought you'd seduce your new lover boy into running away and marrying you. Did you think he cared that much for you? Really? Look at him now. Got himself killed." Her captor shook his head and laughed in an exaggerated tone that made her recoil. Looking at the larger man, he asked, "You sure he's dead?"

The big guy nodded, then kicked Bobby in the face with a booted foot. Bobby did not react. His head simply flopped from side to side.

"Dude, you nearly hurt me for real at the library. You gotta be more careful," Terry squealed like a teenage girl.

The masked man lowered his head and did not respond.

"Why are you doing this?" Mandy whispered fraily.

As he spun her around to face him, Terry re-wrapped his arms around her tightly. The knife was still in his hand, and it grazed the small of her back as his arms encircled her waist. He pulled her hips close to his erection, thrust it hard against her exposed bellybutton and dragged the knife along her denim-protected ass cheeks.

As Mandy twisted against him, he pressed both knife and cock against her harder, making her wonder which she'd rather be impaled upon. His breath smelled like a dead cat, but she made eye contact, hoping to find a trace of someone she once knew. She was still looking into his eyes, dumbfounded, when his over-dramatized soliloquy began.

"Mandy, Mandy, Mandy … Don't you remember little Joey at all?" Terry freed one hand to point at the giant killer standing next to Bobby's body. "He was so in love with you. You were always mean to him. Do you remember spitting on him?" His free hand moved to her throat, grip tightening. "How about when you took that dog shit and smeared it all over his face? Or the time you pushed him down in the clover bed that covered a fire ant hill? I bet he can remember a lot more incidents than those. Yet he remained loving and loyal to you. Ever faithful. He never stopped wanting you for his own.

"That's why I made a deal with him. After you and I were together for one year, he could have you. Of course, by then Bobby had come along and complicated matters, but I see Joey has taken care of that.

"See, Joey doesn't just want to have a date with you, Mandy. He wants to wear your face like a mask. That's why he got a jumpstart last night. I'm not sure he did such a great job taking Gloria's face, but she was good practice. I'm hoping he'll do a better job with yours. You only get one shot at someone's face, you know. We've been talking about ways to preserve it, so you'll last longer. Step closer, Joey. Let her see."

As the hulk stepped out of the darkness, she saw it: Gloria's face, laying right over Joey's, slightly askew. Tears streamed from her eyes, but Terry's hold over her throat prevented screaming.

"I bet you didn't know today is his birthday. Yeah, I know—you're a forgetful, mean girl. Do you remember putting worms in his cupcake when he was six?"

"I didn't forget that one, Te-rry," snickered the child-like giant.

"We were kids, for Christ's sake! It's not like you ever tried to stop me!" she managed, her voice raspy.

"I know, but he's my brother. It's different between us." His smile broadened as he licked her cheek and nodded toward his brother. "Now, Mandy-cane, I'm going to give you and Joey some alone time to get to know one another better. Please don't make him kill you before he's ready. That would not be a very nice birthday present. This is your chance to make up for being a mean bitch all those years. Joey has forgiven you. I know you'll struggle too much for him to skin your face alive, but at least allow him the courtesy of playing with you for a bit before he has to kill you."

A slight moan drifted on the night breeze. Without looking down, Joey stomped Bobby's face to a bloody pulp, wiping his boot on the ground.

"Is there anything you'd like to say to Joey, Mandy? I'll release your throat if you promise not to scream. Joey, take off Gloria's face so Man can see what you look like now. It's been a while since she saw you."

Obediently, Joey removed Gloria's face and dropped it to the ground on top of what was left of Bobby's. As he stepped closer, Terry loosened his grip enough on Mandy's throat to allow a scream to release itself—a scream no one heard except the killer brothers. Mandy began to cry again.

"Don't cry, Mandy. Joey loves you. A lot more than I ever did." Terry twisted Mandy's body around again to present her to Joey.

Taking this opportunity, Mandy bit one of Terry's hands in that soft, fleshy nugget between his thumb and index finger. Her teeth met, and she tasted his coppery blood in her mouth. She spit out the flesh as he yelled and punched her in the face. As she fell, Joey tackled his brother, dropping Terry to the ground and punching him repeatedly, breaking his neck.

Throwing Mandy over his shoulder, Joey carried Mandy's limp body to the cabin like a sack of potatoes, tossing her onto the sofa once inside.

Pacing and mumbling to himself as if talking to his dead brother, Joey did not notice when Mandy opened her eyes, slid down to the floor, and silently pulled her body toward the fireplace.

He did notice when she banged the vintage Ivanhoe knight holding the poker. Startled, Joey, still holding the knife, shook off his trance-like state and lunged toward Mandy.

The tiny gymnast rolled slightly left, holding out the fire poker with all her strength. Joey landed on the poker, but it was like shooting a lion with a needle. She knew it would not keep him down.

All she could do was run. As she exited the cabin, she looked over her shoulder. She did not see Joey. She continued to run. This time she did not look back.

Headlights nearly blinded her as she approached the main road. Throwing herself in front of the sedan, she thought she recognized the driver and his passenger. The car stopped.

Jim looked at Sandra. "Wait here." He stepped out of the car. "What's going on, Mandy? We haven't been gone that long. We took Kent over to Carolyn's since he was no fun without her. Mandy? What's wrong?"

Mandy reached for Jim, who helped her into the back seat of the car. "Joey ... Bobby ..."

"Where is Bobby? What's going on?" Sandra asked.

"Just drive!" Mandy screamed through her tears.

Approaching the main road from the darkness stood a tall, broad man with a fireplace poker embedded in his chest. No one saw him or the knife he was holding, or the face of the woman he was wearing.

THE CLOWN GUY

by Florence Ann Marlowe

Bryan had just gotten home and stepped into the shower when he heard a frantic hammering at his door. He hastily wiped his face and wrapped a towel around his narrow waist. The pounding persisted until he was able to turn the many locks – he pulled the door open, peering through the narrow wedge the security chain allowed him. His sister's frightened, wan face peered up at him.

Claudia was Bryan's little sister – his junior by six years. She was in her third year at Drexell University and her first year in her own off-campus apartment.

"Claudia?" He slammed the door shut and undid the chain. "What the hell are you doing here at this hour?"

Her chin quivered as she tried to speak. "I couldn't stay there another night – it's happening again."

Bryan clutched at his damp towel. There still soap clinging to his chest. "What's happening?"

Claudia dragged a bulging duffel bag into the living room and dropped it on the floor. "You know! It's happening just like when I was a kid."

Bryan shook his head. "I don't know."

"You do!" Her voice was strident. "I'm seeing... *him* again. He's come back."

"Would you shush?" Bryan hissed at her. "It's after eleven!"

Tears flooded Claudia's blue eyes. "He's back. I saw him four times this week. In the library, in the park – I saw him tonight right outside my apartment window. He was looking right in at me!"

Bryan sighed and shook his head. "Aww, Claudie. Not again."

Claudia sobbed and dropped onto the sofa. "Yes, again! You don't believe me!"

"Claudie – listen. You're just not used to living by yourself."

"No! You never believed me about him! I saw him – he's back. The fuckin' Clown Guy is back." She covered her face with her hands, fists clenched.

"Aww, no. Don't cry." Bryan knelt next her, nearly losing his towel. "I believe you – I do! I mean I believe you think you see him, but listen—"

"*No!*" Claudia shouted in his face. "He's real! I've seen him – in day-light, standing outside!"

"Shhhhh," Bryan soothed, taking her hands in his. "Just calm down and tell me what you saw – it can't be the same guy, not over ten years!"

Claudia's face was red and wet with tears. She coughed and sniffed and tried to steady her voice. "I saw him at the library – he was staring at me through the book shelves. I was looking for a special art book and I could see him turning his head sideways, like a confused dog, to look at me from behind the bookcase next to me. It was *definitely* him."

"But the last time you thought you—"

"The last time I saw him was before graduation, when I was coming home from Trina's party."

Bryan tried to stifle a grin, but failed. "You said you saw him on top of the garage roof."

"I did! He was crawling over it – don't laugh!" Her face screwed up and fresh tears flowed.

"I'm not – I'm not laughing. But you were drinking that night. Okay, okay! Was that the only time you saw him at school?"

"No!" She shuddered and pulled her hands free. "I-I've been trying to be more…*active*. So instead of taking the elevator, I take the stairs. I have a late class on the sixth floor."

Bryan nodded. "I remember you telling me – Cultural Influences on Visual Art Today."

Claudia wrapped her arms around her chest and stared straight ahead. "I'd gone down only two floors when I heard a weird sound like – like a giggle. And I looked up and there he was, two floors above, leaning on the bannister and kinda sliding his body down towards me."

"What did you do?"

"I ran! I ran down those stairs two at a time! I nearly fell!" Claudia whispered. "And he was right behind me! He was laughing this high-pitched, crazy laugh!" She scrubbed at her face with both hands.

"You sure it was this...Clown Guy? You sure it wasn't somebody fucking with you?"

"Bry, I *saw* his face! All white with the red mouth and red nose! And who would fuck with me like this? You're the only one who knows about him!"

"And Mom and Dad." He smiled, squeezing his sister's arm. "So, you didn't see him until tonight then?"

Claudia shook her head. "I saw him standing in the park the other day. I sometimes cut through there on my way home. He was standing under a tree in the middle of the day – so it's not a nightmare! He was there, just like a real live person!"

"Okay, okay." Bryan stroked her shoulder to calm her.

Claudia pulled away. "But tonight – oh, my God!" She covered her face with her hands. "Tonight he – I-I was locking up before going to bed and I went to the back door to make sure I'd locked both the screen and inside door." She turned to her brother and met his blue eyes, like hers. "You know how if it's dark outside and you've got the lights on you can't see anything? I thought I saw something white moving outside – it was shifting back and forth near the garden wall, but it was too dark and I couldn't tell if it was a cat or something. So I pressed my face against the glass. There was definitely something out there."

Claudia took a noisy, wet breath and continued. "It was like trying to see a fish in muddy water, watching it scoot back and forth. So I switched on the outside light. And it was him - his face pressed to the glass, his eyes red, grinning, his gums showing. His teeth were stained like with blood. We were less than an inch apart! Just that pane of glass between us. I screamed and he started dancing. I shut that light off so friggin' fast! I couldn't stop screaming – I fell to the floor, but I could still hear him laughing and banging on the door. I couldn't bring myself to look outside until half an hour later."

Claudia turned her damp eyes to him, her face sad. She stroked his thick, blonde curls and shook her head. "You don't believe me, do you? You never believed me."

"That's not true," Bryan said. "I just think there's an explanation. I mean, it can't be the same guy from when you were ten."

She nodded. "He's the same guy – same white outfit, same clown face."

"Claudie, don't you think it's possible this is just a reaction to all the stress you're under?" He continued despite the silent shaking of her head. "You always saw the Clown Guy when you were stressed – at school, when you went away to camp, at cheerleading competitions, when you and Mikey Gleason broke up. Remember how you were crying all the time and you said you saw the Clown Guy peeking out of your bedroom closet?"

He felt some satisfaction when he saw the tension slip from her face.

"Right? You were under a lot of stress every time you thought you saw him."

She sniffled. "I guess. But please, Bry – please let me stay here for a few days – at least tonight. I can't go back there!"

He wiped a tear from her cheek. "Listen, you can stay here as long as you want. Let me get you some nice hot chocolate to calm your nerves."

Bryan went to the kitchen, mixed some powdered chocolate drink with some milk and heated it in the microwave. He added something extra and stirred the concoction before taking it to Claudia.

"Here, sweetie." Bryan offered the steaming cup to her. "Down this. It'll make it all better. I put some Bailey's in there. It'll help you sleep."

Claudia took a mouthful and made a wry face. "It's awful."

"Drink it up. I promise you'll feel better. Let me get you a blanket." He pushed off the sofa and went to the linen closet in the hallway.

Claudia took another slug and stuck her tongue out in disgust. She glanced around until she spotted the rubber plant next to the end table and poured the remainder of her cup into its pot. When Bryan returned with a nubby, blue blanket, she handed him the empty mug.

"Good girl. Now just cuddle up and get some sleep." He draped the blanket around her and kissed her temple. "I gotta go upstairs and get some clothes on! I'm freezing."

She gave him a wan smile and pulled the blanket tightly around her as he clambered up the stairs.

Bryan padded in his bare feet down the hall to his bedroom. He closed the door behind him and turned the lock. For several silent moments, he stood staring into space before letting the towel slip to his feet. His body rocked back until it hit the wall and then he slid to the floor, drawing his knees up to his chest. His jaw stretched open into a feral grin and he crammed his fingers into his mouth, stifling a fit of giggles.

"She's here in the *house!*" he squealed in a shrill, strangled voice.

His eyes were so wide, they were almost lidless. He stared straight ahead, his naked body bucking and hitching with each burst of strident laughter.

"*We've never both been this close to her,*" a deep, guttural voice tore its way up Bryan's throat.

"Not since high school," he responded in the high-pitched breathy voice.

"*And no one else is here.*"

"She's all alone!"

"*Did you give her the allergy medicine?*"

Bryan nodded enthusiastically. "Half a bottle!"

"*She'll be sleepy.*" The dark voice chuckled.

Bryan shook his fists like an excited child at Christmas. "She won't be able to run away!"

"*Remember how she ran away at camp?*"

359

Bryan giggled. "She almost drowned!"

The dark voice snickered. "*She ran right into the lake!*"

Bryan's face became serious for a moment. "I almost made her fall down the stairs at school." He erupted into a series of stifled guffaws. "She could have broken her neck!"

"*We could break her neck,*" the dark voice growled.

An idiot grin exposing Bryan's teeth and gums split his handsome face. "Remember how we hid in her closet?"

"*She doesn't remember that.*"

"She was just a teensy-weensy, itsy-bitsy baby!"

A rumble of sardonic laughter bubbled from Bryan's mouth. "*Remember when we climbed on top of the garage?*"

Bryan tossed his head back and his shrill voice became mournful. "I wanted to pounce on her!"

"*You would have died.*"

"You saved me." A serene, sane expression washed over Bryan's face.

"*We need to hurry – she must be sleeping.*"

Bryan jumped to his feet. "Are we going to kill her?" he squeaked.

"*Not kill her. Not dead.*"

Disappointed, Bryan's grin faltered.

"*Kill her enough so she can never move again, but keep her alive enough to know. Or we can't have fun anymore.*"

Bryan exploded into piercing peals of strangled laughter. He rushed to the mirror on his long dresser and stared at his reflection.

The image that looked back was a crooked, emaciated version of himself. The concaved chest and withered arms bore him no surprise. He gaped into the pale face that was his – only riddled with pock-marks, shiny with sweat. Its eyes were deep red holes drilled into its skull and bloody stripes were scraped into its jaw and forehead. It grinned, teeth clenched, scarlet fluid filtering through it long, predatory teeth. Its nose was a gory gash in the center of its ruined face.

"No one's here to save her!" Bryan said to the mirror, his voice rising to a harsh falsetto. "Mom and Dad aren't here!"

"*They should have known,*" the dark voice rumbled. "*There was no need for another. You should have been enough.*"

Bryan grinned, nodding solemnly. He opened the top drawer of the dresser and chose one of many blue metal tubes. He pulled off the cap, exposing the crimson column of waxiness. Dior 762 Opera, just like the tube he'd stolen from his mother's bag when Claudia was just four. With slow deliberate strokes, Bryan copied the bloody stripes that covered his mirror image's face. He completely colored his eye sockets, lid and all. He drew a broad line across his mouth, extending past the corners of his lips. Finally, he painted his nose with a bright red circle.

"*Take your time. She'll be too sleepy to get away.*"

"No kill?"

"*No kill. Hurt. Maim. Cripple.*"

The mad laughter he had been trying to contain finally broke free and Bryan cackled uncontrollably. He raked his hands through his thick hair, pulling and tangling his curls, leaving a wild nest of snarls and frizz.

He donned the same billowy white top and baggy silk trousers he had worn for years. He left off the nondescript white sneakers so he could sneak up on her easily and slipped into the hallway. He could see Claudia curled up on the edge of the sofa, the blanket wrapped around her like a cocoon. She was softly snoring – it sounded like a dove to him.

Bryan tiptoed down the stairs in his stockinged feet. He crept to the utility room beneath the staircase and shut off the circuit breakers for the electricity. The house plummeted into darkness, broken only by slivers of moonlight that filtered through the windows.

He dropped to all fours and crawled through the living room behind the sofa. He gleefully recalled how he had crept into Claudia's bedroom when she was a little girl, his face painted with his mother's reddest lipstick. He'd knelt by her crib, his face close to the bars, until she woke with a shriek. After a while, she'd begun to complain to their parents about the "Mahnstuh!"

In his excitement, Bryan had bitten his lip, his teeth stained with blood. He scuttled on all fours until his face was level with hers, and patiently waited. His breath came out in steamy puffs, disturbing the fine threads of her thick eyelashes. Her nose twitched and she pulled an arm free from the blanket to rub her face. Her elbow struck Bryan's shoulder and her eyes fluttered open.

"*Nooo!*" Her mouth formed a perfect 'O' as she shrieked. Her arms flailed about as she tried to ward him off and she struggled to escape the confines of the blanket.

Bryan giggled incessantly as his sister floundered from the sofa to the floor. She squirmed away from him, her terrified eyes fixated on the clown face in front of her. Bryan's grin widened, lipless, as he scampered after her, his face floating above hers. Claudia fled, scooting backwards on her butt, her face a rictus of shock. Bryan tried to capture her foot. He wanted to bite her toes and make her cry the way he had when she was three.

Claudia backed into the end table and a lamp came crashing down on her head. A whistling shriek tore from her throat. She stared at the nightmare that came at her on all fours, his bloody teeth and eyes gleaming in the moonlight. A lunatic cackle filled the room as Bryan scuttled after her at what seemed like an impossibly rapid gait. His sister spun around on her hands and knees, fumbling to get up and run. Bryan reached out and grabbed her pant leg. Claudia howled and kicked at him, missing.

The aroma of her panic intoxicated him. A sizeable erection bulged between his legs as he struggled to his feet. Panting, a ribbon of saliva flying from his lips, Bryan pursued her down the hall. In the dark she got confused and turned into a solid wall. Bryan was on top of her in seconds. She responded with ear-splitting screams that set off another cacophony of uncontrollable giggles and squeals from Bryan. He danced a wild, high stepping jig, wiggling his fingers in her tear-streaked face. She flailed helplessly and darted past him, back towards the living room.

Bryan's heart pounded against his rib cage. The thrill of being so close to her when she was in such a state of hysteria was overwhelming. His cheeks hurt from grinning so hard, but he was too focused on his prey to let it bother him. In his high-pitched, squalling voice, he sang out her name.

"Claaaaau-deee-aaaa!" It sounded like a metal rake on the pavement. "Claaaaaaaaaauu-deee-aaaa! Come give us a kiiii-iiissss! Bahaaahahaaahaaaa-haaa!"

He heard her scream, and then the slapping of her bare feet as she ran up the stairs.

Bryan barrelled down the hallway, his socks sliding on the polished wood floors, searching for purchase. He stopped at the foot of the staircase and listened. She was calling his name! He felt light-headed with glee. She was actually looking for him, her older brother, for protection. He had spent many a night lying in bed, fondling his balls, envisioning Claudia's face if she ever figured out her own brother was the Clown Guy. The look of hurt and betrayal he imagined had been delicious. He often climaxed just at the moment that he snapped his teeth on her delicate cheek, ripping off the pale skin.

He slowly mounted the stairs, keeping his head low, searching the darkness for any signs of movement. She must have gone into his room. He could hear her thumping blindly, perhaps looking for a place to hide. Drool ran down his chin and dripped onto the steps as he stalked up them. She was crying, bleating his name – his balls tightened until they hurt.

It was darker than the ground floor, no windows to let the moonbeams leak through. Bryan slunk along the wall past the bathroom to his bedroom. The door was shut and it was quiet. He snickered in the dark, picturing Claudia hunkered down in his closet, her twig-like arms, so breakable, covering her head. Happy tears filled his glittering eyes as he recalled the summer at camp where he had followed his sister – so sure she had escaped the scary Clown Guy for a few weeks. He had chased her into one of the cabins and she had crept beneath a bed, weeping and reciting the Lord's Prayer.

He gently turned the knob and eased the door open. A thread of moonlight broke through the drawn curtains, illuminating his neatly made bed and the pile of objects Claudia had dragged out of his closet. Bryan tiptoed through the debris and gaped inside. It was empty. He shoved aside sneakers, a thermos, several empty boxes and his hockey mask with his foot. There was nowhere else for her to hide. His Spartan bedroom contained just the bed, his dresser and a chair. Glancing up at the mirror, he caught the red eye sockets of his reflection.

"*You've let her escape!*" the ominous voice growled.

"No!" he squealed, pulling at his hair. "There's no place for her to go!"

"*Find her! Do not lose her now!*"

Bryan stumbled into the hall. Without thinking, he tried to flick the lights on, forgetting he'd shut the breaker off. Swearing beneath his breath, he carefully treaded down the hall towards the stairs. Bending forward, he placed the palms of his hands on the floor, slowly ambulating like a big spider.

"Claaaau-deeee-aaa!" he sang, his nearly lidless eyes scanning the dim hallway. "Claaaau-deeee-aaaa – where are you hiding?" Another bout of giggles bubbled up from Bryan's throat. "You can't hide from me! You know I'm gonna find you!" He strained to hear if she had gone downstairs, and a blister of panic erupted in his heart.

What if she had run out the door? He'd have lost her! He might never have the chance to taste her fear so close again.

His eyes swam in the darkness. There were too many shadows and not enough light to tell if someone was moving about. He crept forward, trying to feel his way around the wall, and came to a sudden stop. He could hear her labored breathing – she was close.

"Claaaaau-dee-aaa! Come and play with me!" his shrill, wheedling voice ripped through the blackness. "I'm gonna find you! I always find you!"

A throaty whining sound drifted out of the dark. She was very close. Bryan's hand slid across the wall until his fingers met the wooden doorframe leading to the bathroom. He snickered as he felt for the doorknob.

"Claaaaaau-deeeee," he whispered as he turned the knob.

The door flew open and Claudia leaped at him. He could feel the heat from her body and smell her sweat. Something sliced through the air inches from his face. Bryan reached out with both arms in an attempt to grab her.

Something hard struck his shoulder, sending streaks of pain down his arm. He yelped and instinctively clapped a hand over his arm to protect it. He heard something swish as it passed in front of his face again. Claudia's breath whistled in her throat as she grunted, swinging some invisible weapon at him.

Swish!

It made contact with the side of his head and bright stars of light flashed before his eyes. Before he could recover it struck him again, this time in the ribs, making him double over. As he dipped forward, Claudia brought her weapon down on his head, knocking him to the floor. Her bare feet were inches from his face and he clawed at them with both hands.

Claudia screamed, wielding the unseen instrument again, pummelling Bryan's head and back with it. The blows were too weak to do any damage, but they stung enough to keep Bryan from regaining his stance. Finally, she tossed it away and ran for the stairs.

Bryan's hand fell on the discarded weapon. She had found his field hockey stick. Dazed and angry, he picked it up and hauled himself to his feet. He could hear her naked soles slapping the floor, slowing down as she searched for the staircase.

He charged a shady mass in the darkness. Swinging the hockey stick, he flung himself forward. Claudia shrieked and threw herself out of the way. Bryan's stockinged feet glided across the floor. He tried to spin himself around so he could pursue her, but he slid past her instead. His hip bounced off the mahogany bannister and both feet twisted under him. The handle of the hockey stick ripped through his right eye as he tumbled head first down the steep stairs. His chin hit one of the steps, his teeth neatly nipping off the tip of his tongue, and his heels rolled over his head. Something delicate snapped in his neck as he reeled and bounced down the steps until his body crashed onto the landing, a twisted pile of human wreckage.

Claudia wailed and cried, yelling Bryan's name. Through the pounding of his pulse in his ears, he could hear her searching the rooms upstairs. His one intact eye flickered open and he could barely see through a haze of blood. He tried to pull himself up, but was unable to make his limbs obey. He heard Claudia paddling down the stairs. She stopped several steps above him and gasped. A moment later, she hopped over him. He tried to reach out and grab her ankle, but his fingers simply twitched. Fluid filled his throat and he coughed, spraying blood past his lips.

His sister had made it to the front door. Bryan heard her tear the chain off. She left it open as she ran out into the moonlit street. She'd escaped. She'd got away. He'd lost his chance. Pain sang through his body, but he was overcome by the sense of loss – of being cheated.

"*You let her go,*" a deep, dark snarl purred in his ear.

He was unable to speak. He thought, *I fucked up.*

"*She'll never be yours now.*"

A tear mingled with the blood in Bryan's ruined eye. "I'm sorry. I wanted her. I wanted to catch her, make her your prize, so we could keep having fun with her."

A baleful chortle filled the house, riding up and down the stairs.

"*I have my prize.*"

A bare foot, dripping with blood, stepped into Bryan's view. The toes were sharpened into claws. He was unable to focus his one eye so that he could look up to see who the foot belonged to. A grisly hand reached down and drew a gnarled finger through the pool of blood.

From above him, that dark voice spoke. "*We will continue to have fun.*"

FINIS

Closing Words from the Editors

Veronica Smith

The '80s were the perfect decade. I grew up in the '60s and '70s but the '80s were the best for me. I had graduated from high school and gotten my own apartment; I felt so grown up, so independent. I've always loved horror, so reading and watching it was something I did on a regular basis. It never bothered me at all living alone. I didn't scare easily, until I saw the first *Nightmare on Elm Street*; I didn't sleep at all that night and I didn't stay alone! I don't know why '80s horror has always had a special place in my heart but it does. Slasher films, exotic blood splatters, gory after-sex murders—there's nothing else like it. No other decade really started such a cult following.

When David asked me if I'd like to co-edit Man Behind the Mask, my first thought was, *I would've loved to submit a story to this*. But as a fairly new editor it would be a great learning experience, so I accepted. As a female horror author myself, I love to read stories and books by other women and have shared a place of honor in an anthology of women in horror with others—in fact, several authors in this book. Women *can* do it better than men. (Sorry David and Jonathan – haha - but it's true.) Stephen King may be the king of horror, but after reading these stories I have no doubt there are many queens of horror as well. These stories were vastly different but all of them made me think of the '80s. As I was reading them, it was like watching great slasher films at the drive-in—that unique feeling that gives you the quivering in your chest. You start to breathe faster and you're startled at the slightest noise, jumping in your seat when it really scares you. That's how I felt reading these stories. I was on the edge of my seat and only wanted more each time a story ended. We have a lot of great authors in this wonderful anthology. I'd read some of their other works, but after reading these stories I want to read everything they've all ever written.

I wanted to mention something that I noticed as I read these stories. We all have memories of the more popular names back in the 1980s. Here are few that I noticed were in more than one story. These were in two stories each: Alice, Amanda or Mandy; Bobby, Linda, Stacy, Amber, Charlie, and Jackie. Megan in various forms is mentioned in three different stories. When you see these names, you remember some that were popular not only just in the movies, but in the people that actually lived during that time period. Reading this book brought back a lot of memories for me.

What makes this even better is that all the proceeds go to breast cancer research.

So I thank you, ladies, from the bottom of my heart (even if my heart has been ripped out by some masked stalker and resides, beating, in a glass jar). Thank you for the opportunity to read and edit some truly great writing.

Jonathan Edward Ondrashek

I was six years old when I discovered my love for horror, in 1988. I'd sneaked to a vent shaft overlooking the television in our living room late one night, long after my bedtime. Some poor schmuck appeared onscreen, skinless and malformed, pulling himself across a dusty wooden attic floor. I recall having nightmares for weeks after that—and oddly enjoying them.

Yes, *Hellraiser* had popped my horror cherry.

From there, it spiraled into a love for all things horror: *A Nightmare on Elm Street, Friday the 13th, Halloween, Fear Street* and *Goosebumps.* The heart-pumping, armpit-soaking adrenaline rush which accompanied the indulgence of horror was the greatest, most exciting thing in my world while I fattened up in the '90s (until I discovered masturbation, of course). It didn't stop there. By the time I was out of high school, I had discovered *The Return of the Living Dead, Child's Play,* and other '80s classics I had missed. And now, in my blossoming adult life, I'm an avid horror reader, writer, editor, and moviegoer. Go figure.

When David invited me to co-edit this anthology, I initially balked. We'd worked together on another anthology, and had become close overseas friends for almost two years, so it wasn't his beard or perverse sense of humor that turned me away at first. I simply didn't think I'd have time to take on such an impressive, massive tome. But when he told me all proceeds were being donated to breast cancer research, I knew I couldn't pass up such a noble cause. I *made* time for it. And I'm glad I did.

These ladies delivered what we were hoping to emulate: that classic '80s horror feel. And they delivered it well. This line-up is one for the ages. Though I became known as the word-slashin', dickish editor of the trio, I couldn't be happier to have been involved, and I'm ecstatic to have found 28 ladies whose wet-dream-inducing written work I can stalk from afar.

Thank you, ladies, for keeping the greatest period of horror alive.

Jonathan Edward Ondrashek

AUTHOR AND EDITOR BIOS

Alice J. Black lives and works in the North East of England with her partner and slightly ferocious cats! Alice has always enjoyed writing from being a child when she used to carry notebooks and write stories no matter where she went. She would be the girl in the corner scribbling away while everything went on around her. She writes all manner of fiction with a tendency to lean towards the dark side. Dreams and sleep-talking are currently a big source of inspiration and her debut novel, The Doors, is a young adult novel which originally came from a dream several years ago. Several of her short stories have been included in anthologies and she is always working on more. When she's not writing, she always has a book in her hand and will read from whatever genre suits her that day.

www.facebook.com/alice.j.black.doors
@alicejblack

Audrey Brice writes paranormal thrillers, mysteries, and horror stories where spirits, demons, and occult practitioners are both heroes and villains. She lives along the front range of the Rocky Mountains with her husband and three spoiled rescue cats. Her maternal grandmother is a breast cancer survivor.

www.audreybrice.com

Dani Brown: Born in Oxford but raised in Massachusetts, Dani Brown is the author of "My Lovely Wife", "Middle Age Rae of Fucking Sunshine", "Toenails", and "Welcome to New Edge Hilll" out from Morbidbooks. She is also the author of "Dark Roast" and "Reptile" out from JEA. She's the person responsible for the baby blood bath that is "Stara" out from Jaded Books Publishing. She has written various short stories across a range of publications. When she isn't writing she enjoys knitting, fussing over her cats and contemplating the finer points of raising an army of dingo-mounted chavs. She has an unhealthy obsession with Mayhem's drummer and doesn't trust anyone who claims The Velvet Underground are their favourite band. She currently lives in Liverpool, England with her son and 3 cats.

> You can contact her on facebook at
> https://www.facebook.com/DaniBrownBooks/.
> Amazon: https://www.amazon.com/Dani-Brown/e/B00MDGLYAY
> Official and sometimes updated website
> http://danibrownqueenoffilth.weebly.com/

Dawn Cano is the author of Sleep Deprived, Bucket List, and Final Review, which she co-wrote with her boyfriend John Ledger, along with several other short stories and novellas. She currently resides in central Pennsylvania, and when she's not writing, she loves reading, watching horror movies, and eating everything that doesn't eat her first. Look her up on Twitter: @Dawnzilla_ or on Facebook: dawn.cummings.716.

K.M. Cox started her writing career writing in the Young Adult genre. Currently dipping her toes in the New Adult genre, she is twenty-eight years old and works as a Human Resource assistant at a medical center. She lives in New York with her husband and their two dogs. She's been writing professionally for about eight years.

Debby Dodds is the author of the soon-to-be-released novel Amish Guys Don't Call (Blue Moon Publishers, spring 2017) and has stories in eight anthologies including My Little Red Book (Twelve) and She Writes. "My Mom and The Dead," a story about taking her mom to a Grateful Dead concert, appears in the anthology series Thin Threads. She was interviewed on CBS Sunday Morning on 4/21/13 for a piece featured in the Amazon and Barnes and Nobel bestselling, Things That You Would Have Said (Penguin, 2012). She's a regular contributor and was the Fiction Editor for The Living Dead magazine. She's also been published in The Sun, xoJane, Portland Family Magazine,

FlashesintheDark.com, Stumptown Underground, Zinkzine.com, and twice in Hip Mama. Her humorous essay, Why Sarah Palin Needs Me as Her SAT Tutor, was an editor's pick on Salon.com.

She received a BFA from NYU in Drama/Acting and a MFA in Creative Writing from Antioch University. As an actress, she was featured in many independent films and television shows. She wrote and performed in stage shows at both Disneyland and Disney World. She also appeared in a special with Jerry Seinfeld and in many low-budget horror films: Sex, Chocolate and Zombie Republicans, Bloodbath, and The Protector to name a few. In Portland, OR she performs regularly with the comedy show Spilt Milk.

Fox Emm is the head of Spooky Words Press and loves to write and read about disturbing things that go bump in the night. You can find her on most social media by name, or find her non-fiction horror articles on Wicked Horror, Horror Fuel, and Gores Truly. You can find more of her short story work in BAD NEIGHBORHOOD, or in a full-length novel due for release late 2016 - www.SpookyWordsPress.com

Suzanne Fox is a writer of erotic fiction who is lucky enough to be able to live and work in the beautiful county of Cornwall with her partner and three pussies (cats!). Her work has been published in several magazines, both in print and online, and has also appeared in an anthology of hotel sex stories. She's been an avid fan of reading and watching horror for as long as she can remember but writing it is a new venture for her. She has had great fun expanding her writing skills to include elements of gore and violence. Her first novel is currently in the last stages of editing and she looks forward to seeing it in print.

Rose Garnett is the author of her own misfortunes aka Carnalis (Strigidae Press 2016), first novel in the Dead Central series, along with other assorted monstrosities foolishly liberated from the oubliette of Scottish Urban Horror.

Michelle Garza and **Melissa Lason** are a twin sister writing team from Arizona. Their work has been included in Fresh Meat 2015 by Sinister Grin Press, Rejected for Content 3 by Wetworks, Wishful thinking by fireside press and a handful of other anthologies. Their debut novel, Mayan Blue, was released by Sinister Grin Press on May, 25 2016. They specialize in horror, science fiction and dark fantasy.

A. Giacomi is a wife, and mother to one small human child. She is a Canadian born writer, educator, and artist. She is a zombie enthusiast, lover of all things Tim Burton, Shakespeare, Jane Austen, Marvel, Star Wars and just generally just loves film, essentially she's a fangirl with many geeky tendencies. She is also the author of the Zombie Girl Saga, a four-part series from the zombie's perspective. Eve Brenner: Zombie Girl is A. Giacomi's debut novel. You can catch the latest updates about her and her writing on her blog: www.poeticzombie.com

Kasey Dawn Hill is the author of several books and numerous short stories. She also writes poetry and some non-fiction. To learn more about Kasey, visit her website. https://kaseyhillauthor.com/

Carly Holmes writes weird stories and occasional poetry by the banks of the river Teifi in west Wales. Her debut novel, The Scrapbook (Parthian, 2014) was published to critical acclaim, and shortlisted for the International Rubery Book Award in 2015. Her short prose is regularly published in anthologies and journals. She has a particular liking for the strange and the gothic. Carly is co-editor of The Lampeter Review. She also runs and hosts a spoken word group, 'The Cellar Bards'. www.carlyholmes.co.uk

David Owain Hughes is a horror freak! He grew up on ninja, pirate and horror movies from the age of five, which helped rapidly install in him a vivid imagination. When he grows up, he wishes to be a serial killer with a part-time job in women's lingerie...He's had several short stories published in various online magazines and anthologies, along with articles, reviews and interviews. He's written for This Is Horror, Blood Magazine and Horror Geeks Magazine. He's the author of the popular novel "Walled In" (2014) & "Wind-Up Toy" (2016), along with his short story collections "White Walls and Straitjackets" (2015) and "Choice Cuts" (2015).

> https://www.facebook.com/DOHughesAuthor/?ref=hl
> http://www.amazon.co.uk/David-Owain-Hughes/e/B00L708P2M/
> http://david-owain-hughes.wix.com/horrorwriter
> https://www.goodreads.com/author/show/4877205.David_Owain_Hughes
> https://twitter.com/DOHUGHES32

Crystal Jeans was born in Cardiff, Wales in 1982. She lives there still with her three-year-old daughter. Her debut novel, The Vegetarian Tigers of Paradise, a fictional memoir, was published by Honno in May 2016 and a second novel is due to come out in 2017. She has short stories published in New Welsh Review ('My Bukowski' and 'Split Me in Two, Gareth Moon'), various poems dotted about the place and a pamphlet of poetry, 'Just Like That,' published by Mulfran Press. She takes pleasure in both the literary and the mainstream and is happy to dip her toes into the horror pool....maybe she'll get pulled in. Along with writing she is passionate about karate, feminism, television and hoarding used tampons.

Jaime Johnesee lives in Michigan with her husband and two sons. She spent fourteen years as a zookeeper before shifting her focus to writing full time. Known for her bestselling horror comedy series, Bob the Zombie, she is also currently coauthoring the paranormal horror series, Revelations, as well as her Samantha Reece series for Devil Dog Press.

Links:

> Website: www.JaimeJohnesee.com
> Twitter: https://twitter.com/JaimeJohnesee
> Facebook:
> https://www.facebook.com/AuthorJaimeJohnesee/
> Google +:
> https://plus.google.com/100525684067368354417
> Amazon: www.amazon.com/Jaime-Johnesee/e/B007P5CLDW

Stevie Kopas was born and raised in Perth Amboy, New Jersey. She is a gamer, a writer and an apocalypse enthusiast. Stevie will never turn down a good cup of coffee and might even be a bit of a caffeine addict. She is the author of the bestselling dystopian series The Breadwinner Trilogy (The Breadwinner, Haven, All Good Things) as well as Never Say Die: Stories of The Zombie Apocalypse, released in May 2016. Her other work can be found in the charity horror anthology At Hell's Gates, Volumes 1 - 3. Stevie is also the Managing Editor of the website Horror Metal Sounds and a writer for the site. Offline, Stevie is a telecommunications professional. She currently resides in sunny Florida

> You can visit the official website at http://someonereadthis.com and connect on Facebook via http://facebook.com/thebreadwinnertrilogy and also follow Stevie on Twitter @ApacoTaco.

Lisa Lane: In addition to writing dark speculative fiction for over twenty-five years, Lisa Lane has earned a black belt in karate, sang the National Anthem for the opening of a Dodger's game, and sung lead and backup vocals in bands ranging from classic rock to the blues. She currently lives in the dusty outskirts of Sin City with her husband, an editor and educator, and the recently departed spirit of one very spoiled cat.

Florence Ann Marlowe started out as a journalist, writing for local newspapers and radio stations. Since 2008, she has been a published fiction writers for E-magazines and hard copy publications such as Macabre Cadaver, Demon Minds, Pseudopod, 69 Flavors of Paranoia, Dedman's Tome, Death Head Grin, Fantastic Horror and Wiley Writers. Her stories have also appeared in the anthologies Reflux, Peep Show Volume 2, The Pulpateers, Fantastic Horror's Temptations and Other Sins, Fear's Accomplice and Fear's Accomplice: Halloween and in the next issue of Black Candies and the upcoming installment of Ladies and Gentleman of Horror. She has just finished her first novel titled The Bitter Dead and is currently looking for a publisher. Originally from Hoboken, Florence has lived from one end of New Jersey to the other and currently lives on a small farm in southern New Jersey. Her closest neighbor happens to be the Jersey Devil.

Christine Elise McCarthy has been acting professionally for 28 years and is recognized primarily for her roles as U4EA-popping bad girl, Emily Valentine, on Beverly Hills, 90210, as Harper Tracy on ER, and as Kyle, the gal who killed Chucky in Child's Play 2. She has also appeared in recurring roles on China Beach, In the Heat of the Night, and Tell Me You Love Me. Among her other film roles are Abel Ferrara's Body Snatchers and two films starring Viggo Mortensen: Vanishing Point and Boiling Point.

As a writer, she has written three episodes of Beverly Hills, 90210 as well as characters and storylines for the series, a pilot that was optioned by Aaron Spelling, and comical true-life essays that she performed at the Upright Citizens Brigade and Naked Angels theaters in LA. She maintains an irreverent food porn blog called www.DelightfulDeliciousDelovely.com for which she provides recipes, photographs and sometimes shares details of the triumphs and, more frequently, the humiliations of her own life. She has a

MAN BEHIND THE MASK

great passion for photography (www.MyPinUpArt.com) and has shown her pin-up and decaying Americana imagery in the United States & Paris. She has been on the selection committee of Michigan's Waterfront Film Festival since its inception in 1999, she is co-director of the Victoria Texas Independent Film Festival, programs for the Self-Medicated Film Festival and The Lady Filmmakers Film Festival, and consults & judges for many others. Her directorial debut, Bathing & the Single Girl, was accepted into over 100 film festivals and won 20 awards.

Bathing & the Single Girl, inspired by the short film, is her debut novel.
www.BathingandtheSingleGirlBook.com
Check out her Bathing & the Single Girl playlist on Spotify
Follow her on Facebook –
www.facebook.com/christine.elise.mccarthy and
www.facebook.com/BathingandtheSingleGirlTheBook
Follow her on Twitter – www.twitter.com/celisemccarthy
Follow her on Pinterest –
www.pinterest.com/foodpornsite
Follow her on Instagram –
www.instagram.com/christineelisemccarthy
Follow her acting career –
www.christineelisemccarthy.com

Stacey Leah Mewse was introduced to the world of horror at a young age thanks to the likes of R.L Stine, and then the accidental viewing of one of the halloween series at the age of 8 years old. She instantly developed a taste for horror and has never looked back. An avid reader of horror fiction, and watcher of horror films, she enjoys the writings of Dean Koontz, Richard Laymon and Stephen King. Not only is Stacey an author, but also a keen animal lover, artist and cancer survivor. She has a passion for unusual animals and is especially fond of hairless pets. She was diagnosed with cervical cancer and then treated in 2013, and is now thankfully in remission. One of her biggest wishes is to use her talent as a writer to earn money to donate to the hospital where she was treated.

Rachel Nussbaum is a writer and artist living on the Big Island of Hawaii. Since a young age she's had a fascination with films that featured the strange and bloody, something that's helped shaped her writing style. Rachel loves experimenting with many different genres: her favorites are science fiction, urban fantasy, and horror. In the future, Rachel plans on writing and illustrating her own original novels and comic books.

Jonathan Edward Ondrashek loves to spew word vomit onto the masses. He's had an array of poetry, reviews, articles, and interviews published in the past decade. His short stories have appeared in the anthologies Fifty Shades of Slay and Rejected for Content 4: Highway to Hell, and his first book in The Human-Undead War series debuted in April 2016. He also co-edited the horror anthology What Goes Around (KnightWatch Press, June 2016). If he isn't working, reading, or writing, he's probably drinking beer and making his wife regret marrying a lunatic.

You can stalk him on Twitter (@jondrashek), Facebook (www.facebook.com/jonathanondrashek), or his Dark Randomosity blog (www.jondrashek.com).

Delphine Quinn is a new horror/extreme horror author who has had early success submitting shorts to various publications. She is currently working on an upcoming collection of stories titled Asylum, as well as a full-length novel, both of which she plans on self-publishing. Delphine lives in the central United States with her husband and her cat, Coco. In her free time from work and writing, she likes to binge watch TV shows and movies, or indulge in her unhealthy obsession with reading about sociopaths and serial killers.

Delphine Quinn would like to dedicate her story in this collection to her mom, Kathy, who fought a long and arduous battle with a rare form of breast cancer herself, and came out victorious. Your strength and grace in the face of chemo, radiation, and surgery were nothing short of inspirational, and she is proud to call you her mother.

You can find out more about her via her newly created Amazon Author page: http://www.amazon.com/-/e/B01GUKYHV6 Or her Facebook page: http://www.facebook.com/delphine.quinn.5

Briana Robertson is an emerging speculative fiction author, working primarily within the genres of fantasy and horror. Her love of authors such as Stephen King, Shirley Jackson, Patrick Rothfuss, and J.K. Rowling has developed her own need to put pen to paper. Her short stories have been published in several anthologies, and broadcast on online podcasts. Her debut novel is in the works, set to release in 2017. She currently lives in the Midwest, with her husband, three daughters, and their Maine Coon, Bagheera.

Charlotte Ros' early life was influenced by her tough father, a successful entrepreneur who ruled his business empire with a fist of steel and who lived to indulge his only child with everything she could ever want. Although she was born into a life of privilege, she never shied away from an opportunity to develop her business acumen. Following the sudden and traumatic deaths of both of her parents, Charlotte went to live with her aunt, a remarkable and inspiring woman who played a major part in nurturing Charlotte into the forceful and imaginatively creative woman she has become until her own untimely demise. This is her first, albeit somewhat chaotic, venture into writing.

D.M. Slate resides in Colorado, where she's lived for most of her life. She attended college at the University of Northern Colorado and now works as a financial analyst. Danyelle is married to her high school sweet-heart and together they have a daughter and son.

D.M. Slate's first sci-fi horror novella was released in 2009, followed by two novels and many more short stories. Her first audio story was recorded in 2013, and in 2014 she was named Most Wicked Woman Writer at Horroraddicts.net.

2014 also marked the year that Slate became involved with screenplays and independent film directing. Her short films were selected as runner up in the Colorado Creative Short Film Contest in both 2014 and 2015 at the Mile High Horror Film Festival.

Veronica Smith lives in Katy, Texas, a suburb west of Houston. She has been married to her husband, Kelly, for over 25 year and has a son, Zach, who just graduated from college and is also a writer. She always loved writing and although her overall school grades were only average, she always got A's in English. Her current project is her first full-length horror novel, Salvation, for Helheim Games Studios. It is based on the world of Survive: Zombie Apocalypse CCG. She also has several short stories published in anthologies: 47–16 : Short Fiction and Poetry Inspired by David Bowie – Volume II, A Very Zombie Christmas, Bite Sized Offerings, Crossroads in the Dark, Eight Deadly Kisses, Fifty Shades of Slay, Grynn Anthology, ODDisms, and Unleashing the Voices Within. Look for more of her stories in anthologies to be published soon: Dead Silent Zombies, Edge of Darkness, and Kids Volume Two. In addition to her writing, she's a co-editor for the Man in the Mask Anthology and Unleashing the Voices Within Anthology.

www.facebook.com/Veronica.Smith.Author
https://www.amazon.com/author/veronicasmith
https://kvzsmithwordpresscom.wordpress.com/

Kindra Sowder was born and raised in Rancho Palos Verdes, CA until the age of 12, when her family moved to Spartanburg, SC. She graduated from high school in 2006 with full honors and as a member of her high school Literary Club and the Spanish Honor Society. In January 2014, she graduated with her second degree in Criminal NeuroPsychology. She married her husband Edd Sowder in May 2014 and still lives in Spartanburg, SC where she is basing her company Burning Willow Press. Her works have earned multiple award nominations and accolades, earning her a coauthorship with The Walking Dead actor, Santiago Cirilo.

Tamara Turner was born in Lafayette, Louisiana. She's spent most of her life editing for magazines and other authors. Tamara currently resides in North Los Angeles County with her muse (a scarlet macaw) and her favorite grey tabby, Gus.

C.A. Viruet is a wife, mother and Army veteran who writes as much as she can, but horror is her favorite genre to write. She has been previously published in the Dark Chapter Press anthologies Flashes of Darkness and Eight Deadly Kisses. She also has a couple of short stories in the Sirens Call Publications ezine, The Sirens Call, issues 25 and 26. You can find her on Facebook at www.facebook.com/C-A-Viruet-1675626722653321

A CLOSING NOTE FROM THE PUBLISHER

Each of us has been affected in some way by breast cancer. We, the authors, editors, cover artist, and publisher, chose to dedicate this book to breast cancer research because research is important when it comes to finding a cure. I imagine it's unanimous when I say that we all hope there will be a cure in our lifetimes. As a publisher, this cause is important to me personally because my maternal grandmother is a breast cancer survivor.

That said, the proceeds from this book will go to fund breast cancer research. Every quarter I will make payments to the authors' and editors' breast cancer research charity of choice.

We would like to thank our readers for reading, and thank our authors and editors for donating their time and hard work to this special project.

Thank you.